Lightning Strikes

Death on Willow Pond

by Ned Crabb

North Country Press

Lightning Strikes

Library of Congress Control Number: 2014948652

ISBN 978-0-945980-82-7

North Country Press
Unity, Maine

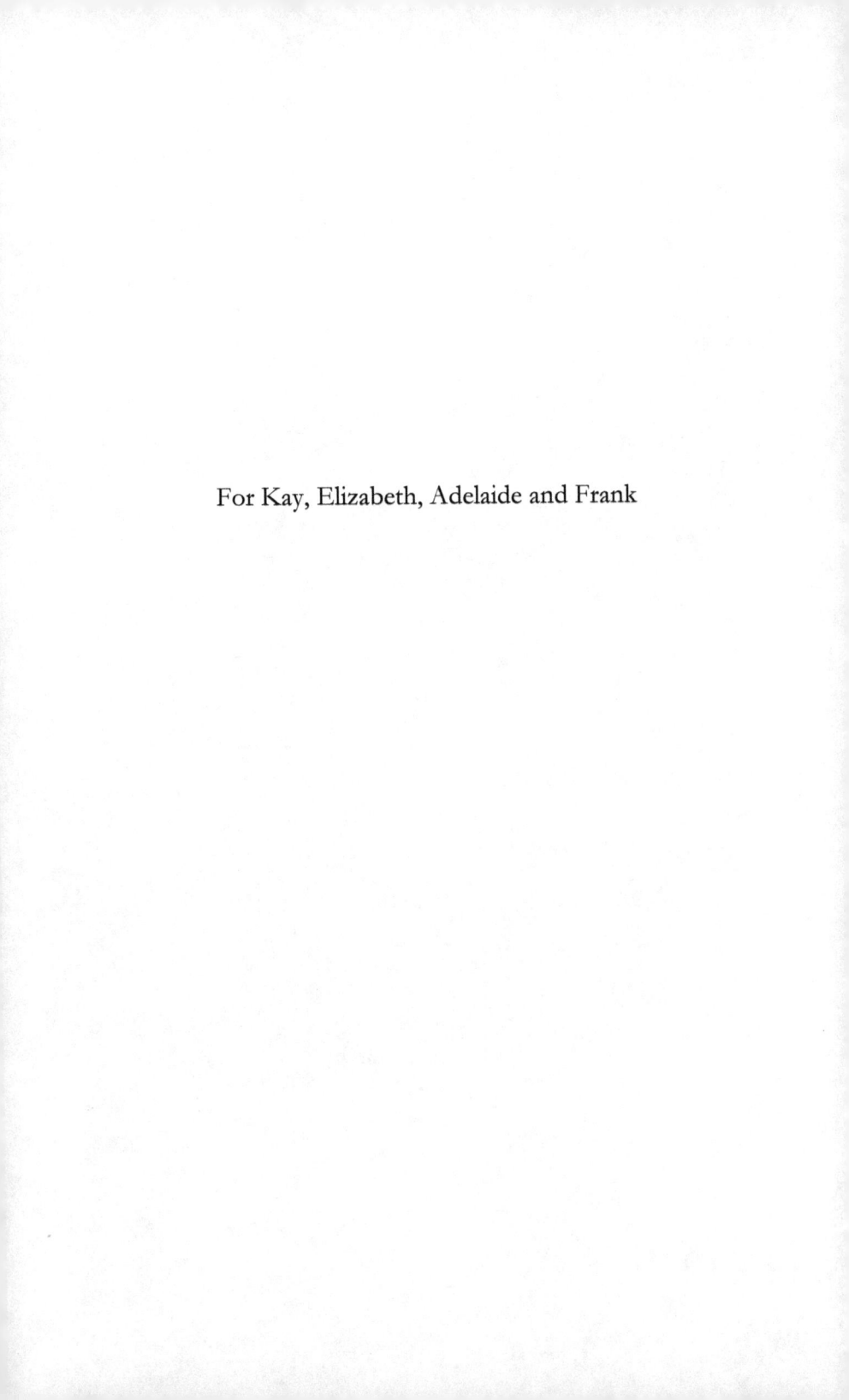

For Kay, Elizabeth, Adelaide and Frank

Storm Coming

hot July day still
as death cicadas
humming
white sun blazes soft
breeze rises leaves
whisper dark
clouds tower storm
coming *

* from the uncollected, unpublished, unread poems of Preston Thorndike
Seldon Hawthorne Whittier Garfield Godwin.

Prologue

At 6:30 on a particular bright July morning at McCorkle Camps on Winsokkett Pond in Maine, in the third camp going north from the east-west camp road that wound for a quarter-mile up to the state road, the camp from which the agitated whir of a coffee grinder competed with the matutinal concerto of finches, warblers, sparrows, jays, wrens and chickadees in the thick surrounding woods, retired Professor of English Alicia Godwin, a six-foot-two example of how middle age does not necessarily diminish physical comeliness, stood nude in the modest-sized kitchen, savoring the aroma of ground Costa Rican coffee beans as she watched retired Professor of History Six Godwin, also nude, emerge smiling from the bedroom and walk toward her past the big stone fireplace and easy chairs.

"Ahh," Six pronounced, professorily, "did Orpheus, strumming on his lyre, awaken to a vision surpassing thine own?"

"Strumming on his what?" Alicia asked.

"Lyre."

"Just checking."

Six came to the kitchen and embraced his wife and looked down into the face he still adored after these many years. Few men were physically able to look down on Alicia, but he was six-feet-six, regarded by the Godwins' friends as an exceptionally appropriate height for a man named Six. It had been only a scant fifteen minutes since they were embracing in a more sustained manner, yet the kitchen hug elicited a physiological reaction in this lanky Orpheus that caused his Eurydice to giggle and look down to regard the sudden action.

"Well, my goodness gracious," she said, "were you not sated in our bed of lust?"

"The beast aroused."

"So it seems."

"I wouldst gather thee once more unto our bower."

"How about some coffee first?"

"Excellent suggestion. What today—Ethiopian, Kenyan or Guatemalan?"

"Costa Rican."

"Straight from the mountain sides?"

"Picked and processed day before yesterday." Alicia smiled up at Six and pinched one of his prominent cheek bones. She too had become re-aroused, so to speak.

Six and Alicia's vigorous outdoor life had kept their long-muscled bodies in fine shape, now enhanced by deep tans from days under the sun in their bass boat on Winsokkett, as well as on other waters close at hand, such as North Pond, Great Pond, Willow Pond, Lake Salmon and McGrath Pond. Alicia's hair had whitened prematurely when she was just past forty and Six's hair had since then also gone white. And typical of outdoorsmen, they wore their hair short, completing their aspect of a matched pair.

Thirty years before, Six and Alicia had been very young, newly constituted assistant professors—she taught English literature, he, history—at the same small Massachusetts campus. They first clapped eyes on each while striding across the quad and they had immediately liked what they each saw, which wasn't surprising, as they were so physically corresponding. As would be expected for two such tall young people, they were remarkably attenuated, seemingly all legs and arms and elbows; each of their long faces, though not classically handsome, were enhanced by large brown eyes and sweet, wide-mouthed smiles.

Their first two mutual sightings on the quad had rendered them both dumb with simultaneous embarrassment and longing. On their third approach, Alicia decided that something had to be done; she stopped squarely in Six's way, blocking him, and smiled and stared at him with a look that said, "What the hell are you waiting for?"

After learning they were related to some of the same old guard New England families, Six did some frantic research and found, to his and Alicia's mutual relief, that they were only third cousins.

Once that was established they quite sensibly fell in love. When Six discovered Alicia was also a fisherman, he knew there was a God.

While they both continued to teach, Alicia bore them two daughters, whom they had loved dearly and raised to well-adjusted (allegedly; one never knew for sure) adults. Once the girls had taken wing, Six and Alicia took a big financial risk by retiring after only twenty years of teaching and established an antiquarian mail-order book business. Their respective parents—also academics of modest resources—had been able to help a bit with finances, but one of their many cousins—an impressively wealthy one—had splashed out with an impressive no-interest loan. The book-selling profits and Alicia's watercolors, which were big sellers at three galleries over on the coast, paid for their Winsokkett Pond camp and enough free time to fish to their hearts' content.

At 8:15, following breakfast, another round of coffee and another round of love-making, Six and Alicia walked out to the end of their T-shaped dock and sat in their sagging, faded director chairs, whose cracked, sun-bleached frames popped and creaked under the strain, and regarded the warm, still day before them.

"Might have to get new chairs one of these summahs," Six announced.

"Ayuh. Might." Alicia didn't want to think about it. Once she got used to a chair she didn't want to ever give it up.

On the far western shore, other camps similar to McCorkle and nestled in the thick forests that ringed every mile of Winsokkett were barely distinguishable without the use of binoculars. Forested hills rose behind the southern and western shores, and to the northwest and north, ranks of hills and eventually mountains, in varying shades of green, undulated to the horizon. Except for the gleaming black 50-horse Evinrude on the Godwins' 17-foot bass boat, there was nothing to indicate to the eye that the year was not, say, 1946 rather than 2010.

Six and Alicia's fishing ensembles did not sully the illusion. They wore tattered fishing caps with long, fraying visors, faded, knee-patched jeans cinched with cracked-leather belts, threadbare khaki camp shirts mottled by fish and oil stains, and biodegrading blucher moccasins with splits sewn together by fishing line. Young people paid substantial prices for this sort of "distressed" clothing in such establishments as Old Navy and Gap, with one significant difference—the garments the youngsters purchased were new; the professors Godwin had distressed their outfits themselves by constant wear over a period of years. Once Six and Alicia got accustomed to fishing in particular items of clothing, they hated to ever give them up, and when at long last a shirt, or a pair of jeans or moccasins were no longer wearable, they hung them on pegs in their bedroom and left them there, much like other sportsmen hung trophies of mounted fish and animals over a fireplace.

The Godwins' yellow Labrador retriever, Rudolph, ambled out to the end of the dock, chose a spot next to Alicia's chair, circled three times, flopped down with a lusty sigh and began inspecting his private parts. Their cat—a marmalade cat efficiently named "Marmalade"—soon followed, but in a desultory fashion, stopping several times to gaze intently at swallows darting down from overhanging branches to drink from the water's surface.

"I've got an idea," Six proclaimed brightly.

"Do we need ideas this early in the morning?"

"Let's get all the work caught up today and tomorrow—just a little fishing morning and evening—and then treat ourselves to a couple of days and a night over at Gene's place. We haven't fished Willow Pond this summer." Iphigene Seldon—Six's second cousin, Alicia's third—was the relative whose generosity had given Winsokkett Antiquarian Books the wherewithal to be launched. She owned the historic and famous Cedar Lodge on Willow Pond, an immense lake of wild beauty just west of North Pond. It was the premier fishing and hunting lodge in central Maine.

"I was wrong," Alicia said. "It's *not* too early for good ideas. Let's do it. If all the rooms are full we can at least fish there."

"All we need is tackle. Gene has plenty of rental boats."

"Excellent," Alicia said, smiling at Six. "Let's have another cup of Costa Rican and plan our frenetic agenda."

As so began another day of quiet splendor for the professors Godwin in the heavenly lake country of rural Maine.

Unfortunately, as the mythologies of various religions warn, trouble eventually will break out in paradise. As Six and Alicia sat on their dock, regarding the day before them in Taoist-like placidity, murderous evil, a human condition foreign to the Godwins' experience, was lying inert but poised beneath a benign surface at Cedar Lodge. Six and Alicia could not have known it, of course, but in a matter of days that evil, once manifest, would envelop them in its terror.

A death storm was brewing to the west and it was heading their way.

One

Brad Seldon stood at the end of the dock watching Sam, their dock boy, showing one of the bass boats—three fishing chairs, fore and aft trolling motors—to Brad's fishing party, a couple who had arrived late last night and gone to bed exhausted. Brad was already imagining what the scrumptious blonde woman would look like stretched out on his bed wearing only her skin. Take it easy, stud, he thought, mocking himself. No chance. Here with her husband. That's if he *was* her husband. Neither of them wore wedding rings.

Married or not, Brad noticed—how could he not?—that the woman—Terry? was that her name?—was already giving him the big eyes and the wide smile. The pair had come to Cedar Lodge saying they loved bass fishing and wanted some first-rate angling. *Allll riiight, Brad decided, I'll knock their socks off with jumping, fighting, tail-dancing smallmouth bass and rod-bending largemouths. Might throw in a pike or two for big grins. Get the little lady excited.* Fishing, Brad had found during his twenty-two years as a Maine guide, was often very nicely arousing for women.

Some women. The ones who dig manly men stuff. Plaid shirts and romance by the campfire frying the day's catch. Straight off an L.L. Bean catalog cover circa 1950. Ayuh, Brad reflected, manly men and smoke dreams.

Brad Seldon was all too aware that he may be drinking his life toward a ditch, but, by God, he was manly. He snickered at the thought as a rude song from college jingled through his mind: *We are the manly men, we hump all the . . .* Whoops! There went the couple back toward the lodge. What the hell now? He walked down to Sam and said,

"What's the prob, Sam?"

Sam, a college junior back for his second summer, rolled his eyes. "Their picnic basket and thermoses."

"Their *pic*—oh, Jesus."

"They seem nice, though."

Brad shot Sam a dark look and said, "I'm going up to the porch," which the dock boy knew was code for "I need a drink." Ten-thirty in the morning and already Brad was longing for a comforting 86-proof buzz. Well, it was the guests' fault, he decided—Terry? and . . . who was the guy? Some godawful name like Jason—had demurred at the suggestion of a sunrise outing. Drinking didn't affect the purpose soon at hand, however, because even pants-wetting drunk he could bring a boatload of fish out of any water. Out of a park fountain. Out of a bathtub.

Brad paused and looked out on Willow Pond, the second-largest lake in central Maine. On its western shore and the part of its eastern shore nearest to Cedar Lodge at the south end there were a great many private camps, some new, some very old, dating back to the teens and twenties; the newer wooden camps were mostly built in the traditional style, with big screen or open-air porches, and one or two stories under a peaked roof. These days, even the old camps had been renovated to install heating. There were three islands in the lake, all of them covered with huge weeping willow trees that overhung the desiccating ruins of ancient camps and docks.

The lake was calm now but was subject to sudden tumultuous change when violent storms or hard winds roared over the mountains to the west and north and swept across, raising whitecaps. Here had been his boyhood and his youth on this huge, deep, lonely and haunted lake where his parents had died violently, where the only woman—girl, really, at the time—he had ever loved had drowned. Here . . . oh, dear God, he needed that drink.

Had a first-time observer seen this man striding up the dock toward his secret hidey-hole on the lodge's enormous first-floor porch, he or she wouldn't have seen an alcoholic wreck, but a handsome fellow who moved with athletic assurance. He was not overly tall, about six feet, with wide shoulders, trim, though getting waist-line soft from too much good bourbon. Various antique New England bloodlines had coalesced into features that suggested early Errol Flynn (also ruined by booze) and perhaps a bit of Ronald Coleman. And, as genetic chance would have it, Brad had a topper of thick, curly, russet-colored hair. The combination was deadly to women who, one, preferred the dash of Golden Age movie stars to the sulking beauty of today's film brats and, two, were missing a shark-detection function on their personal sonar systems.

He walked up the wide front steps to the first-floor porch and over to the flower box nestled among the Adirondack and wicker chairs that held his bottle of George Dickel and a shot glass. At such moments as this Brad followed his father's firm admonition: "A gentleman never drinks good whiskey straight from the bottle." Just as he was pouring his first shot of "spiritual uplift," as he called it, a loud voice bellowed, "Sam! After they're off, get three canoes from the rack and set 'em up!"

"Yes, ma'am!" Sam shouted back.

The owner of the rambunctious voice came marching toward Brad down the long porch. Iphigene Seldon, his aunt and owner of Cedar Lodge; "Il Duce," Brad called her, the re-incarnation of Benito Mussolini in an old woman's body. A still somewhat hard body, though, Brad had to concede. Her white hair was cut short, she was tanned like a South Pacific surfer, and her face had skin like a coconut shell. Today, he noticed, she was featuring one of her signature ensembles, dubbed "the Hemingway" by Brad's sister, Merrill—loose white fishing shirt with four pockets and loops for tackle, khaki shorts with multiple pockets, and blucher moccasins. The shirt was rolled up above her elbows, exposing sun-blackened, muscular forearms. Seventy-seven years old and still able to lift a 20-horse motor off a boat transom and carry it to the dock. "I can take the nuts off a bobcat," was her favorite self-admiring statement.

Amazingly to Brad, especially as he studied her now powering toward him, she was still sexually active. Every season she managed to seduce at least one of the unattached elderly fishermen who came to the lodge in appreciable numbers from late April through early October. A handsome silver fox had registered yesterday around noon and by the evening Gene, as she was called, was sending him drinks at the bar. Brad's mind reeled at possible bedroom images.

As perpetually, Gene's sad-eyed bloodhound, Amos, sloped along right at her heels. Ten summers before, another silver fox, a wealthy old boy from Georgia had checked into Cedar Lodge and fallen for Gene's rugged idea of romance, telling her she reminded him of farm girls back home when he was a boy who had done it up against the wall behind the barn. Gene was actually charmed by the comparison, slapped him on his bare backside and told him to come see her the next summer. He did do that. And he brought her a bloodhound puppy, too. Every good woman, he had declared, should have a bloodhound at her heels.

And on this day nine years later, that's just where Amos was. He followed Gene as she strode up to Brad, put her fists on her hips and thrust out her chin. "What the hell's going on? Thought you were getting underway." Brad reached down to stroke Amos. He hated his aunt, but he liked her dog.

"Picnic basket."

"I beg your pardon. Are you drunk already?"

"*I* am not drunk and *they* are getting a picnic basket."

"Jesus."

"Just what I said."

"Fill the boat with bass. These two are important."

"I always get fish, you know that. And why are they important?"

"Potential investors."

Brad's eyebrows went up on that one. "Oh? We need investors?"

"I've got plans."

"You've always got plans."

"I hear your party coming down the stairs. Got everything you need? Your bottle, your dick—you don't need your brains."

Brad stared at Gene and realized not for the first time how much he'd love to watch his auntie dear drop dead.

"Get stuffed," he said.

Gene smiled, enjoying the moment, enjoying the mutual hatred. How she'd love to punch Brad right in his face. Merrill too. They were just like their parents, Reg and Annice, so beautiful, so smugly vain, so cruel in their disregard for anyone not like them. She longed to be rid of them, but they were much too valuable. As fishing guides, nobody in this part of Maine, probably in the whole state, could touch them.

They knew huge and sometimes deadly Willow Pond better than anyone and were also experts on the nearby smaller lakes and the rivers. They had become the image of Cedar Lodge, Maine. There they were, smiling out from full-color ads in every classy sporting magazine in the U.S., Canada and Europe, their gorgeously thick auburn hair ruffled by the wind, faces suntanned and freckled, as they held aloft glistening champion-sized bass, trout or pike. "Come fish with Brad Seldon and Merrill Beauchamp, Maine's premiere freshwater guides!" Anglers far and wide logged on to the lodge's web site or picked up the phone and took the lure.

As Brad's couple emerged onto the porch, with the man holding a wicker basket, Gene came over all hearty and beaming. "Good morning again, folks. I know you're going to have a splendid time. Brad's the best there is."

The woman said, "Oh, I'm sure he is."

Gene widened her smile and said, "Are you folks in a hurry? There's something I want to show you. We're expanding at Cedar Lodge and I'm kind of proud of my latest purchase."

They assured her they were not in a hurry and then followed Gene and Amos toward the new dock that had just been completed. Two brand-new 18-foot sailboats had been put in the water the previous day. As the trio walked way, the woman turned to flash Brad a brilliant smile.

Brad smiled back and then glared at the quick-marching figure of his aunt and muttered, "You goddamn phony old weasel. Now, God, right now, strike her dead—how about it?" Only he didn't believe in God anymore. He had stopped believing in God the day he watched lightning fry his mother and father in their boat just as they were tying up to the dock. Eighteen years ago. He'd been thirty at the time—and he'd been a drunk ever since.

As Brad poured another shot of blessedness, he heard the soft tread of designer espadrilles on the porch stairs and turned to see Renee, his wife, second only to his aunt as an object of loathing, descending. Twice a month she drove over from her apartment in Bar Harbor, on the Maine coast, to Cedar Lodge to get her monthly separation-agreement check personally and to see if perhaps Gene were getting feeble or, her fervent wish, dying. She was desperate for Brad to inherit his part of the lodge so she could get a sizable wad of the cold, hard by granting him a divorce.

"Hello, my poisonous flower," Brad said. "Want a divorce?"

"Yes. Do you have two million?"

"One of these days."

"Gene looks disgustingly healthy. Why don't you kill her?"

"Why don't you?"

This was their usual joke routine, only to Brad's mind it was starting to not sound so funny anymore. Lately he had been subject to dark ruminations, in which he fantasized ways to murder his aunt. Murder. Dear God, this was not him. This was not the man in his mirror. Was it? What the hell was happening? His soul was decomposing.

Renee sat beside him and was silent for awhile, looking out at the lake and swinging an elegant leg. Finally, she said, "Look, Brad. I'm sorry we got trapped. We need to set each other free. But I need money. I intend to have money. I don't intend to grow old sitting in Bar Harbor's tourist bars."

"Why don't you marry one of those rich bastards over on the coast and get off my back?"

"You know damn well I'm not going to marry again, Brad. And especially not just for money, much as I might want it. I want my *own* money. I want to go where I want when I want, do what I want. I'm thirty-eight. I want the beautiful places with the beautiful people. It's where I belong. I want to be seen."

"Yeah. You're right, Renee. I don't like you, but I gotta admit, you're still a looker."

"I don't like you either. Funny how we got married."

"Yeah, it's a frigging riot."

"I think it was sex."

"Yeah, it was sex. Want a drink?"

"Before noon? God, no. Please don't drink yourself to death before you inherit."

"And after I inherit?"

"Be my guest."

"My special angel."

"Speaking of angels, are you going to poke that little blonde you're taking fishing?"

Brad scrunched up his features and turned to stare at Renee. "Am I going to *poke* her? *Poke* her? What kind of damn language is that?"

"It's a British expression. Rather evocative, wouldn't you say?"

"Oh, Jesus, are you hanging out with Brits again?"

"I have some English friends, yes. I certainly find them more appealing than the average American jerk."

"Swell. Gotta go." Brad rose, a tad unsteadily, and lumbered down the stairs and toward the bass boat. Renee ignored him and pulled a paperback mystery from her bag. The cover, which showed an old and forbidding house with tall, creepy windows and the title "Death at Broadmoor Manor," was just the sort of presentation that most often made her buy a book. Murder and Anglophilia—lovely combination. And that set her quick but not especially deep mind trotting along a familiar path: Wouldn't it be a treat if someone would actually put down—"put down" was a term her English friends used—Iphigene Seldon, the old horror.

Renee was starting to despair. Any year now, gravity, as the saying went, was going to start pulling at her body and face. She needed that damn money.

* * *

Sam was helping the couple aboard the bass boat. Come on, sluggo, Brad told himself, get it together for the customers. As he came up beside the boat he put on a big charming-devil smile, bowed from the waist and said:

"Hello, my name is Brad and I'll be your guide today. Would you like to hear our specials?" Whoops, Brad warned himself— "specials" sounded more like "sheshals." Better watch it. Don't alarm the guests.

The woman giggled and said, "I'm Tory Bolston, and I already know who you are—Brad Seldon. I saw the picture of you and your beautiful sister on the lodge's web site and in a big ad in *Field & Stream*."

Brad climbed into the boat. "Ah, yes. The bodacious Merrill. She leads fly-fishing expeditions as well as bass outings, if you're also interested in getting some trout."

Tory flashed a thousand-megawatt smile of gleaming ivories. "No. I came here for bass fishing. With *you*."

Whoa! Brad thought. What's this? He looked quickly over to the man just as Tory said, "Brad, I'd like you to meet my brother, Nelson. I think he wants to go fly-fishing."

"Weh-hell, Nelson! How do ya do? Pleased to meet you."

"Thanks," Nelson said, smiling. "Nice to meet you." Brad looked him over: He wasn't the equivalent of his sister in looks, but he was a big guy, well built. Probably an IT executive, Brad thought—*everybody's* an IT something these days.

Brad settled behind the wheel, started the 75-horse outboard and eased away from the dock in a state of amused wonder. Yessir, he told himself, this is something new—a brother and sister team on the hunt in fishing camps. Suddenly, the day looked a lot brighter, and his mood lifted as he checked for his flask under the dash and smiled over at the blue eyes regarding him.

As if cued by a director, two big loons surfaced not far from the boat and one of them opened his great dagger beak and called a ghostly *aaaWHAAhaooo* that echoed in the dark forests and hills surrounding Willow Pond.

"This is just what I dreamed of," Tory purred.

Brad glanced at her and silently replied, Me too, little darlin'— me too.

* * *

Over on nearby Winsokkett Pond, Merrill Beauchamp lay beside Bruno Gabreau in a cocaine-and-three-orgasms-induced euphoria. God, how she loved Bruno! She was crazy about him. And she didn't yet know what she was going to do—especially what she was going to do about a particular large and boring husband, one Huntley Beauchamp. But she was going to do something.

Gene Seldon depended on Huntley to manage Cedar Lodge's investments, but that didn't mean she, Merrill, had to stay married to the great lump. Huntley had told her three years earlier, just before their separation, that Cedar Lodge, its investments, the land it occupied and the land purchased at other lakes in central Maine for Cedar Lodge Enterprises Inc. were worth more millions than even she realized. The thought of all that money made her weak with longing, and it also made her angry. Why couldn't she have her part of the inheritance now? Oh, God, it was so unfair. She had begged Gene to let her cash out her share now, but all she'd gotten in return was a bellow of derisive laughter.

"You know how to fish, little lady, but that's about it for major skills," Gene had said. She could never resist sneering, Merrill thought bitterly. What a ghastly old termagant.

"You don't know a goddamn thing about money," Gene had continued. "Cash in your inheritance ahead of time? Nobody does a thing like that. Besides, the money's all tied up. I'm making it grow like duck weed. You and Kipper and Brad will be rolling in it, so hold your horses until I've registered at the great fishing camp in the sky." Gene had chuckled maliciously. "I licked big C, so it looks as though that registration is a long way off. Enjoy your middle age."

That last remark had sent Merrill into another fit of despair; she was forty-five, still an auburn-headed knockout, but time seemed to be galloping by. The self-centered Huntley hadn't wanted children and had tricked her by having a vasectomy. During a violent quarrel he'd unintentionally let that little fact come slithering into the light. Enraged, Merrill had demanded a divorce and he'd shrugged and said, sure, fine with me, but not until he received a settlement of over a million. So he had moved from Cedar Lodge to Boston, which suited him grandly, for he had grown sick of all the Orvis-clad hardiness of the great outdoors. He preferred tailored clothes, striped ties, cocktails at the 19th hole at a country club. Women, he'd decided in his first year of bachelorhood, were for sexual pleasure; who needed to live with one, enduring her demands and complaints?

Merrill was terrified of trying to have children at her age, but at least she could have someone who truly loved her—she could have Bruno. On this day, following another confrontation with Gene, she had run to Bruno for the comforting he always knew how to give. He was outdoor rugged but kind, he was French and handsome and always calm, and he made love like a god.

Gene had learned of her affair with Bruno—secrets were a rarity around lake camps, which were even more vigorous in their delectation of gossip than small towns; the Winville general store was like a trading floor for local data. Merrill could do whatever she pleased with her body, Gene had told her, but her talent as a fisherman belonged to Cedar Lodge.

"I need you living right here, on the spot. You and Brad are two of the lodge's top assets, a true cruelty of fate as far as I'm concerned. The kitchen is getting famous, but it can't keep the rooms and the boats filled with customers. Don't even *think* of taking up residence on Winsokkett Pond with Bruno Gabreau. If you do a thing like that, I'll slice you out of my will with a ten-inch fish knife."

Merrill had shouted back, "Goddammit, Gene, Winsokkett is twenty minutes away. I could come here whenever I'm needed."

"No, damn it!" Gene had bellowed. "Twenty minutes driving time plus thirty minutes or more getting-ready time—*if* you happen to be home at the time—while I've got high-rollers doing a slow boil cause they're missing a guide. It's deadly for business."

"Hire another guide. There are plenty of them."

Gene had reddened with fury. "Je-sus *Cuh-rist!* Don't be deliberately obtuse, Merrill! You and your drunken brother are like fishing-world movie stars. All our promotions point to the fact that the two of you are an integral part of Cedar Lodge, not just hirelings. That you live here, that your lives *are* Cedar Lodge."

"Brad and I are doomed, aren't we?"

"You and Brad are lucky. He's an alcoholic—he'll be a pants-pisser in ten years—and you're a cokehead. And you're both over forty. How far do you think either of you'd get in the outside world?"

The hideous truth of Gene's words crept into her euphoria now as she lay beside Bruno. Tears welled up and then ran down her lovely tanned and freckled cheeks. The thought of being without money terrified her more than contemplation of late-age childbirth. Oh, Jesus, Jesus, the brutal unfairness of it, she thought. If she had the money that was rightfully hers, her part of the fortune *her* parents had begun creating, not Gene, then she and Bruno could set up their own fishing camp, be free to live as they pleased. She sank into further anguish thinking about her beautiful parents, killed so horribly. And that thought led her to another, too-familiar source of her almost constant anger—her mother and father had not made a will. And under the terms of her grandfather's will, Gene had inherited everything.

Oh why couldn't the old bitch just die and make everyone's life happier? Why couldn't someone kill her? What an ugly wish, Merrill told herself as she sat up and reached for the glass of white wine on the bedside table. Ugly but hard to put down. If anyone deserved being murdered, Merrill decided, it was "Il Duce," Brad's nickname for horrid Aunt Iphigene.

* * *

Huntley Beauchamp sipped a scotch on the rocks and gazed forlornly from a window seat at the Copley Plaza. It was two-fifteen in the afternoon and he was already tight. He *had* to drink. Only drunk could he endure the fear and tension that gripped him.

He was in bad, bad trouble. Fortunately, only he knew about it. He was the sole proprietor and only officer of Beauchamp Portfolio Investments, Inc. and therefore Iphigene Seldon knew nothing, as yet, of his little "personal rewards." He had told her—using his rich, purring baritone to its fullest effect; a voice that could've reassured a window-ledge jumper that he would bounce—that things were humming along splendidly despite the effects of the recent recession. Cedar Lodge's securities had mostly recovered from that misfortune and new mutual funds were producing impressive increases.

That, basically, was the truth. What was not said—and what did not appear in the spread sheets—was that Huntley Wooster Beauchamp, bearing an oak room and fine leather name he had devised for himself, had been living like a Dubai sheik for the past two years. A Bentley convertible sedan rolled him majestically to his clubs—the Somerset and the Tavern—a twenty-two-foot sailing yacht glided him gracefully across the harbor on weekends, and a six-room, antique-stuffed, private elevator apartment awaited him upon his return.

He shuddered when he thought of the four million he had picked from the fat ($48.5 million in assets) pockets of Cedar Lodge Enterprises—and that amount was in addition to his robust monthly fees for managing the investments.

Misallocation of funds was bad enough, but discovery of outright embezzlement meant disaster: criminal charges, permanent loss of broker's license, and, most likely, jail. At the end of this merciless gauntlet would be the worst specter of all—a return to the poverty that Jack Spurling, late of the dreaded proletarian class, had struggled with insane determination to leave behind and become Huntley Beauchamp, respected and admired as a true man of class and discernment.

The former Jack Spurling had made a marvelous discovery twenty-nine years before when he was a scrambling twenty-two-year-old at a financial services corporation. He had discovered, by concentrating on the techniques of the power men around him, that appearance and B.S. were the touchstones of success in the investment industry. And he knew he had the qualifiers: looks, voice, charm and high I.Q. What he needed was to disappear from one city, and, with a legally changed name, pop up in another city as a different person, get into a good firm by virtue of the University of Virginia education he had purchased from a very expensive document maker, and then . . . begin playing the big game. One had to have nerves and ego both made of steel to stay the course for this sort of endeavor, and back then he had them.

But now, at age fifty-one, and with so much at stake, his nerve was weakening. Sure, he'd been in tight corners before and, sure, he'd bobbed and weaved into the clear. But this coming meeting with Gene Seldon and her family at Cedar Lodge was like nothing he'd ever faced. As far as life as he knew it was concerned, it had the potential effect of a roadside bomb.

Someone in a board meeting or at a club or cocktail party regarding "Hunt" (as he was called by acquaintances) Beauchamp would have seen an impressive figure—tall, broad-shouldered, hair wavy brown with gray temples, carefully tailored clothes and . . . and then, the voice, a soft, mellifluous baritone redolent of good breeding, and the smiling charm, with a hand on one's shoulder imparting sincerity. Huntley was a convincing package, just as his father had been, though his father had never gotten farther than an auto dealership and had drunk himself into an alcoholic ditch.

But now, sitting in the Copley Plaza working on a mid-afternoon buzz, this suave figure was a nervous wreck. A week previously Gene Seldon had called him with a heart-freezing demand.

"Hunt, my man," she had bombasted, "I'm calling a big meeting in two weeks. Everybody. The whole family, you—well, you're still technically family (a hearty chuckle). Our lawyer, our accountant, the whole shebangaroo. I'm changing my will and two of the heirs are going to do a war dance. We need to look at the books on everything and show the savages just how rich they'll be even though their slice of the pie is being narrowed."

Having reassured Gene that everything would be there "in superb shape," though his marvelous voice squeaked twice as panic hit him like a bullet, Huntley had hung up the phone and sat for an immobilized half-hour with his mind popping and fizzing as gruesome possible scenarios flashed before him. *Oh, bloody Christ. The lawyer and the accountant. A double-barreled shotgun aimed right at the lapels of his English summer-weight worsted.*

There was no way to hide that missing four million with phony spreadsheets; Huntley knew he did not have that kind of accounting talent. He was certain his fiddled statements would never get past an accountant. He'd shown them to Gene several times, but she was easy. She thought she knew everything about business, just as she thought she knew everything about everything, *the obnoxious old braggart,* but the truth was she didn't really know how to study financial statements.

Finally, Huntley had gotten control of his panic and started thinking. Inevitably, his thoughts led him to the only person he believed could help him out of this hole, a very private, intensely discreet businessman, who spoke only in discreet coded phrases, who was in touch with talented specialists who knew how to provide escape for cornered rats. But the cost would be substantial, he was told. Fine, fine, he had responded. He could borrow the money, he told himself, sell his boat and car, his apartment. Anything just to get clear and start again.

A specialist, using a bogus individual name employed by a bogusly named corporation, was found who contacted Huntley and assured him that by the time of the fateful Cedar Lodge meeting two weeks hence, all problems would be covered. Huntley had to send printouts on Cedar Lodge Enterprises and a large cashier's check as a deposit (he'd maxed out an entire bank credit line) to a post office box in Rhode Island.

"This specialist firm," the discreet businessman had told him, "is imaginative and responds quickly to difficult or surprising turns of events. In addition to resolving your, um, central problem, the firm will create phantom companies—even providing them with, say, fifty-year corporate histories—that will look as solid as gold and prevent embarrassing questions afterward."

Huntley ordered another double Scotch from the waiter. *If Gene Seldon could just conveniently drop dead, all would be well. All would be well.* But the tough old bird gave every indication of continued good health.

Two

Six Godwin was standing in the bow of his bass boat in the middle of Winsokkett Pond battling a pike when his cellphone rang. Well, dammit, he thought. Perfect timing. The thing rang an enraging ten times while he lurched about with a seven-foot rod almost bent double, struggling to reel the monster in. Uh oh, here it comes, he told himself, get ready. A big, torpedo-shaped fish with a long mouth containing rows of sharp teeth came slowly to the surface, rolled over on its side and floated, inert, while staring at Six with a big, dark eye.

OK, this is the moment, this is the bugger's big trick . . . steady, steady. Just as Six was reaching ever so slowly for the net, his cellphone emitted the merry little voice mail jingle and the pike, which had worked the fishing line to the back of his mouth, shot forward, snapping the line, crunching the lure and causing Six to fall backward.

"Oh, sonofabitch," Six muttered as he grabbed the fishing chair and pulled himself up. Typical. Wasn't the first time. Pikes were notoriously hard to land, and though Six and his wife, Alicia, were excellent bass fishermen, they'd gotten only about a half-dozen pikes on board during the past few summers.

He wondered if Alicia could possibly be the one calling him. She knew he was fishing, and being an angler herself, she would never ring him unless there was an . . .

Oh, no. Emergency! He hurriedly pulled the phone from his jeans pocket and punched in the voicemail code. "*One. New. Message. Message. One.*" A loud, boisterous female voice said, "Six! It's Gene. I need your help over here at Cedar Lodge. Nothing complicated. Could you call me back first chance?"

Six smiled for two reasons: one, relief that there wasn't an emergency, and, two, at the image that always came to him when he heard Iphigene Seldon's un-dulcet tones—a sea captain, hands on hips, bellowing at the crew. Of his many cousins, Gene Seldon was one of the few to whom Six had ever been close. She was an outrageous character, egotistical and dominating, Six had to admit, but he had always gotten a big kick out of her, and she had returned his regard for her with some big favors over the years, including the loan for his and Alicia's book business. Cousinhood was a big issue in Six's life. His peculiar name was a result of being related to basket-loads of New England cousins. His charmingly deranged parents, exceptionally proud of their lineage, had thought to include as many cousinly bloodlines as possible in his name—Preston Thorndike Seldon Hawthorne Whittier Garfield Godwin. In prep school, his classmates, with admirable logic, had edited his moniker to Six, and the name had endured.

Because Gene had several times unburdened herself to him when she'd over-served herself at the lodge's bar, Six understood why his cousin approached the world like a . . . *hmm, like a what? he pondered. Ah! Like a pike.* She told him how she had suffered from her parents' indifference. Not neglect—no, she was well cared for, well clothed and well educated. What she had endured was the cruelty of indifference. She had not been like her brother, Reginald, a sun god in his mother and father's eyes. She had been an awkward, unattractive child, which had embarrassed her elegant parents. At parties, Reg the Beautiful's achievements had been expanded upon to guests while she sat silently nearby, smiling rigidly and accumulating hatred.

"Hatred, Six," she had said to him years ago, wagging a cocktail glass at him, "is a vile and very powerful thing. I wouldn't recommend it." And then, Gene had continued . . . and then, Reg, just out of college and rotten with the vanity fostered by his parents' adoration, had married someone equally beautiful and vain, Annice, also from a determinedly outdoors, sportsman family. She even modeled for catalogs such as L.L. Bean and Orvis.

"But during all this time I had fooled everybody by growing to womanhood with some bodacious curves. My face grew into its nose and ears and I wasn't so bad looking, though far from the glowing perfection of Reg and Annice." God, how she had loathed them, she'd told him. "They treated me with . . . oh, what's a good description . . . amused contempt. How would you like that in daily doses?" Six had agreed it sounded appalling. "Because of my bumbling, ugly duckling childhood, I suppose, I was often a social jerk, full of faux pas. Like I told you—curves, exuding sex and all, but no social graces. So that's how we aged together, all tucked into Cedar Lodge, 'cause by that time it had grown into the goddamnedest gold mine that none of us was going to leave. Besides, Reg and I had grown up there, it was home. It was huge and it was home."

Now, Six wondered what was up over at Willow Pond. Cedar Lodge was prospering, gathering more fame yearly, but he knew Gene had her hands full because she trusted no one else to manage the place. The youngest of Reg and Annice's children, Kipper, who, Six guessed, must now be in his late thirties, was the only one of the three who took an active interest in the business side of the lodge, and he had made a huge success of the restaurant with a gourmet chef. Gene worshiped Kipper and despised Brad and Merrill, his siblings, who had fought her claw and fang in court for control of the lodge. She had won, so they were all trapped in a situation of mutual hatred coupled with mutual benefit: Brad and Merrill, two of the best fishing guides in Maine and the much-advertised image of Cedar Lodge, probably attracted a good third of the yearly revenue, so Gene had to keep them there; Brad and Merrill, on the other hand, could get outstanding jobs anywhere there was water containing bass and trout, but would be cut from Gene's will if they left, throwing away the millions they were due to get. And they knew the promised inheritance was real because the lodge's lawyer had shown them the will—a three-way split among brothers and sister.

Six punched in Gene's number, heard three rings, and then Gene's voice answering.

"Hello, Gene. It's Six."

"Six, my man! Thanks for calling back so quickly!" Six had to hold the phone away from his ear. "How are you and the bodacious Alicia?"

"Couldn't be better."

"Fine, fine! Look, Six, I was wondering if I could get the two of you over here for a little visit, this weekend, Friday, Saturday and Sunday?"

"Sounds wonderful, Gene. We always love coming to the lodge. Anything special going on?"

"Ayuh. There's something special all right—an explosion."

"Gene! You're an al Qaeda target?"

Six winced as laughter boomed from the cellphone. "If it was al Qaeda I could handle it. It's worse—it's family. There's gonna be an explosion of familial rage at a special meeting I've called. The whole family plus lawyer, accountant and investment manager. That's Huntley Beauchamp, you know . . . Merrill's husband, only they're separated. He's coming in from Boston."

"And you need Alicia and me to serve drinks?"

More laughter, and louder. "Goddammit, Six. That's why I love you. You always break me up. No. I need you two for moral support. I mean, we *are* cousins—aren't we second? And Alicia's about a third or fourth. And, well, Six, this damn thing isn't gonna be easy. You're more like a brother to me than Reg ever was."

"I'll call Alicia right now. I'm sure it'll be fine, we never have anything going."

"Call? Where are you now?"

"Out on the lake."

"Catch anything good?"

"Just got a big pike up to the boat, but he got away."

"Someday I'll show you how to land those buggahs. Meantime, call me back, and when you and Alicia get here I'll explain what's happening."

* * *

"Seems like we don't have to reserve a room at Cedar Lodge," Six announced as he walked into the camp to find Alicia busy at her easel. "Gene called while I was out on the lake and insisted we come over for two or three days."

"No kidding? What's the occasion?"

Six pulled up a chair next to his wife and said, "Well now, let me tell you all about it." When he had finished repeating his conversation with Gene, Alicia said:

"I wouldn't miss it for the world. A weekend at Cedar Lodge *and* high drama."

"I don't know what's up, but it's got to be serious. Gene, as usual, covers anything she may be feeling with a lot of Long John Silver heartiness, but this is an unusual request."

"Well, with the whole family and lawyer, accountant, Indian chief all there, do you think it's possible that some major corporation has made an offer?"

"Ermm." Six fumbled in his pockets for his pipe and tobacco pouch and lighter. (Why, he questioned himself rhetorically, were the damn things always in separate pockets?) "Oh, I guess it's a possibility, but I can't see Gene ever selling Cedar Lodge. It's been her whole life. For that matter, that's true for the nephews and nieces, too. They've never known anything else." Six filled his pipe bowl with No. 79, a special mix he bought from a Boston tobacconist that featured in its blend a bit of honey, a smidgeon of rum, and the cuts of three different Turkish leaves, and puffed up a cumulo-nimbus of fragrant smoke.

"From what I saw when we were there last September," Alicia said, "she's really mean to Brad and Merrill. I mean, the insults she casually threw at them were downright nasty."

"A couple of times I saw them give it right back to her."

"Yes, I remember that, but she just grinned and walked away, as if it's a big game. She owns the toy box and they have to play by her rules."

Six puffed and chuckled and said, "To be a devil's advocate—the devil in this case being Gene—would you want to deal with Brad and Merrill on a daily basis?"

Alicia laughed as she picked up her tackle box and began rummaging for some swivels for putting Carolina rigs on two of her lines. "Lord, no! They're beautiful, but what a handful. Brad's always sloshed or on his way to an insloshment and Merrill, if I'm not mistaking a couple of symptoms, may be on cocaine."

21

"Oh, you're right there. Gene told me Merrill is a cokehead. There's damn little she can do about their addictions—I mean, they *are* over forty—and, to tell you the truth, she doesn't care as long as they can get paying anglers to where the fish are."

"And they're doing that?"

"Amazingly, they are doing that as superbly as ever. Gene says she doesn't see one damn hint of their skill being affected. It's a real marvel—two ace guides high as kites most of the time." Six puffed for a minute, contemplating the curious Seldon family. Then he blew smoke rings. "I guess it's not so surprising when you consider that they grew up in bass boats on the lakes and hip boots in the rivers. Fishing is part of their DNA."

"Then we probably shouldn't try the booze and coke fishing-enhancement method."

"Probably not."

"Want to go fishing anyway?"

"For sure. You finish your painting?"

"Ayuh. It's a beauty. Something a little different this time."

"Oh?"

"Bass boats at sunset."

That was a knee-slapper for both of them. Alicia's watercolors were bringing in more money each year from sales at galleries in nearby Waterville and in Rockport, on the Maine coast. Her themes were fishing, loons, sunsets, approaching storms and combinations of the four. Chopin nocturnes wafted serenely from the CD player at their feet as their equally serene yellow Labrador retriever, Rudolph, sprawled flat on the dock boards behind their chairs with his legs straight out. He was tucked close to their chairs to catch the shade of the blue-and-white awning-striped umbrella held by the lichen-covered redwood table between Six and Alicia. In naming the dog, Six had theorized that "Rudolph" somewhat imitated dog sounds—"ru," *rurrr*, for a growl and "dolph," *rawf, rawf,* for barking—and therefore it would be easier for their pet to learn his name. Alicia thought such theorizing was piffle and that a dog of yellow Labrador intelligence could handle "Ebenezer" just as well. Meanwhile, their marmalade cat, efficiently named Marmalade, having exhausted herself stalking chipmunks, was napping at the base of one of the oak trees that shaded their camp.

The professors Godwin, like their dog and their cat, were also in a mood of tranquility, regarding with pleasure their gorgeous lake as they drank coffee from white mugs adorned with leaping bass and trout. Six blew out three smoke rings in quick succession, then turned to Alicia and said:

"Damn hot weather, wouldn't you say, kiddo?"

"Been hotter than hell's hinges all week," Alicia replied.

"Think it's global warming?"

"No such thing as global warming, Six. You know that. Bunch of hysterical rubbish."

Six chuckled as he puffed up another cloud. He was amused that he could always get a rise from Alicia on certain subjects. "Didn't you see the picture of that poor little polar bear floating around on a chunk of ice?"

Alicia turned and glared at Six. "Speaking of ice, the stuff you're skating on right now is getting remarkably thin."

"Prob'ly be palm trees in Portland by next year."

"SIX!"

Just as Alicia finished assembling her second Carolina rig, Six said:

"You know what this weather does to me—hot and no breeze?"

"Can't imagine."

"Gives me the fantods."

"Which is . . . are?"

"Fidgety and tense."

"You don't look tense. You always look like you were born relaxing."

"The symptoms are deceptive."

"Only one thing to do for it," Alicia responded.

"And that is . . ."

"Go fishing."

"Right you are."

23

They arose from the decrepit chairs and walked to their boat, which was tied up to the dock fully gassed and with rods, tackle, sandwiches and thermoses already aboard. Their blue-hulled 16-footer was typical of boats designed for bass fishing: It rode low in the water and had high fishing seats fore and aft; in the middle was a steering wheel and driver and passenger seats. Though their craft bore the dents and scrapes and faded paint of ten summers on the lakes, the outboard motor was a big, gleaming-new 60-horse Evinrude they'd bought just the previous summer. Getting to the fishing holes speedily was of foremost importance to the professors.

They climbed aboard and untied the bow and stern lines. Alicia got behind the wheel, lowered the motor and started it up, then Six sat beside her and they pulled away from the dock, gliding slowly across the estimated 200-foot "no wake" zone. Before them was a calm lake glittering with sunlight; puffy, harmless clouds squatted over the western hills.

"So, kiddo," Alicia said. "Where do you reckon the fish are today?"

"Where the sky meets the sea."

"Oh, very funny."

* * *

At Cedar Lodge, Gene paced up and down the second-story porch deep in thought about the coming turmoil she was going to cause. (Amos hated this back and forth routine so he stretched out at one end of the porch and kept a wary eye on his mistress's movements.) Brad and Merrill were unmatched as guides and were popular charmers in the main dining room and the bar. But neither of them would ever be able to properly run the lodge. Brad couldn't get through a day—couldn't get through a *morning*—without little doses of "spiritual uplift," his cute little term that made Gene want to barf. And Merrill was unlikely to give up cocaine and whatever else kept her going. If Gene left the lodge to them they'd destroy it. Even if they each shared one-third with Kipper, together they would have enough leverage to dominate their little brother and make a mess of things.

And so she had called the attorney who had won her inheritance case and asked her to come to the lodge to advise and witness a change of will. Her darling Kipper, her genius, was the only one who could preserve Cedar Lodge. She intended to give him 55 per cent and his siblings 22.5 per cent each. The howling would carry all the way to Waterville and probably cause a moose stampede, but she was ready for it.

An accident of wicked fate had awarded her Cedar Lodge Enterprises.

Annice and Reg, so narcissistic, so convinced they were touched by the gods, believed they would never die, and so they had never even bothered to make a will. James Rutherford Seldon's will, made when Iphigene and Reginald were teenagers, gave sixty percent of Cedar Lodge, which he had founded, to his son. Even if Gene had been the sun goddess equivalent of her brother, the sixty/forty split would have been the same, for in "Big Jim" Seldon's mind, why on earth would a father give controlling interest to a daughter? His will stipulated that if one sibling predeceased the other, then the entire kaboodle would go to the survivor. And therefore that will had still been in effect when Reg and Annice were killed.

Brad and Merrill—Kipper was a minor at the time of his parents' death—hired a lawyer who was a notorious will-breaker, but Gene countered with a man considered to be Boston's best estate lawyer—Adrian Bucksaddle, Esq. He cost a small fortune, but was worth it, for he won the case. Annice and Reg's children were told by Mr. Bucksadddle—Gene was so enraged by the legal battle that she wouldn't speak to them for weeks—that Gene would forward them each $50,000 to live on while they searched for employment, or . . . or, they could "go fish" for Cedar Lodge and be included as heirs. As they had never known any life other than at the lodge, and fishing, they chose to "go fish," and became employees of Cedar Lodge, their home—it was a galling, humiliating situation.

Gene stopped pacing when she'd passed the center-hallway screen door for the umpteenth time. She decided to quit fretting, go downstairs and do one of her favorite things: peruse next week's menu with Kipper and the chef, Jean-Pierre LeMaire. Thank God for Kipper, she thought. He was so clever. It had been his idea four years ago to hire a gourmet chef, and it had worked out superbly. Cedar Lodge had always been known for its hearty meals for active fishermen and hunters (the lodge didn't emphasize hunting as much as fishing, but Gene had hired a first-rate winter guide). Now, it was getting a reputation for four-star Cordon Bleu cooking that was bringing in diners from nearby lakes and towns. And what was even better was that Kipper's hiring of Jean-Pierre had resulted in Kipper settling into a permanent relationship, for he had fallen in love with the man. Jean-Pierre was too pretty for his own good, Gene thought—he looked like a girlish Johnny Depp—and he was something of a snip. But if Kipper was happy, then that was all. And oh lord how that little snip could cook! During the winter, she especially loved watching some of the big red-steak-eating hunters look at their plates and say, "What's this crap?" and then beg for more a half-hour later.

* * *

Downstairs in the kitchen, things were not going well. As Jean-Pierre stared at Kipper, his lower lip began trembling and his eyes flooded with tears. Suddenly, he ripped off his apron and fled to the big screened-in back porch, letting the screen door go slappity-bam behind him.

Kipper dashed after him, heart pounding, panic rising, his usual hysterical reaction every time the little Frenchman threw a hissy and made Kipper have painful visions of losing him. Oh, dear God, how he loved Jean-Pierre. Each time he looked at him he wanted to grab him and squeeze him. He was so cute and adorable—except for moments like this, when he threatened Kipper with emotional chaos and despair by saying he would leave if he didn't get his way.

"Please, *please*, Jean-Pierre. Don't do this to me," Kipper implored.

Jean-Pierre's big eyes widened. "*I* am doing this to *you*? Oh, no, no, Kee-pair—this is something *you* are doing to *me*, over and over."

"But I don't have the money yet. You *know* that."

"It has been four years, *mon cher*. You promised. A restaurant in New York. You see how even these big thugs in plaid shirts go *fou* when they taste my food. I need to be known, the world needs to know my cooking, Kipper. I'll be famous . . . and so will you. *Four years*, you said."

"But that was when Gene was very ill. No one knew it but me. I thought she was dying. She had cancer."

Jean-Pierre's beautiful little face was suddenly suffused with renewed hope. "She has cancer?"

"*Had*. She *had* cancer. Ovarian. She was cured by chemo. It wasn't as dire as breast cancer."

"She *has* breasts?"

Kipper moaned and looked up at the ceiling in despair. "Oh, Jean-Pierre, I love you to death, but you can be so *callous*."

"Shit, merde, crap. Look, my sweet man, we are not talking about a nice person. Gene is a mean bastard. Look how she treats your brother and sister. She torments them. She has them trapped."

"She pays them big salaries. I know."

"They are trapped. And she insults them every time she opens her mouth."

"Brad and Merrill are free to leave." Kipper silently admitted that that sounded like a good idea.

"All they know is to feesh. You know very well they cannot risk their inheritance by leaving."

Kipper ran a hand through his tangled hair, which was redder than his siblings' deep auburn; he also had more freckles than they and less of their facial beauty; he often worried about how a little doll like Jean-Pierre could be in love with *him*, Kipper the Not So Handsome. He sighed and met Jean-Pierre's eyes. "You're right.

They're trapped." He paused and looked out toward the nearby woods. "I'm trapped, too."

Jean-Pierre softened his voice. "Yes, my sweet man, you are trapped. And I love you. But I also love myself . . . and my cooking. And I do not wish to be trapped."

"But look how famous your kitchen is becoming *here*. People are coming from farther away each month. And lots of them don't even feesh. They come only to eat." Kipper thought the "feesh" would get a smile from Jean-Pierre, but it drew only an irritated stare and downturned mouth.

"Kipling Seldon, mon amour, being famous *here* is like being the most famous wart on a hog's ass."

Kipper exploded, his freckles deepening in color. "Goddammit, Jean-Pierre, how can you say such a thing?"

"I just said it."

"How the hell can you be so insulting and ungrateful! I've done everything for you. I've spent hundreds of thousands setting you up. I . . ."

"I can bear this no longer. You are shouting and cursing at me. It breaks my heart, Kipper, but I am leaving."

As Jean-Pierre tried to move past him, Kipper fell to his knees and grabbed him around the legs. He began sobbing as he spoke. "Oh, dear God in heaven, *please*, Jean-Pierre. Please, *please*. I can't lose you. I'll kill the miserable old bitch if I have to. Just please don't leave me."

Jean-Pierre looked down in shock at the tall man clutching his legs, and then looked up and stared through the windows at the magnificent, gleaming ovens and stoves and cabinets. Though basically a person devoid of true evil, Jean-Pierre at that moment seriously contemplated how heavily a murder done for his sake might weigh on his conscience.

* * *

Just as the sobbing subsided and she heard Kipper and Jean-Pierre go through the screen door, Renee stepped back from the position she had frozen into and walked carefully back down the porch on the lodge's east side. The porches ran all the way around Cedar Lodge on all three floors; only the first-floor porch at the back, by the kitchen, was screened. Renee had been about to open the porch door and head for the kitchen to see what was cooking for lunch when the quarrel had erupted.

Holy crap, she thought. Gene's love object, Kipper. The phony. The way he slobbered over her was disgusting. *Oh Gene, darling . . . Oh Gene, my dearest.* . . . But despite what he'd just threatened, she thought it was something blurted in the agony of the moment to keep his French queen from bolting—snotty little frog; she couldn't stand him. She didn't think Kipper had the big ones to actually commit murder. I, on the other hand . . .

Renee was an instinctive pagan—life was everything, death was nothing, extinction, and the purpose of life was pleasure and getting what you wanted. The idea of actual physical violence appalled her, but the idea of murdering someone who deserved it by . . . hmm, how would she phrase it . . . by *remote* means seemed positively civilized. Gene, she had decided, was sadistic and . . . what was that word she'd read in her latest murder mystery? Ah yes— malevolent. Gene was malevolent. She deserved to be killed. She was in everyone's way. Who would care if she died?

Poison was the obvious choice. Renee had read umpteen mysteries in which various poisoning methods were outlined in generous detail. She would use one of those superb poisons that were undetectable except by the most exhaustive autopsy. Why didn't most murderers choose such a method, she wondered? Perhaps the poisons were difficult to acquire. She would have to find out.

Three

Brad had taken the Bolstons to the far northern section of Willow Pond, which was nine miles long and five miles wide. They were now beyond North Island, inhabited by otters, minks, small deer, loons and, high in their big tree-top nests, two families of ospreys and one of bald eagles. Here, there were no camps on the northern and eastern shores, and the forests that crowded the rocky shores were thick and dark and brooding, home to moose and bears.

Using the stern-mounted trolling motor, Brad eased the boat toward large boulders protruding above the surface some twenty to thirty feet from the island.

"You see those rocks?" Brad said. "Down in there is a dining establishment featuring crayfish, minnows, worms, frogs and whatever else a bass can get his big mouth around."

"Is it lunchtime yet?" Tory asked.

"Oh, probably." Brad smiled at Tory. The woman was just full of delights. For instance: Just as they had swung by Duck Island and were out of sight of the lodge, Tory announced, "I just *cannot* fish wearing a bra. It's just *too* constricting. Shouldn't have put it on in the first place." As she began unbuttoning her white fishing shirt, she giggled and said, "I hope you don't mind."

Brad had flashed a Rhett Butler grin and said, "Not at all, ma'am. If I had a bra I'd take it off too."

Laughing, Tory opened her shirt and deftly removed her bra, taking time to stuff it in her canvas bag before buttoning up, giving Brad a chance to savor the sight of her tanned breasts.

"OK," she said, fastening a few buttons, "let's go fish."

"That we shall do. But first . . . a little oogie-oogie."

Nelson, sitting behind Brad and Tory, laughed and asked, "Oogie-oogie? A native ritual perhaps?"

"Well, sort of. This native, anyway." Brad put the motor in neutral and as the boat slowed he reached under the dash and brought out his fifth of George Dickel. "Oogie-oogie is a little fisherman's pick-me-up. We toast the lake and we toast the fish and the lake gods will favor us. Nelson, there's some small glasses in that case right by your chair. Cheers!"

That had been forty-five minutes ago. Now, as they anchored near the North Island rocks, Brad was curious to see if this lusty little woman really could fish. She had insisted that she and her brother knew how to handle spin-casting rods, which spared Brad the tedious casting lessons for neophytes.

Brad had put Tory in the forward fishing chair and Nelson in the stern. "Tory," he said, I see you have one of your rods fixed with a Carolina rig. Put this lizard on your hook." He held up a five-inch, dark-green plastic lizard with black spots.

"Thanks," she said, taking the lure; she inserted the hook through the lizard's nose, brought it out the throat, twisted it around and brought it up through the lizard's back.

Brad went through a similar routine with Nelson, giving him a dark-red grub with a long wavy tail, and watched as he also expertly hooked on the lure. Okey-doke, Brad thought—they know how to deal with lures, let's see how they fish.

"All right now, I want each of you to cast to either side of that biggest rock, and then dead-stick the lure for about two minutes, then start twitching it and dragging it very slowly across the bottom."

To Brad's delight, both Tory and Nelson whipped out neat casts into the water he'd indicated. They didn't reel in or pull on their lines, so obviously they knew what "dead-sticking" meant—letting a lure lie inert on the lake bottom. Weh-hell, Brad thought, we've got a couple of troupers. As they each began a slow reeling in, Brad poured himself another spiritual uplift, studied Tory's profile and wondered if her honey-colored tan covered everything relevant or if there were rude tan/white demarcations here and there. Tory Bolston, he decided, didn't look like the sort of lady who sported swimsuit lines. We shall see, he merrily told himself; we shall see.

Tory got the first hit. She properly "bowed to the fish"—dipping the rod slightly until the fish tap-tapped again—and then jerked her rod back over her shoulder and set the hook. The fish dived and circled, bending Tory's rod far over—a big one with a lot of fight, Brad guessed. From the stern came a surprised exclamation from Nelson as he began fighting a fish on the end of his line.

Brad poured another whiskey and smiled. Nothing like satisfied customers.

* * *

When Gene barged through the big swinging doors of the kitchen and yelled, "Hiya, boys!" Kipper and Jean-Pierre, standing with their backs to the doors and with their heads together in mumbled conversation, jerked with spasms of alarm that only the guilty experience. They whirled around and stared at Gene like small animals frozen in the path of an oncoming vehicle.

"Let's take a look at those menus, shall we?" Gene was headed for the white wooden chairs arranged around a big butcher-block table in the kitchen's center when she stopped abruptly and frowned at the two gaping figures.

"Uh. Anything wrong, boys?"

Kipper and Jean-Pierre broke into rictus-like grins.

"No, Gene, darling. Nothing at all. Everything's fine, fine."

"Bon jour, madam. All is well." Jean-Pierre's voice squeaked on two syllables.

During the long menu discussion around the big table the two men were rigid with tension and spoke in short, clipped phrases. Gene was extremely annoyed, for she always enjoyed these sessions, but she put a lid on her irritation and attempted to jolly them up, but it was no go. Probably had a lovers' spat, she decided. May as well ignore it.

When they had finished and she got up to leave, Kipper said, in as cheerful a voice as he could manage, "Gene, darling, do you have time to talk in your office?"

Gene had a big pine-paneled office whose walls were covered with eighty years of Seldon family photographs, most taken in the great outdoors, punctuated by mountings of champion-sized bass, pike and trout. A polished oak table in front of a leather sofa contained wooden carvings of birds and fish. But for Gene, at the moment, the entire room could've been covered in bubble-wrap—she could see only Kipper's worried face, his blue eyes, his red hair, his freckles. She was trembling with the effort to keep control. She simply could not bring herself to shout and curse, her usual reaction to obstinacy or stupidity in others, at her darling boy.

On the other hand, her darling boy had just given her a terrible shock. As she continued to stare at him she took deep, somewhat calming breaths and formed a response.

"Kipper, you must listen to me very carefully." Even when Gene tried to modulate her voice there was still an "all hands on deck" quality to it.

"Yes, Gene," Kipper said. He could see that there was a bomb behind his aunt's eyes and that she lacked only a detonator.

"I . . ." She closed her eyes for an instant, took another breath. "I am looking . . . You, Kipper, are the hope for the future of one of Maine's most famous sporting establishments."

Kipper's eyes widened but he didn't speak.

"You must be the one who takes over from me. Your grandfather founded this business and I don't intend to see it die. On the contrary, it is going to grow and become more famous. You are the only one who can do it."

"But what about . . ."

Gene's big right hand shot up, palm outward, and silenced Kipper. "Don't even say their names. You know goddamn well your brother and sister are seriously addicted and that at the rate they're going they won't be able to find a fish in a bait bucket in about fifteen years. Meantime, they'd screw around and mismanage everything. If the three of you have equal shares there'll be a constant catfight and things wouldn't get done."

"We could hire a top manager, and then . . ."

"Kipper dammit!" Gene shouted. Then she lowered her voice and continued. "That would be the worst thing in the world. The very worst. A place like Cedar Lodge must be run with love as well as business sense. It must be family run. Someday my portrait will be out there above the fireplace beside the portraits of Big Jim, Reg and Annice, and then eventually your portrait will be beside mine."

Kipper couldn't believe what he was hearing. "And whose portrait will go next to mine? I am gay, in case you've forgotten, and good luck on Brad or Merrill coming up with heirs at their ages."

"Don't you worry about that. I've got my eye on several young Seldons being nurtured by first cousins."

Kipper flopped back in his chair and threw up his hands. "I don't believe this!"

Gene realized she might lose her dominance of the conversation so she slammed her fist on the desk and gave in to shouting and cursing. "Well you goddamn well better believe this! The meeting I've called this weekend is to announce a change in my will and witness the signing. I'm giving you fifty-five per cent of Cedar Lodge and splitting the remaining forty-five between Brad and Merrill."

Gene stood up. She was on the poop deck now and bellowing orders to the first mate. "So the answer is no, goddammit, you cannot have your inheritance now! The very idea that you'd ask such a thing makes me want to throw up!" She fought for control and came down a register. "You're going to manage Cedar Lodge and keep it prospering, Kipper. It's your heritage."

Kipper was silent for several moments and then, speaking as calmly as he could manage to forestall more bombasting from his aunt, he said: "Gene, please hear me out." Gene frowned and opened her mouth and Kipper blurted, "Please! Just listen. I never imagined a thing like this. Of course I love this place, it's my home, it's all I've known. And that's just it—I don't want to spend the *rest* of my life here. And now I've found Jean-Pierre, the only person I've ever loved."

That hit Gene hard. She sat down slowly but didn't speak. In her heart she had adopted Kipper as the child she never had. She had never given genuine love to anyone else in her long life, men had been only for pleasure. But Kipper had been twenty years old when his parents died and so she'd never been able to speak the tender words of a mother as she could have to a child. Instead, she had bonded with Kipper in a masculine way, as his pal, always admiring of him, deferential to his wishes, teaching him how to manage the lodge and become her unofficial co-manager. What did she expect, she asked herself now. That he would love a tough old crow like her in return? She had been deceiving herself. *And so every time he said "Gene darling" and put his hand so affectionately on her arm, he was just oiling up the old auntie with the money.* Gene felt numb at the moment, but by God she was still going to have her way. She'd calmed herself, but her voice held steel.

"You cannot desert me, you cannot desert Cedar Lodge. You cannot go to New York with Jean-Pierre." She stopped as a troublesome thought occurred to her. "If you leave anyway. . . If you perhaps have stashed away enough money to start this restaurant in New York and move from here, I will cut you from my will—you won't get an Indian head nickel."

* * *

Brad headed toward the lodge with a triumphant Tory and Nelson, who had landed a total of thirty bass and, unintentionally, three fat perch. They'd taken photos of themselves holding the largest bass. All the bass were returned to the water, for sport-fishing of bass was the rule at Cedar Lodge. The perch they had kept; Brad intended to take them to the kitchen. When they came in sight of the lodge his cellphone buzzed in his pocket. He'd been cruising along in 86-proof bliss chatting with the Bolstons; the buzzing was a rude intrusion. Answering, he heard Kipper, sounding a bit unhinged, asking to see him as soon as possible.

Merrill was in her Land Rover driving back to Cedar Lodge for her 3 p.m. fishing party when her cellphone rang. By the time she'd found a place to pull over on the heavily wooded road, the call had gone into voicemail. She punched in her code and listened:

"Merrill? Kipper. This is important. Please come see me as soon as possible."

Thirty minutes later they were all three gathered in Kipper's room. Kipper had his hands over his face, muffling his voice. "Oh, Jesus God, I don't want this. I had nothing to do with this. She took me completely by surprise."

"Calm down, little brother," Merrill said. "We believe you." She found she couldn't concentrate. Her brain was still somewhat fuzzed with cocaine and in twenty minutes she had to deal with three randy fishermen who said they'd fallen in love with her picture in Gray's Sporting Journal. She knew that the shock of what Kipper had just revealed would hit later. One thing for sure: Her post-coital bliss had been shot to hell.

Brad was less sympathetic than Merrill. "Oh, for Christ's sake, Kip, don't tell me this was a surprise. You've kissed her ass for years. What did you think was going to happen? She thinks the morning sun rises out of your freckled backside. I thought this was just what you were gunning for."

Kipper looked at Brad in open-mouthed shock. "Goddammit, Brad. You just stop right there. I have never *once* in all my life mentioned anything to Gene about our inheritance or money or anything. Until today, when I begged for at least part of what would be coming to me. She threw a hissy."

"Oh did she," Brad sneered. "And how do we know you're not just making up all this crap so Merrill and I won't . . ."

Kipper, red-faced and shaking with fury, jumped up and shouted, "Don't you *dare*, you sonofabitch! Don't you *dare* say such a thing!"

"Oh, get screwed, Kipper."

"No, *you* get screwed, you goddamn drunk."

"Sticks and stones . . ."

Kipper walked from the room and slammed his bedroom door. "That went well, don't you think?" Merrill said.

Four

Brad was at the end of the long bar in the lodge's clubroom—
which served as bar and dining room—nursing a whiskey and water while he waited for Tory and Nelson, who weren't due to meet
him for at least a half-hour. He seldom "nursed" anything with
alcohol in it, preferring to knock it back and let his chemistry readjust as quickly as possible, but tonight he wanted to avoid the
embarrassment of slurred consonants, so he nursed. Tory Bolston
was a bright-eyed class act, and she'd made it extravagantly clear
from her first bouncy little trot down the dock this morning—
which now seemed like a long time ago to Brad—that she was at
Cedar Lodge for pure damn fun. And what he needed, right now,
more than anything, was fun.

The afternoon meeting with Kipper had left him in a simmer-
ing blue rage that had taken him hours to quell. But now he was
determined not to let anger deprive him of pleasure. When Tory
arrived he would reach into his grab bag of fishing adventures and
a few amusing anecdotes to set the stage, and then, employing a
technique fostered by his observation of current feminist sensibil-
ities, he would focus entirely on her, becoming increasingly enthralled as the evening wore on by her life story and
accomplishments. If he didn't get too drunk, it usually worked like
a charm.

Nearly as strong as the promise of a new, exciting woman, Brad
was discovering, was the energizing emotion of hatred. And there
at the other end of the long mahogany bar, now crowded with the
lodge's guests and those who had come in for dinner, was the object of his loathing, Iphigene Seldon. Auntie dearest was laughing
and talking with the handsome old fisherman she was still trying to
pin to the mattress, and she was—whoa! Goddamn!—she was
wearing a *dress*. A blue seersucker dress that contrasted vividly with
her dark skin and white hair. The silver fox was in trouble, Brad
surmised; Gene put on a dress only for special targets, men she

was especially keen on. This fellow had the look of one of those patriarch-type models that preppy catalogs posed at the tillers of yachts.

An alarming thought materialized in Brad's troubled mind: Was the old crow trying to find a mate? Was "Il Duce" looking to share the golden years of her tyranny with a husband? Oh, please Jesus no. What of the will then? As of this weekend, according to Kipper, he and Merrill were each due for an eleven percentage point reduction in their inheritance. What if they got cut out altogether?

Slow down, stud, he told himself. You're zooming way out in front on nothing more than Gene doing what she usually does every summer, which was to amuse herself with good-looking old gents. It nauseated him to see her portraying the aging playgirl, throwing her head back laughing, squeezing the man's arm, ruffling his hair, pressing against him shoulder to shoulder. The fox seemed to be enjoying it, too, as in *really* enjoying it, a sight that made Brad look away in disgust.

Where was Merrill? he wondered, looking around the room. He could use some sisterly shoulder-to-shoulder right about now; he needed a comrade in misery. Oh yes Christ she probably was over at Winsokkett with Bruno. Damn. She was spending too many nights over there with that guy. He would never begrudge his sister, his best friend in the world, his *only* friend in the goddamn world, the pleasure of a lover, but the truth was, Bruno worried him. He was an excellent guide, no bad stories about him that Brad had ever heard, but there was something about the quiet, saturnine man that Brad found . . . well, he thought, now that he'd wandered into this wool-gathering moment—what did bother him about Bruno? Menacing; that was it—he seemed menacing. But why? The guy never said much, and was always nice as hell to Merrill. *It's the way he always seems to be studying everyone around him with his dark eyes. Never says anything about himself. Just watches everyone and smiles.*

Brad giggled at his own thoughts. They sounded like something out of one of those damn novels Renee always had her nose in, "Love's Abandoned Hope" or some crap like that. It was either that or "Death Creeps at Midnight." Uh, oh. Speak of the devil and who should appear in a puff of smoke.

Renee stood in the doorway of the clubroom wearing a white silk dress cut in a deep V down to her stomach, revealing a generous amount of honey-tanned skin for the delectation of the men and prompting eyeball-rolling from the women, most of whom were hardy outdoor types in casual après-fishing outfits. She scanned the room until she spotted Brad and then began drifting toward him.

Oh damn, he thought. What now? He'd told her about his soon to be diminished slice of the Cedar Lodge fishcake and she had reacted viciously, cursing Gene and wishing her dead. He didn't want to hear more narcissistic yapping and he didn't want her here when Tory and Nelson arrived. Maybe he should just . . . Oh, Jesus, auntie dearest was heading right for him with the silver fox in tow. And why was she grinning so smugly? Renee saw her and darted in another direction.

"Brad, I want you to meet Roberston Weller. Bob, this is my nephew Brad."

"Very pleased to meet you," Weller said. "I've been told by Gene that you and your sister are two of the best fishing guides in Maine." The man's voice was pleasant, his accent educated, his smile warm beneath a thick white mustache that curled at each end.

"Ohh, well, I'm not sure how our standing is statewide, but we usually manage to keep the customers smiling. How about you? I can get you some fish."

"I love to fish, Brad, and I did go out with Merrill, but I'm here on another sort of expedition." He paused and looked into Brad's eyes. "I don't think you recognize me, do you? I've been here three times before."

What the hell was this all about, Brad wondered, but, ever the gentleman, he lied and said, "Aha. Now I remember. Welcome back."

Gene said: "You don't remember crap, Brad. But I think you'll remember this. Mr. Weller is courting me. Don't you think that has a nice old fashion ring to it?" Her blustery voice attracted attention, and several people turned and looked at her, obviously incredulous.

The shock left Brad speechless. He made a sound, but it wasn't a word.

"As a matter of fact, the courtship's over. We're getting married." Brad could only gape at Gene, whose eyes registered his stupefaction with a look of malicious delight.

Weller gave him an "old devil" sort of smile and saluted as Gene dragged him away by his arm.

Brad covered his eyes with his left hand as his right hand tightly gripped the cocktail glass. *Oh. My. God. I was right. I can't believe it.* For a woman her age, Brad admitted, Gene had a good body and her face was still attractive if leathery. But she definitely was not in the looks and charm class of Weller. Brad guessed the old bastard had come here to fish, seen this spectacular lodge, smelled those millions and had swum in for the kill. If they actually got married, then hers would become his. She would probably change her will again, leaving good old Bob a huge share of Cedar Lodge Enterprises. The old bandit was probably insisting on it up front.

Brad felt his knees weaken. And people thought living on a lake was so serene.

"Brad. Brad!"

His head swung up and there was Tory, concern in her baby blues. Nelson was behind her.

"You were moaning. Are you ill?"

"Uh, no. I just had a big shock. Family matters." He smiled ruefully. "Nobody died. Yet." Come on, get it together, he told himself. Standing before him wearing a simple pale-blue cotton dress that successfully clung everywhere it should cling was the delectable saving grace of a perfectly gruesome day. He stood up straight, smiled at Nelson then looked into Tory's eyes and smiled.

"All better now for seeing you. Will the two of you have a drink? On the house."

Nelson was craning around, looking for someone, then stopped and waved. "If you don't mind, Brad, and I'm sure you don't, I'm going to slip away. I met this knockout woman named Renee his afternoon and she said to look for her here. See ya."

Brad again covered his eyes with his hand.

"You're groaning again," Tory whispered in his ear.

"That's my wife."

"What?" Tory stepped back, anger sparkling in her eyes. "I had *no* idea you were married. I've been flashing you all over the place and you're *married?*"

Brad grabbed her forearm. "I'm not! I mean, I am but we're separated. Have been for a long time. Hate each other. She doesn't live here, lives over in Rockport."

"Oh yeah? Then, why don't you divorce?"

"We both want to but we're in a trap for the time being. It's more complicated than you can imagine. And it just got more complicated about ten minutes ago. Please believe me, Tory. We can go over there right now and she'll tell you we are not a couple."

"No, don't do that. I believe you. But why does she come here?"

"She comes once a month to collect the money she's due under our separation agreement and she . . ." Brad chuckled mirthlessly ". . . well, she comes to see if perhaps Gene is feeling ill."

Tory's eyes widened. "I beg your pardon?"

"Look, it's just a mess, and it's boring. I'd rather concentrate on you, my lovely little fisherman. What'll you have to drink?"

Tory's lips and eyes smiled in unison. "Whiskey and water on the rocks."

"Ah, we have something in common." Brad got Armand the bartender's attention and ordered two whiskies. When the drinks arrived, they clinked glasses and Brad secretly vowed to dismiss all troubling events from his mind and, with a voluptuary's true sense of what was important, satisfy the primal urges.

"Now," he said, "can we go back to flashing?"

Tory laughed, touched his hand and said, "Flashing or fishing?"

"Flashing."

"I've gotten my fish. Let's flash."

* * *

"More bad news, Bruno," Merrill said as she closed her cell-phone. She was sitting on the side of the bed, having just taken a call from Brad. She was naked, of course; she and Bruno were always naked when they were together.

Goddamn this family, Bruno thought. What now? He didn't say anything, simply waited for Merrill to speak.

"That was Brad. Gene is hauling some elderly sex symbol around the bar saying they're going to get married." She sighed and was silent for awhile.

"Can we please make some drinks and go sit on the dock? I've got some thinking to do."

"Of course," Bruno said, getting up and putting on some shorts. Merrill did the same, not bothering to put on a shirt. If you can't sit on the dock at night with your ta-ta's hanging free, she thought, what good is there being on a lake?

As they sat in the darkness listening to the loons and the muted voices from other camps, Merrill wondered desperately if she would ever be free. Forty-five years old and trapped. Trapped by Cedar Lodge, trapped by Iphigene Seldon; God, how she hated that woman. And she was still chained to Huntley Beauchamp. He wanted money for a divorce, lots of it. He always wanted money. That tall, ever-so-elegant man who'd dazzled her a dozen years ago had become a venal sonofabitch. Two years into their marriage she had realized but not acknowledged how selfish he was, but she'd stuck it out for six more years, God knows why. Yes, why, she asked herself now. Why? Why, when there were men like Bruno Gabreau? Well, to be honest, she'd never met anyone like Bruno until last year. She'd had offers from wonderful men, wealthy sportsmen over the years who'd begged her to bag the husband and come with them to Montana, Wyoming, Minnesota, Georgia—Jesus, how many states had she been offered? She recalled several weak-kneed moments when she had almost capitulated, but . . . no, she had stayed true blue to the bastard, who, in their first years of marriage, had given her physical love like she had never known—until Bruno, of course, who was in a class by himself in love-making *and* affection; Huntley had the emotional depth of a lizard. But, then, gradually, incredibly (incredible because any cheval mirror she stood in front of unclothed reflected a body that most men and a number of women would've loved to take in their arms), the love-making had become mechanical, absent of eroticism, and Huntley was more often in Boston or New York or Philadelphia cutting deals.

In the four years since her separation from Huntley, Merrill had taken several lovers, but Bruno had driven all thoughts of other men from her mind. She glanced over at him now, studied his (to her) divine profile. She could never lose him. Never. She knew she was still a knockout in looks, but the reality of being forty-five to Bruno's thirty-seven worried her constantly. She needed to keep him by marrying him, and to do that she needed to be rid of Huntley, and to do that she needed the money that should rightfully be hers. Whenever she got into this train of thought she wanted to weep, but she definitely did not want to show despair to Bruno.

Also, in these moments she grieved for and longed for her beautiful parents. If they had not been killed then everything now would be so perfect; Mom and Dad had always made it perfect. In recollection they seemed like gods—so glamorous and dashing and dynamic. Although her grandfather had founded Cedar Lodge in 1926, restoring the old 1882 building that had housed the Abenaki Sporting Club and then expanding it with a third floor, it was Reg and Annice who had made the lodge famous. It had been a wonderful world then, and the whole family had worked together superbly. Her mother and father had inspired everyone with their humor and sunny nature. Everyone except Gene, of course. Gene was not inspired. She worked very hard, always, and was the principal fishing guide until Merrill and Brad were primed. But her cold dislike of her brother and his wife was apparent in all their interactions. Merrill had tried a number of times to get to the source of it, but Reg or Annice always fobbed her off with, "Oh, she's always been like that. Don't let it bother you."

And then in one hideous second of roaring thunder and blinding light, that world—hers, Brad's, Kipper's—had been shattered. Brad had been the first one to reach the boat following the lightning strike; she had been at the back of the lodge and ran out the front door thirty seconds later. Brad had run toward her sobbing, his face distorted with horror; he'd grabbed her and dragged her, struggling, back inside, begging her not to look.

"Bruno?" Merrill whispered.

"Yes?"

"What do you really think of me?"

"You are beautiful and I love you and I want to marry you."

Merrill sighed. "And *you* are beautiful and I love *you* and I want to marry you. We'll think of something, Bruno. Something will happen soon."

As Merrill grew silent beside him, Bruno simmered. The situation was maddening but, as always, he kept his emotions hidden, never evincing outwardly anything but calm. He didn't really love Merrill, but he sure as hell wanted to marry her. For him, the wonderful possibilities offered by this woman was a rare chance. He knew he'd never get close to this kind of wealth again. He had his looks and sexual prowess, but he was nevertheless an uneducated fisherman, working alone as a guide with no assurance of sufficient income month to month. Men in his position met few women dripping in diamonds and pearls.

Cedar Lodge itself and the millions that Merrill said lay behind it made Bruno dizzy with longing. And now here was yet another obstacle thrown up by that leathery old bitch. Merrill said everyone hated her. When Bruno first heard that, he had thought, in his very basic way of approaching life, *So, if everybody hates her, why doesn't somebody just kill her?* Bruno could think of any number of "accidents" that could be orchestrated around a big sporting lodge. He was going over to the lodge tomorrow night to stay with Merrill until the dreaded Sunday meeting. He promised himself while

there to reconnoiter the building and the docks for safety viola-
tions.

* * *

Renee rolled languidly to the side of the bed, arose and walked
slowly to the bedroom bar table, exaggerating the swing of her
hips, so that Nelson could have a leisurely view of her perfect (in
her estimation) ass. This suite on the second floor had a cheval
mirror, one of her favorite pieces of furniture, for it allowed her to
appraise the thing she loved most—her body. Now, in the faint
glow coming through the window from the dock lights below, she
looked herself over, pleased with all she surveyed, a form honed
by countless hours of gymnasium sweat and toil. The only little
bitty worrisome flaws were the tiny lines at the corners of her eyes,
whose pupils were greenish brown, and the ever so slightly notice-
able crinkly bits at the corners of her lips, which were generously
full, the bee-stung look, only hers was naturally so. Her face
formed a soft triangle framed by dark, thick, waving hair. Her eyes,
which slanted upward like a cat's eyes, regarded themselves in the
mirror.

I am like Maggie the Cat, but without the pain-in-the-ass Brick. I own
myself. I own this body. But in ten years my ownership will begin diminishing
as age relentlessly calls in the mortgage.

Other than herself, Renee loved many other things, prominent
among them the exquisite pleasure of sex. She loved men's bodies,
she loved women's. Nevertheless, she was not promiscuous. Sleeping around, going upstairs from a wild party with an aroused
man—or for that matter, woman, only women usually were more
circumspect and gentle in their entreaties—was tawdry, to her
mind. Her body, she sincerely felt, was a gift to a lover, and not to
be cheaply thrown down on a bed to be urgently groped by some
drunken, or doped, fool. Besides, she didn't need to be fondled or
caressed to become fully aroused: Simply being looked at by the
hungry eyes of men or women stimulated her to vigorous autoe-
roticism once she was in the privacy of her bedroom.

Therefore this particular night of making love to a man she'd met two days before was unusual for her . . . and somewhat surprising. This fellow who looked like Mr. Conservative Businessman was a sexual bronco rider. She hadn't had so much fun in six months. Perhaps a semi-regular arrangement was possible, she thought. She sure as heck wasn't in the market for a *regular* arrangement, but a periodic night in the saddle with Nelson the cowboy seemed very appealing at the moment.

"Nelson?"

"Hmmm?"

"Wanna drink?"

"Got gin over there?"

"Yep."

"Got tonic?"

"Yep."

"Let's see what they taste like together."

Renee giggled. "You're witty, Nelson. I hate dull people."

"I've met a few."

"I don't throw compliments at men just to ratchet up their rotten-ass egos, but I gotta say, cause it's true . . . you're a stud."

"And you're dynamite."

Renee brought Nelson's drink over to the bed, handed it to him and sat on the edge of the bed. "Would you like to meet sometimes, maybe over in Bar Harbor, where I live?"

"Sometimes sounds perfect. I never settle down. How about Boston?"

Imitating the Maine accents she kept hearing all around her, Renee said, "Ayuh, Bahston sounds like a winnah."

Nelson grinned. "I'll call you next month."

"Cool. I never settle down either."

"Wait a minute, I thought . . ."

Renee quickly cut him off—"Except that once! Yes . . . I got married to that lush holding up the end of the bar downstairs. Neither one of us can remember why the hell we did such a thing."

"The obvious question comes next: Why don't you . . .?"

". . . get divorced. Because I need the two million dollars Brad can give me when he gets his inheritance out of this thirty-million-dollar fishing hole."

"Sounds reasonable. And when does he get this stack of chips?"

"When that horrid old dragon cashes in *her* chips."

Nelson arched an eyebrow and smiled. "You would be referring, I guess, to Iphigene, the Duchess of Cedarshire?"

Renee loved that. She laughed loudly and patted Nelson's head. "You're a kick, funny-bunny. Yes, she's the duchess and her courtiers are getting restless. We're all hoping she drops dead or gets hit by lightning."

"You people are a rough crowd."

"If you were around her long enough you'd hate her too." Renee climbed on top of Nelson and swung her breasts lightly across his chest. "Wanna do it again?"

* * *

Kipper was drunk and alone, looking despondently out the window of his third-floor room at the docks below. It was a pretty scene: There were shaded lights on stanchions every 25 feet along the white-washed docks, illuminating the boats and throwing sparkles of light on the water. The bass boats were blue and white, the canoes deep green, the sailboats white with blue sails, and the runabouts white. His gaze shifted to the post on the second dock to the left where his parents had tied up in the midst of a gigantic, fast-moving lightning storm that had roared in suddenly out of the northwest. They were lifting gear from the boat to the dock when a shaft of lightning struck the boat, enveloping it in an aureole of crackling blue electricity that killed Reg and Annice instantly, burning their bodies piteously.

He'd been twenty when it happened, home for the summer after his sophomore year at college. The tragedy had plunged him into depression and chronic use of marijuana, and he stayed stoned for a year, refusing to return to college. When eventually he did go back to complete his junior and senior years, he stayed on for a two-year MBA degree; then, under Gene's tutelage he'd become a deft co-administrator of the lodge.

But now he wanted out. All his life, except for college years, had been spent in rural Maine. He wanted New York City and everything in it. He wanted to take Jean-Pierre there and live with him forever.

The drunker he got the more he despised his aunt. The truculent old bitch was denying him his happiness. The memory of their meeting that afternoon, the image of her quivering, belligerent face and her berating voice filled him with rage. "Goddamit!" he screamed into the empty room. *If I lose Jean-Pierre because of Gene I will kill her and then kill myself.*

* * *

Jean-Pierre was buzzing around the kitchen supervising the three members of his staff but, busy as he was, his mind kept drifting back to that afternoon's tearful conversation with Kipper. The old woman was going to ruin everything. Jean-Pierre believed he really did love Kipper to a certain extent, but if Kipper was truly trapped he would have to seek another life with someone else who was rich enough to give him his dream restaurant. Venal, yes, but then what the hell else was he to do? He'd saved a good deal of money at this job—where *was* there to spend money locally? He would have to leave; he would set himself up in Manhattan and allow fate to be good to him. These thoughts upset him but he was determined to go.

Perhaps, he jokingly pondered, someone will shoot the old turkey.

* * *

Though he'd received several reassurances from the specialist that he would be rescued, Huntley Beauchamp was in a heart-stopping panic as he whispered—why was he whispering he wondered?

Who the hell was listening?—into his office phone, "This is Thursday. The meeting is Sunday afternoon. What is happening?"

The voice that answered him, as on previous calls, was ghastly, a raspy, metallic uttering, as though it were being filtered through a Brillo pad. "Stay calm. By the time of the meeting all will be resolved. Documents will be delivered to the site that readjust any, shall we say, inadequacies."

"By Saturday? Things will happen by Saturday?"

"Yes," the voice replied. "Be calm, Mr. Beauchamp." The connection was cut, leaving Huntley gripping his phone in a trembling hand. He was not convinced. It was just too frightening. In case things went wrong, he'd already withdrawn several hundred thousand from a bank account; then he'd flown up to Canada and rented, under an assumed name and paying cash, a camp on a remote lake. Once there, he would have to devise a plan. He couldn't just sit here and let them nail him to the wall.

Maybe he could fake his own death. That was it. Disappear. Plenty of guys had done that. And he'd already had experience at identity change.

He was due at Cedar Lodge the next night, Friday. There he would be trapped right in the middle of them all—Gene, Brad, Merrill, Kipper, maybe even Renee. The thought of them filled him with fear and loathing.

Five

Six and Alicia entered the clubroom at Cedar Lodge wearing some of their "good clothes," a category that, between the two of them, took up six hangers and two dresser drawers. Their ensembles had been purchased from a Brooks Brothers summer catalog of forgotten vintage when the models looked like someone you might know: pleated khaki trousers, striped camp shirt with rolled up sleeves for Alicia and blue linen blazer and rumpled white duck pants for Six. They had, of course, also brought their disgraceful fishing outfits, for they'd had a superb day of hauling in the big ones. Gene had insisted they come on Friday morning for fishing, with the understanding that they would meet privately in the evening in order for Gene to explain her concerns about the possibly tumultuous family gathering on Sunday.

Gene waved at them from the end of the bar and so they headed that way, fascinated, as they looked around, at all the prosperous-looking suntanned men and women Cedar Lodge usually attracted. The place was *not* cheap. But what the guests got in return for a big bill were the best guides Maine could offer, luxurious rooms that still held that old-style fishing camp ambiance and gourmet cooking.

As they neared Gene, Six and Alicia noticed that an exceptionally handsome elderly man with a big white mustache was standing close to their cousin with a decidedly proprietorial air.

"Six! Alicia! Come here and have a drink." She shook their hands warmly; Gene did not go in for cheek-kissing. "I want you to meet someone very special," she said, turning to beam at the man. "This is Robertson Weller. And I'm going to marry the glamorous sonofabitch."

Six and Alicia were caught off guard, but they managed not to gape or go slack-jawed. However, it did take them about two blinks to register the incredible statement; they gushed simultaneously. "Gene! Fantastic. Gene, darling, how thrilling!"

"Bob, these are my wonderful cousins, Six and Alicia Godwin. They have a camp over to Winsokkett Pond."

Bob's lips parted in a gleaming smile that showed perfect teeth. He extended his hand to Alicia. "Alicia, so very pleased to meet you." And then to Six. "And you, Six. I've heard so much about both of you." His mellow voice wafted over them.

Good lord, Alicia thought. This boy is Hollywood central casting. Gene was in superb shape for seventy-seven years, but she was a tough piece of old leather. Good ole Bob Weller, she quickly surmised, was digging for gold.

As he shook Bob's hand, Six noticed that the fellow was tall as well as sporting a great physiognomy. Six was six-feet-six; he estimated Bob was six-one or -two.

"*What* a surprise," Six enthused. From his accent Six guessed Bob was Boston old guard; he also cynically guessed that he was Boston old guard sans 401(k).

Gene put a fist gently into Six's shoulder. "You and Alicia look sort of knocked out." She smiled broadly at both of them and said, "Look. Relax. Bob's marrying me for my money, obviously. And I'm marrying him because he's a stud. He may be a shark, but he's an honest one."

Bob let out a mellow baritone laugh and said: "Well, there's no use denying anything around Gene, but the fact is, Gene and I have been testing this thing for awhile and have found that we're very good companions. We enjoy each other's company immensely."

"Alicia and I can certainly testify to the value of that," Six said. "We've been best pals most of our lives. Anyway, the two of you look happy. Congratulations."

"So," Gene said, "did you get in some good fishing?"

"We sure did," Alicia said. "We went out with Errol Flynn—I mean Brad."

Gene chuckled. "Yeah. He's a good-looking SOB, but at the rate he's drinking he's going to go down fast. Anyway, after dinner I'd like to talk to you about this Sunday meeting. It's going to be a knock-down-drag-out. Everybody's getting tense and spooked."

54

She scanned the room. "Most of the dramatis personae are here now. Brad you saw today, don't know where he is now, but there's Merrill down at the other end of the bar with Bruno Gabreau. Wants him here this weekend for emotional support, I guess."

Six and Alicia waved at the pair. Merrill waved back, Bruno smiled slightly and nodded.

"Bruno's a neighbor of sorts on Winsokkett Pond," Six said. "I've spoken to him a couple of times at pond association gatherings. Seems all right. People who've been out with him say he's a superb guide."

"How did they meet?" Alicia asked.

"Last year they both had four-day fishing parties at the same place over to the Kennebec River. Each had one wealthy couple apiece, going for trout and salmon. So they all pitched their tents next to each other and had a lot of time to get acquainted."

"Kind of romantic," Alicia said.

Gene shrugged. "Well, yeah. They're both cokeheads, so I don't put much future in it. Also, she's still tethered to Huntley. I'm sure you remember him. He's over there now at one of the window tables."

Six and Alicia turned. "Oh, yes, I see him," Six said. "Wow. Look at his clothes. Snazzy."

Gene said, "He's a pompous windbag, but he knows money. He's handling our investments."

"Oh, isn't that Brad's wife two tables down?" Alicia asked.

"Ayuh. The viper in vamp's clothing. She's stalking Brad for money. I'll tell you all about it later."

"And she's with a good-looking man."

"Ah, yes. Now *that* is real funny. That fellow and his sister came here together. Brad's already nailed the sister and now Renee is closing in on the brother. It's a real circus around here."

"Is Kipper here tonight?" Six asked.

"He's in the kitchen with our chef, Jean-Pierre, who is also his lover." Gene chuckled wickedly. "Hot place, Cedar Lodge, wouldn't you say? Everybody's got somebody. Except Huntley. He's only here with his clothes."

* * *

"Well, that's it. The whole damn bucket of fish," Gene said. She and Six and Alicia were in her three-room apartment on the top floor sipping whiskey and water while Gene described to them her plans for changing her will and the confrontation with Kipper the day before. Amos was curled up at Gene's feet, his big eyebrows curling upward whenever emphatic statements were uttered.

"Kipper really upset me," she told them. "Goddammit. He's my fair-haired boy. He's got to take over after me. He's the only one in this family who can do it, and we've got to keep this lodge a family business. That's part of its fame."

Six pulled out his pipe and started searching pockets for his tobacco pouch. "Gene, is it all right if I smoke?"

"Go right ahead. I like the smell."

"Thanks." Six got the pipe filled and fired up. "I think better when I'm sucking on this thing. Now. It sounds like you've got the makings of a real catfight. What do you think is going to happen Sunday?"

"I thought I had everything under control. I was just going to surprise them all with the new terms. Brad and Merrill would scream and yell, I would roar and slam the table, and that would be the end of it. But Kipper shocked me when he came begging to cash out on his part of the inheritance, so I told him the whole deal. I shouldn't have done it. I'm convinced he told Brad and Merrill, and I bet they told Renee and Bruno. Now everybody is tense and angry and won't even look at me. Except Bruno. He just smiles and stays calm. But I think he's a shark circling what he expects will be bloody water. After money, like the rest of them."

"And do they know about Bob?" Six asked.

"Oh, yeah. They know. I figured as long as everybody was in a frenzy anyway, I'd throw another bomb in the water and let all the fish rise to the surface. The fact is, I have no plans to change my will in Bob's favor. I was hoping to scare them all, make them think they could lose everything, make them shut up and behave."

Six and Alicia exchanged raised-eyebrow looks that indicated the same question hitting them, simultaneously, but Alicia asked it: "Gene, how do we fit into all this?"

"Well, frankly, like I told Six when I called, I need moral support. Even before everything about this will got out in the open I knew this meeting was going to be rough. I'm a tough old bird, but it was going to be me on one side of the room and everybody else on the other side opposing me and some of them yelling their heads off. Even Huntley. He won't say anything in opposition but I know what he wants—he wants me to give Merrill her millions so he can have a million and then he'll give her a divorce. He's just like Renee. Brad can't get loose of the bitch until she gets a couple of million. And now Kipper is bawling for his share. They're all crazy as loons and they're all waiting for me to die." She paused as her eyes filled with tears, and her voice was tight as she continued. "Even Kipper. I've been such a fool. I thought, with his sweetness to me and his devotion to all the work in running the lodge, that he was actually returning the love I've given him all his life."

"Gene, I'm so sorry," Six said. "Is it really as bad as all that?"

"Ayuh, Six, I know my people. The atmosphere around here is getting damn fraught. On Sunday I simply want some family members on my side of the room, physically and metaphorically. You *are* on my side of the room, aren't you, metaphorically speaking?"

Six said, "Yes, of course, Gene. I understand your thinking about the reworking of the will. You've devoted your lifetime to Cedar Lodge. You want it to endure."

"Yes, we'll be with you," Alicia said.

"I guess you don't want us to say anything, just be there, right?"

Gene looked out a window and was momentarily silent. Heaving a big sigh she said, "Well. I don't know. We'll have to see how it goes. I might have to call on you for some calming wisdom." She smiled at them. "The two of you are good at calming wisdom."

There was a knock on the locked door and a rattling of the knob. "Who's there?" Gene asked.

"Brad. Important."

"Goddammit," Gene said sotto voce. "Hold on." She walked to the door, unlocked it, swung it open, whirled right around and walked back toward her desk without even looking at Brad. Six and Alicia saw cold fury in his eyes.

"Hi, Brad!" Six called as cheerily as possible.

"Good fishing this morning, Brad," Alicia said. "Much appreciated."

Brad managed a smile and started to speak, but Gene cut him off. She was enormously irritated that Amos had ambled over to Brad and was receiving head and ear rubs from him.

"What is it?"

Oh dear, Alicia thought. Rude.

Brad ground his teeth. Venomous old bitch, he thought. He wouldn't have subjected himself to this little humiliation in front of Six and Alicia if his message weren't vitally important. "I don't give a damn if you're irritated, Gene. I've got something you better listen to."

"What?"

"I've been looking at my instruments for hours. We're in for trouble."

Now Gene looked directly at Brad, and Six noticed that her expression and manner changed abruptly. "Storm?" she asked.

"Not just *a* storm, a huge, wide storm front and it's piling up very high. I think there might be a supercell in with the front. The national service is getting worried and the weather channel is starting to hyperventilate, but I'm better than all those characters. They don't know yet how really bad it is. I do."

"Oh, Jesus," Gene said, leaning back in her chair and staring at the ceiling. "Just what we need. You're sure?"

"Please don't bother asking. You know damn well I am."

"Supercell," Alicia said. "I think I know what that is." She turned to Six. "Remember that doozie last summer? We read up on supercells right after."

"Enormous revolving storms, like small hurricanes," Brad said. "Heavy winds, torrential rain and lots of hail. Five years ago one had baseball-size hailstones that put a two-foot cover on the ground in the area north of Great Pond and felled trees, broke windows, dented cars. The bastards can also spawn tornadoes."

Gene studied her whiskey glass for about fifteen seconds then looked up at Brad. "When do you see it getting here?"

"Late tomorrow night, early Sunday morning."

"Okay. First, we'll have to tell all the guests, see who wants to get out. Probably no one. Then we'll get the windows shuttered. If it's reasonably calm in the morning, then we'll let people fish, but we'll take in the sailboats. In the afternoon we'll get all the boats out of the water. Nothing to do after that but sit tight." Gene turned to Six and Alicia. "What about you two—you'll have to go back to your camp, I reckon."

Six said: "We'll go over in the morning, put the shutters up, get the boats out of the water." He paused, looked at Alicia. "But I think we'll come back and ride it out here. That okay, kiddo?"

"Sure," Alicia said. "Back in time for suppah."

Brad looked at them with curiosity, then said, "All right, see ya."

When he'd gone Gene said, "Brad's apartment is filled with barometers and such, the best you can buy. Always knows the weather. When he says something's coming, it's coming."

"Is this a hobby?" Alicia asked.

Gene barked out a mirthless laugh. "Hobby? Unh-uh, it's no damn hobby. With him it's deadly serious business. He's terrified of storms because of what happened to Reg and Annice."

"Ah!" Six replied. "Ohh, yes. Of course." He frowned and puffed a little cumulo from his pipe.

"Seeing his parents fried by lightning sort of knocked him off course."

Alicia's eyes widened as she stared back at Gene. She knew Six liked her and Alicia was grateful for the loan to start their business, but she was beginning to have uncomfortable feelings about the old woman. She was not only tough, Alicia decided—she could be brutal.

"He has four activities," Gene continued, "fishing, drinking, women and weather. The first three he can do without even using his pickled brain. The fourth, weather, he studies like a scholar."

"Well, Gene, if we've been properly briefed, I think Alicia and I would like to take a stroll around the docks before dinner."

Gene smiled and said, "Majors Six and Alicia, you have your briefing and are now dismissed."

Her guests laughed and they all walked downstairs together. At the bottom of the stairs Gene said she was going to start talking to any guests in the bar and dining room about the coming storm. "I'm going to find out if anyone wants to chicken out. See ya."

* * *

After dinner, Six and Alicia stood at the end of the sailboat dock looking up at the starlit heavens. "I don't like it, Six," Alicia said. "This whole thing makes me nervous, but of course we'll see it through. We owe her some gratitude."

Six rummaged through his pockets, found his pipe and tobacco pouch and began filling up for another smokefest. Alicia waited patiently, knowing he would speak eventually. She was accustomed to every quirk of the lovable man standing next to her, and she was certain he knew *her* every idiosyncrasy. It was a good, peaceful marriage. How many people were as lucky? she wondered.

A waxing gibbous moon rose above the trees to the southeast. Loons called to one another out in the darkness. The honey-like smell of Six's tobacco wafted over them.

"I don't like it a damn bit either," Six said. "I'm very uneasy about this Sunday meeting and now this storm has me sort of jumpy."

"Gene's absolutely brutal to Brad."

"Yes, she is. I do wish she wouldn't do that, but on the other hand don't let Brad's good looks fool you. He's a tough bastard, too. If he was the owner of this place he'd kick *her* around, for sure."

"Yep. Reckon you're right."

They heard soft footsteps behind them and turned to see Kipper and a short, dark-haired man walking toward them.

"Good evening, Six, Alicia."

"Kipper, how nice to see you again," Alicia said.

When the two of them drew close Alicia and Six were intrigued to see that Kipper's companion looked like a miniature version of Johnny Depp. He was wearing white linen trousers, a green and yellow Aloha shirt and pale yellow espadrilles. Kipper looked down at him with an expression similar to that of the Magi adoring the Christ child.

"Six and Alicia, I'd like you to meet Jean-Pierre LeMaire, Cedar Lodge's famous chef."

Jean-Pierre treated them to a traditional Frenchman routine by bowing ever so slightly and air-kissing Alicia's hand and saying, "Enchanté, madame," and then gripping Six's hand and graciously uttering, "Monsieur."

"Delighted," Alicia said. "Your cooking is heaven."

Jean-Pierre's dark eyes softened as he beamed a thousand-watt smile at Alicia and murmured, "You are too kind."

"We often drive over from Winsokkett Pond for dinner here, Jean-Pierre," Six said. "Never had better food."

"Merci."

"Are you here just for dinner?" Kipper asked.

"Uh, er . . . Gene said she . . . well, we wanted a break from our camp and needed some superior fishing, so we came for the weekend." Six and Alicia had agreed ahead of their visit that they would not reveal their requested presence at the Sunday meeting to any of the three siblings. Six had almost blurted it out.

"Well, it's so nice to see you again, and I especially wanted you to meet Jean-Pierre because . . ." Kipper's blush was detectable under the glow from a dock light. "Well, because, you see, he and I . . . uh . . ." Jean-Pierre looked at Kipper with a raised eyebrow and an expression of delighted amusement.

"Because you love him," Alicia said.

Kipper gaped at her.

"Kipper, my dear, Six and I are older but we're not fuddie-duddies. We think it's marvelous."

"Fuddie-duddie?" Jean-Pierre said. "I am intrigued."

Six said, "People who disapprove of everything, especially if it means other people are having fun."

They all laughed. Kipper and Jean-Pierre said their goodnights and walked away arm in arm instead of rigidly side by side as when they had approached Six and Alicia.

Speaking softly, Alicia said, "I wonder if there's going to be heartbreak there."

"I wouldn't be surprised," Six answered. "This place is Heartbreak Hotel. If that French fella gets loose in New York without Kipper it'll be all over."

As they neared the lodge front steps Alicia gave Six an elbow nudge and nodded toward the porch. Sitting in wicker chairs on the porch and visible by the light of a battery-operated Coleman lantern on the table between them were Bob Weller and Huntley Beauchamp. The back of Huntley's chair was turned toward Six and Alicia as they ascended the steps. He was leaning forward, talking intently and gesturing as Bob listened. Bob waved, Huntley turned and waved, and then they put their heads together again.

"Would you buy a used car from either one of those characters?" Six asked.

"A bicycle perhaps, and even then I would hesitate."

"I'd road test it first."

Six and Alicia were standing in the front hall before the big stone fireplace regarding the portraits of James Rutherford Selden and that of Reg and Annice posed arm in arm. Trophy-sized bass, trout, salmon and pike decorated the cedar walls on either side. To the left of the fireplace, above the door to the clubroom, a snarling bear's head greeted incoming lodgers.

Shall we walk beneath the bear and have a nightcap, kiddo?" Six asked.

"Certainly, my love."

In the clubroom they got some whiskies and settled at a table by a window.

"Oh, look," Alicia said, "there's Merrill with Bruno walking on the docks."

Six watched them for a minute then said, "Funny. They're stopping to examine each boat. They live in boats. Why not look at the moon?"

"Aren't you a grumpy bear. Other than the moon, boats *are* the only things to look at around here."

"Now they're being joined by Kipper and 'Louis Jordan'— what's his name?"

"Jean-Pierre."

"Look at them. They're all having a big flapdoodle about something."

"Six . . . look."

"Well, well. Huntley and Bob the Magnificent. Are they going toward the others? Damned if they're not. Looks like a party and we weren't invited."

"Want to crash it?"

"Naw, I'm too tired. Sitting feels too good to stop."

Gene strode into the clubroom, saw Six and Alicia and came to their table. "Just as I thought," she bellowed, as if loud-hailing the first mate. "No one wants to leave because of the storm. They want the thrill of seeing a real Maine piss-rippah up close."

"Join us for a nightcap," Six said. Gene pulled out a chair and said," Don't mind if I do. Have you seen Bob?"

Six nodded toward the window. "Out there."

Gene pulled a pair of glasses from her pocket and stared out the window. "Good God, look at those desperados. They'll bend that boy's mind." Outside, Bob happened to look in their direction, prompting a big back-and-forth wave by Gene. Bob said something to the others and then walked toward the lodge, waving at Gene.

"Atta boy," Gene said in a tone that would've been cooing by someone else but by her sounded like Popeye. "That's a good puppy. Come to mama."

A minute later Bob came through the clubroom door and walked toward their table. Watching him, Alicia saw that he moved with an easy, swinging grace. Probably was an athlete, she thought, and he must have been quite the guy in his day; even now, in old age, he was an impressive-looking man. She calculated that he must be fifteen to twenty years older than she and Six.

He came up to the table, leaned over to plant a kiss on the top of Gene's white hair, and said, "How's the old girl?"

Gene laughed and said, "The old girl's horny tonight. Hope you've had plenty of rest."

Astonished couples at two nearby tables giggled at Gene's raucous announcement of sexual excitement.

Bob seemed to take Gene's coarseness in stride. (She's a handful, Alicia thought.) He smiled widely, flashing his beautiful teeth, chuckled and said, "Well, I have taken my enhancement pills."

"You're gonna need 'em, buster," Gene chortled, merrily whacking him on the back.

Bob gave her a wink and turned to Six and Alicia. "It's so nice to see the two of you again. May I stand you a round of whatever poison you're having?"

"Sure, Bob. That's very generous," Six said.

"Oh, that's all very well," Bob responded. "Gene's set me up with an open-ended bar tab. Sort of a stud fee, you might say."

Gene whooped joyfully and pounded the table, alarming the entire room, which became suddenly quiet, perhaps fearing a violent disturbance. When they saw it was only another outburst from the lodge's outlandish owner, they laughed in relief and resumed their chatter. Nearly all the guests were return customers who had become accustomed to Gene's oversized personality.

Gene beamed at Bob. "Robertson Weller the fourteenth or whatever the hell purebred title you have, you are hot stuff. I'm a lucky doxy."

When the general hilarity subsided (the occupants of neighboring tables having convulsed with laughter), Bob said, "Now, where were we? Oh, yes. Drinks. Alicia?"

"Bourbon, rocks and water. Hmm, Wild Turkey, please."

"Same for me," Six said.

"Excellent choice." Bob rose and headed for the bar.

Gene said, "Lucky old me," then knocked back a small glass of straight Scotch and sighed. In keeping with her overall ruggedness, she could drink like a timberjack when she wanted to, the "when she wanted to" being significant—unlike her dipsomaniacal nephew, Gene seldom took a drink before the imaginary sun was over the metaphorical yardarm.

Six, meantime, had been affected by Gene's sex banter to the point that his thoughts began jogging down familiar paths that led directly to Alicia, whom he now turned to with a happy smile and mumbled, "Room service tonight." Quick off the mark, Alicia, who'd been thinking along similar paths, returned the smile, arched an eyebrow and mumbled back, "Room service indeed." A night together away from camp in a romantic setting . . . the game was afoot.

Gene grinned at them. "You kids having fun?"

"Couldn't be better," Six replied.

Just as Bob returned with the drinks, a subtly glamorous couple appeared at the table. "Hello, Ms. Seldon," the man said. "I'm Colin Trimble and this is my wife, Daphne." To Six's ears, his accent was definitely Queen's English. "So sorry to come barging"— he flashed a smile round the table—"but just wanted to say that as first-time campers we're absolutely heads-over with your splendid chalet."

Gene sized up the couple and liked what she saw: Colin was weathered and strong-looking, probably late forties, wearing khakis, plaid shirt and moccasins with kilties; Daphne, similarly plaid-shirted and moccasined, was a graying beauty who looked as though she was born to hunt and fish. The hostess aroused, Gene grinned broadly, grabbed Colin's outstretched hand in her brown paw and boomed, "Welcome to Maine, Mr. Trimble. You landed in the right place." She gestured at the two empty chairs. "You and your wife take a seat on the log and we'll pass the whiskey jar."

"Oh, dear," Colin said. "Hadn't meant to intrude."

"No, no!" Gene sang out—God, she loved people with class— "I insist. We were just flapping about one thing and another. Sex, mostly."

"Brilliant," Daphne said. "Shall we contribute?"

"Hah!" Gene blurted, then thumped the table and said, "Good lookin' *and* a sense of humor. You'll fit right in. Colin and Daphne, this is Robertson Weller, you can call him Bob, and these lovebirds are my cousins, Six and Alicia Godwin."

Handshakes were shaken and break-the-ice pleasantries exchanged as Colin and Daphne took their seats. Bob again good-naturedly played the host, took drink requests from the Trimbles and ambled to the bar.

Gene was obviously proud of luring a sample of England's upper class to Willow Pond. "How did you folks learn about Cedar Lodge?"

"We saw a smashing advert in *The Sporting Magazine*," Daphne told her. "It's one of the oldest hunting and angling rags in the U.K."

"Don't recall it, myself, but then I probably wouldn't—Kipper does most of that, placing ads in magazines and on the Internet. But anyway, good for you! Glad to have you here. Getting some good fishing?"

"Superb," Colin said. "We were out with Merrill this afternoon. Lost count of the bass we landed—large-mouth, small-mouth. Real fighters, those small-mouths."

"What did you think of Merrill?" Six asked.

"Brilliant guide," Daphne replied. "Knew where the fish were feeding, knew what lures to use, how to play them. Quiet woman, though. Dreamy sort of personality."

Six smiled and he and Alicia exchanged a knowing look. "Dreamy" was close to the mark. Six tried to imagine the reaction of this very English couple if they'd known their guide had cocaine runnin' round her brain.

Just as Bob returned with the Trimbles' drinks, Gene spotted Tory and Nelson drifting in.

"Bolstons!" she bellowed, nearly scaring the trousers off two inebriated fishermen walking by the table. Tory and Nelson lurched to a halt and looked about in wide-eyed alarm until they saw Gene directing a semaphore at them. When they got to the table, Gene said:

"Join the party! Get some chairs from another table and belly up to the trough. Drinks are on me . . . er, they're on Bob . . . which is actually me." She laughed heartily and gave Bob, standing beside her chair, a slap on his rump. The Bolstons looked properly mystified, but did as directed and scraped some chairs across. Everyone shifted and smiled and made pleasant noises until all were again seated, and then Bob said, "My name is Bob and I'll be your server tonight. Now, what would you like?"

Nelson leaped to his feet, gave Bob a big smile and said, "*Oh* no. If you're buying, I'm getting. I know what Tory wants. Anyone else ready?" he asked looking around the table. "No takers? Be right back."

When Nelson returned and everyone was settled, Gene's selected table companions discovered they were mutually amiable conversationalists, and so the evening wore on with lively discussions of fishing, naturally—with some intriguing stories from Colin and Daphne about fly-fishing in Scotland—sailing off the Maine coast, moose-hunting in the unbelievably primitive forests of far northern Maine (Gene's contribution), skeets, trapshooting (Tory and Nelson said they were avid), canoeing and the proletarian awfulness of jet-skis desecrating the ambiance of Maine's glorious lakes.

Gene sat back and took it all in, for the most part, satisfied for once not to be featuring herself as the main attraction. She enjoyed evenings like this at the lodge when she could preside over a sort of captain's table of favored guests.

Six smiled at Tory and Nelson and said, "The Trimbles here are like you—first-timers for Cedar Lodge. They found out about the lodge from advertising in a British outdoors publication"—he looked at Daphne and asked, "What was that thing?"

"*The Sporting Magazine.*"

Colin said, "*Sporting Magazine* readers are a fussy lot, mostly poncy layabouts—although Daff and I earn our board, we've no inherited wealth . . ." He emitted a deprecating laugh, wrinkled his brow and said, "Now where was I?"

"You were 'laying about'," Tory giggled, squirming in her seat and giving Colin a cheerful leer.

Oh, please, Gene thought, glaring at Tory. Save the tootsie routine.

"Ah, just so," Colin said. "Well, readers of this rag are forever on the alert for adventures across the pond, having fished and hunted most of the prospects in the U.K. And Ireland, for that matter."

"And we'd love to fish in England," Six said, "though we probably never will. Too damn lazy just sittin' on our dock watching the world go by."

"But you came here from somewhere, though . . . right?" Nelson asked.

Alicia laughed. "Oh, yes, we came from somewhere. We live on the next lake to the east of here—Winsokkett Pond. We have a small camp there."

Turning once more to the Bolstons, Six said, "So, what I was about to ask is how you folks discovered Cedar Lodge." Six noticed that Nelson looked uncomfortable and possibly bored. Priggish sort of fellow, he decided.

Tory, however, was full of perk and breathlessly announced that, "Oh, we've heard about Cedar Lodge for years." Her pretty, round face lit up with a wide smile, supported by twinkling in her big blue eyes. "Nelson and I are originally from Oklahoma. We went our separate ways after college and then . . ." She giggled and twinkled ". . . then years and years later we both wound up married and living in New Brunswick. Would you believe it!"

"Enthralling," Colin said, smiling with sincere enthusiasm. "And then?"

"Well." Tory's bright smile vanished and was replaced with a tragic pout as she looked down at her folded hands. "Things did not work out for either Nelson or myself." A meaningful pause ensued. "We both have suffered through difficult divorces."

"Christ," Gene muttered into her glass as she gulped more Scotch.

Then Tory caught herself, looked up at everyone with bright eyes and said, "But we're fine now. We were always close as brother and sister, and we supported each other and now . . . well, I know it's a bit unusual for brother and sister to be traveling together, but we decided . . . well, what the hell?"

Following this slightly embarrassing revelation, Bob Weller, ever the gentleman, raised his glass to Tory and said, "What the hell!"

There was a general following of suit as everyone round the table raised their glasses and exclaimed, "What the hell!"

But Tory wasn't finished. "And so," she chirped, her smile making dimples in her tanned cheeks, "living just next door in New Brunswick, we've heard about Cedar Lodge for just the longest time. So we looked at your web site, thought it looked just like *our* kind of place and decided . . . what the hell!"

Again, everyone saluted with their glasses and sang out, "What the hell!"

Nelson, obviously embarrassed by his effusive sibling, looked around him like a man seeking any excuse for a rapid exit. Nevertheless, he smiled stiffly and joined in the absurd toasts.

Gene was amused by his discomfiture. He was a fairly good-looking fellow with an athletic body, but she thought he had no "cool"—much too tight-assed. Probably was a boring computer exec or some such. Tory, on the other hand, reminded her of all the obnoxious cutie-pies she'd endured through college, forever ass-wiggling their way around campus surrounded by a cluster of tongue-dragging males. Perfect airhead for Brad.

* * *

Tory Bolston woke from a thirty-minute nap with that wonderful feeling of satisfaction and release of tension that usually results from vigorous sexual congress. She looked at the bedside clock. 1:30 a.m. She propped up on her elbows. Where was her congress mate? Ah, there he was, sitting in the nude over by a window in the shadows staring out, unmoving.

"Hey," she called out.

No response.

"Brad. Brad!"

"What? Oh. Tory. Welcome to the middle of the night."

"What are you doing?"

"Nothing. Thinking."

She giggled. "Here's something to think about—I just woke up horny."

Brad turned his head to smile at her. He sighed and said, "You're a scrumptious little woman, Tory. So different from Renee. Wish I'd met someone like you back when."

"What a lovely thing to say, Brad." She cocked her head and gave him a puzzled look. "You sound different."

"Yeah, well. I should. I'm sober. It is not, how shall I say . . . it is not my customary aspect." He got up, turned on a lamp and walked over to the bar table. He picked up a bottle of George Dickel and said, "So I must take the cure. Would you like an ante meridian cocktail?"

"Sure." Tory let her gaze sweep around the room. "Brad, what are all these instruments and dials and things?"

Brad walked over to the bed with her drink and said, "I guess you'd say it's my hobby. I'm a one-man weather bureau. Those two are barometers, the thing by it is a hygrometer—measures humidity—those right there are various kinds of thermometers. Then over there is a rain gauge, the next is a wind meter, and that little bugger is an anemometer, which measures aspects of wind. All weather stations have them."

Brad went over to the long instrument table and picked up a blue, handheld device that looked a bit like a digital scale. "And this is the *pièce de résistance*—a lightning detector."

"Wow. That is totally impressive."

"I always know what's coming." Brad sat down beside Tory and lightly stroked her thigh. She made purring noises and tongue-kissed his ear. "And I may as well tell you now—by tomorrow night we're getting hit with an enormous, dangerous storm front. It's entirely possible that one section of it will create tornadoes."

Tory stopped purring, pulled back from ear-nibbling and said, "Good lord! Tornadoes?"

"Only a possibility. But for damn sure it's going to be one hell of a storm. You and Nelson might want to leave."

Tory grew silent, occasionally sipping the whiskey Brad had given her. "Oh. I don't know. Nelson and I aren't usually chicken about things. I'll have to ask him. A big storm sounds like fun. But a tornado sounds like sudden death."

"I hate storms . . . any storm."

"Sometimes they're fun. Lightning and thunder—when you're inside a house, of course."

"Not for me. I think they're evil."

"Evil? Brad! That's . . . that's . . ." Tory almost said "ridiculous" or "absurd," which was how she really felt, but she didn't want to anger him, so she fumbled for "strange."

"Yeah? Well, I guess it is." Brad stared down into his glass of whiskey. "You see, I'm terrified of storms."

"Oh. I see." Tory looked at the weather instruments. Maybe, she thought, this beauty sitting next to her was a nut. A strong, macho 48-year-old hiding under the covers during a storm? Oh, please.

"No, you don't see," he said sharply. He knew what she was thinking. Then he softened his tone. "Well, how the hell could you? I'm not scared of storms because I think they're going to kill me, I'm terrified because every storm brings back the picture of my mother and father lying in a boat out there by one of the docks burned to death by lightning, burned like they'd been in a frying pan."

"Jesus, Brad, I'm . . ."

"I was the first one up to the boat." He rose abruptly and went over to the window and looked down at the docks. "I was the first one up to the boat," he repeated. "I loved my mom and dad. Their names were Reginald and Annice, like people in an English novel. They were charming and beautiful and I loved them dearly. They made this place famous with their hard work. And when they died my Aunt Iphigene got Cedar Lodge. Nasty old witch. I wish someone would throw water on her and she'd melt screaming, 'My world! My beautiful world!' "

* * *

Kipper gasped his way through the most incredible orgasm he'd had in his life. The most incredible orgasm he'd ever had in his life before that was about 20 minutes previously, and the one before that had been about 30 minutes ago—and so the evening had progressed.

As the tremors and little shooting spears of pleasure gradually subsided, Kipper flopped back on the bed and lay very still, until his breathing regulated and he was sure he wasn't having a coronary. Dear God, he thought, never had he experienced such ecstasy with women—and he liked women and had enjoyed sex with women. But now . . . to hell with women. If this was homosexuality, he was signing up forever. This gorgeous young man—well, 34 years young—whose head now lay on Kipper's stomach, looking up at him, was a champion.

"Jean-Pierre."

"Hmmm?"

"To say that the past couple of hours were extraordinary *beyond* belief is doing you an injustice. Words, English ones at least, can't express the pleasure I've had."

A chuckle came from Jean-Pierre. "It sounded like you were having a good time."

"Oh dear God, yes, I must've *bellowed* like a buffalo. You must forgive me."

"I was yelling a bit, too," Jean-Pierre said. "It's part of the fun."

"Perhaps the ancient Egyptians had hieroglyphs to express these sorts of mind-blowing moments. I mean, they *must* have been sexy devils. Their tomb paintings show them boozing and cavorting practically naked."

Kipper sat up and reached for the whiskey and water he'd left on his bedside table; next to the cocktail glass was a saucer with the gray ashes of the two marijuana spliffs that had enhanced his and Jean-Pierre's enthusiasm for their just-completed exertions.

"Jean-Pierre dearest?"

"Hmmmm?"

"I don't want to ever lose you. *Ever.*"

Jean-Pierre sat up quickly and his eyes filled with tears and his accent got loose. "Oh, non, Kee-pair. Do not put me through these *tourmente* again. I am going to do what I am going to do."

"No, no, no, puppy! Please, I know. We're not *going* through all that again. I am telling you that I am not going to lose you ever because I promise you that my aunt will not stand in our way. I'll make sure of that. We are going to New York and I am going to buy you a restaurant. You'll see. Oh, Jean-Pierre, my darling darling. You'll see."

* * *

Huntley sat in the leather armchair in his first-floor room dressed in a floor-length, gray-and-white-striped summer-cotton dressing gown from Brooks Brothers and wearing burgundy English-made Peel & Co. soft leather slippers. He loved his beautiful clothes but tonight he was so frightened and desperate and miserable that he could've been wearing a gunny sack and wooden clogs for all the comfort his garments gave him. He had been drinking and staring into a bleak future for hours, and though he was staggering drunk he could not sleep or relax. With trembling hand he took his cellphone from a pocket in his robe and carefully dialed the dreaded number.

Only cessation of ringing and the sound of someone on the other end breathing told Huntley that he had made contact.

"Beauchamp here. Tomorrow's Saturday. Please tell me something."

The ghastly, rasping metallic voice said, "Our representative is already on the premises where you are. You will receive your results and documents tomorrow."

The connection was cut. Huntley's gin-soaked brain struggled to process what the eerie voice had said. Someone was *here*? Someone he'd perhaps met, talked to? What was he supposed to do tomorrow? Sit tight and wait. That's all he could do. Sit tight and wait, but be ready to drive to Canada.

Six

Brad was up at 10 a.m. and moving around the bedroom, having showered and dressed in clean fishing clothes, and he was feeling fine. Despite the fact that he had gotten spiffed again by 3 a.m., he had no hangover. He seldom had hangovers—during his eighteen years of steady drinking every cell in his body seemed to have been conditioned to metabolize alcohol and spit it out.

Tory was amazed, and irritated—a night of sex and drinking more than her usual limit had left her with a groggy, aching head. Screwing a gold-medalist drunk, she decided, had its drawbacks.

Brad noticed that Tory was awake and giving him the evil eye. "Good morning," he said.

"Good nothing. I'm wrecked. Going back to sleep. Wake me at noon."

"Fine. I'll take you and Nelson fishing then, and I won't even put it on your bill. I'll show you a new place. I figure the storm front will start coming in around six. Typically, ahead of a front the weather is beautiful and the fishing's superb, and we can take a spin for about an hour."

"Sounds great, but don't worry about Nelson. He's gone somewhere, Bangor I think. Don't know why. Said he had to get something important. By the way, he's got the hots for your, uh, wife."

"He's welcome to her. She'll eat him for lunch."

"Hey," Tory said. "You were really spooked about the storm last night . . . uh, earlier this morning. Are you still worried?"

"Oh, I'm worried, all right. That's why I've got to stay sober. I don't like staying sober, but I must. This damn storm front is big and dangerous, and I've got to keep monitoring it."

Brad walked over to a window and looked out and continued talking. "I've got to stay sober up until the storm, help the boys get the boats out of the water, get the furniture inside, then I'll get drunk. Nothing to do in a storm except get drunk and ride it out.

Gene will be all over the place, bashing around and shouting, getting everybody screwed up. I'll make sure everyone's inside. People think they're safe, watching a storm like it was a show. They don't know, they just don't know. Dumb bastards, they'll be out there like it was a cocktail party."

He turned to look at Tory. She was asleep.

* * *

"There it is," Brad said, speaking softly, almost reverently. "See that dark tree trunk rising just above the water's surface? It's huge. Thirty years ago it was about eight feet above the water. Its big limbs kept it up for, oh, I don't know, maybe fifteen years."

They were in the northern reaches of Willow Pond, where only huge rocks and thick forest lined the shore. There were no camps, no docks, no evidence at all of human intrusion. It was one-thirty in the afternoon, hot and still. Finches, warblers, orioles and flycatchers chattered and flitted back and forth, up and down on the tree limbs. A gathering of cormorants and gulls stood on nearby rocks and a family of mallards bobbed for food. Two ospreys circled overhead watching the lake for unwary fish swimming near the surface.

Brad had cut the boat motor and now he stared silently at the tree trunk. He was silent for so long—staring, not moving—that Tory became uneasy. She broke the spell by saying, "It must be a fabulous fishing spot. Shall we cast?"

"No, we'll go somewhere else. I'm sure it's got good bass, but I never fish here. This is where Leslie died."

Tory turned quickly toward him. "I beg your pardon?"

"Leslie. We were eighteen. I loved her."

Tory wasn't sure what to say, so she waited. But when Brad lapsed into prolonged silence she got antsy and said, "Uh . . . what happened, Brad?"

"This was a favorite summer hangout when we were teenagers. Pull up in boats, have picnics with beer, mess around in the water getting sexed up, but the biggest deal was to climb on that trunk and dive. We'd get drunker and the diving and games got wilder."

A long silence ensued before Brad continued. "We'd been diving off that tree for years, because the water right under it was clear of rocks so we believed there was no danger. Well, actually, there *wasn't* any danger—except that something weird happened. Leslie did this big comic dive, thrashing her arms and flipping over backward off the log. She hit the water head first but the position her head was in snapped her neck. None of us ever knew such a thing could happen. We'd all grown up in and around the water but we never . . ."

Brad pulled himself from the reverie, started the motor and said, "Well, enough of that. I'll show you another place we loved when we were kids." He motored to the east a couple of hundred yards, steered the boat slowly toward the shore and put the motor in neutral. "See that?" He pointed toward a marshy area with high reeds.

Tory hesitated. "I . . . well, I'm not sure what I see."

"Right through that marsh and behind those trees is a creek that goes over to the next lake, Rocky Pond. It's about three miles long. We call it a serpentine because it winds and curves so much. There used to be this old commercial fishing camp on Rocky Pond that had a beach. Sand on these lakes is unusual but they had a big one. We'd canoe or kayak all the way over there just to play on the beach and rent sailboats."

"Sounds like fun." Tory managed to flash a hundred-dollar smile to hide the fact that she was getting profoundly bored. Relief came when Brad wheeled around and sped away.

Speaking loudly over the motor's roar, Brad said: "I'm forty-eight years old and I've lived on Willow Pond all my life. I've gone to Europe, Caribbean, out West fishing. But I've always lived here. I don't want to die here."

Tory privately agreed. Nice place to visit, she reflected. Wouldn't want to live here, sure as hell wouldn't want to die here.

* * *

"I always assumed we'd die here at our camp." Alicia was speaking; she and Six were standing at the lake end of their big T-shaped dock looking back at their camp to make sure they'd secured everything properly in preparation for the predicted storm. "What if our camp gets destroyed while we're over to Cedar Lodge and we lose everything?"

Six needed a smoke when Alicia got like this, so he poked about in his pocket, located his pipe, filled it from his tobacco pouch—which seemed always to be in another pocket; why, he wondered, could he never stuff both into the same pocket?—and fired up. Alicia was a calm woman, sensible, seldom given to fear, but she was very sentimental about their camp and about Winsokkett Pond and their neighbors. They had bought the camp twenty-five years ago, when they were still teaching, and when she got on a tear about losing "everything" it was her one foray into anxiety. For November through March they had a tiny house in Waterville; it was pleasant enough and they conducted their book business from there, but their hearts belonged to the lake and their camp and fishing. So Six knew what she meant, and he loved their lakeside life, but losing their camp wouldn't be *everything*.

"We could always . . ." puff, puff ". . . we could always rebuild. Put up an architectural statement."

"Very funny."

"We've been in plenty of storms, my darling kiddo. And we've had tornado warnings before. You usually don't fret about these things."

Alicia took a deep breath then blew it out slowly. "Well, yep, that's true. I think I've been spooked by all the hullaballoo over to Cedar Lodge, especially Brad's Cassandra performance. Did you see him, Six? He was more than intense, he was frightened. He was also sober, which I surmise isn't his customary condition."

"Yep. I've got to admit, he had me a little jumpy, too." Six turned and looked at Alicia. "So. Do you want to stay here and ride out the storm then go over to that damn meeting at Cedar Lodge tomorrow?"

"Ohh, well, no. I mean we've got the place all battened down and we have the computer with us and all the files on disc. If the camp took a direct hit then we couldn't prevent the books from getting destroyed even if we were here. Besides, we'd probably be dead anyway and Winsokkett Antiquarian Books would be immediately defunct and who would give a hoot anyway?"

Alicia gave Six a brilliant smile full of the frisky humor that first charmed him when they were college teachers. Seeing that smile Six knew that his wife was back on a steady course. And just at that moment, fate, which also has a frisky sense of humor, chimed in with a call from Gene Seldon. As the merry little tune played over and over, Six slapped on his pockets until he found his cellphone and answered it.

"Six? Gene here!" She was back on the loud-hailer again, and Alicia would hear her distinctly as Six held the phone away from his ear and rolled his eyes.

"Yes, Gene?"

"Are you and Alicia squared away over there?"

"Yep. All set. We'll be heading back soon."

"Excellent, excellent. That's what I wanted to hear. Was afraid you might not want to. Think I need you more than ever, Six."

"Oh? What's happening?"

"Something truly weird. I got a death threat in the mail."

Six and Alicia stared wide-eyed at each other. "Oh, for God's sake," Six told Gene, "that's straight out of Agatha Christie. Do people actually send death threats these days?"

"Apparently they do."

"It's got to be a joke."

"Don't think so, Six. Damn note is strange, and personal. It's definitely from someone at Cedar Lodge. Here's what it says: 'Why don't you unleash the puppies and give them their goodies? It will be mutually beneficial—they'll be happy and you will continue to live'."

"Holy catfish. That is a *verbose* death threat. And articulate. You're right. It's weird."

"Wait'll you see the goddamn thing. It's computer generated, I'm sure of that. The letters are ornate, a Gothic-like dark script. I looked on my Word format and sure enough, there it was, a typeface called Blackmoor LET. Looks somewhat like the type used for death notices in newspapers."

"I don't like this, Gene."

"You ain't the only one, bustah. Meantime, it's like a psyche ward around here. Brad has been completely sober all day and is even more of a jerk than when he's drunk. He's wandering around the place mumbling to himself and looking like he's seen a werewolf. Merrill won't look at me when I talk to her and won't speak. Kipper just sits in his room and drinks, as if he's taking Brad's place for the day."

"Hoo, boy."

"Even Hunt seems spooked, pacing back and forth on the porch and peering at all the guests. An hour ago I went up to him at the bar, I guess he didn't see me coming, and when I spoke his name he jumped about a foot and then giggled to hide his nervousness. I think one of them sent me that note, Six. Not Hunt, of course—what does he have to worry about, his name isn't Seldon. But I can tell you one damn thing for sure. Some member of my precious family is trying to scare me. I've got a news bulletin for 'em—it won't work."

Six and Alicia's last duty before going to Willow Pond was the transfer of Rudolph and Marmalade to their neighbor's next-door camp. Chuck and Lottie LaFray had two dogs, Labradors like Rudolph, and a calico cat. All were acquainted, so there was no customary ritual of the beasts—growling, hissing, circling and smelling.

That accomplished, they got into their Jeep and headed up the camp road.

"Ayuh," Six said. "Two storms on the way, one courtesy of mother and the other . . ."

"I beg your pardon? Mother?"

"Mother Nature, of course. And the other storm courtesy of the changing of a will."

"Sounds like the beginning of a crime novel."
"Which do you think will be worse? Weather or will?"

* * *

As Gene had said, Huntley Beauchamp was indeed spooked. He was as spooked as a rabbit in an owl sanctuary, but he was, he believed, doing a superb job of hiding it. He had to keep himself calm in order to schmooze with the guests and spot who was new, who had registered today and the day before. He wanted to find this "representative" that the frightening voice had told him was already at Cedar Lodge. Here it was midday Saturday and still no "documents," which were one half of the specialty firm's guarantee. If the sonofabitch was here, why hadn't he—or she; Huntley was aware that it could be a woman—done anything? Of course the "representative" might not want to be known or seen but couldn't he or she at least have slipped a discreet envelope under Huntley's door or given him some kind of sign that all was well? The damn meeting was tomorrow and Huntley was getting panicky, unable to eat, but he *could* drink, and the scotch and a few valiums were holding him steady, allowing him to function outwardly as Huntley Beauchamp the tall, golden-voiced man of success and not as the cornered, red-eyed rat that was cowering within. Part of his brain screamed at him that he had been suckered, that he was *not* going to be rescued, and that he should get on the turnpike toward Canada immediately, but Huntley suppressed the dissonance and concentrated on the task at hand, *viz,* chatting up the newly arrived fishermen at Cedar Lodge.

Now, as he slowly strolled the length of the front porch, smiling and murmuring pleasantries to the people who had just come in from fishing and were awaiting the luncheon bell, he looked like a man who had the world by its tail. With each leisurely swing of his legs, Huntley's tan, full-cut gabardine trousers rippled luxuriantly. Over a white shirt he wore a navy linen jacket with white buttons, a yellow pocket square flowing from its breast pocket.

Ah, there was that English couple who came in late Thursday—Colin and, um, what was her name, something terribly British sounding. They were still on his list of potentials. The secret firm's representative didn't need to be a lone operative, Huntley had reasoned; two of them posing as a married couple would be ideal in a place like Cedar Lodge.

"Hello there again, hah-hah. Huntley Beauchamp. I met you the other day. Splendid day, isn't it, just splendid, hah-hah."

The man waved Huntley into the chair next to him and said,

"Colin here, wife Daphne." Daphne, a glorious example of what Huntley thought of as upper-class everything, smiled pleasantly at Huntley.

"Brilliant day," she said. "Lovely."

"Hah-hah, lovely, yes, just lovely." Noting that the couple were sporting shorts and fishing shirts, Huntley asked, "Been fishing this morning, what?" (He recalled that Englishmen said "what?" at the end of sentences.)

"Damn straight. Fabulous. We, uh . . ." Colin turned to his wife. "What's that yank expression?"

"Hammered them," Daphne answered.

"Ah yes, we hammered them. Between us, we brought in twenty-three bass in three hours. The guides here are some of the best we've encountered."

"Hah-hah, ah yes, yes they are."

"Merrill took us out. I gather she's the niece of the owner. Oh, just a mo'—her name is also Beauchamp. Your wife, your sister?"

Huntley chuckled his rich, low confiding chuckle—"huh huh huhhh"—and ran a manicured hand through the thick hair that curled down over his shirt collar. "My wife. We're, uh, not together anymore. She's kept the name Beauchamp. Likes the sound of it, huh huh huhhh."

"Oh dear," Colin said. "Didn't mean to poke a stick into troubled waters."

"Not at all, not at all. We're still friends and all that, hah-hah. I no longer live here at the lodge. I'm down in Boston."

"Oh really. Daff and I have a little place there. Half-year in Boston, half-year in London."

Huntley became alert. *Boston. They just came from Boston.* He took a sip of his scotch and surveyed the sunlit lake beyond the docks, studying it carefully, as if he were thinking of going out fishing. "Two of the best cities in the world, hah-hah. You've got the best of both sides of the pond." (Hah! Huntley thought. Good one. Just remembered that British "pond" thing for the ocean.)

"Oh, we think so," Daphne said.

"Sooo, have you taken early retirement, enjoying the sporting life and all that? Hah-hah."

"Well, we're not slogging away in some dreary office," Daphne responded, "but we still sort of . . . what's the Hollywood bit? Oh yes, players. We're still players."

"Yes," Colin said, leveling his gaze directly at Huntley. "We're punters in commercial sporting outfits." He paused to take a sip of his gin and tonic. "Much like this one."

Huntley's heartbeat began step-dancing. *It's them. Holy shit, I was right. They're the ones.* Calm, Huntley told himself. Stay calm. Drink some scotch. Look at the water. Make like it's just chit-chat, nothing more.

"And you, Mr. Beauchamp? Law, business, stealing horses?" Colin gave Huntley a big grin.

"Welll, hah-hah," Huntley purred, recrossing his legs and straightening the crease in his trousers. "That's quite a coincidence. You see, I'm in charge of investments for Cedar Lodge Enterprises." *You know that, goddamn it. Tell me now. Tell me everything's in place.*

"Well, that's splendid. Isn't that splendid, Daphne?"

"Why yes," Daphne smiled. "You're just the chap we're looking for."

Huntley was seething. Outwardly, showing all his pearlies in a rictus grin. Inwardly, seething. Roadside bombs were going off in his brain. *Yes, I'm the chap you're looking for, you dirty bastards. Tell me something now!*

"Absolutely," Colin said. "We heard that some investment opportunities were opening up here."

Huntley felt like he was going to explode. Cold perspiration was dampening his collar. He tried to drink more scotch but his hand was trembling so he just gripped the glass.

A ship's bell rang from inside the lodge. "Ah, there we are," Colin said merrily, rising and helping Daphne to her feet. "The luncheon bell. Well, cheerio, Mr. Beauchamp . . . or may I call you Huntley?"

"Huh huh huhhh. Yes yes, huh huh," Huntley uttered through his teeth. He watched them walk to the front door. *You miserable bastards. Playing me along. Just dangling me for the fun of it. 'Stealing horses.' Oh, nice touch, you cretins.*

His hand shaking in rage and fear, Huntley lifted his glass and knocked back the rest of his scotch.

Inside the lodge, Colin turned to Daphne, raised his eyebrows high and curved his mouth down in a comic expression of disdain. "Oh dear," he said.

"Yes, appalling. Just like he was described."

Seven

In the late afternoon of what had been a hot, deathly still day, the massive storm front, stretching hundreds of miles, swept across Maine unleashing a torrent of nearly incessant lightning and thunder, blinding, wind-driven rain, baseball-sized hail and, here and there along its calamitous route, small tornadoes that ripped through forests, croplands and towns.

At Willow Pond, shortly after 6 p.m., the front appeared as a seemingly benign dark line over the mountains to the north and northwest. Soon, there was a faint booming as white puffs of cloud grew all along the horizon. The kind of flashes people often mistakenly call "summer lightning" accompanied a distant timpani. Fifteen minutes later majestic cumulonimbus clouds arose, billowing rapidly and punctuated by stronger flashes of light and a constant low rumble like a bombardment in some faraway battle. Another half-hour and the clouds had turned into a roiling, darkening mass, riven by jagged rivers of lightning that loomed over the western and northern landscape. Thunder boomed seconds behind the lightning—the storm was nearing quickly. A breeze, harbinger of coming violence, rippled the lake's surface and chilled the air.

Six and Alicia, leaning on the front porch railing beside Gene and Bob, felt a tinge of fear along with the sudden coolness. Amos, usually hard by Gene, didn't need Brad's weather instruments to tell him something bad was in the air, so he'd slunk off to what he considered the best refuge—a corner in the clubroom.

"It's magnificent and it's frightening," Alicia said. She chuckled. "An irresistible combination."

"Ayuh," Six replied, "I can remember being out in the middle of the lake, standing there in a metal boat, just gawping at some storm covering the sky and getting little thrills of excitement, forgetting that I could be fried any moment. Lightning, you know, can strike ahead of the storm itself."

Gene looked at Six and gave him a crooked smile. "That's for sure—lightning out of nowhere is sort of famous around here."

Six stood up straight and looked at Gene with embarrassment. "Oh. Damn. Forgot. Sorry."

"Don't apologize," Gene said. "Doesn't bother me."

Bob was intrigued. "What's this about lightning at Cedar Lodge?"

"My brother and his wife—parents of Kipper, Merrill and Brad. They'd just come in ahead of a storm and were standing in the boat at the dock—it was that dock over there on the left. They were lifting out tackle and gear. Thought they were safe because the storm was still to the north and the sky over the lodge was clear. Damn huge shaft of lightning seemed to come right out of the blue sky and hit the boat. Incinerated Reg and Annice."

Bob said, "Good Lord, Gene. I'm so sorry."

"Don't be. I loathed them. Anyway, it was eighteen years ago."

Bob's eyes widened in shock as he looked over Gene's head at Six. He didn't say anything, but it was obvious to Six that the man had just received a nasty jolt in regard to the personality of his fair betrothed. Better now than after the swapping of rings, Six believed. If this dashing gray fox needed Gene's money to keep him in the style to which, etc., then he must learn to live with a woman who was as tough as steel rivets. Six was accustomed to Gene's coarseness and was fond of her despite that—and, of course, he was eternally grateful for her financial help in the past—but he couldn't imagine living with his cousin. She was rough. Rough and strong-willed.

Gene was unaware of any reaction to her cruel statement and would've shrugged it off if she had known. Nothing like brutal honesty, she always felt. Bob, quiet and thoughtful, stared at the docks.

"Storm's comin' in damn fast," Gene said. "Glad we got the shutters closed and locked." She was dressed in her customary outfit of fishing shirt, khaki shorts and camp moccasins. Bob was sporting a similar ensemble. A matching pair already, Six thought as he looked over at them; no dinnertime elegance tonight—they were dressed for battle.

Farther along on the porch were three other couples watching the approaching chaos. The rest of the lodgers were in the clubroom, having been advised to get dinner early in case of a blackout.

Gene said: "When we go back in I need someone to help take flashlights to the bar. I have about two dozen in boat bags behind the reception desk. If we lose power I don't want people stumbling around in the dark trying to create a legal action."

"Sure," Six replied. "But I thought you had a generator."

"We do. It's in a little house hidden in the woods way out back. Didn't want the damn thing intruding on the sylvan ambiance. It's an old one and takes about fifteen minutes or so for it to gin up enough juice to get everything lit up again, just enough time for some damn fool rugged outdoorsman, drunk as an owl, to break his neck. I'm gonna get a new generator next season."

The breeze from the lake became a hard wind, raising white-caps on the water. The four of them watched, enthralled, as the menacing tempest spread farther west and now east and soared upward until it was a towering universe of churning blackness, turning day into twilight.

Alicia cried out, "Look! Look at the far western edge—it's dip-ping."

"Is that a tornado?" Bob asked, startled from contemplation of his intended bride's possible barbarity.

"Oh, Christ," Gene said. "It could be one starting to form. There could be funnels any minute."

"Good God," Bob said. "I've been in a lot of storms but this one looks like a real bastard."

"Ayuh," Gene said. "Don't like it. Could be real bad."

As if her words had been a challenge to the cosmos, heavy rain and powerful wind hit suddenly like an airborne tidal wave. Every-one on the porch yelped and stampeded toward the big double-doored entrance.

"Goddammit!" Gene shouted as they made cover. Explosive cursing was her customary reaction to turmoil or danger.

As he and Bob were closing the doors, Six stopped abruptly and grabbed Bob's arm, blurting, "Bob, look, a funnel! It's dipping over there to the west!"

Gene slipped forward and glared at the horizon. "Oh, God-dammit, Goddammit!" she erupted, as if with further blasphemies she could hold back nature's anarchy. Heaven answered with an ear-shattering blast as a great shaft of lightning speared down from the blackness onto the nearest island. Everyone ducked in fright reflexively and retreated from the doorway.

"Holy crap," Bob whispered as the thunder faded.

With blinding light and a terrifying explosion, lightning struck a huge oak tree near the lodge, causing all of them to recoil farther back inside. The tree split in half to the ground, and half of it top-pled onto the west end of the front porch, crashing through the roof and smashing wicker chairs and tables below. The four of them crept to the doorway and peered out in disbelief at the wreck-age.

"God's teeth!" Gene screamed. "There goes ten thousand dol-lars."

As Six and Bob closed the doors, Alicia said, "This is getting a bit horrifying."

The lodge's lights flickered, went out, then came back on. "Dammit, we're gonna go dark," Gene said as she rushed behind the reception desk and pulled up two boat bags, which she placed on the counter. "Six, could you take these into the clubroom? Tell everybody in there what they're for."

A crowd of men and women, led by Colin and Daphne, emerged from the clubroom, drinks in hand. "What was that al-mighty crash?" Colin asked. "Everything holding up?" Gene grinned at them—her self-trained reflex was to always smile at guests, even in the midst of a raging tumult. "Lightning felled a tree right onto the front porch," she told him.

"Bloody awful," Colin said. "Anything we can do to help?"

Now that, Gene thought, was a perfect example of the quality of her average lodger. Pampered ninnies at some worthless resort would be squealing for management to protect them. Fishermen waded in to lend a hand.

"As a matter of fact, you can," Gene replied, handing Colin and Daphne the bags of flashlights. "If you could take these bags of flashlights to the dining room and the bar and parcel them out among everyone, I'd greatly appreciate it. If we go dark it'll take a good quarter-hour to get the generator going."

"Of course," Daphne said. "Splendid idea." Enormous blasts of thunder rattled the building; Daphne raised her eyebrows and looked around her. "Are you going to survive this little rumpus?" She laughed to acknowledge the facetiousness of her remark.

Gene also chuckled. "Don't you worry about Cedar Lodge. It's endured a hundred and thirty years of vicious Maine weather. Tough old building." She flashed Colin and Daphne and all the others behind them a lop-sided grin and said, "And I'm a tough old broad. Drinks are on the house, folks. It could be a rough night. I've already told the bartender."

"Good show," Colin said, reaching for the bags of flashlights. "We'll just pop these round to the glittering hordes." As Colin and Daphne gathered the small crowd and returned to the clubroom, Gene turned to Six, Alicia and Bob and said:

"Fishermen are in a class by themselves."

* * *

*"Rain, rain go away,
Come 'ginn shum other day."*
Brad sat in his bedroom singing to his weather instruments as thunder provided a percussional accompaniment. Next to the hygrometer was a bottle of George Dickel with only inches of its amber liquid remaining. He had knocked back enough fine, smooth, branch-water-distilled bourbon to feel very fine and smooth himself. The more he had drunk the more the old terrors

and hideous visions that came with each big storm had receded, until now he was in the mood for auto-amusement.

"Ish raining, ish pouring,
The old man ish snoring."

Tory, he felt, was being rudely unresponsive to his amusing songs and patter. He looked around in irritation. *Whoopsie, Toryish gone.* Funny. He didn't remember her leaving. Damn woman. Philistine. Must've walked out during his rendition of "Si mi chiamano Mimi." Tory seemed classy, he thought—shocking to learn she's a Philistine. I mean, if one isn't moved by *La bohème*, he told himself, then one is numb to beauty.

"Tory, Toryish's gone away,
"She'll come back shum other day."

Brad grabbed the bottle of bourbon, poured the remaining inches into his empty glass and then attempted to stand up, but the captain's chair kept teetering and swiveling—as it was designed to do, albeit for sober people—and he found it hard going. Finally, he put down the glass, grabbed the edge of the instrument bench and hoisted himself erect. "Aha, just so," he muttered, then lurched to the drinks table in the living room for ice and water. These he dropped and sloshed all about him on the floor, though he did manage to get some into the whiskey, then he re-lurched to the bedroom and dropped heavily into the captain's chair, which he merrily spun around several times, coming to a halt facing his beloved instruments, all now busily scratching away on graphs or readjusting dials or slowly revolving.

"Ahh, my pretties," he purred, "what have you got for da-da?" He carefully examined each instrument while sipping his bourbon. "Oooo, barometric proos . . . prezhur is plunzing. Very bad. And wha's zis? Wind verocity sixty-two! Oooo. And you, my pet—Ah! Prepris . . . presoup . . . pre.cip.eye.ta.shun . . . wait for it . . . One hunnerd percent! Wow! And now you, my new little feller." Brad smiled as he picked up the small blue instrument and pressed a button. "What're *you* telling us? Ah hah! Bress your heart, you're shaying there's major occurrence of . . . LIGHTNING! Ah, hah hah hah! Of course, of course!" he shouted, holding his arms wide in an all-encompassing gesture. "You're all telling me, my pretties, that . . . that . . . we're . . . having . . . a . . . STORM! Ahh, yes. We're having a whoppero. Thaz Italian for whopper. A big whoppero, bad-ass storm. And tonight, my children, tonight, I mush go out in the whoppero. Oh, yes, I mush go out. Tonight's the night when I do it, when I . . ."

Brad jerked in fright and dropped his glass as thunder exploded as if lightning were coming through the wall. He jumped up, enraged that the blast had scared him, and screamed "Goddammit!" and threw the bourbon bottle against the wall. Seconds later a rumbling crash that shook the lodge caused him to stumble back against the instrument table, knocking over a barometer as he reached out to steady himself. "Jesus, Jesus!" he screamed. "What the hell?"

* * *

No one will ever suspect me, Kipper thought as he sat before the new double-screen PC in Gene's office. No one will ever suspect Kipper the Straight and Narrow. He giggled at his self-designation. He was diligently depositing computer-generated checks on the Cedar Lodge Holdings account into one of three holding companies that existed in name only in accounts he had opened at three different banks in three different cities. Kipper whispered a little song as he worked: "Oh, clever, clever, me," it went. "The money no one will ever see."

Being one's own business manager made this sort of thing child's play for Kipper. Gene, he'd realized early in his tutelage to become the lodge's manager, thought she knew everything about business and finance, which was not surprising, considering that she thought she knew everything about everything. But he had soon learned how naïve she really was. The lodge's day to day accounts and transactions bored her. All she really cared about were the quarterly investment statements from Huntley Beauchamp and he knew she didn't know how to read those accurately, though of course she was certain she was an investment wizard from way back. It wouldn't surprise Kipper if that weasely bastard Beauchamp was ripping them off in grand style. God, how he detested that smug, condescending bastard. *Kipper, lad, how's it hanging? Hah-hah. Getting enough pussy?* The cretin knew he was gay. *Everyone* knew Kipper was gay. But Huntley thought it was ever so witty to tweak him about it. Pompous fop. Kipper hated all the white shoes and ascots and sweaters over the shoulders.

Fortunately for Kipper's bit of financial treachery, Gene contracted with an accounting firm for the investment funds only, and her old troll of a lawyer, Adrian Bucksaddle, kept his ugly nose out of the daily ledgers. In regard to daily and weekly business, Gene had left everything entirely to Kipper, who had made the fictitious holding companies' corporate names match the names that were actually painted on the local trucks that delivered food, condiments, kitchen supplies, laundry or boating and fishing supplies to the lodge. For filing of taxes and infrequent reports to regulatory agencies, Kipper relied on the Waterville CPA who had been his roommate and best friend at Colby College. His friend (bless his heart, Kipper thought, smiling to himself) forthrightly signed off on Kipper's meticulous bookkeeping, and why should he not? The figures for employees' salaries, Social Security and FICA withholding were always flawless and the calculations on debits, revenue and net income were marvelously exact.

Gene had had him educated much too well, he thought with amusement—business administration, accountancy, marketing and advertising. The latter two skills he employed with outstanding success via magazine and online advertising to lure ever more wealthy patrons to Cedar Lodge year-round. He should win a CLIO for his ads, he thought. His full-color layouts made Brad the Dipso and Merrill the Cokebrain looks like gods. If sportsmen knew the truth about "Maine's Premier Freshwater Guides" they would pack their Orvis luggage and kick up dust and small stones getting away from Cedar Lodge. His brother and sister amazed him. He hated them, but they *were* amazing fishermen. Brad hid his bourbon breath by chewing tin after tin of Altoids, and as he was nearly always intoxicated his boozy fog was accepted as normal.

No one could smell cocaine, so Merrill didn't have a breath problem, and as she was nearly always stoned, the people in her boat accepted her dreamy aloofness with unconcern. Fishermen in boats cared about one thing only—fish on the line. If the guide was a little peculiar then who cared? Most fishing guides were peculiar.

No matter. Brad and Merrill got fish into every boat that went out. Sometimes it was twenty, thirty, forty or more; sometimes it was only a few on the days when truly evil weather buggered everything, but they never came back to the dock with disconsolate fishermen in a boat in which no bass or perch or pike had been caught. Kipper's siblings had been on the lakes with rods in their hands since they were toddlers (so had he, but he'd never really loved fishing nor did he have any skill), and their guiding techniques were a mix of instinct and prodigious memories of seemingly every square yard of water that had at one time or another yielded a fish.

But Kipper wondered how long they could maintain their mastery before their personal habits defeated them. When that time came, he had decided, he wanted to be well shot of the lodge. He'd instituted his rake-off scheme two years earlier, after Jean-Pierre's entreaties concerning the New York restaurant had become more and more urgent. Kipper feared (fear that had been so viciously— to his mind—confirmed earlier in the day) that Gene would never forward him money from his anticipated inheritance. Therefore, he would secretly build a fund of his own. Thievery, embezzlement? Oh, not really, he had firmly rationalized to himself. Had not his business and marketing acumen resulted in impressive profit gains the past seven years, especially the concept of a gourmet restaurant in the boonies? More than that, *he* should be one-third owner of Cedar Lodge now, "right *now*," he muttered, angrily punching the send key on the latest of his larcenous transactions. Hideous fate had robbed of him what should be his *this* very moment. Then there would be no "Il Duce" with her boot on everyone's neck—there would only be weird old Auntie Gene, whom they tolerated, awarding her secondary tasks to earn her keep.

Despite his rage at Gene, Kipper experienced a gnawing guilt at having sent her that outrageous death threat note. At the time, he had admired his own artistry, with the arch wording and the funerary typography. But now he was feeling that it was a bit asinine and useless. Something like that would never frighten his ballbusting aunt. The note wasn't serious—he didn't really want to kill her, he didn't want to kill anyone, he just wanted Gene to drop dead on her own.

He had not yet "appropriated" enough money to enable him to bolt from Willow Pond to New York City with Jean-Pierre, establish a restaurant and be certain the two of them could live decently. At least another year of peculation was necessary. He hadn't told Jean-Pierre what he was doing because he simply couldn't risk it—no one, not even his lover, must know about it. Also, if he told him and Jean-Pierre became frightened of being an accomplice to thievery, what then? All would be lost. No. He would not lose Jean-Pierre. He would rob the damn place bankrupt first.

This was the madness of passionate love, the madness he'd never believed was real. It was portrayed in novels and film, but he'd never thought it truly possible, especially for someone like him. But now he knew. It was real and it was frightening. It was an emotion so implacable that someone in its thrall would do anything necessary to possess the love object. Its demands negated personal ethics and morals.

Kipper tilted his head back, massaged his neck and closed his eyes. Images of his life at Cedar Lodge appeared unbidden to his mind's eye: the idyllic boyhood summers, his first girlfriend from a nearby camp, and then the smiling face of the woman with whom he'd once thought himself in love. Charming memories, but there was no sense of loss or regret. Now that he thought about it he realized that his one adult romance had been rather tepid. And now? This . . . this *thing* that possessed him, where had it come from? Whence this aching desire for another human, for this beautiful little Frenchman? For Kipper, stricken by pitiless Eros, Jean-Pierre LeMaire had become his sole reason for living.

An explosion of thunder like a bomb rocked the building. Kipper lurched forward in his chair and then jumped to his feet. Seconds later he heard the crack of splintering wood on the porch below.

"Oh, God," he whispered. "Now what?" He ran from the room.

* * *

Renee had just put on her Barbour foul-weather gear and Wellingtons—imagining herself part of a tweed-swathed shooting party in Scotland, just like the ones pictured in the Barbour catalogs (oh, dear God, how she lusted for that life)—when the tree crashed onto the porch, causing her to nearly jump out of her skin.

Certain that something had hit the lodge and damaged it, she listened tensely for another crash. Sudden thunder made her flinch. How bad was this storm going to get? she wondered. The thought of a tornado terrified her, and yesterday and today Brad had been maundering on about the storm front "spawning tornadoes." Her breathing became quick and shallow as she allowed her thoughts to panic her. What did a tornado sound like? She'd read newspapers quoting victims describing a noise like a freight train. Tornadoes flattened everything, killing hundreds. You couldn't get out of the way. It was useless to run because the damn things constantly changed direction. People died quickly and horribly.

She couldn't die. She could *not* die. How could there be a world without her? Possessing a narcissist's approach to humanity in general, Renee didn't give a damn who died as long as it wasn't her. She experienced a secret thrill when watching TV reports of disasters in various parts of the world, for the accounts of faceless hundreds or thousands dying violently made her feel that her own beautiful flesh increased in value. Other people died, not her.

Get a grip, you silly bitch, she admonished herself. It's thunder and lightning, nothing more. You've been in it plenty of times. You're not doing to die. She walked unsteadily over to the little drinks trolley, found some brandy and poured some into a snifter.

Her hand trembled ever so slightly as she raised the glass, but after a few bracing sips she grew calmer. She looked down at her classy, dark-green wellies and her elegant rain wear and felt the urge, which possessed her at least a couple of dozen times a day, to admire her reflection. Once in front of the cheval mirror by the bed, she turned this way and that and smiled wickedly at the mirror as she stroked herself, sighing in momentary pleasure. How could anyone so gorgeous, she reassured herself, be a pathetic statistic in some tawdry little disaster?

And how could someone so gorgeous be stuck in Maine when the world was waiting? That enraging situation was going to end tonight, she had decided. That selfish, leather-skinned old bitch had everyone trapped—Brad, Merrill, Kipper—and of all the people in the world who died in typhoons, earthquakes, fires, bombings, wars and . . . murders, none was more deserving of joining that list than the Abominable Auntie.

Why, Renee wondered, was murder considered so awful if the victim was not only unloved and unwanted but also viciously denying happiness and freedom to others? In many of the English murder mysteries she read so avidly, those murdered were often mean, tyrannical old men or women whose elimination made the world a better place. Okay, so they weren't always old, she thought, but they were usually evil. If they deserved to die, good. Renee had felt sympathy for any number of fictional killers. If they were British and upper class, they often reacted with a crooked smile and a shrug as they were led away. That was real class in Renee's book; the undaunted aristocratic sneer for the lower orders laying hands on him (or her).

But Renee had no intention of playing that particular endgame. She was not going to get caught. She believed she had devised the perfect scheme for escorting Gene quietly from the land of the living to the land of the graveyard. Unfortunately for Renee, she, like so many people of moderate intelligence who are not given to critical self-analysis, was blithely unaware that she was not nearly clever enough for this sort of business.

Nevertheless, she was about to institute a plan for grievous bodily harm to one Iphigene Seldon, "Il Duce," the object of general loathing. Unable to imagine a way to get her hands on any of those simply marvelous poisons featured in those marvelous English mystery novels, she had settled for the next best thing: Elavil. She'd first learned about Elavil from "The Ghost of Moorland Abbey," in which a villain rendered his victim unconscious by slipping the anti-depressant into the person's glass of whiskey. Internet research further informed Renee that an excessive dose of Elavil could have severe effects on an inebriated person; fatal effects, for instance.

Getting some Elavil was simple—fake a depression. Problematically, since she needed the drug right away, she'd had to fake a depression on the phone to her doctor in Bar Harbor. But that, too, had proved to be sublimely easy, for her doctor had impetuously revealed that he was mad for her and had demonstrated his feelings by becoming aroused during each of her last two physicals. Naughty, naughty doctor. *I'm really suffering, and I really need the pills, and I won't ever tell what you did in the examination room.* A prescription had been called in immediately to the Rite-Aid in nearby Oakland.

Surely, Renee reasoned, warming to her scheme, if she could somehow get an excessive dose of Elavil into Gene's whiskey, it would render the old devil permanently unconscious. The problem was opportunity. She somehow had to get next to Il Duce when Gene had booze in her hand. That would be doable tonight, Renee reasoned, because with the storm raging there was nothing else for everyone to do except go to the bar and drink. Surely Gene would be there with the old stud she had on a leash.

Thunder boomed and lightning flashed through the cracks in the shutters. Renee was afraid of running out into the storm but she had no choice. Stupidly, she had left the damn envelope containing the pill box in the glove compartment of her little BMW sports convertible, which she'd had repainted British racing green. She recalled what she'd been told about thunderstorms: Lightning, she had been assured, always hit the tallest object in any area. The back parking lot was surrounded by tall trees; she would be safe from harm.

Eight

Ripped out screens flapped wildly on the back porch, and over-turned wicker chairs and tables and shattered vases of flowers lit-tered the porch floor. Renee hurried along through the debris, crouching against the driving wind and rain. Glancing toward the windows she saw that the kitchen was dark. She was almost to the back door to the parking lot when she jumped in fright—a figure was there in the dark leaning against the back wall.

"What?" she snapped angrily, "who's—oh, it's you, Merrill. What the hell are you doing? You're practically in the middle of the storm."

"I love the raw power of nature!" Merrill shouted, sounding a big maniacal, and then she broke into loud giggles. "It's so beauti-ful! Isn't it beautiful, Renee?"

Renee rolled her eyes. "Christ, Merrill. Are you stoned?"

Merrill simply smiled; Renee moved closer toward Merrill's drenched figure and peered into her eyes. Yep, she thought—Little Orphan Annie eyes; blitzed on coke.

"You all right, Merrill?"

"Oh, I'm alll riiight. Juust fiiiine."

"You're coked up. Why don't you go back inside?" Renee said. She was not being solicitous about Merrill's well-being (worrying about others being an alien concept); she didn't care a damn if Merrill snorted a kilo of coke and danced naked in the lightning. She just didn't want Merrill watching her run out to her car and possibly start wondering what was up.

"Don't woo—worry 'bout moi."

Thunder and a flash of lightning made Renee recoil and glance around her in fright. She turned back to Merrill and said,

"Where's Bruno?"

"Bruno?"

"Jesus, Merrill. Bruno. Dark, French, shares your bed."

"Oh, wow. Bruno. I don't know. I guess he's around some-where."

Renee blew out her breath. This was exasperating. "Are you sure you're safe here?"

"Whassa matter, Renee? You the frigging angel of mercy or something? I'm staying right here. I'm having a goood time."

There was nothing for it. The bitch was so stoned she probably wouldn't remember seeing me, Renee decided. So she fastened her Barbour coat, switched on her flashlight and bolted through the screen door.

Merrill watched her go with relief. Surely, by this time, Bruno had ducked out of sight. Their prearranged signal was a shouted "I love the raw power of nature" if anyone approached while Bruno was getting things ready at the edge of the woods beyond the park-ing lot. The lightning splitting the oak tree had inspired Bruno. He told Merrill that he had figured out a way to solve the Aunt Iphi-gene problem. It had come to him in a flash, he said (they both laughed at that one). Clever Bruno. Earlier in the day he had talked to her long and hard about what they must do. Ordinarily so reti-cent, he had spoken to her at great length, gently and convincingly reasoning against her moral misgivings. It wasn't just for them-selves, he insisted; they would be freeing others, too, others trapped by Gene's heartless tyranny.

Then they had coked up and made ecstatic love, exhausting each other with their passion. Merrill knew then that she could never live without Bruno. She had wept and held him tightly, fiercely. Bruno had said:

"She is mad, Merrill. She is criminally insane, sadistic."

"Bruno?"

"Yes, my love?"

"Okay. I believe you. But I don't want to do it. Can you do it? Just you?"

"I'll find a way."

"And you'll never leave me."

"I will never leave you."

100

Two hours later the lightning struck the tree and Bruno was struck by murderous inspiration, but Merrill didn't want to know the details. "Don't tell me ahead of time. Just do it." But she had agreed to be his watcher in the dark while he—in his words—"prepared the scene." Now, she watched Renee, crouched low, running back toward the lodge. Vain, repulsive woman, Merrill thought. How, *how* had her brother ever married such a monster?

The monster was coming through the screen door. Time for Merrill to resume her stoned-senseless routine. I should've been an actress, she thought.

* * *

Bruno very slowly and cautiously crept from behind the generator shed just beyond the parking lot and stood unmoving for several minutes. Merrill's raucous "raw power of nature" shout had done the trick for a danger signal. Now he must wait. Steady, he told himself, don't be impatient. He was regretting not having devised an "all clear" signal with Merrill. Too late to worry about that. Just wait awhile.

Bruno checked his luminous watch. Five minutes had passed. Crouching, he moved back out to the fallen tree next to the parking lot, where he'd been when Merrill raised the alarm, and began dragging the tree toward the shed. Thunder boomed nearby and light flashed in his face, but not from lightning. Goddamn! It was a flashlight! Someone was coming from the generator shed and shining a light all around. He dropped the tree, leaped behind it and hit the ground, hoping he'd not been seen. Christ, he thought, what the hell? Suddenly it's like a shopping mall out here.

Peeping over the tree, Bruno could just make out a dark figure in the shed's doorway. He flattened himself as the figure moved toward the cars and passed by the tree; he—or she, never underestimate women, Bruno reminded himself—was covered in foul-weather gear with the hood over the head. The person looked neither to the left nor right as he walked into the midst of the cars. Bruno watched him until . . . suddenly, no one was there. Must be behind a car, Bruno decided. Damn. What now? Nothing to do but lie here in the damn rain and wait.

The person in the dark hooded rain gear was also thinking, *What now? What is that f'ing jerk doing out here? Damn it. What's the next move? Nothing for now. Can't do anything about him tonight.*

* * *

Gene had an audience and she was playing to it, regaling the men and women in the clubroom with outlandish though true adventures of her father, founder of Cedar Lodge, and of herself, of course. She had just finished telling them how she'd single-handedly rescued two fishermen whose canoe had overturned on the swift-running Kennebec River. In response to the call for drinks on the house, most of the forty-two registered guests—eighteen couples, six singles—seemed to be gathered within the clubroom's knotty-pine walls, which were decorated a la Maine backwoods with trophy-sized mounted fish, five deer heads with impressive racks and one extravagantly antlered bull moose head gazing down glassy-eyed from behind and high above the bar, which was a long, three-foot wide slab of darkly gleaming oak, its sheen resulting from more than seventy-five years of linseed oil rubbed into its grains. Glittering bottles of more than two hundred types of alcohol were arranged on four shelves in front of a big mirror that ran the length of the bar.

Among the animal heads and fish were scores of framed black-and-white photographs. A number of them, starting just before World War II, were of lodge guests holding up the big bass or brown trout they'd landed, while many others were of sportsmen going back through the decades to the 1880s, pictures that Gene's father had acquired along with the building when he'd purchased the Abenaki Sporting Club in 1926. The old photos were of men posing with fly rods and dressed in the style of the day—tweed jackets, vests and ties, wide-brimmed hats and knee-length, lace-up boots. Across New England after the Civil War, wealthy outdoorsmen—fishing in the good old days was something of an elite pastime for gentlemen—had established sporting fraternities and then erected impressive buildings in wilderness areas for the benefit of their members. As wealth and membership faded away following institution of the income tax in 1913, the lodges began closing down; most became hotels or, like Abenaki, commercial hunting and fishing camps, while others were simply abandoned.

The barroom's *pièce de résistance* was a magnificent example of the taxidermist's art, an entire nine-foot grizzly bear—arms and claws extended in attack mode, fangs exposed in wide-open jaws— standing in the southeast corner near the windows that opened to a view of the large boathouse and the woods beyond, that is, when they *were* open; they were shuttered now against the storm.

"My father shot that big sonofabitch in 1933, when I was just a pink, cherubic one-year-old . . . if you can imagine such a thing looking at me now."

Appreciative chortles sounded up and down the bar.

"He was one hell of a sportsman, I can tell you," Gene continued, employing her Captain Ahab voice to fill the room. "This area was a lot more primitive and remote in those days, and bears were something of a regular nuisance. Worse than jet-skiers today, but not by much."

Loud guffaws erupted on that one; lake cowboys roaring about on jet skis were the bane of fishermen everywhere.

"And in my immodest way, ladies and gentleman," Gene bellowed, laughing at her own immodesty, "I'll tell you that I'm just like Big Jim Seldon, a rough and ready outdoorswoman from sunup to sundown. So is every member of my family, all of whom live here at Cedar Lodge. And that's what makes Cedar Lodge special—I don't think you'll find its equal in Maine."

Applause and a few whistles and delighted hoots answered Gene's last words, though they were suddenly overwhelmed by powerful blasts of thunder, over and over, that shook the walls. Lightning flickered around the edges of the shuttered windows.

When the booming finally subsided, Gene shouted, "Do you reckon that was a positive or a negative comment?"

That brought the house down.

"All right, everyone!" Gene shouted again. "Drink up! Don't know how long this storm's gonna last. Just tell Armand what you want."

Armand, a local fisherman, was one of the two men Gene employed to bartend. He was large and hearty, outfitted in plaid shirt, cord trousers and a hunting knife strapped to his big belt. A wide grin flashed perpetually beneath his walrus mustache. Having remembered what most of the guests were drinking, he already had glasses lined up and was pouring out refills before the first requests were called out.

Six and Alicia were next to Gene and Bob at the western end of the bar sipping glasses of bourbon and water. Tomorrow, Sunday, was the day of the gunfight at the Seldon family O.K. Corral. And as soon as *that* contretemps had passed they wanted to rush back to Winsokkett Pond to see if their beloved camp had been damaged by the storm.

Six said, "I don't see any of the family around tonight, Gene."

"I wouldn't expect them to be here. Brad must be drunk and wetting himself every time there's thunder, Merrill's probably making the two-backed beast with Bruno and I'm sure Kipper's in the kitchen with his hand up Jean-Pierre's ass."

Six glanced over at Bob, who had been quiet since they'd run in from the storm, and saw him lean on the bar and put his hand over his eyes in reaction to this latest charming articulation from his betrothed. Smiling to himself, Six recalled some lyrics from his favorite musical comedy, "Little Mary Sunshine—"Young ladies from Eastchester Finishing School are ever so properly bred . . ." Robertson Weller, Six thought, gave every appearance of having been "ever so properly bred." He was going to have to hang on tight if he intended to bed down permanently with an outback princess like Gene.

On the other side of Six a lethally anxious Renee Ranger (her maiden name) Seldon gulped scotch while working up nerve for her criminal debut. She felt as though she had a small animal in her stomach. I may barf, she thought; I may projectile vomit straight across the bar onto Armand's plaid shirt. The loud, bragging fishermen crowded around her added to the ordeal. Her usual venue over in Bar Harbor was a nightclub with glassy-eyed stoners draped around a grand piano and digging a cabaret warbler. For the past half-hour she'd been gradually working her way up the bar toward Gene and now only Six and Alicia Godwin were in the way. Renee ground her teeth as she listened to them sucking up to Gene—Christ, they were irritating; seedy old bastards, she thought. She reached into her purse and fingered her silver lip-blush case containing the Elavil; she'd ground the pills into a fine powder, ready for sprinkling into Gene's glass. And then . . . bingo. Knockout. A sudden worry entered Renee's mind: She didn't know if the drug acted immediately or had a delayed effect. She hoped it was the latter; Gene keeling over at the bar would look suspicious, no doubt about that. She would have to sprinkle and make a speedy exit.

She flinched in fright and turned around quickly as someone touched her elbow. Nelson was standing there smiling at her with carnality in his eyes. *Oh, damn. Not now.*

"Nice weather," Nelson said. "Perfect weather for . . ."

"Why, Nelson," Renee interrupted, arranging her features into a delirious happy face. "Where *have* you been all day?"

"I drove up to Bangor. Wasn't sure I'd make it back."

"Uh, Bangor. Oh, ah, how interesting." Gene was ordering another drink and Renee eyed her nervously. "Why did you, uh, you, uh . . . go up there?"

"Business. Tory and I have a business deal going."

At that moment, following more thunder, the lights flickered, went out for a few seconds, blinked on and off a few times, then stayed off, damping the voices in the room. Armand switched on a couple of flashlights. Other flashlights came on, filling the room with dancing beams. Then minutes later, the power came back up.

Gene turned to Six and Alicia and said, "You got your flashlight?"

"Right down there," Alicia said, swiveling on her barstool and pointing down at the floor below her feet. "We're ready for action."

"There may be some, and soon," Gene told her. "If we have a power outage then I'll be going out back to the generator. I'm the only one I trust to get the thing going. Last summer some jughead nephew damn near ruined the thing by throwing the wrong switch." She saw Nelson looking at her with a big smile. "Why, hello, Mr. Bolston. Enjoying the weather?"

"Charming," Nelson said. "But I think I'd best get used to Maine weather."

"Oh? Planning to stay awhile?"

"Actually, Tory and I are thinking of buying a big commercial fishing camp up near Bangor. That's where I was today."

Gene's smile faded. She had regarded the Bolstons as potential investors in a Cedar Lodge fishing gear line she'd been planning with Kipper. The news that they would be competitors instead was an exasperating surprise. "I hope you know what you're doing," she said and looked away.

At that moment Tory came up to the group, flashed a smile all around, and said, "I enjoyed your stories, Gene. I'd like to hear more."

"Stick around. I've got about a hundred."

Oh, please, Six moaned inwardly. Don't get her started.

Now I *know* I'm going to barf, Renee thought. She hated little bubbly cutesy-pies like Tory.

"That would be swell," Tory chirped, "but right now I have to drag my brother off for a little business conference. She grabbed Nelson by the arm, laughed musically and twiddled her fingers bye-bye.

Renee wanted to slug her, but at least she was getting Nelson out of the way. The last thing Renee needed was a large male next to her getting tumescent when she was attempting murder. And then she got her second break.

"Bob," Gene barked, "watch my drink. I'm going to the head. Be right back."

Amos dutifully sashayed out of the clubroom behind her.

Nine

Renee's rattled brain started screaming at her. *Now, now! Think of something, think of.* . . . Ahh—Bob Weller suddenly looked her way and smiled. He seemed drunk, and no wonder, Renee thought, facing marriage to the dragon. Poor old bastard must be desperate for money. With her right hand she took the silver case from her purse and closed her fingers around it. Scooting into the space by Bob and turning her back on Six and Alicia, who had their heads together chuckling about something, she leaned on the bar with her left arm and draped the flowing sleeve of her silk blouse over Gene's glass.

"Mr. Weller . . ."

"Pleezsh, call me Bob."

Renee's hand moved stealthily across the bar's surface and under her sleeve.

"Well, Bob," she said, smiling sweetly and pitching her voice low, "I couldn't help wondering, looking at you just now . . . Did you ever do any modeling?"

"Ohh, years 'go, years 'go. Brugz Buggers catarog."

"I beg your pardon?" She got her thumbnail under the snap and opened the case.

"Bru—brook . . ."

"Oh, Brooks Brothers!" Laughing generously, Renee threw her head back and tossed her dark, flowing tresses in a manner that never failed to engage male eyeballs. Into the glass went the powder. "I just knew it! You have that classic look."

Bob grinned stupidly and attempted to reply, but the only utterance to get past his lips sounded like "scrimjus."

When Renee saw Gene barreling through the door she said, "Here comes your . . . *intended* . . . so I better scram. So nice talking to you."

"Brizziljim."

Renee didn't dare even glance at Gene as she passed by her. However, as she stood just outside the barroom door, she looked back to watch Gene and was rewarded by the sight of "Il Duce" knocking back the entire glass of scotch.

Just as Renee turned to hurry from the scene and just as Gene frowned down at her empty glass wondering what the hell she'd just swallowed (it certainly wasn't her favored brand), a sudden, horrendous pounding against the walls of the lodge, like rapid cannon fire, shocked the barroom revelers into silence. Renee backed against a wall and whimpered, "Oh, no, a tornado. Oh, please, God, no." (Renee became a believer during moments of fear.)

At the bar, Six spilled his drink and Alicia said, "Dear God, what now?"

"Hailstones," Six told her. "Must be damn big ones."

Once more Gene emphasized her displeasure toward nature: "Goddamn it!" Everyone at the bar turned to look at her. "Hail!" she bellowed. "We're getting hit by hail, folks."

"Must be the size of tennis balls," Six interjected.

Gene continued her shout-out: "It could bring down the power lines! Keep your flashlights nearby." She paused, her mouth widening in a lascivious grin. "And no cheap feels in the dark."

Listening to the resulting laughter from inside the clubroom, Renee put her head back against the wall and sighed in relief. *Got to get out of here before Gene drops dead.* She hurried up the stairs.

Voices were raised against the din of the hailstorm but Gene's voice easily carried above all of them as she called out to Armand. He came hulking down to her and said, "Yes,m?"

"Armand, that last drink tasted like fish crap. You sure you put the right stuff in my glass?"

"Ayuh, damn sure," he said, smiling and brushing the ends of his mustache. "I wouldn't do that to you, would I? Glenmorangie. You might've grabbed someone else's glass."

"Yep. Maybe. Don't think I'll have any more. Thanks, Armand." Gene, who never let age slow her down, was feeling tired. Well, she thought, stands to reason—it's been one helluva day. She looked over at Bob and said, "Christ, Bobby. You okay?"

"Scamraddin," Bob said, his glassy eyeballs rolling as he attempted to focus on his immediate environment.

"Oh, Jesus." Gene turned to Six and Alicia. "I've got to get the stud up to his bed. If the power goes while I'm upstairs could you guys keep everybody laughing until I go out back and get the generator going?"

Six said, "I don't know if I want to be here in the dark with all these drunk, horny women."

Alicia glared at him. "Six, will you please behave yourself? Are you sneaking extra drinks?"

"Civilization breaks down in the dark. The primal beast becomes aroused. So to speak."

"You're not a primal beast."

Six turned and looked into Alicia's gray-green eyes. "I could be. If asked."

"Is that so? Well, now that you mention it I was just thinking that perhaps . . ."

The lights went out, interrupting the Godwins' vocal foreplay.

Six emitted a low snarl and said, "The beast arises from the murky depths." He edged closer to Alicia and kissed her on her neck.

"Hmm. Not bad. But the beast better watch it. The lights will probably switch back on at any moment."

But this time darkness persisted, making the clamor of the hailstones seem louder and more threatening. Flashlight beams again danced about the room. A man with a good baritone voice began singing "Dancing in the Dark," provoking laughter and applause.

Gene said: "I'll have to wait until this hail stops before I can go out to the generator. Also, I can't take Bob upstairs now. How ya' doing, handsome?" She reached over to him and found that he was head-down on the bar. "He's passed out. Probably a good thing. Don't want him stumbling around in the dark."

"Want me to take him up?" Six asked.

"If he's unconscious it'll take two of us," Gene answered. "He's a *big* boy. Wait till I get back. The hail's easing up now, so I'm gonna start getting my gear on. See ya." She switched on her flashlight and picked her way through the tables toward the door, swinging the beam back and forth. By the time she made it to her office and began pulling on her Wellingtons she realized that she was definitely feeling fatigued. Her movements were getting slower. Goddamn it, she thought, I will *not* give in to old age. I'm as strong as I ever was. The tiredness, she decided, was simply the result of constant tension throughout a hellacious day.

Out in the hallway she heard Amos raising a fuss about something, whining and growling. Storm's getting on his nerves, she thought. She put on her yellow hooded foul-weather coat and walked in the hall, but now Amos wasn't there. "Amos?" she yelled. No Amos. Must really be spooked, she thought, as she followed her flashlight beam down the hallway and then to the left toward the kitchen and through the double swinging doors. She played the flashlight around the kitchen, illuminating the gleaming steel surfaces of the ovens and stoves and the rows of knives, and of the long counters with cooking instruments hanging above them.

"Anybody in here?" she called. No answer. The deserted kitchen seemed creepy and menacing. She walked slowly to the door opening onto the back porch. As she opened it she detected a small noise behind her. A sort of swish. She swung around and pointed the flashlight at the swinging doors and then all around the kitchen. Nothing. Nerves, you old bat, she scolded herself. Since when have you been afraid of the dark?

"Amos?" she said. "That you, boy?" Nothing. Where had he got himself off to? Odd. He never wanted to miss anything and was always trailing in her wake. She shone the flashlight all around the floor and called out again, "Amos? Where are you, boy?" Ah, well, get on with business, she told herself.

Out on the porch she saw the ripped-out screens and realized the wind must have been gale force, though now it had suddenly died down to a breeze; the rain and hail had also ceased, though lightning persisted. She pushed open the screen door and walked out between the cars. Lightning flashed and boomed nearby but Gene kept moving, though her legs felt strangely heavy and her breathing was labored as she plodded toward the generator shed. Oh damn it damn it, she thought—what the hell is happening to me? The ground seemed to tilt and she fell sideways, landing painfully on her left arm. The joint in her shoulder throbbed as she struggled up onto all fours; her muscles seemed drained of strength. "Goddamn it!" she choked out. Rising unsteadily to an erect position she stumbled forward, fighting to keep her balance. The shed was only yards away when a blaze of pain tore through her head and down her body. She shrieked and crumpled to the ground, losing consciousness as she swirled into absolute darkness.

Ten

Alicia slapped Six's hand and hissed at him: "Six, will you stop that!"

"I thought you liked that sort of thing."

"I do, but the lights could come back on any second. I do *not* intend to be caught in public in a posture of indecency."

"Oooo. 'Posture of indecency.' Sounds a bit Cotton Mather-ish."

"I just don't want your hand where it is now when the lights come on."

Six withdrew his wandering hand and said, "Who's gonna notice in here? Everyone's concentrating on the concert." Six and Alicia had relented on their intention to have only one drink each and Six, at least, was feeling frisky. Alicia actually felt frisky, too, but much preferred to frisk in the privacy of their room. To her mind, she and Six were much too old for displays of intimacy in front of others. Now she was certain that Six had gotten excited and had knocked back a drink or two when she wasn't looking.

In the darkness, the clubroom had evolved into a sort of *son et lumière* show of laughter and excited conversation amid dancing, flickering flashlight beams. Fishermen in general being a jolly sort, they naturally tended to get jollier when lubricated; now they began a sing-along, with various men and women taking turns belting out old standards and those who remembered the words joining in. At the moment, a tenor who really knew the old, *old* standards was offering a sweet rendition of the 1930s Tommy and Jimmy Dorsey hit "Night Wind."

*"Love was blown away by the night wind
And the dreams we shared fell apart . . ."*

"That song is certainly appropriate for the current circumstances," Six said. "Do you remember it? Can't recall it myself."

"Well, yes, I do . . . vaguely. You know, my mother and father were big on romantic tunes of the twenties and thirties, so I heard a lot of the old ones."

"By the way, how's old Bob doing?"

Alicia turned on her flashlight and illuminated the slumbering figure of Robertson Weller. He twitched and said "Mmpf" when she shined the light on his face.

"How anybody can sleep sitting in a chair and slumped across the bar is remarkable."

"I reckon if you get drunk enough it's better than the floor."

As the roar and rumble of the storm persisted beyond the walls, a chorus of three or four men began singing "Thunder Road."

"And there was thunder, thunder
Over Thunder Road
Thunder was his engine
And white lightning was his load . . ."

More people joined in the song until it sounded as though everyone in the clubroom was singing.

Alicia leaned over and spoke into Six's right ear: "Six, I think something's wrong."

"Whad'ja say?"

"Something's wrong! The lights are still out!"

"No need to shout."

"Six, pay attention. Gene's been gone a long time."

Six switched on their flashlight and looked at his watch. "By God, you're right. Almost forty-five minutes. I better go check on her." He swung around and hopped off the bar chair and directed the flashlight toward the door.

"I'll go with you," Alicia said, falling in behind him.

"Wait. What about Bob? He might fall off the chair. You better stay with him."

Alicia weighed her concern about Six going out in the storm by himself against the possibility of Bob Weller seriously injuring himself. She and Six would look like fools and Gene would be furious.

"Oh damn. You're right. I'll stay with old Bobby."

"See ya," Six told her, and started moving away.

"Six! Get some rain gear. I saw some in that room behind the front desk."

Six found an old, heavy Gore-Tex jacket with a hood hanging behind the front desk; it was a couple of sizes too big for him but he put it on anyway and headed down the hallway on the west side of the big fireplace; if he was remembering correctly, you took a left at the end into a hall that led to the kitchen. Ah, yes, there they were, the swinging double doors to the kitchen. Directly opposite them was another set of swinging doors that led into the clubroom. Six went through the double doors and shone his light around over the white tile walls and the steel cabinets, counters and ovens. He reckoned a great deal of money had gone into modernizing the kitchen; everything in it looked new and expensive. It had certainly paid off, he knew that. Cedar Lodge had been four-star in hunting and fishing for decades; now its dining room had acquired a fourth star.

"Gene?" Six called out. He didn't really expect her to be in the kitchen but then you never knew; too, she could be out on the porch or somewhere nearby. "Gene?" he shouted. He walked through the kitchen and through the back door. Passing out into the parking lot, he trudged toward the woods between two of the three rows of the kind of SUVs favored by outdoors enthusiasts— Rovers, Jeep Wranglers, Suburbans, etc., and big four-door pickups—playing his light all around and bellowing "Gene! Gene!" He caught the generator shed in his beam and headed toward it, and as he got closer he saw a flash of yellow—someone was lying beside a fallen tree just yards short of the shed.

"Oh no," he cried, certain that it must be Gene. "Gene!" he shouted again. "Gene, Gene!" Something was terribly wrong: At least half the yellow coat was blackened, and smoke—quickly dispersed by the breeze—was rising from it. *Oh no, dear God, lightning.* He rushed up to the face-down figure, grabbed the left arm and rolled it over.

And jumped back screaming.

Eleven

It was Gene, or what was left of her. The spikes of short gray hair and the prominence of what had been the nose made it obvious. Her face had been scorched to the bone and her hands were shriveled, blackened claws. The smell of burning flesh overwhelmed Six and he fell backward to the ground; he staggered to his feet and turned to run from the horrifying sight, but then vomited down the front of his coat and trousers and fell on all fours, dropping his flashlight.

He shuddered violently and gasped for air as his stomach kept heaving. Finally, the retching eased and he rolled over to a sitting position and held his head in his hands. Dizziness overtook him and he felt that he couldn't get up.

"Help!" he shouted, picking up the flashlight and waving its beam back and forth. "Help! Out here!"

But who the hell was going to hear him?

Amazingly, a voice called out, "Who's there? Who's there?"

"Here, here! By the shed!"

A crouched figure came around from behind the cars on the eastern end of the parking lot and battled through the lashing rain shouting, "What's happened?"

As the figure drew closer Six recognized Brad. Gene's hound dog, Amos, was with him. Six tried to rise but his trembling body couldn't make it, so he raised his right hand and shouted, his voice hoarse and broken, "Brad! No!"

"Six! What's the matter, man?"

"Don't come any closer, Brad, don't . . ."

"I'm coming to help you."

"Aww, Jesus." Six started dry-heaving. He thought he was going to faint.

Brad lurched up to Six and reached down to grab him but Six hollered, "No! Christ. Don't lift me. I'm sick as hell."

Brad stopped but leaned over to look closely at Six. "God, Six, what's happened?"

Six put his head down to the ground and moaned. Brad stood up straight and said, "Look, Six, I can't leave . . . Jesus! Who's that?" Brad spotted the body and started moving toward it.

"No, don't go there, don't . . ." Six collapsed and rolled over onto his back. Seconds later Brad passed by quickly and shouted, "I'll get help!"

Six lay still and gulped air. The wind had ceased abruptly and only a light drizzle was coming down. The rain felt good. God just let me lie here, he thought. Just let me lie here.

A frightened Amos approached within six feet of Gene's body, then jumped back at the powerful smell and began whining and then running in frantic circles around her, barking and yelping. Finally he came to a halt and stood, his pitiful, anguished howling resonating in the rain-sodden forest.

He heard voices. How much time had gone by? Only minutes, surely, but it seemed much longer. Lifting his head he saw two figures coming toward him wearing rain gear with the hoods up. When they got up to him he saw that it was Kipper and Armand, the bartender. Kipper stared down at him, obviously terrified, then glanced at Gene's body and turned away. Armand crouched beside Six and said, "You all right, Prof. Godwin?"

"I'm okay," Six gasped. "I'm just sick."

"Six, oh, Six!" Alicia ran toward him as Armand walked toward Gene's burned corpse. She hadn't bothered with a raincoat and her clothes and hair were drenched. "Oh, my sweet boy," she cried, flopping down beside him and lifting his head to cradle in her lap. "Brad came in the bar looking frightened and said Gene had been killed. I was terrified that it was you, too, that you'd been hurt or killed."

"I'm not injured, Alicia. Just sick—been throwing up. Gene's up there burned beyond recognition. Must've been lightning, direct hit."

"Oh, dear God," Alicia said. "That's horrifying."

"Don't go near her, Alicia. Please don't go. You don't need to see anything like that." He looked up at Kipper, who was trembling and staring ahead at nothing, seemingly. "Don't look at her, Kipper."

Kipper shook himself, as if emerging from a petit mal. "What?" he asked.

"Don't go look at Gene's body."

He shook his head slowly but said nothing.

"I can't believe it," Alicia said, starting to cry. "We were just talking to her."

"It's awful, Alicia. Ungodly. I didn't know lightning could do so much damage."

There was a commotion near the lodge. "I hear voices," Six said, sitting up straight.

"Brad was frantic when he came in to get Armand," Alicia told him. "People at the bar heard what he said. He just blurted it out. I bet they're coming this way."

Kipper said, "People coming from the back porch."

"Oh, Christ, Kipper. Don't let them come out here! Get Armand. You've got to stop them." Six braced his hands on Alicia's shoulders and got himself standing but nearly fell over again. Alicia stood quickly and supported him. "Armand!" Six yelled. "Come here, quickly!"

Armand ran up to the three of them and said, his voice choked, "God, that's the whuss thing I've evah seen."

"Armand," Six told him. "Please don't let those people come out here. Kipper, help him. Keep them back. Alicia, can you go find Sam, the dock boy, and Brad? We need them out here. Bruno even. We've got to get some kind of control."

"Will you be all right, my darling?"

"Please don't worry about me. Just go . . . please, kiddo."

As Alicia hurried off, Armand and Kipper walked back through the parked cars holding up their arms and shouting for everyone to keep back. "There's been a terrible accident, folks!" Armand bellowed. "The police will be here soon."

Though he was still nauseated and his knees felt like jelly, Six flipped open his cellphone, called up his contacts list and scrolled to "Sheriff." He'd never had occasion to call the sheriff, but it had seemed sensible to have the number close by because the sheriff's department responded to emergencies on the lakes.

"Somerbec County Sheriff's Department," a no-nonsense woman's voice announced.

Six kept it as brief as possible. "My name is Six Godwin. I'm at Cedar Lodge, near Rome, on Willow Pond. The owner of the lodge, Iphigene Seldon, has been killed—by lightning, we believe. We need help."

"Please spell your name and tell me your phone number."

Six complied and the woman said, "Help will be there shortly. I'll dispatch a car right away."

After snapping his phone shut, Six headed for the generator shed to try to get the lights back on. Fighting waves of nausea, he picked up the flashlight and walked unsteadily toward the shed, making a big circle around the gruesome remains of what had been his cousin Iphigene. She had seemed to him like an immutable life force, but she'd been destroyed, hideously, in a moment by one of nature's most unpredictable killers.

Six entered the shed. The generator itself was a huge box-like thing with louvered vents; on top of it was a big cylinder lying on its side. He played the flashlight around the shed until he located a wall-mounted wood box with three metal switches. Three pipes that he assumed must contain electrical cables descended from the box straight down into the concrete floor. There was no way to tell which one ran to the generator. What was it Gene said? Something about . . . oh, yes, he remembered now. She'd said that the previous summer a nephew had nearly ruined the generator by throwing the wrong switch. There were three switches—surely more than one of them was connected to the generator; perhaps all three were. That must mean, he decided, that the switches had to be turned on in proper sequence. He sighed and leaned against the wall. What to do? Nothing. He couldn't risk blowing the generator.

He trudged back to the door and walked outside. All around was silence. No thunder, no wind, not even a breeze. The misty rain had stopped. Six looked up to see a clear, star-dazzled sky. It was an eerie contrast to the recent violence of the storm and the pathetic, blackened corpse left in its wake.

A far distant wail penetrated the stillness. Sirens. The sheriff, Six thought. The sheriff is on the way.

Twelve

Sheriff Benson Doucette sped through the inky night across state road 225, just north of Great Pond, as fast as he dared with siren wailing and dome lights flashing red, blue and white against the thick woods that encroached only a few yards from the macadam. Narrow, two-lane route 225 was hazardous enough at noon in bright sunlight; at 10 p.m. it was potentially lethal at any point along its eight-mile stretch as it wound through a series of hills and valleys. Houses were few, except in the hamlet of Rome, and traffic sparse, and so those familiar with the road tended to tear along at 60 to 65 instead of the posted 40 mph. Plus there was always, *always*, the added Maine hazard of night-roaming creatures suddenly dashing onto the road from the trees—deer, foxes, wild turkeys or, especially and terrifyingly . . .

A moose, Benson thought, as he bumped across a small concrete bridge and whipped around a steep curve. That's all I need right now is a damn moose galloping onto the road. People get killed every year hitting moose on highways, even on wide I-95. At the KMD Driving School over in Waterville the first lecture class for beginning students always included instructions on what to do if a moose appears in front of you. The instructions were not reassuring: Slam as hard as possible on the brakes then release them just as the car hits the moose so that the front of the car lifts and throws the moose over the car, thus preventing him from smashing through the windshield—which, of course, can render the driver quickly dead.

"Jesus CHRIST!" Benson screamed, slamming on the brakes. The squad car fishtailed and then turned sideways, tires screeching and laying burnt rubber streaks on the pavement. A small tree, now only several yards beyond the car, had fallen across the road. Benson put his forehead on the steering wheel and said,

"Hoo damn. That was close."

Beside him, Deputy Sgt. Caleb Cobb, a very large man who never seemed to let anything rattle him, said,

"Ayuh. Bit of a surprise."

Benson cut the siren but left the flashers on as he and Caleb got out of the car and walked to the tree.

"What the hell is going on around here?" Benson growled.

And Caleb said, "Look around, sheriff." He unclipped a flashlight from his belt and played the beam around on both sides of the road. "Trees broken all over the place. Musta been that hail."

"Damn. You're right. Reckon we better go a little slower."

Though small, the tree, a maple sapling, was still heavy enough, but Caleb's immense strength made the lifting much easier for both men. The previous year Caleb had saved the lives of a couple and their two children by wrenching a door from their overturned and burning SUV and pulling them up to safety. Five minutes later the car had exploded. And Caleb's name was legend in the town of Skerridgewock for two raids he'd made on the notorious Bob's Good Time Tavern to break up armed brawls. During one of the raids, witnesses swore they had seen drunks airborne as Caleb decanted them through the front door to a backup team of Skerridgewock patrolmen. Benson Doucette thought the world of the huge man and tried always to have him alongside when serious trouble arose.

Benson and Caleb heaved the tree onto the narrow dirt shoulder of the road. Once they were again strapped into their seats Benson decided not to reactivate the siren but left the flashers on as they continued west at a more circumspect speed.

And what was the hurry anyway? Benson figured. This was an accidental death. Lightning strike, the dispatcher had told him. Iphigene Seldon struck down by lightning, just like her brother and his wife so many years ago. He marveled at the incredible odds on such a coincidence; lightning deaths were much fewer in Maine than in the South and Midwest, with only two recorded in the state in 2008. The ultimate, savvy woman of the outdoors—caught in the open in the middle of dangerous storm. Well, it must've been out in the open, he figured. How else?

Gene Seldon suddenly dead. Benson could hardly believe it. A complete force of nature in one old woman's body. She was famous in this part of the state and Cedar Lodge, he knew, had an international reputation. Brad and Merrill, whom he'd known since they were teenagers, had also garnered fame of their own among serious sportsmen—when it came to fresh-water fishing, no one in Maine could top them.

As the squad car headed down a hill, Benson saw the headlights of another car appear at the top of the hill and was not surprised to see the car pull to the shoulder and stop. Out here in the far reaches of lake country, sirens or emergency flashers were uncommon, and people tended to react quickly to them. Benson knew that a siren in the night would be remarked upon by anyone in the region who heard it, either to themselves or to someone nearby. A siren piercing the profound quiet of rural Maine could be frightening.

They passed the stopped car and continued west toward route 27, driving over scattered branches and leaves but, fortunately, encountered no more felled trees.

Caleb said: "Who called us from the lodge?"

Benson pulled a small notebook from his shirt pocket and switched on the overhead light. "A fellow named Six Godwin. Unusual sort of name."

Caleb's face brightened. "Unusual sort of guy."

"Oh? You know this character?"

"Ayuh. Character is right. He's a professor."

Benson looked at Caleb with an amused expression. "He's a professor therefore he's a character?"

"Unh uh. Didn't say that. Prob'ly plenty of professors that are dull as a wet Sunday. This one's a character. So's his wife. She's a professor, too."

"I should've guessed."

"Damn nice people. Smart as hell, too."

"You sure do get around, Sgt. Cobb. How did you meet them?"

"They solved a burglary case for me last year."

"I beg your pardon?"

"Ayuh. Don't you remember we had all those calls last fall about camp break-ins around Winsokkett Pond?"

"Well, yeah, I recall something about that."

"By the time I got out there to McCorkle Camps, Six and Alicia—that's his wife's name—had interviewed all their neighbors who'd had break-ins and then called over to the other side of the lake to friends who'd reported the same thing. Then they sat down at the end of their dock and solved the whole thing."

"Now wait a minute."

"It's a damn fact, sheriff. I pulled up, went out to their dock and there was Six sitting smoking a pipe and casting surface lures into the weed beds. Had the whole thing wrapped up."

"Oh, Jesus. Sherlock Holmes."

Caleb chuckled. "Not much similarity other than the pipe. Seems that he and his wife had found out that nothing had been stolen from a single camp. The refrigerators had been raided, cans of salmon and tuna opened and eaten, and then dishes carefully washed and left in the sinks. The professors deduced—I just love that word, don't you?—that it had to be that old hermit who camps out in the swamp by the serpentine creek between Winsokkett and Great Pond. He didn't steal anything—just wanted to eat."

"And it was him?"

"Yep. I got one of our boats out and went in there with Billy and we found where he'd built this lean-to kind of camp. He was scared when we showed up and confessed to the break-ins without much urging. Crazy old guy, all hairy and dirty. Has a canoe he drags back in there. Slips around the shoreline in the canoe at night, looks for an empty camp and goes in for a snack."

"Hah! So what'd you guys do?"

"Told him to stop doing it cause it scared people and that jail would be horrible for a guy like him. Thought he was gonna faint. So we worked out a deal. Once a week the campers will leave a few cans of food out on the ends of their docks and old Fred—the hermit said his name was Fred—can slip by in the moonlight and collect them."

Benson looked over at his sergeant in absolute amazement. This large human, constructed like one of those frightening TV wrestling hulks, had a consistent tender heart for the world in general. Benson knew that Caleb, a college graduate, had wanted to be a biologist or something along those lines. Why he'd ever gotten into police work, Benson didn't know, but he had to admit that, tender heart and all, the man was very good at it.

"Caleb, you are a good man. I don't want to embarrass you"— Benson had seen Caleb flush scarlet when given any sort of compliment—"but you damn well are."

Caleb could feel the heat rising up his neck and over his face, but he figured that at least Benson wouldn't see it in the semi-darkness of the car. "Well, I don't know," he muttered. "It just seemed logical, that's all. Save everybody a lot of trouble, including us."

Benson smiled and decided not to say anything more.

For his part, Caleb thought back to his first meeting with Six and Alicia Godwin. Having been told that they were retired university professors who ran a book business, he had expected a couple of geezers in summer tweeds and sun hats pottering about in the garden. What confronted him were two surprisingly tall middle-aged fishermen in top physical form and tanned like leather. They also looked like fishermen living on welfare checks. Their incredibly shabby outfits and their warm smiles had quickly put Caleb at ease, for he had been concerned, before meeting them, that former professors summering at a lakeside camp would be intellectual snobs from away who treated Mainers in general with benign condescension. Caleb still chafed at the memory of humiliation at the hands of one pompous English Lit. professor at the University of Maine who had snickered at the young Caleb's Down East accent when he had attempted to read aloud several verses of Keats and then suggested that he invest in accent-reduction therapy.

But the Godwins, Caleb soon learned, were Mainers from generations back who, despite the Ph.D.'s they held in their respective disciplines, had never smoothed the edges of their native accents.

Plus, they were two of the most comfortably open people he'd ever met.

Since the time they had all collaborated on the Winsokkett Hermit Mystery, as Caleb privately thought of it, he had remained fond of the Godwins, though his demanding schedule left him few opportunities to visit them. Now here they'd popped up in the middle of the action again.

Benson stopped the car at the juncture of 225 and 27 and turned north; five miles later he turned onto Red Fox Lane, a dirt road that ran south of Willow Pond. About a mile and a half in their headlights illuminated a large sign to the left, painted forest green with gold lettering announcing "Cedar Lodge, Willow Pond." The camp road, cut through a forest of steep pines and oaks, had been graded and resurfaced, so the bouncing was minimal as they headed slowly down to the lake, although they noticed that the storm had carved out a few big rivulets.

"Lights on top of the poles are out," Caleb said.

"Maybe the lightning or the wind took down their lines."

"Figured they'd have a generator."

"For sure—lightning musta hit that too."

The road curved twice then widened gradually into the clearing around Cedar Lodge. All was in darkness except the yellow flashing of the EMS truck Caleb had called for.

"Whoa," Benson said. "Everything's out."

He again cut the siren and left the flashers going as he stepped out of the car, switched on the big door-mounted spotlight and played it around the parking lot. He saw a large number of people standing by the lodge's back porch; a smaller clutch of people, including the two EMS medics, were across the parking lot near what Benson guessed was the shed housing the generator.

In the spotlight's beam two tall figures, like gunfighters on the old "Gunsmoke" series, Benson thought, strode toward them. Benson and Caleb moved out to meet them, and as they got closer the man cried out, "Caleb! This is just horrible."

"I'm awful sorry," Caleb said, taking Six's outstretched hand. "This is Sheriff Doucette. Sheriff . . . Six and Alicia Godwin."

Benson, at 5-feet-11 and wide-shouldered, was a physically substantial man, but he felt like Tiny Tim as he looked up at these people looming over him. Six's white duck trousers and blue blazer were wet and muddied; Alicia's striped seersucker dress was also mud-splattered. Her long, brown arms and legs jutting from the dress reminded Benson of a spouting teenager wearing last year's clothes. They shook hands with him silently and Benson saw they'd both been crying. Six tried to speak, choked and shook his head.

"Mr. Godwin," Benson said, speaking gently, "it's Gene Seldon, isn't it? I'm so sorry. I know her."

Six nodded vigorously and then managed to croak out, "Ayuh. Gene. Burned up. Horrible."

Benson and Caleb exchanged a look. They had witnessed horrendous sights during their years on the force—hunters with their heads blown off, ripped-apart bodies in car wrecks—and they'd never gotten used to it. Contrary to popular myth, cops usually didn't get hardened—they pretended to be hard, to keep themselves steady. The look between them said, in essence, "This one's bad. Keep it together." Benson closed his eyes, took a deep breath, and said, "We better go over there."

Caleb spoke up: "All the lights here are out. Lightning musta hit a transformer."

Alicia looked puzzled. "Uh . . . you mean all the lights in this area?"

"No," Caleb responded. "Everybody else has lights . . . there was only a brief outage over to Oakland. Look out at the lake—you can see other camps."

Six and Alicia turned toward the lake and noticed for the first time that camp lights along the western short were twinkling through the darkness. "You're right," Six mumbled. He stood silently, gazing at the lake.   Benson said, "We're going over to the truck, Mr. Godwin. You and Mrs. Godwin don't need to go with us, but I do need to talk to you later."

When Six failed to respond or turn around, Benson shrugged and said to Caleb, "Let's get it over with."

As they neared the EMS truck they saw the two medics squatting by a form on the ground; one was holding a large, intensely bright spotlight. The medics stood and turned toward the sheriff and his deputy, as did the three other people standing nearby. In that trio, Benson recognized Armand Dupuis and Kipper Seldon; the third was a tall, weathered-looking man wearing a plaid shirt and khaki trousers.

Armand said, "Sheriff. Caleb." Benson and Caleb nodded back. Kipper didn't say anything, just stared blankly at the ground.

The two medics were Warren Cobb, Caleb's cousin, and Johnny Bolduc. After years of responding to medical emergencies countywide, including countless car wrecks, they knew everyone in the sheriff's department and the police forces of six towns. They came up close and Warren said,

"Fellas, this here's a bad one. Not seen nuthin' quite like this. I mean, we've tended folks hit by lightning, but, well... godamighty, this is strange."

"What's strange about it, Warren?"

"Well. Considerin' the huge storm we just had, it sure seems like lightning, and . . . well, there's a tree down near her that's got burn marks on it, but . . ."

"But," Benson said, still keeping his eyes away from the body. "Tell me."

"I just don't think it was lightning."

Thirteen

"Don't touch me, Bruno!" Merrill shrieked as she backed across the room. She'd been looking around for a weapon; seeing none, she scrunched her right hand into a hard fist and drew it back, ready to hit at Bruno's face.

Bruno stopped, riven by shock, and stared, disbelieving, into the beautiful eyes that only hours ago would've glowed adoringly at just the sight of him. Merrill had only her fist, but Bruno knew she could probably use it damn well; she was a strong outdoors woman seasoned by a lifetime of daily physical exertion. She hadn't been a doper long enough for coke to weaken her body; so far, only a small part of her brain had fizzled.

Of course Bruno could overpower her, but that wasn't the point. Why would he *want* to? Why would he ever want to brutalize Merrill? He stood very still and studied her face, raw from crying, for some clue as to what the hell was happening. Had she gone mad? Was this a cocaine delusion?

"Merrill," he said, keeping his voice soft. "Please. What is wrong?"

"What is wrong!? What is *wrong?*" she yelled. "You maniac, how can you stand there and say that?"

Now Bruno was sure that at least one of them was totally nuts. Was he dreaming? *No. I am not dreaming*, he thought. *Merrill just came screaming into the room and woke me. Coke. She's had a massive dose and is freaking. Had to be.* He blinked and opened his mouth to say something but nothing came out. This was scary. Merrill's eyes were darting and frenzied.

"You burned her up! You incinerated her, Jesus Christ how could you do that, you goddamn savage?"

"I did *what?* What the hell are you talking about?" Bruno's voice got higher and louder as he spoke. He was losing his cool . . . and possibly his mind. This confrontation was *not* making sense. *Careful*, he reminded himself. *Careful. Get some facts first.*

But Merrill kept shrieking. "How can you stand there and say that? You know goddamn well what I'm talking about!"

"Is it Gene?" Bruno asked. A horrible feeling began creeping into his mind that something very weird was going on in this lodge. After his attempt to devise an accidental death site for Gene near the generator shed, he'd gotten spooked by the other figure coming out of the shed and darting through the parked cars, so he had crept back to his room, knocked down three glasses of whiskey to steady himself and hit the mattress. He'd been in a deep sleep since that time. He glanced at his watch—an hour and a half ago. "Has Gene been killed?"

"Has Gene been killed?" Merrill's eyes got wilder and she backed farther toward the door. "Jesus, JESUS!" she brayed, her voice becoming ragged, "you horrible . . . godawmighty! Yes, she's dead, you sonofabitch! You said just a tree hitting her . . . just a TREE, for God's sake, and I said . . . I said okay, but you, you. . ." She began sobbing in howling bursts, gulping and gasping. She was hysterical with guilt. She'd colluded in Gene's murder but she never imagined Bruno would do anything so horrifying. This beautiful man to whom she had given herself heart and soul had just cremated her aunt as if she were in a Nazi death camp.

Bruno remained frozen in position, waiting. The hysteria would surely abate and he could try to get her to listen. Merrill's sobs gradually lessened and she took in deep breaths; she let her hands fall to her side and stood staring at Bruno in apparent exhaustion. After another couple of minutes of mute standoff, Bruno took a chance and said, calmly, softly, "Merrill, you must listen to me." Her eyes widened and Bruno feared she would explode again. "Please, I beg you," he said.

"You burned her up." Merrill's voice sounded strange—a rasping monotone. Her eyes and lips were puffy.

"I did not. I did not kill Gene."

Merrill's words came out quietly, almost trancelike. "Brad told me. He's in the bar in the dark. He told me what she looked like."

"Listen. Hear me. There was some—"

"I've got to get out of here."

"*Listen!* Someone else was out there." Bruno spoke rapidly. "Someone came out of the shed while I was dragging the burned tree and I hid, don't know who it was but I lost my nerve, came up here, went to bed."

"You're hideous." Her eyes burning with rage and fear, Merrill backed to the door, jerked it open and ran from the room and down the hall.

Bruno remained motionless as he tried to calm himself. Now he was scared too. Someone had burned Gene Seldon to death while he was asleep. That hooded figure coming from the generator shed. Had to be. Someone frighteningly brutal. Killed the old bitch and set her on fire. Bruno shuddered.

Then a scary new thought chased the others from his mind: Did the bastard see me?

* * *

Renee stood on the second-floor porch looking down at the scene below, mesmerized by the emergency vehicles' multi-colored lights flashing a lurid disco strobe against the surrounding forest. The yellow crime scene tape and the lights reminded her of *Law & Order* or *CSI*, two of her favorite programs.

But this was real and it wasn't fun. She gripped the porch railing tightly to try to stop her arms from trembling. Her knees felt weak, and they banged together as her legs shook. She didn't want to look at the ghastly yellow-jacketed body just beyond the parking lot, but the compulsion was irresistible. Slowly, ever so slowly, her gaze traveled from the sheriff's car to the three figures outlined in its headlights, to the generator shed, down to the EMS truck with its yellow flashers still revolving and then to . . . Oh God. She wheeled around, hand over mouth, feeling that she was going to vomit—the burned head beneath the spiky white hair had been clearly visible under the harsh glare of the EMS spotlight. This was horrible, horrible. What am I going to do? Murder outside the pages of a country house thriller, real murder, was not exciting. It

was terrifying. How had she ever imagined that she had the courage to be a nerveless killer? Now, the very thought of emulating
those insouciant fictional aristocrat murderers who curled their lips
at plodding coppers snapping cuffs on their wrists appalled her.
They couldn't ever do that to her. Not to *her*—Renee Ranger; beautiful, desirable Renee Ranger.

Oh, please, God, don't let this happen to me (there was that
deity again, creeping back into her fevered brain and receiving yet
more supplication). Get me out of here. Right now I should be
over on the coast in a yacht club barroom with beautiful people or
. . . anywhere on the coast, anywhere, except here on this dismal
lake. I need to get out of here. But wait—how could she? Her car
was parked down there right in the middle of the action. More cops
would be coming. Trapped. She was trapped in Cedar Lodge with
all the others.

She tried to recall what she had learned about autopsies from
the many mysteries she'd read. After any suspicious death an autopsy was automatic. Wasn't it? She was sure it was. And they
tested for what was in the stomach and the blood stream. Would
they find the Elavil? Would it still show up in a badly burned body?
The doctor who had given her the stuff had warned that alcohol
mixed with just one or two of the 20mg tablets would knock her
flat for hours and engender a truly evil hangover. Renee remembered how she'd ground fifteen—*fifteen*—of the pills into a fine
powder, hoping for a chemical death blow.

She walked slowly down the porch, around the corner and toward the front of the lodge, and as she walked she made a supreme
effort to get control of her nerves. Okay—here's what to do. Go
to your room, undress, get in bed and don't come out. When the
inevitable knock on the door comes, fake a drowsy stupor and insist that you've been in bed since leaving the bar after talking to
Bob Weller. Don't panic.

Renee climbed the outside stairs to the third-floor porch and
went to her room, whose windows looked out onto the docks and
the lakes. She felt her way carefully to the drinks table and poured
a brandy, knocked it down, then poured another. The room was

warm and stuffy so she moved to a window and opened it and stood before it sipping the brandy and gazing at the lake, amazed to see, so soon after the powerful storm, that the water now twinkled with moonlight under a star-dazzled sky. Also winking through the darkness were pinpoints of lights from other camps, but Renee's thoughts were so tumultuous at this point that she didn't register the fact that Cedar Lodge was the only camp with a power outage.

The brandy's sharp tang was good. Another sip, another deep breath. Now. Get control. You know you're a good actress. Don't volunteer information. Just answer the questions. Throw in some distraction: thighs, tits. By the end of the second brandy her trembling had stopped and her panic was gradually succumbing to the false confidence-building of strong booze.

She began peeling off her clothes. Time to get in bed and play sleeping princess until . . . Whoa! What's that down there? A movement in the moonglow. She put her face to the screen. Definitely someone there. A figure, barely discernible, standing at the end of one of the docks. Not moving now. Just standing there. Creepy.

* * *

"*Bippity, boppity, hooley gazam,*
rastabangus blamity slam."
Brad giggled at his own instantly composed doggerel and took a sip of bourbon from a jigger.
"*Wistelfarcus himmitybuck,*
Boligojingus nominysuck."
This was fun, he thought. It was black dark in the barroom. Only thing visible was the moonlit outline of the window. Every time the vision of Gene's burned head darted into his brain he quickly began blurting out new doggerel or singing old Beach Boys songs.

The darkness was comforting, and he was going to stay here having fun. *Fun, fun, fun till her daddy takes the T-Bird away.* Heh heh. Beach Boys. Geezers now but still singing, still having fun, fun,

fun. Suddenly, an image from his boyhood—*why does the brain summon these things out of nowhere?*—was before him, a promotional tourism ad. Sun-drenched beach, striped awning, a beautiful bikinied woman balancing on one foot while holding above her, with both arms, a huge red beach ball. "Fun In The Sun!" is emblazoned across the azure sky. The woman's mouth is joyously open, flashing perfect teeth and her eyes are alive with excitement. Brad sees it perfectly with his ten-year-old eyes and remembers wondering how holding up a big red ball could engender so much ecstasy.

The woman's mouth and teeth suddenly became the gaping cavity in a macabre, melting skull and so Brad quickly belted out:

"Bippity, boppity, hooley. . . Jesus Christ!" He jumped up in fright as furniture crashed at the other end of the room.

"Help!" a man's voice cried out. "Goddamn! What the hell's happening?" More banging around, sound of glasses breaking on the floor.

"Who's there!" Brad called out.

"Bob! Bob Weller. Help me."

"Okay, don't move. Gotta find a flashlight." He walked Frankenstein-style with his arms straight out and took baby steps toward, he hoped, the bar. Ouch! Damn. Table. Over to the left. Okay, now he could see the outline of the bar. He knew there were flashlights there because he'd used one to find a bottle and a glass. He got to the bar and put out his left hand as he walked slowly forward. Ah! There was one. He turned it on and shined it around the room.

"Here!" Bob called out. "End of the bar."

Brad shined the beam in that direction and saw overturned stools. He moved quickly up to them and discovered Robertson Weller sprawled out flat and grasping the brass rail. His hair was a wild mess, his clothes were crumpled and he looked, at this moment, more like a guttered bum than a silver fox.

"What happened?"

"You're drunk."

"I know that, dammit, I mean where're the lights and all the people? What time is it?"

"I don't know the time," Brad told him, "but the lights went out a couple of hours ago, and . . . uh, well, everybody's out back, I believe."

"Where's Gene?"

Brad stooped and put his hands under Bob's armpits and began hoisting him to his feet. "First, let me get you up." Bob was none too steady in a standing position so Brad levered him over to a chair and sat him down.

"Need a drink?"

"God, no. Where's Gene?"

"Well. That's just it. That's why everybody ran out of here. I've got some very bad news for you, Bob."

* * *

Jean-Pierre LeMaire perched on a stool in the darkened kitchen among his beloved steel counters and pots and pans and knives. He was traumatized with fear as he looked out through the damaged porch to the bizarre scene of a crowd of heads outlined by flashes of blue, red, white and yellow. Someone had told him what happened but he didn't want to go anywhere near the horror. Kipper was out there but he didn't want to see him. Anyone but Kipper. His lover's last words to him earlier in the evening now filled him with dread.

* * *

Huntley Beauchamp, clad only in undershorts and sitting by an open window hoping for a cool breeze, raised a glass of claret in a toast to himself as he regarded Willow Pond in the moonlight. Here's to me, he thought. Clever me. Job well done.

He loosed a deep, satisfied sigh of relief. The dreadful old bitch is dead, and I am home free. During the past two days, his long-ago old self, the rapaciously venal Jack Spurling, laid to rest these many years under a mound of documentation giving birth to Huntley Beauchamp, had resurrected himself in Huntley's psyche as a terrified, rat-eyed Valjean. But now . . . hah, hah, the confident, self-adoring master of the universe had regained control and all was well. Repressing the memory of his recent bowel-loosening terror, Huntley now murmured out loud, "I knew it would all come right. Good show, Beauchamp old man. Good show."

He put the wine glass on the window still, turned on his flash-light and examined once more the papers on his lap, which had arrived about an hour earlier via a manila envelope slipped beneath his door. A soft *swiiish* had alerted him to its arrival. The papers were a masterpiece—spreadsheets and investment summaries that covered over his every treacherous footprint through the portfolio of Cedar Lodge Enterprises.

Smiling lovingly at the several dummy corporations that had been fitted out with detailed histories and impressive earnings charts, he once more chuckled at his favorite—Bearscat Industries, the maker of hunting products that featured a donuts-and-syrup formula irresistible to bears. Hah, hah, very witty. All very clever and splendid. Nothing could be traced back to him. Nothing. He was certain of that. All he had to do was wait it out. Nevertheless . . . nevertheless, after everything had calmed down and he'd gotten his divorce settlement from Merrill, he intended to slip noiselessly away to Toronto and start another life for that ever-resourceful, debonair Huntley Beauchamp. Hah-hah.

Fourteen

Benson and Caleb squatted beside Warren Cobb and took their first close look at Gene Seldon's burned corpse. The sheriff was a psychologically stable man, a tough cop who had seen many of his fellow humans mutilated—sometimes literally ripped to pieces— by highway tragedies or by the savagery of other humans. Since early days on the force, he had internalized those dreadful memories, some of which occasionally returned to haunt him in agonized dreams; however, eventually he had conquered the fear of facing each year's inevitable new slaughters. But the sight on the ground before him now was in a class of horror by itself. He had known Iphigene Seldon, had gone fishing with her. This couldn't be her. Gene Seldon, the strong, boisterous fisherman and hunter, had been reduced to incinerated flesh.

Benson held a handkerchief over his mouth against the choking smell emanating from Gene's pathetic remains; his eyes filled with tears, and he didn't trust himself to speak, waiting, instead, for Warren's analysis. Caleb also had a cloth over his nose and mouth; he felt like screaming. This big man, so admired for his unflappable courage, often wanted to scream and rage against unmerciful fate. Violent death upset him, always, and the murder of children engendered in him an agonized grief, as if he had been the father of the victims. These emotions were his secrets; to survive as a lawman he had disciplined his inner self to keep outwardly silent. Just as he and Benson had squatted down he'd emitted a soft "Jesus!" which he was sure Benson had heard, but that was it for expostulation—his mind's screaming went unheard.

Warren turned to his assistant standing behind him and said, "Johnny, bring that light in closer." Gesturing with his rubber-gloved hands, he said, "Well, Benson, there's several things that are really puzzling. Number one, I didn't know lightning could do this kind of damage. I've worked two lightning deaths—the last was three years ago over to Rocky Pond. God knows they were badly scarred, but nothing even close to this. Number two, well . . . understand I'm feeling my way here . . . it's these clothes, especially this rubber foul-weather jacket. I mean, when Johnny and I got here the clothes were still smoking, and . . . just look, they're mostly burned up and, I don't know, I'm no expert but do clothes burn with a lightning strike?"

"I don't know, Warren," Benson replied, his voice muffled by the handkerchief. "But it doesn't seem unreasonable. I know lightning can set off forest fires."

Warren was silent for several moments and then said, "You know, that's right, of course. But this damn thing's thick rubber." He blew out his breath. "Well, anyway, number three. Look at this." Inserting his gloved fingers underneath the body, he lifted it about three inches. Rubbery, unburned flesh hung in loops. Benson closed his eyes and took a deep breath. Caleb grunted softly, feeling his gorge rise. "Neither the flesh nor the clothes are burned underneath the body," Warren pointed out. "Can lightning do that? Just burn down one side of the body? I guess it can, but it sure seems strange. Like I said, I'm no expert on this kinda thing." After a pause, he said, "Right here next to her is this burned tree, which I'd say was obviously split by lightning, so that means lightning did strike here." He stood up and Benson and Caleb did the same.

"But there's another damn thing, Benson. When we first jumped out of the truck I swear to God I got a whiff of gasoline. Don't smell it now, but I'm sure I did then. It's probably burned off. Do you guys smell it?"

"No," Benson said, "I don't. Caleb?"

"Nossuh."

They walked away from the body and Benson said, "Warren. Good work. You're a medic and a forensic team rolled into one."

"Ayuh, well, not really. I was just saying what I thought was obvious in case you wanted your guys in here."

"I sure as hell do now. I'm gonna treat this as a possible crime scene. Caleb, phone over to the station and get Tom Barclay to put together a crew and get here as fast as they can. And you need to contact the pathologist, too."

"Yessuh, will do." Caleb turned toward the squad car to use the radio. Cell phone links were tenuous in some parts of the county.

"And Caleb . . ." Benson called.

"Yessuh?"

"Call Central Maine and tell 'em I need lights in this place. Fast."

Benson went over to where Armand, Kipper and the other man were standing. "I'm sorry, Kipper, truly sorry. This is just godawful." Kipper looked at the sheriff but didn't respond. He seemed dazed, his eyes blankly serene. "Armand?" Benson said, turning to the bartender.

"Sheriff?"

"Is that your doing?" He gestured toward the crowd of people near the lodge's back porch. "How the hell did you keep 'em back?"

"Well, I did my roaring mountain man act, but I also had some help from this gentleman here," Armand said, indicating the plaid-shirted man Benson had noted when he'd first arrived. "Fella's got a voice that makes you sit up straight and behave." The man strode forward and extended his hand, saying, "Hello. Colin Trimble, sheriff."

English, Benson guessed. Something of a rarity in Maine's lake country. He shook the man's hand and said, "Benson Doucette. You a guest at the lodge?"

"I am. My wife is here with me. Afraid I shoved myself into the action without being asked, Sheriff Doucette."

Armand told Benson, "I'm damn glad he did. Mr. Godwin was upset and screaming that he didn't want people looking at Gene."

"Royal Navy," Colin said. "Retired. Accustomed to bellowing at poor sods sluicing the decks, I suppose." He glanced toward Gene's corpse. "Ghastly business. Shocking."

Wordlessly, Kipper turned from them and walked away, not toward the porch, but toward the lodge's west wall, as if heading for the lake. Armand pulled at the ends of his big mustache and said, "Kipper was doing his part, too, yelling and waving his arms. Seemed to go crazy for awhile, sounded like he was crying, and then he clammed up. Ain't said diddly since then."

"Sheriff!" They all turned at the sound of Six Godwin's voice and saw him and Alicia emerging from the darkness to the west, near the camp road. As the two of them neared, Six seemed excited, and he had found his voice again. "Sheriff, this was no power outage. The line from the road's been cut. And so's the line from the generator."

Benson shut his eyes briefly, took a deep breath and said, "Oh, Christ. This is bad. What the hell is going on around here?"

Six ran a hand through his curly white hair and, staring down at the ground as if there might be a helpful answer scrawled in the dirt, said, "Ayuh. Kind of scary."

"Caleb," Benson said, "we need to start gathering people up as soon as the power company guys fix the lights. We've got some interviewing to do."

"Always my favorite thing," Caleb said.

"And Caleb?"

"Yessuh?"

"We need to find something around here that's sharp enough and strong enough to cut through a power cable." Benson turned to Six and Alicia. "Do you know where there's a tool shed?"

Six pointed toward the western end of the lodge. "Big boathouse out front. Got a tool room."

"We'll wait till later to take a look, when the power's back on."

Benson and the Godwins walked silently toward the lodge. What was I thinking just the other day? Benson wondered. Ohhh, yes. I was thinking how peaceful July had been so far. No drownings, one knife fight, two stolen boats and several car crashes, none of them fatal.

Never, ever again, think a thing like that, Benson told himself. The gods of chaos love it when, during a span of sunny days and serenity, you look around and think, "Isn't this nice?"

Fifteen

After erecting a white tent over Gene's body, Sheriff's Det. Lt. Tom Barclay, the forensic team and the county pathologist had put on paper anti-contamination jump suits and were now examining the body and the surrounding area and bagging samples of anything that looked in the least relevant. Two deputies in a second squad car had arrived, at Benson's request, to guard the camp road just in case any of the lodge's guests or staff got an inadvisable urge to leave. And, a Central Maine Power crew had come with a boom-lift truck to patch in new cables, and now the lights had been restored to Cedar Lodge.

With the lights on, Benson could start worrying about everything else—and everything else included the possibility of a reporter. Worse, a reporter *and* a photographer. Even worse than that, multiple reporters and photographers. Yes, this was the boonies and, yes, the first reports were of death by lightning, but in today's world even temporary isolation of events was no longer possible. In the years before cell phones and laptop computers, Benson could have kept a murder probe at such a remote site as Cedar Lodge isolated for this first night and all the next day before some eager newshound studied the incident log at sheriff's headquarters or got a tip-off from someone who'd been at the scene.

Now, Benson thought, *now* every damn one of the thirty-six registered guests at the lodge had a cell phone and most likely a laptop. And Cedar Lodge, having full service equivalent to its fame in the sporting world, had Internet access in all its rooms. Everyone carried the toys, everywhere—everyone, that is, except the occasional grumpy, I'm-above-it-all Luddite. After Gene's body had been found, probably all the guests had piled out of the lodge through the back porch until they were halted by Armand, Kipper and the stentorian Englishman. By now they all knew what had happened and private reports of murder at Willow Pond were without a doubt darting through the atmosphere just at this moment, as he and Caleb, with the help of Armand and Colin Trimble, began rounding up those very cellular-toting guests. A half-hour later they'd been herded into the front lobby.

Benson stood in front of the big stone fireplace and said, "Folks, I'm Benson Doucette, sheriff of Somerbec County, and this is Sgt. Cobb. There's been a tragedy here tonight, as you know, and we're working to . . ." He ran his hand through his curly auburn hair, causing strands of it to spring up in places. "Well, to be quite honest, there's some things that don't look right."

His words caused a buzzing of comments throughout the small crowd; he heard a couple of people say, "I told you so."

"And we need your help," he continued. "So, I'm asking . . ."

"Suspicious death, sheriff?" a woman called out.

Oh, goddammit, he thought. Well, what did he expect?

"Frankly . . . yes." As the hubbub grew in volume, Benson held up his hand and shouted, "Please. I can't say more, but I do need to ask your help. My deputies and I have to talk to the family and the people working here. It's going to take awhile. Could I ask all of you, please, to meet me here in the dining room tomorrow morning about . . . oh, say, eleven? Is that a good time? Is anyone planning to leave?"

"I don't think anyone's checking out just yet," Colin said. He looked at his fellow guests. "Is everyone in for the night?"

A chorus of assents answered him.

"Eleven a.m. good for all?" Colin asked.

No one said a nay. Benson then told them: "After we've met with you tomorrow, then you can probably all leave, if you want to, unless something extraordinary happens. Things are most likely going to be disrupted around here and I don't know if the Seldons are going to get the camp running tomorrow. Maybe by Monday they'll have things back to normal. You'll have to ask them. Meantime, if you will please try to recall anything—anything, no matter how insignificant it seems—that we should know about, please let us know."

* * *

Later, inside the lodge's kitchen, under high-watt ceiling spots, Benson and Caleb sat with Six and Alicia. The Seldons, their spouses and the other principals at Cedar Lodge would be arriving, as forcefully suggested, any minute.

"Sheriff?" Alicia said. "Are you treating us as suspects?"

Benson looked at Alicia, studied her big brown eyes and sweet smile and realized that she reminded him of his English teacher. "Well, Mrs. Godwin . . ."

"Oh, do please call me Alicia."

"Well, OK . . . Alicia. We're not calling anybody suspects just yet because we're not calling it a murder." Benson felt uncomfortable as Alicia regarded him silently. He cleared his throat and said, "Yet."

"But you're going to, aren't you?" Six said. "How could lightning have done that frightening damage to Gene?"

Benson leaned forward on the steel counter, folded his hands under his chin and thought about what he should say. After several moments of silence he made a decision, sighed, and said, "There's the possibility that a direct lighting strike on Ms. Seldon could've set fire to her clothes, which then kept burning. But . . ." He paused again then said, "But I don't think so. And neither does the emergency crew. However, I'm waiting for confirmation one way or the other by Lt. Barclay and the forensic guys. Meanwhile . . . well, meanwhile, Mrs. . . . er, Alicia. . . I really don't think you and your husband qualify as suspects. Sgt. Caleb here has spoken very highly of both of you and, well, I can see how very upset you are by this, uh . . . death."

"Thank you, sheriff," Alicia said, smiling at him.

"We were very fond of Gene," Six said. "We would never have harmed her. Besides, we're family."

Benson raised his brows. "Oh?"

"Yep. Cousins. Actually, we're cousins to a lot of people in Maine."

"Yeah, well, I know how that goes," Benson said. "When you're French-Canadian background like me you're related to probably half the state."

Alicia said, "Sheriff, there's something you need to know. Gene had scheduled a big family conference for tomorrow to announce a change in her will and to sort out the investments. Lawyer was coming. Accountant. She told Six and me that she expected a huge fight and that it would be her versus everybody else. So she wanted at least some family in her corner."

"Also," Six interjected, "She got a written death threat yesterday. Had to be done on a computer. It's remarkably creepy."

"Do you have a copy?"

"Gene showed it to us in her office. We can probably find it in there."

"OK. We'll look for it later."

Benson was stunned by what had suddenly fallen into his official lap. A family quarrel over inheritance, a death threat and now a terrifying murder. He had to think things through very carefully, and he certainly needed to be certain that he had all contingencies covered at Cedar Lodge and the surrounding area. He was grateful that he had Tom Barclay and Caleb Cobb nearby; this was probably going to be a nerve-wracking night.

Ah well, he reminded himself—you wanted to be sheriff.

He studied this unlikely pair, Six and Alicia, sitting regarding him solemnly with their big eyes, and made a decision based on instinct. They seemed like good and intelligent people.

"Professors," he said, giving them an encouraging smile, "how would you like to be temporary cops?"

Surprised, Six and Alicia looked at each other and then back to Benson. "You mean like deputies?" Six asked.

Benson chuckled. "Well, no, in order to deputize you I'd have to send you off to the academy. Don't think you'd like it."

"More than likely not. Cuts into fishing."

"What I have in mind is the two of you helping us without us saying that you are. You know the whole family, all the ins and outs, and probably a lot of the tensions—I mean, you were supposed to be part of this family conference Sunday."

"We do know quite a bit, Sheriff Doucette," Alicia said. "And Gene told us a good deal more yesterday when she had us in her office."

"We'd be eager to help in any way we can," Six told Benson, then turned quickly to Alicia. "Wouldn't we, kiddo?"

"Of course we would."

Benson slapped his knees. "Excellent. Now, for this first interrogation I'd like you to sit with the others facing the sergeant and me . . . as if you *are* suspects."

At that moment, the big double doors swung open and Brad, smelling like a Tennessee distillery, meandered in, stopped and drunkenly focused on the four people watching him. "Ah. Sheriff," he said. "Sergeant. Godwins. Bon soir and comment ça va and all that crap."

"Très bien, Bradley," Alicia replied without hesitation. "Et vous?"

Brad grinned. "Alicia. You're a pistol." Then he shuffled over to a stool and plumped down. Six and Alicia got up, walked behind Brad's counter and sat near him.

Kipper came through the doors with Merrill right behind him. Kipper kept his eyes down and avoided looking at anyone. Merrill, disheveled and vacant, glanced at Benson and the others, tried to smile, then took a seat and stared down at her hands. Was this grief? Alicia wondered. She and Gene had fought like wolverines, and yet here she was with puffy, red eyes.

The others all drifted in. Benson wasn't at all sure who was who, but he knew he'd be finding out. Armand he knew, of course; the young fellow standing next to Armand must be the dock boy, he figured.

Robertson Weller had been taken to his room after Benson had Warren Cobb check him over for possible clinical shock. Also, Benson realized, the man was reeling, drunk as a coot. Benson had not known of his existence and was amazed when Brad had introduced him as Gene's fiancé. Wonders never ceased, Benson reflected.

"Is this everyone connected with the lodge?" Caleb called out.

Kipper's head rose but his gaze settled above Benson and Caleb. "Because . . ." He seemed to gag, cleared his throat and continued: "Because the storm was coming I sent everybody home—the sous-chef, two cooks, waiters, the girls who clean the rooms. We served cold cuts and salad for dinner."

Benson cast his eyes over the morose gathering and shuddered. This, he decided, was going to be murder. Well, actually, it already *was* murder, wasn't it? He glanced through the list of names Caleb handed him and realized that at some point he was going to need help from Barclay, the best interrogator in the sheriff's department. It had required a considerable job of hunting all these people down in the lodge, so Benson was determined that once he'd gotten them all in the kitchen he was going to keep them there for awhile, until he somehow uncovered something, anything, that would indicate—simply an initial hint, please God—just what the hell had happened in this place.

Iphigene Seldon's shocking death had occurred on his ground. He was sheriff of this county, he had nine deputies, two sergeants, one detective, and a state-of-the-art forensic lab with two technicians. No way around it: His department was on the line. Just at the moment, the thought depressed him. When he had fugitives on the run then he could depend on help from the state troopers and from various town and county police. But this one was his. He glanced through the windows at the white tent, hoping he'd soon see Tom Barclay heading toward the kitchen.

Benson stood and said, "A number of you know me, but for those who do not, I am Benson Doucette, Somerbec County sheriff, and this is Sgt. Caleb Cobb. First, let me say that I am shocked and saddened. I've known Gene Seldon for a good many years. We responded to what we thought was a lightning death, and further investigation may prove that to be true. However . . ." Benson noticed small movements during his pause. "However, we are now treating it as a possible—and I emphasize possible—homicide." That produced some gasps, a few small expostulations, and a number of exchanged glances among the assembled.

Benson turned and gestured toward the white tent. "As you can see, we've begun an intense examination of the death site. That's all I have to tell you right now. We've just started and we have no speculation about who may've been involved in this tragedy." Again, he paused and prepared to watch the faces as he announced, "Ms. Iphigene Seldon was burned, beyond recognition."

His blunt statement elicited further muted verbal reactions, but the faces he searched told him what he suspected: Everyone had already heard, from someone else, the nature of Gene's hideous death. "Obviously, I need to ask everyone here some questions. I am asking you to please be patient and stay together here in the kitchen and sit this one out with me. If I let everybody scatter then we would waste a lot of time finding you again for individual interviews. If you need to leave the room for personal reasons, then of course you may. Just please return as soon as you can. Now. Is this agreeable to everyone?"

Silence.

"Anyone? No? Thank you." The faces told Benson that it was not "agreeable" at all, but obviously everyone accepted the sense of it.

Okay, he told himself—time to fish. Catch and release. Let's get the small ones out of the live well first. He checked the list of names, looked at Sam—muscular, tanned and blond; standard dock boy—and said, "Young man, your name is Sam Wiley?"

"Yes sir!"

"And you live at the lodge during the summer?"

"Yes sir. This is my second summer. Sir!"

Either he's nervous or he's ROTC, Benson decided. "And you attend college at . . ."

"Colby. Sir."

"Sam, where were you tonight during the storm and the blackout?"

"I was asleep, sir. After we hauled all the boats on shore and tied things down I was exhausted. Ms. Seldon told me to knock off and get some rest. I was in bed when I heard the storm hit, but I fell asleep anyway. I never knew about the blackout until Mr. Seldon woke me up about . . ." He looked at his watch. "About an hour and a half ago."

"Which Mr. Seldon?" Caleb asked.

"Oh, uh, it was Mr. Kipper Seldon. Sir."

"And what did he say?" Caleb continued.

"He said his aunt had been killed by lightning."

Benson studied Sam's alarmed face. By college age, Benson knew, no young person was without some degree of disingenuousness, but this boy, he concluded, looked about as honest as you could get 'em these days.

"Okay, Sam. You can go. Thank you."

"Yes sir! Thank you." He turned to go. "Sir!"

Once he had left the kitchen's swinging doors swinging, Benson turned to the bartender and said, "Armand?"

"Benson?" Armand replied. "Uh, sheriff?"

"That's all right. Benson's fine. We've known each other for some time. Now. During the storm and the blackout you were behind the bar?"

"Ayuh. Well, I took one whiz." Armand looked abashed and quickly said, "Sorry. I visited the porcelain. Before the lights went out, I'm happy to say."

"Came back quickly?"

"A prolonged absence in my case woulda set up a howl, sher— Benson. What with the storm and the singing and the whole hullabaloo, folks were accepting Ms. Seldon's offer of free drinks at an impressive rate."

"Gene was there during all this?"

"Right there at the end of the bar with Mr. Weller," Armand replied.

"And after the lights went out?"

Armand chuckled. "Damned if I know. All I could see was everybody's flashlights jumping all around."

"Oh?" Caleb said. "Everybody had flashlights?"

"Well, not everybody, but Ms. Seldon had passed out a whole bunch of the things. People started playing games, scary faces and stuff like that, and they started singing."

Six raised his hand, and, receiving a nod from Benson, said, "I can tell you what happened. Before the blackout Gene went to the head once, quickly, and then when she returned she asked Alicia and me to help her get Mr. Weller up to his room."

"Mr. Weller was sick?"

"Well, uh, you might say he had overserved himself at the bar," Six replied. "The lights went out for good shortly after that, so we figured it would be dangerous stumbling around in the dark up the stairs with Bob between us. He isn't what you'd call diminutive."

"He isn't what?" Caleb asked.

"Small."

"Ah hah. I like that word."

Benson rolled his eyes. "So then what?"

"Gene waited until the hail let up and then left with a flashlight saying she was going out to the generator shed."

Alicia spoke up at that point: "Gene was gone for a long time but we didn't notice it because . . . well, because for one thing, the lights were out and we weren't paying attention to the time passing, and also there was a lot of singing and carrying on and, well, we just got caught up in it.

"Finally, it dawned on me to shine a flashlight on my watch, and I was startled when I saw the time. She'd told us it would take her only fifteen minutes at most—almost an hour had gone by. I told Six I was worried, so he went to look for her, and then. . . well . . ." She took Six's left hand and held it in both of hers. "Then when Six didn't come back I got very anxious, and I was just about to go looking for him when Brad suddenly came up to the bar right beside me and called for Armand. He told Armand that Gene was hit by lightning and to come quick . . ."

Det. Lt. Tom Barclay, wearing jeans, camp shirt and yellow work boots, appeared at the kitchen door. Her penetrating, blue-eyed stare slowly swept across the alarmed faces and then came to rest on Benson and Caleb.

"Compadres," she said, her voice low but nonetheless heard by everyone in the silence of the kitchen, "we have a murder."

At first there was profound silence, and then Merrill sank face down on the counter before her and began softly crying.

Lt. Barclay leaned over and spoke softly: "Benson, there's also a man and woman from the Sentinel in Waterville out by the road-block."

Benson drew in a deep breath and blew it out noisily. "Damn. Now everybody can have fun."

Sixteen

Colin and Daphne Trimble had not gone up to their rooms, as had the other guests. They had retrieved two porch chairs and taken them to the end of the center dock, beyond the last dock light, where they now sat sipping the astoundingly expensive single-malt scotch they had brought with them. They had turned their chairs to face Cedar Lodge. It wouldn't do to have someone padding up quietly behind them while they were talking. Wouldn't do at all. The couple certainly wouldn't want anyone to overhear anything they were discussing privately and, conversely, it would be potentially quite dangerous for anyone to unwisely creep up behind Colin and Daphne. Quite dangerous.

"Nice night," Colin said. "Considering."

"Hmm, yes it is, considering," Daphne replied.

The air was warm and calm and the storm seemed to have driven off the mosquitoes, for now. Loons were calling and chattering to one another out on the lake.

"So, what do we do now?" Colin asked. "The situation has altered considerably."

"Yes. I know. I think we should sit tight and keep playing the sporting life."

"Even now that the old woman is dead?"

"Yes," Daphne replied. "I want to play it to the end. Don't you?"

Colin sighed heavily. "Well, yes, actually I do. Especially as we did not collect the fee up front. But we have to be very careful."

"Very careful indeed. What do you think of Doucette and his crew?"

"Can't tell just yet. Past experience tells us never to underestimate local studs wearing uniforms."

Daphne gestured toward the figure stepping onto the far end of the dock. "Here he comes now. Back to the poncy accents."

"I'm beginning to enjoy it. Have we done British before?"

Daphne thought for a moment. "Yes. Yes, we have. Remember that job in Miami in ninety-nine? Eduardo what's his name—the Brazilian hood."

"Oh, yes," Colin said, smiling, as if recalling a fond memory. "He died rather badly, didn't he?"

"Yes."

"Hello, old horse," Colin said as Sam approached them.

"Hi." Obviously nervous, Sam looked back the way he'd come and then examined the two other docks.

"Easy does it, laddie," Colin told him. "All the peepholes are covered."

Sam didn't say anything. He never knew what to make of this man's expressions.

"Do you have anything for us?" Daphne asked.

"No, ma'am. I tried, like, ten times to get in his room but he always locks up. Not everyone does that at Cedar Lodge, but he does, always. Also, I've been watching him, like you asked, but I haven't seen him do anything random."

"Random?" Colin asked. "Oh, dear. What do you mean?"

"Sorry," Sam blurted. "It's a college expression. It means, like, weird or, or, like stupid or something. Random."

"Very well. Now, look here, laddie. You assured us you had the requisite skills for this sort of enterprise."

Colin's sudden change of tone frightened Sam. "I've done it before," he blurted. "Plenty of times. Sir."

"Easy. Keep your voice down."

"Yessir. I've tried the old credit card trick and the hairpin. They worked in my dorm."

"Did they indeed?" Colin snapped. "I would imagine, young Sam, that Cedar Lodge has a more sophisticated security system than your dormitory."

"It's all right, Sam," Daphne told him sweetly. "You've tried very hard to do an important job—as we've told you, we're with the government. Hasn't he been diligent, Colin?" Daphne's sugar-sweet voice frightened Sam as much as Colin's angry snap. "Now. Colin and I will carry on from here. This is for you." Daphne held out an envelope to Sam; gingerly, he took it, folded it and stuffed it into his shorts.

"Th-thank you, ma'am," he said.

"And what is it you're *not* going to do, Sam dearest?"

"Ma'am?"

"You're not going to tell anyone, anyone at all, about this. Are you?"

"No!"

"People can get into very serious trouble by telling secrets, isn't that so, Colin?"

Colin frowned at Sam and said, "It certainly is. Serious trouble, indeed."

"I-I-I won't say a thing. Honest to God."

"Very good, Sam," Daphne purred. "Now run along."

Sam wheeled around and walked up the dock without looking back. They watched him step carefully up the porch steps and through the front door.

"We've got to get that laptop," Colin said. "Tonight."

"Yes, we do. We do indeed." Daphne leaned back in the deck chair and stretched out her legs. "Since our little chap can't manage it, then . . .?"

"Of course," Colin assured her. "Of course. Necessity dictates."

Many years before, after two harrowing instances of discovery *en flagrante* burglary, Colin and Daphne had decided that, though they themselves had magic fingers vis-à-vis locked doors, they would rely whenever possible upon the venality of petty criminals to carry out petty crimes. Also, they enjoyed playing games with people while they were, as they termed it, "on location" carrying out assignments for clients. It amused them to see how much of the dirty work they could assign to others as the two of them sat back and watched the show. They were growing jaded, were Colin and Daphne, and the risks they often took of hiring on-location dupes provided an extra dollop of thrill. Because they were experienced in the disappearing arts, they were, in the blink of an eye, nowhere to be found if "embarrassments"—another of their terms—arose. Their real names had long ago fallen into a bureaucratic oubliette. Potential clients had to contact them through a double layer of "employment agencies" that communicated exclusively by means of typewritten letters hand delivered to commercial mailbox stores.

Daphne said, "We're not going to brutalize Sam, are we?"

"Not necessary, really. We've got him pissing in his pants. Sorry," he said, reverting to an Oxford drawl—"wetting his knickers. By the time our quarry is bagged we'll be other people in some other place."

Daphne was quiet for awhile, swinging her leg and listening to the night sounds. Finally, she said, "Oh, about that other . . . matter?"

"Other matter? Er . . . oh yes. Of course. I was right—same ghastly individual. Different name this time, of course. Very ugly customer."

"We'll have to be careful."

"Damn straight," Colin said, maintaining his Britishisms. "I'll take care of it."

* * *

In his small, third-floor room that faced the woods, Sam Wiley drank a cold beer and tried to calm his nerves. He decided that right now, from this moment on, his very short career of larceny was ending. Looking back at the spring semester he wondered what compulsion had driven him to enter other students' rooms and take things. None of what he'd stolen was valuable. But he'd gotten a rush from the adventure; he had the skill to slip through locked doors and never leave a trace; what a sense of power—he imagined himself like that totally cool guy in "White Collar," the jewel thief, the handsome dude who knocked chicks silly just by looking at them.

But his dashing internal TV persona had quickly regressed to a frightened nineteen-year-old when confronted with the suave but menacing real-world Colin and Daphne. He had thought English people were like David Niven and Audrey Hepburn from the old movies he watched on Turner Classics. *These* people were cold and hard. At first, he'd even had fantasies about the woman, though she was much older—her sexuality had riveted him, especially when she and Colin had recruited him.

Over drinks, they had adroitly and circumspectly discovered that, yes, he had little extra money at college and would like to earn more. They persuaded him that they were British government agents working under deep cover and that their "quarry," as they called him, was laundering money for an Islamic foundation that supported terrorists seeking to strike civilian targets in the U.S. What he would be doing would be patriotic in addition to gaining him three hundred in cash for a few minutes' work and did he per- haps have keys to the various rooms? Daphne had said, treating him to a view of sun-tanned thighs unobscured by her short skirt as she crossed and re-crossed her legs.

He had told them, barely able to speak around his dragging tongue, that Gene Seldon guarded the keys like a nesting eagle and gave them to the room-cleaning girls each morning. But he, by that time feeling very worldly in the presence of such exciting people, had assured them that they were not to worry—he could get through doors like Houdini.

Once they had sealed the arrangement and Daphne had slipped Sam a hundred dollars' advance, she'd purred, "Good lad, Sammie. Welcome aboard." That night, Sam had lain in his bed consumed by teenage lust. He didn't know women Daphne's age could *be* sexy. He figured she must be at least the same age as his mom. That thought worried him—he wondered if there was something wrong with him.

Now he lay in his bed consumed by the realization that he was a prize-winning dickhead. Never, never again. From now on he was hewing steadfastly to the straight and narrow.

Seventeen

Thomasina Barclay, sheriff's detective, Ph.D. in criminal psychology and visiting criminology professor at the University of Maine, was "Tom" to all who knew her; nobody in rural Maine was going to put up with a name like Thomasina, especially Thomasina herself. Her mother had been unduly charmed by a Disney movie about a runaway cat and had given her firstborn the name of the feline star.

Tom, a big, attractive woman with generous curves, had a round, pleasant face and thick brown hair worn in a bob. Her eyes were large and very blue, and when she trained them on someone else's eyes they seemed to penetrate to the person's soul; it enabled her to be a superb interrogator. Lt. Barclay herself insisted that the thousand-watt stare that made those of an uneasy conscience so readily uncomfortable was an accident of nature. She said that when she conducted an interrogation she was simply listening carefully and trying to gauge the other person's candidness. She had learned to adopt a completely flat aspect. "I just go blank and ask polite questions," she once told Benson. "No matter what kind of hooey or outrageous lies they utter, I don't react, just keep looking straight at 'em and nodding. For some damn reason, it gets most people really upset."

Now, she and Benson were talking to the reporter while the photographer was using a minimally intrusive small digital camera with flash. Benson said: "Ms. Iphigene Seldon, owner of Cedar Lodge, was killed tonight sometime between nine and ten o'clock. Initial indications are that she was struck by lightning during the storm. We're investigating, but there's nothing else . . ."

"That's not what we heard," interrupted Jennifer Libby, who was on her own private fast track to get out of Waterville and onto a big-city rag. "We've been getting calls and emails from people inside the lodge that someone suspects that murder is possible."

Jennifer masked her wolverine instinct under a pretty face and a constant light-bulb smile.

"Oh? And who would that someone be?" Benson said. He'd run into this woman before. She was damned insistent, he remembered, but not nearly so rude as some others.

"I can't give you names," Jennifer said. "They asked me not to. They said a crime scene tent had gone up and that forensics people were here."

"Standard procedure," Benson said.

Jennifer gestured toward the parking lot, where the white tent was being folded up by the two technicians. "Sheriff, do you deny that you're conducting a murder investigation?"

Fortunately, Benson thought, Gene's body had already been put in a black mortuary bag and placed in the department's forensic van. That would've made some uncomfortable pictures. "As I said, standard procedure. Now, you'll have to excuse us. We're real busy right now."

As he and Tom walked back toward the lodge, Benson smiled and said, "Just that 'standard procedure' line will give her enough room to fatten out a thriller for the front page without me committing to anything." When they got back to the kitchen door, Benson leaned inside and gestured for Caleb and the Godwins to come outside. When they were all gathered, Benson said:

"OK, Tom, tell us the gruesome facts."

"The pathologist says a lightning strike seems unlikely but he can't commit to anything before an autopsy. I believe you definitely can rule out lightning. Only an accelerant, in my estimation, could've caused the flames to persist and burn flesh down to the bone in some places. I sniffed around the ground and so did the others, but I couldn't detect any gasoline."

Six said, "Could it have been one of those things people squirt on their cookout coals?"

"Well, yeah," Tom answered, "it could've been most anything like that. But the fire would've burned off the odor." She was surprised that Benson would include the two professors in a police conference, but, then, maybe it was a good idea. Who knew? She was anything but a rigid, by-the-book officer, which made her a good match for Benson and Caleb, who operated on common sense and openness to ideas.

"What about lab work?" Benson said.

"Naturally I'm hoping they'll pick up any accelerant trace in the clothes, what's left of them, but I doubt if that's gonna happen. Despite the extensive destruction of the body, an autopsy probably can still turn up anything unusual internally or whether the victim had been injured before the fire."

Six said, "Can it tell whether Gene was dead or alive when she was set on fire?"

Tom blew out her breath. "Prob'ly not."

Six winced and Alicia shut her eyes. "Jesus," Caleb muttered. In his mind he let loose a silent scream.

"There's another thing," Tom said.

"Oh?" Benson said.

"That tree next to her body was hit by lightning, all right, but not right there. It had been dragged over from close by, where there was a stump. Now, it was near enough that maybe, just maybe, lightning could've hit the tree and bounced off and hit her, but I seriously doubt it. I believe the tree had been moved after it had been struck. I think it was already lying out there when the victim was killed and the killer dragged it closer to make it look like a lightning death."

"This is a bad one, isn't it?" Caleb said.

"Yes, Caleb," Tom replied. "Yes it is. So. What's next?"

Benson nodded toward the kitchen and said, "We've got a hen house full of chickens. We've got to get to them fast, right now. Do you feel like playing fox?"

"Sure. I'm cool."

"When you got here I told you about the sequence of events before the body was discovered. Do you need to know anything else? What the people are like?"

"Nope. Thanks. You know I like to go in cold. Helps me concentrate on the face and the answers." She turned toward the door, stopped and asked: "Who do I know in there?"

"Well, you know Armand."

"Right."

"Did you know Gene or her nephews and niece?"

"I've heard of Gene Seldon for years. Never met her, or the others."

Benson went through the other names quickly and when he was finished, Tom said:

"Gabreau. I know Bruno Gabreau."

Oh, damn, Benson thought. Tom Barclay had never, as far as he knew, said a single thing about her private life to anyone in his department, but he got the feeling that she liked men. (Had to be careful on that subject these days.) And this Gabreau was a real beefcake. Tom was a stratosphere above the guy in education, but when it came to sex, he figured, all cats were potential academics in the dark. Benson tried to keep his voice casual as he said,

"Oh? You know this character?"

"Ayuh. I hired him to take me fishing over to Winsokkett Pond last summer."

"He's good is he?"

"Excellent. But he's poor as Job's turkey. Has two ancient boats, rents a shack."

Caleb chuckled. "Well, here lately he's been making a two-backed beast with Gene Seldon's neice, Merrill." He glanced at Benson, who gave him a sour look. "Ahem. Or so we're led to believe."

"That so?" Tom smiled. "Then he'll probably be over to Mid-Maine Marina soon shopping for a new boat. Okay. Let's ruffle some feathers."

As he and Alicia followed the others, Six ducked to get his head under the door jam and whispered to his wife, "This is kind of weird, isn't it?"

Alicia whispered back: "Yes, I know. We've lived long enough to become cops."

The first thing the lieutenant noticed when she re-entered the kitchen and had another look around was that no one was sitting close to anyone else. Also, not a one of them was looking at any other person nor was anyone talking. Well—no one except Armand, who smiled and gave her a little flick of his hand. Tense, she thought. Something's up with this crowd. After tragedies people, especially if they were family or lovers or just friends, tended to huddle together for emotional support. Well, she thought... let's open the cellar door and see what scatters.

She told them: "I'm Detective Lieutenant Thomasina Barclay, of the sheriff's staff, and I would like to ask each of you a few questions. We'll get you out of here as fast as we can."

"Bippity boppity boopy."

Tom, careful to maintain her famous blank face, turned toward the speaker, a deeply tanned, handsome man wearing a rumpled khaki fishing shirt. He looked belligerent and drunk. Real Hemingway type, she decided. "And you are, sir?"

"Bippity boppity boopy."

Displaying not one flicker of emotion, Tom said, "Intriguing name, sir." Then she stared at him placidly until finally Brad rolled his eyes, drew in a deep breath, released it noisily, and said:

"I'm Bradley Winship Seldon. I own, as of this very night, one-third of this fishing shack."

Tom heard an intake of breath from one direction and a disgusted grunt from another, but she couldn't tell who made the sounds.

"I'm also drunk. Do you like poetry, Thomasina?"

"I do, Mr. Seldon. Let's discuss that later."

Brad sputtered with laughter but Tom simply regarded him placidly and said, "Then you are a nephew of the woman who was killed here tonight? Ms. Iphigene Seldon? Is that correct?"

"Good work, Thomasina."

"Lieutenant, if you don't mind."

"Lieutenant, if you don't mind," Brad shot back.

A smirky giggle erupted from the big-haired woman flashing her breasts from a partially unbuttoned shirt. Oh, crap, Tom thought—right from the git-go I get these buggers. This reaction, needless to say, didn't register even as an eyelid blink on the detective's calm face. She stared at the woman for about ten beats, eliciting a flip of the hair and curl of the lip.

"And you are, ma'am?"

"Renee Ranger . . . Seldon. Soon to be former wife of the comedian." She leaned over and glanced down the counter at Brad, giving him an exaggerated wink.

Mr. and Mrs. Sunshine, Tom thought, but she said: "Mr. Seldon, can you please tell me your movements during the storm and the subsequent blackout?"

"I was playing with my instruments."

Renee giggled again. No one else, Tom noticed, seemed to think Bradley was funny. Two seats away from him the woman who had been crying just stared miserably down at the counter and the red-haired man on the other side of Bradley kept his eyes closed and his arms folded across his chest.

Her voice level and neutral, Tom said, "Could you explain that, Mr. Seldon?"

"My wevver—my weather instruments. Up in my room. I was studying them while I, uh, had cocktails. It was cocktail hour when the storm hit and I wanted to, uh, hmmm, monitor . . . yes, monitor its progress."

"Couldn't you have looked out the window?"

"Christ, Lieutenant Thomasina—the windows were shuttered. How long you been around here?"

Tom ignored his remark and turned to stare at Renee for about fifteen seconds. Renee refused to play who-blinks-first and studied the ceiling.

"Ms. . . . Ranger? Seldon?"

"Ranger will do."

"Could you please tell me where you were during the storm and blackout?"

Renee performed a little cute-cheerleader parody with her head cocked to one side, a forefinger on her cheek and her eyes slanted upward. "Hmmm. Oh, YES, of course. Now I remember. I was in the bar for just the longest time, drinking with . . . oh, I don't know who. But I got bored and left. All those fishermen talking about their big ones." She looked at Tom and simpered. "You know how they are."

Tom's big blues studied the overtly sexed-up Renee for a few beats and then, never modulating her voice beyond a pleasant monotone, said, "Yes, I do, Ms. Ranger. I'm a fisherman and I certainly like to boast about my big ones."

Armand burst into laughter then turned away quickly and clamped a hand over his mouth. How could he help himself? Tom's buxomness was something one noticed either right after or right before one noticed her amazing eyes. Benson bit his lip and Caleb got intently interested in the ceiling, thinking again what a treat it was to watch Tom work. Renee studied her bright red fingernails and faked disinterest. Tom noticed that the large senator-looking guy in the back was chuckling.

"Did you leave the bar before the blackout, Ms. Ranger?"

"Why yes I did, as a matter of fact. I was in my room when the lights went out."

"Very well. Did you see the deceased in the bar before the blackout? And did you speak with her?"

"No, I didn't speak to her, but I certainly heard her. Actually, you could've heard her on the third floor."

"She was shouting?"

Renee smirked at Tom. "She had a voice that could scare a dead moose."

"Intriguing description, Ms. Ranger."

"She was bragging about killing a bear and all the drunks were lapping it up. Like I said, I got bored, went up to my room."

"Did you go anywhere else other than the bar and your room during the storm and blackout?"

"No, I did not go anywhere else. Why should I?" Renee snapped. She was sick of this slab-faced bitch harassing her.

Only Merrill knew Renee's answer was a lie, but in her present state of mind she didn't give a damn what Renee said, or what anybody said about anything. What difference did it make? Bruno had murdered Gene, and she was terrified. She was an accessory to the murder of her own aunt, and she sure as hell wasn't going to say anything about her encounter with Renee on the back porch while Bruno was setting up the burned tree. And now this creepy woman cop was going to stare at her with those strange, accusing eyes. She knew that Bruno was sitting at the counter behind her—she had made sure to sit where she didn't have to look at him. She couldn't look at him; she never wanted to look at him again.

Merrill had loathed the very sight of her aunt, and had wanted her dead, had prayed for Gene to die; but now, oh dear God now, she was looking back with horror at the great abyss between wanting to kill and actually killing; an abyss with no return bridge—the burned corpse being transported to the Thayer Medical Center in Waterville was a merciless reality.

But there was one small mercy, at least for now—the cocaine she had inhaled before coming down to the kitchen—and she'd taken a big hit—was, just this moment, coursing its anodyne way throughout her fevered brain. Ahh, yes. Yes. So much better. For the first time since she'd sat down, Merrill looked up from the counter's surface and around the kitchen. Suddenly she saw things as they really were—she hadn't killed Gene; she had not burned her body. Time would heal her conscience; Gene had been evil. Meantime, there was no way the sheriff or this female deputy would ever find out that Bruno was the killer. I'm certainly not going to betray anything, I feel fine now, I feel cool. And Bruno ... he'll just stare back at the woman with his black eyes. She hated Bruno now, but she knew he would never break. He was too tough.

Tom noticed that the crying woman was now dry-eyed and peering around the room. She had russet-colored hair and a sprinkling of freckles like Bradley, and their facial structures were similar. Had to be the sister. She glanced at the list—Merrill. Studying her, she realized Merrill was a beauty—no artifice, no makeup or any of the other standard crap used by a woman like Renee, just natural beauty. She looked like she lived on the water. Of course, Tom suddenly remembered—on her day of fishing with Bruno Gabreau last summer he'd described brother and sister guides who lived on Willow Pond. Merrill was a fishing guide, one of the best,

Gabreau had said. Was that before or after he had started bedding down with her, Tom wondered. And if they were lovers, why wasn't he sitting beside her?

Uh-oh. Something was wrong. Now Merrill was looking straight at her, Tom, and smiling rapturously. She was either nuts or drugged.

"You are Merrill Beauchamp?" Tom asked, returning Merrill's gaze.

"Hmmm?"

"You are Merrill Beauchamp?"

"Oh yes," she drawled dreamily. "Yes, that's me."

Stoned to the eyebrows, Tom concluded. She must have taken a hit before she came in. Coke, probably. Could be grass, although marijuana's harsh smell tended to persist even if the smoker stood in a stiff wind. Tom could smell a lit spliff two blocks away, and she detected no familiar odor now.

"Perhaps you heard what I asked your brother and Ms. Ranger. Where were you during the storm and the blackout?"

"Where was I?" Merrill's head lolled to one side as her smile widened. "Ohh, I don't know, I wasn't anywhere that I remember." She chuckled softly. "That's right—I wasn't anywhere."

Oh, brother, Tom thought. She's out for the night. "Thank you, Ms. Beauchamp."

Merrill's dumb show amused Renee and Huntley, both of whom laughed and smirked in her direction. Just who was that big, fleshy guy? Tom wondered, once again going down the list of names in her hand. She indicated the three male names as she leaned over and whispered to Benson, "Who's his lordship?"

Benson drew her closer to him and pointed to Huntley's name. "Merrill's husband," he whispered. "They're separated. Robertson Weller's in bad shape. We'll get him tomorrow, and Jean-Pierre's the little guy in black."

Tom stood up straight and took a bead on Huntley: "And you sir. You are . . . Huntley Beauchamp?"

Tom pronounced it bo-shaump, which delighted Huntley, eliciting from him a rumble of deprecatory laughter. Using the mild but obviously condescending tone he reserved for social inferiors, he said, "Bee-chum, my dear. Bee-chum. Hah-hah. It's pronounced the English way." He was hoping for a reaction, but was annoyed to see that the plump woman cop simply stared back at him, with not a flicker of emotion crossing her implacable face.

For her part, Tom had been insulted at least a hundred different ways during her law-enforcement career. Put-downs rolled off her like rain off a rubber ducky. She studied Huntley as if he were a previously uncatalogued species: Wavy salt-and-pepper hair, tanned but running to jowl, white trousers, loafers with no socks, and a cotton sweater draped over his shoulders. Oh, please, Tom thought. It's roasting in here. She had to admit, though, that the big, wide-shouldered guy had probably been a hottie in his youth.

"Excellent—Bee-chum. Thank you. Are you a guest at the lodge?"

Huntley's amused laughter rolled across the counters. "Oh, no, my dear Lieutenant Barclay . . ." (well, Tom reflected, at least he gave me a title) ". . . I am, somewhat loosely defined, you understand, a member of the family. I am the investment adviser for Cedar Lodge Enterprises and I am, ahem, married to Ms. Seldon . . . uh, Merrill. We have found that we, are, um, hah-hah, no longer compatible."

Oh for the love of Mike, Tom thought. She glanced at Merrill, who was looking around like Alice observing giant butterflies.

"We are, hah-hah, legally separated, you see."

"So you do not live here at the lodge?"

"Oh, no, no, not by any means, hah-hah. I came here this weekend to advise Iphigene on some financial matters. However, now that she, uh. . . . ahem, the situation has of course tragically changed." Huntley put on his best shocked-and-saddened face. "I am terribly shocked and saddened, Lt. Barclay. I was very fond of Ms. Seldon as a business colleague . . . and, uh, mmm, of course as a mother-in-law."

Phony bastard, Brad thought. *Liar, creep*, Kipper whispered to himself. Merrill wasn't hearing anything.

"Now, Mr. Beauchamp, where were you during the storm and power outage?"

"Ahh, yes, well." Huntley uncrossed then recrossed his legs, carefully hitching up his trousers by the crease. "I was drinking with all the others in the barroom during the course of the storm. Nothing else to do, actually. I was there when the lights finally went out for good but I stayed and joined in the singing, lending a good baritone, if I do say so myself, hah-hah, to the songs that I knew." Which was another lie. Huntley had been angry and frightened at that point in the evening as he cautiously stalked Colin and Daphne, hoping that they would reveal themselves as his mysterious rescuers. He couldn't have croaked out one bar of a song. "I was still there when Brad came in to announce that Gene had been struck by lightning."

Let's get jumping, Tom told herself. She turned abruptly toward Jean-Pierre, who visibly flinched under her glare. What an improbable little man, Tom thought. Almost doll-like. Put a cross-dressing outfit on him and you'd have a woman.

"Jean-Pierre LeMaire?"

"Oui!"

"Vous être le chef de cuisine?"

Jean-Pierre's liquid brown eyes widened in surprise. "Oui, Lieutenant!"

Benson and Caleb stared at Tom. The woman was full of little surprises.

"Est-ce que vous avez aimé Iphigene Seldon?"

Jean-Pierre was alarmed. He turned and beseeched Kipper with his eyes. Kipper shook his head ever so slightly. He was conversant enough to know that Tom had just asked Jean-Pierre if he had liked Gene. What the hell was this damn cop doing? Tom saw the exchange between the two men and mentally filed it away.

"Madam . . . Lieutenant . . . je ne sais pas . . ."

Tom said: "That's all right, Mr. LeMaire. I'll soon be running out of college French." She paused and gave Jean-Pierre a tiny smile. "How long have you been chef?"

"Quatre . . . hm, four years."

"Can you think of any reason why anyone would want to kill Iphigene Seldon?"

"Oh, no, no, madam. It is shocking."

Looking quickly over at Kipper, Tom said, "Mr. . . . Kipling Seldon? Correct?"

"Yes. Kipper." He refused to engage Tom's high-caliber eyes.

Tom studied him: Red hair as contrasted with his siblings' auburn tones and much more extensively freckled than they were. His face was pleasant rather than handsome. Though just now that face was unsurprisingly sullen.

"Mr. Seldon, did you speak with your aunt during the course of the storm and blackout?"

"I did not. Jean . . . Mr. LeMaire and I served the guests cold meats and salad. I had let the cooks and the waiters leave early before the storm arrived. I saw Aunt Gene during dinner but did not speak with her. After that, I had *no* desire to spend my evening with a crowd of drunken fishermen, so I worked on my computer up in my room. Until the power went out, of course."

"Can *you* think of any reason at all why anyone would want to kill your aunt?"

Kipper's slight hesitation was just enough to grab Tom's notice. "No! Of course not."

"Now . . . let's see . . ." Tom looked up at the overhead lights for a few seconds then slowly lowered her gaze to Bruno. "Mr. Gabreau." Pause. "You are a guest at the lodge?"

Bruno played Tom's game. He folded his arms across his chest and stared at her without answering, his dark face emotionless. He remembered Tom from last summer, though he had had no idea at the time that she was a detective. Now here she was grilling them like she was some tough cop on *Law & Order*. It disgusted him. To Bruno, women police officers were an aberration of nature.

"Mr. Gabreau?"

"I'm here by invitation."

"Of . . ."

"Merrill Seldon." Well, Tom reflected—no peepin' and a hidin' there. She glanced at Merrill, but Merrill wasn't paying attention;

she was still looking around at something none of the others could see.

"I'll ask the same question I asked the others: Where were you during . . ."

"Boozing."

"And did you . . ."

"No, I didn't speak to Gene and no, I don't know who killed her."

"You're very decisive, Mr. Gabreau."

"Ayuh. Always."

Tom turned abruptly and focused on Brad. "Mr. *Bradley* Seldon, can you think of anyone who would've wanted to kill your aunt?"

Brad laughed. "Can I—oh, wow, Lieutenant Thomasina. How many do you want? Four, five, six?"

Tom was caught off guard and she could feel her normally controllable face register the surprise. Damn it, she thought. Now what? "And they are?" she asked, making certain her voice did not betray her astonishment.

"Find out for yourself. We're all here in this room."

Eighteen

"That was as strange a thing as I've seen," Tom said. "He accused everyone else of wanting Gene Seldon dead and *then* put himself at the top of the list."

"And then promptly denied he did it."

"Naturally."

Following Brad's remarkable declaration, a cacophony of angry denials had erupted from Renee, Kipper, Jean-Pierre, Bruno and Huntley, with Brad drunkenly laughing at them as they raged. Merrill had turned to stare at him vacantly, struggling to understand what all the fuss was about. Armand had simply frowned and begun a furious mustache twisting.

"Oh, no, my dear lieutenant-if-you-don't-mind," Brad had said, "there's a big difference between fantasizing murder and actually committing it, isn't there?"

"But you admit that you wanted your aunt to die?" Tom had asked.

"Admit? I *admit* it? C'mon Thomasina, I didn't suddenly collapse under your intimidating grilling. I volunteered my guilty thoughts, didn't I?"

At that point Kipper, red-faced and shaking, had spat out, "Yes, and you volunteered the rest of us, you dirty bastard. . . . Didn't you?" he had added, mocking Brad.

But Brad had kept ranting: "Gene hated our mother and father, she hated us, and she was cruel. She had all of us nailed to this place."

And Kipper had shouted, "Shut up, Brad! I did not kill Gene, and neither did Merrill! Why don't *you* drop dead!"

Kipper's angry shouting had jarred Merrill from her funk, and she had begun crying again. Tom had been intrigued to observe that Jean-Pierre also had begun to cry, placing his hands over his face.

After another forty-five minutes, with the family members in an emotional turmoil and with Tom making no headway against the implacable denials of everyone except Armand that they had not been anywhere near Gene, Benson had called a halt.

Now, after the others had cleared out, he sat in the kitchen with Tom, Caleb and the Godwins. Tom said, "Brad's a tough SOB. Is he always like that?"

"He's always drunk," Six told her.

"I think he's a little deranged," Alicia said. "And Gene told us Merrill was on cocaine."

"Oh, yeah, that's gotta be a definite," Tom said. "She was really floating around in there tonight. But why do you think Brad's deranged?"

Alicia looked thoughtful. "Well, perhaps deranged is too strong a word. He's usually somewhat acerbic and disagreeable because of the alcoholism, but I was thinking about his obsessive fear of storms. That's what Gene told us. She said he won't ever go out in a storm, and has his rooms full of weather instruments—he always wants to know if one's coming."

"Good lord," Tom said. "The *stud* is afraid of storms? The mind reels."

"Yeah, I know it seems ridiculous," Six said, "but there's a reason. Brad, Merrill, Kipper—they really loved their parents, Reg and Annice. We knew them. Lovely people, very charming. About, oh, nearly twenty years ago, they were killed together by lightning while standing in their boat at the dock. Brad was first on the scene and then dragged back his sister and brother before they could look. Reg and Annice, from what Gene told us, were badly burned. Apparently Brad was so affected by the sight of his parents dead and burned that he turned to booze after that and never stopped. And he's scared as hell of lightning. Definitely won't go outside in a storm."

Tom was intrigued. "That is totally wild. I mean, considering what happened tonight . . ."

Six began fumbling in his various pockets for his pipe and tobacco pouch, which were never in the *same* pocket, he thought wonderingly; often, pipe, pouch and lighter were in three separate pockets. *Ah, well.* As he began stuffing tobacco into the pipe bowl he realized that the others were watching him intently. He looked embarrassed. "Oh. Sorry. Does anyone mind?"

No one minded, and Benson said, "Believe I'll join you." He fished around in his inside jacket pockets and located two cigars. "Anyone else?" he asked, waving them about.

There were no takers, so he lit up just as Six released an impressive nimbus of smoke from his pipe.

"Reg and Annice had not made a will," Six continued once he'd stoked the pipe sufficiently. "When they got killed then Gene got complete ownership. The three children had never liked Gene, but when she inherited what they believed was rightfully theirs—can't really fault them on that, I reckon—they loathed her. They had grown up at Cedar Lodge, had never known any other life but here, and never knew how to do anything except fish. So they were trapped. Gene paid them big salaries, making them employees in their own home, you might say. She told them she'd disinherit any one of them who left Cedar Lodge. They couldn't walk away from an inheritance that would give them each more than ten million dollars."

"Never had such a perplexing problem myself," Tom said. "So they were hanging on, waiting for her to die."

"Ayuh. Only Gene seemed healthy as a moose and looked to be having a long span."

"Did they go to college?"

Benson said, "Oh, they went to college, didn't they, Six?"

Six blew away the smoke wreathing his head and said: "Yep. Brad and Merrill went to Colby. Alicia and I remember when they were college kids. They loved their parents and the lodge so much that they didn't want to go away to school. Kipper was a freshman when the parents died. He dropped out of school, went totally into a ditch with drugs."

"But he must've pulled out of it at some point."

"Well, now, that's a peculiar thing. According to Gene, she was the one who rescued him, got him dried out, sent him back to

Colby, then taught him how to manage the lodge. She told us she tried to love him like a son and was enraged when he asked for his part of the inheritance so he could move to New York and set up Jean-Pierre with his own restaurant."

"You know," Tom mused, "I've got a real ugly thought about all this. Maybe it's occurred to the rest of you."

Benson said, "Don't hold back."

"Well, lightning killed the parents and burned them badly. To-night, Gene Seldon gets killed and her body is burned. If it wasn't lightning—and we're almost sure of that—then it looks like some-one could be making a vengeful statement."

"What kind of black-hearted person would do that?"

Alicia said, "Tongue nor heart cannot conceive nor name thee!"

"Ma'am?" Benson said.

"Oh. Line from Macbeth." Alicia looked embarrassed at throwing in erudition. "Sorry."

"Don't be sorry," Tom said. "Perfect description."

Alicia suddenly pulled at Six's arm. "Six! All this has reminded me of something. I forgot it and so did you. When you called for help, right after you found Gene, you said it was Brad who ran up to you."

Six grimaced and squeezed his eyes shut. "God, yes. How could I have forgotten?"

Alicia turned to Tom. "Brad was the one who came into the bar in the dark and told Armand to go out back. He came up right next to me—I could tell he was wet. Brad had been out in the storm when he heard Six shouting."

"But maybe he'd been on the porch when he heard Six calling out," Benson said.

"No, no . . . wait a minute," Six said. "I remember now. I was crying for help and then I heard a voice shouting, 'Who's there, who's there?' And then I saw him—didn't know it was Brad at first—coming from the eastern end of the parking lot, from behind the cars."

"I guess we'll have some questions for him in the morning," Caleb ventured.

Six knocked out pipe ashes on his shoe heel and said: "Kinda looks that way."

* * *

Benson drove with Tom sitting beside him and Caleb in the back as they traveled east across 225 at one-thirty in the morning; the occasional set of eyes shining in the headlights indicated that night creatures were on the move.

Tom turned around as far as the harness would permit so that she could see both men while she spoke. "Tell me something. If Brad Seldon is always drunk, then how the hell can he, as advertised, be one of the best fishing guides in the state?"

"It's the damnedest thing, ain't it?" Benson replied. "I don't know how he does it. And I wonder if Merrill gets coked when she takes people out."

"They're a real pack of rascals, aren't they?"

"What did you think about Brad ratting out everybody in the room?"

Caleb said, "You know, I'm thinking he might've created all that commotion just to throw suspicion off himself."

Tom looked at him and said, "That's a damn good point, Caleb. He might be doing just that. *Damn* good point."

Her words pleased Caleb more than she could ever have imagined. Caleb had carried a secret yearning for Det. Lt. Barclay for years but was terrified of ever saying anything to her. She was a superior officer, a detective—damn smart one, too—a criminology professor, and . . . Well, God knows what else she was. Nevertheless, Caleb just couldn't help himself. To him, she was a drop-dead attractive big woman and he was a big man and he was hankering for a mate of size. This, he often ruminated, must be love, but he sure as hell wasn't going to do anything stupid, such as suddenly blurting it all out to Tom. Being a man of self-discipline, Caleb was going to keep a lid on it until . . . well, until that magic something or other simply happened and guided her into his life. Hope springs eternal, he thought, an expression that had tickled him ever since the time he'd seen a cartoon of a woman named Hope leaping about in a vast meadow.

"Deer!" Tom cried out.

Benson hit the brakes. The deer stepped from the trees and halted on the right shoulder of the road. Her head flicked toward the car, her eyes shining in the lights, and then she turned and shot back into the woods.

Tom was deep in thought for awhile as Benson regained speed. Then she said, "I didn't do so good with that bunch."

"You handled them fine," Benson told her. "Don't see how you could've done it better, but . . ."

"But I didn't get a damn thing out of them," Tom finished. "None of them knew anything, saw anything—none of them talked to Gene Seldon during the storm and blackout, and not a one of them would ever have laid a dainty finger on her. Heavens!"

From the back, Caleb laughed and said, "You know every one of them was telling one or more lies."

"That's a real hothouse there," Tom replied. "Too damn many attractive people stuffed into an explosive situation. I could've done with just one or two ugly ones."

"Well, Armand's big but he ain't pretty," Caleb said.

"Oh, he's all right, but I wasn't really including him. I mean, we've known the guy for years, and can you imagine him ever doing such a thing as burning someone to death?"

"It does defy common sense, I'll say that," Benson said.

"He was in a couple of rude fights a few years ago," Caleb offered, "and I had to run him in on one of them. But I honestly cannot see him doing this." Plunging back into the moment, he said, "We're on the hotdog grill for this one, aren't we?"

"Ayuh," Benson said. "It's the worst damn thing I've been faced with since I first became a deputy. We own it, and we've got to make an arrest. No way out of it." He sighed deeply. "I sometimes wonder why I gave up being a fish and game warden."

"For the big bucks?" Caleb said.

"Oh yeah. Yeah, I forgot about that. The county payroll is just a real cornucopia, isn't it?" He was silent for a minute and then said, "Just think about it. We had a killer right there in that kitchen. A really evil bastard, too. It has to be one of them, don't you think?"

"It seems like it must be, although prudence would dictate that we consider someone among the people staying at the lodge. I don't think that's the case, but . . . well, you never know."

"You're right, Tom. We do have to do just that. I'm just worried as hell, thinking about all that crowd of people horsing around during the storm, sneaking around during the blackout. I'm just hoping to narrow the field. Tomorrow morning we'll talk to them in a group, then get complete contact information from each of them. Could be someone there from Gene's past, some long ago rage that's been festering."

"Or maybe some business deal," Caleb said. "Think about that. Didn't Mr. Godwin say Cedar Lodge was worth forty-eight million?"

"Damn good point, Caleb," Tom said, turning to smile at him. "We need to talk further with Huntley Beee-Chump. What a piece of work. I didn't know people talked like that outside of movies."

"He's a right pain in the ass, Tom," Caleb told her, warming to the subject. Privately, he was thinking that if Tom paid him one more compliment he was going to get aroused.

"Also, we've got that lawyer who was coming to the family conference," Benson said. "We need to confirm this change in her will. Six and Alicia said Gene told them she was giving Kipper a controlling interest, fifty-five percent, but I'd like to see all the details."

Benson slowed and stopped the squad car as they came to the intersection of roads 11 and 8 north. "Look there!" Tom said.

To their right, barely visible in the moonlight, two foxes slipped along in the weeds bordering a wooden fence.

Benson suddenly recalled a much-loved song from his childhood. To the astonishment of Tom and Caleb, he began singing:

"Oh, the fox went out on a chilly night,
He prayed for the moon to give him light . . ."

* * *

"Sweet Jesus," Six said, taking off his socks, balling them up and throwing them somewhere. Who cares where they land, he thought. He was in a mood. The vision of Gene's hideously burned head kept appearing repeatedly in his mind. Now, sitting on the edge of the bed, exhausted and bewildered, his soul (his agnostic left or right side of the brain; which was it?—often wondered if there was a soul, but the other side insisted that there must be) burdened by the confrontation with heartless savagery, he remembered that cell phone call from Gene only days before as if he'd been Agamemnon taking a call from Cassandra. It seemed that long ago.

He was down to his undershorts and ready for bed, but despite his exhaustion he was worried that sleep wouldn't come. Thank God he had Alicia, his port of love in any storm. He watched her undressing and thought how wonderful she still looked despite time's corporeal ravagings. Had this been a normal weekend, a normal night away from home, which usually inspired arousal in most couples of any age, they would've been up to their old tricks; under the current dreadful circumstances, all thoughts of pleasure seemed indecent.

Alicia came to sit beside him. "Oh, Six, this is just the awfulest, awfulest thing." Her eyes filled with tears as she lay her head on his shoulder. "Who could've imagined such evil? I still can hardly believe it. We were with her, right beside her, most of the evening, and then for her simply to go outside and be murdered—*destroyed*—in such a horrifying way, it just . . . oh, dear God."

"Yes. I'm having a hard time taking it in."

"And you were the first to see her. My poor boy. How terrible."

"Never want to see a thing like that again."

"What are we going to do tomorrow?"

"Benson told me that if we didn't have to hurry back he'd appreciate it if we sat with the rest of the lodge guests when he and Tom and Caleb question them. Thought maybe we might hear or see something. Or just stick our oar into the Q and A. How's that sound to you?"

"Oh, of course. We have to help if we can," Alicia said. "Are we still cops?"

"Reckon we are. We can go back home tomorrow afternoon or evening." They were silent for a few minutes until Six said, "You know, kiddo, there's already some damn thing nagging at the edge of my brain. Something . . . oh, I don't know. It's as if I've forgotten something important I should've told Benson. Perhaps it was something I heard or saw. My synapses are starting to sputter with age."

"You'll think of it, my old boy. I'll tell you what I think."

"Whassat?"

"I have an uneasy feeling we're in for a big shock when the killer is found. It's going to be awful, I just know it. And he's here, Six, here somewhere in this lodge."

"Yep. Got to be. Benson posted a pair of deputies to block the road and there's no boats in the water, so unless the murderer is desperate enough to strike out through the woods then he's still here in the henhouse, as Benson called it."

* * *

Following the interrogation by Lt. Barclay, Merrill, though still stoned, had rallied herself to action and groped her way out of the kitchen and up the stairs as fast as she could manage. By the time a worried Bruno arrived at the door to their room, he found the door locked and his suitcase and clothes on the hallway floor.

He rapped on the door and said, "Merrill. *Merrill.* Please open up. I've *got* to talk to you." He waited. Silence. Goddamn the bitch, he thought. This was getting serious. In her state of mind she might spill out everything to the sheriff and that detective.

"Merrill!" He rapped again, harder. "Merrill, for God's sake let me talk to you!"

A door opened down the hall and the large face of an annoyed fisherman glared at him. Bruno gathered his things and went in search of a place to bed down.

* * *

Jean-Pierre trembled, tears running down his cheeks, his hands tightly clasped before him, as he sat on the edge of a chair and watched Kipper, who was drinking gin and getting into an ugly mood. Kipper was only an occasional drinker, so the gin was hitting him hard.

"You frighten me, Kee-*pair*," he said.

Kipper made a noise of disgust. "Oh, give me a break."

"You are acting so different. You are acting so . . . mad."

"I'm mad at my eff-ing brother, not you, my little darling. I'd like to kill the arrogant bastard."

"No, no, no. Please do not say these things. I am afraid that you murder Gene."

"Damn it, Jean-Pierre! We've been all through this. I'll repeat it for the umpty-umpth time—I did not kill the old . . ." His voice trailed away and he knocked back more gin.

"But I hear you say you are doing something to make us free."

"I. DIDN'T. KILL. HER!" Seeing Jean-Pierre flinch, Kipper softened his face and said, "Look, my dear little frog. I love you, and now we are free. The wicked witch is dead. We are free to do whatever we want."

Jean-Pierre eased back into the chair and closed his eyes, but he could not stop trembling.

* * *

Huntley was getting nervous again. The "creative" spreadsheets on the dummy corporations had been skillfully integrated into the Cedar Lodge Enterprises financial statements, Iphigene

Seldon was quite conveniently dead and the planned Sunday family conference was obviously moot, but Huntley nevertheless felt an urgent desire to put some long miles between himself and Cedar Lodge. Gene's ferreting old bastard of a lawyer would be poking his snout into everything. If he looked long enough and deep enough, the situation could become very tense for Beauchamp Portfolio Investments Inc. And now there was this goddamn fat-ass cop on the scene acting like a "CSI: Miami" wannabe. She made Huntley distinctly uneasy. That whole scene in the kitchen was an ugly surprise. He thought rural Maine would produce nothing more intimidating than some beef-brained Andy Griffith sheriff in a big hat. Instead, the Somerbec County officers looked and acted more like businessmen wearing gunbelts; and then up jumps a detective. A *detective*, for crissake. He didn't know county sheriffs *had* detectives. He did *not* like the way Det. Lt. Thomasina Barclay looked at him. Those eyes. During those moments when her eyes had locked remorselessly onto his, Huntley Beauchamp had felt Jack Spurling squirming inside him. It was all he damn needed to have the lawyer *and* the detective sniffing around for the scent of a money trail.

Now, Canada once more occupied Huntley's thoughts as an attractive destination. Not that he feared anything imminent. For the nonce, all bases were covered. True, he still owed the "discreet businessman" three-quarters of a mil, but that would easily be covered by the sale of his apartment and boat. No, there was nothing frighteningly imminent such as a knee-capping or whatever it was hoods used these days as a collection technique. He simply wanted to take a little vacation until the investigative smoke cleared. He had about a hundred thou running money and he could run Beauchamp Portfolio from his laptop. Then, once Cedar Lodge and environs returned to normal, he could grant Merrill a divorce and get his $1.5 million reward. After that . . . another city, another fresh start for the silver-tongued devil.

* * *

Renee paced the porch outside her room, unable to sleep. Anxiety, in the form of the sheriff's department and its goddamn scary detective, pulled her one way; excitement about her coming life as a wealthy international playgirl pulled her the other. Her fear about the Elavil she'd given Gene turned to relief when she convinced herself that even if the drug were discovered in an autopsy, how would anyone know that she was the one who'd poured it into Gene's glass? The old man had been dead drunk, her back had been turned to Six Godwin, and her sleeve had blocked any possible sighting by Armand or the bar patrons of her hand emptying the lip-blush case.

Smiling to herself, she began plotting her itinerary. Once Brad had exchanged two million dollars for her granting of a divorce, it was first stop Montenegro. The image of herself swanning into the casino wearing the kind of dress Eva Green had worn in Daniel Craig's *Casino Royale* made her warm with unspecific desire. (Maybe, she thought, Nelson Bolston would be up for some more gymnastics tomorrow.) James Bond movies. That's the life she wanted, with those kinds of men and women. Film fantasy and reality were beginning to merge in Renee's fevered but modestly IQ'd imagination. She intended to visit every glamorous location in every Bond movie. After Monte Carlo, London. Then Jamaica. From there it was Miami, for that *Goldfinger* effect. Then Venice, Geneva, Cairo, Istanbul, the list went thrillingly on and on, and for each new destination she would have . . .

Renee was so self-entranced that the lone figure she could see standing at the end of the center dock didn't actually register in her consciousness.

* * *

"Free at last! Free at last! Thank God Almighty, I'm free at last!" Brad said out loud to the river of moonlight streaming across Willow Pond's still waters to where he was standing on the dock. Yes, he knew—it was ridiculous to apply Martin Luther King Jr.'s elegiac cry to his own pathetic life, but the sensation was nonetheless genuine. He was free at last, but was it perhaps too late for sustained joy? Was he free at last only to forever be dragging guilt and remorse behind him?

He had wished Gene dead almost daily. He had prayed to God to strike her dead. But in the end, God had not been needed, only the murderous hand of a person pushed too far by her unyielding control of everyone and everything about her. And now that she *was* dead he wanted to weep. Achieving happiness by another's death now seemed to be the saddest thing in the world. The feeling will pass with time, he told himself, surely the feeling will pass.

I will go away. Kipper and Merrill can manage Cedar Lodge, he decided. Running it and working his ass off every day was the last damn thing on his life list at the moment. If they didn't want to run it, then what the hell, sell it. He wanted his share paid out anyway. Then, with his blessed millions, he could cruise peacefully along for the rest of his years. There would be new women, wonderful women with sunny charm, no more viperous Renees. And there would be new fish in sunny waters. He would cast his line in tropical seas and afterward sit on shady porches and drink. He knew he could never stop drinking. He didn't *want* to stop drinking. Golden-hued bourbon soothed the savage breast and engendered bliss. If it shortened his life, what difference did it make? Who cared? Life extended as the result of dreary days of soul-flattening sobriety held no appeal.

He turned and headed slowly toward the lodge, feeling at last that sleep would come. The next few days would be nerve-wracking. He just had to get past the sheriff and his cold-eyed detective.

* * *

Armand drove south on route 27 toward his humble camp on Long Pond just outside of the village of Belgrade Lakes. He had seen a lot and endured a lot in his fifty-seven years, but he couldn't name anything worse than what had happened on this night. His boss, a woman he'd known for fifteen years, long before he started bartending at the lodge, had been burned up like some animal on a hunter's fire. He'd poured her a drink, the lights had gone out and she had walked outside to a painful, nightmarish death. Maybe she hadn't been alive when she'd been burned. He prayed that was so. Maybe she'd been killed first by a blow to the head or a gunshot.

Meantime, Armand had a problem of his own. He felt he should tell Sheriff Doucette what he'd seen, but he was not at all sure if what he had seen had any significance in Gene's death. He loved Cedar Lodge, he'd liked Gene Seldon, cantankerous old villain that she was, and he was fond of Merrill and Kipper and Brad—especially Brad. The guy was hilarious, and the most amazing fisherman he'd ever seen; and he treated Armand affectionately, like a buddy. Brad's wife, on the other hand, he definitely could do without. How a man like Brad had ever got tangled with a hard case like Renee was beyond him.

It was on Renee that his problem centered.

He had seen the damn woman doing something peculiar at the end of the bar. When Gene had left the room, he'd noticed Renee quickly taking her spot next to Bob Weller and flouncing around and smiling up at him, tossing her hair, doing the whole vamp routine. Armand may've looked and acted like a big, humorous Paul Bunyan, but he was a quietly sharp-witted man, accustomed to reading the myriad natural intimations that made the difference between a good day and a bad one when fishing or hunting. And he had carried that outdoorsman's keen watchfulness into his part-time bartending career, a job that he'd grown to love. He prided himself on seeing nearly everything at once, all the constant movement and hubbub of bar patrons, so that he could usually anticipate when a drinker was going to raise his or her hand in the familiar "Oh, bartender!" gesture.

And that's why he had spotted Renee's unusual movements as she approached Weller. She had swept out her left arm widely, rippling the voluminous material of her sleeve, and then had leaned awkwardly far over on the bar so that her sleeve enveloped Gene's glass of whiskey. Was it simply a dramatic flourish to catch the old man's attention? Armand didn't think so.

When Gene had appeared in the doorway, Renee had darted from the room. And then . . . the moment was blazoned on his mind . . . Gene had downed the whiskey and declared that it "tasted like fish crap."

Armand knew what he saw. It didn't look good. The more he thought about it the more he was convinced that Brad's bitch of a wife had put something into that whiskey.

* * *

Robertson Weller awoke during the morning's wee-est hours to the torment of a barbaric hangover and the horrifying realization that Gene had been murdered. Dear God, how could it be, how could it be? Spears of pain shot from his eyeballs back through his brain, his throat was parched and his lips felt baked together. He smacked his mouth open, gasped and moaned. Must have water. *Water!* He sat up in bed with infinite care but just that slow movement engendered dizziness and nausea. He got over the edge of the bed one leg at a time and summoned the courage to stand. The room rocked and his gorge rose as he stumbled with desperate need toward the bathroom and downed three glasses of water. He doubled over as his stomach cramped but he held on to the sink until the pain passed. Then he downed four extra-strength aspirins with more water and groped his way back to bed. He lay back gingerly and breathed deeply for five minutes until the whirling subsided and the headache eased.

He reviled himself for his self-pitying binge. He had been drunk and useless—passed out on the bar like some proletarian lout—when Gene had been killed. He could have protected her; he could have saved her life. But all he could dwell on at the bar the previous evening was how far down he'd come, a pathetic playboy grown old, his inherited fortune exuberantly (at the time) dissipated on two wives notable for their glamour and narcissism, gran turismo Ferraris and Maseratis, speed boats, airplanes and houses on islands, all of them now just memories in the mist.

That ghastly face he'd just seen in the bathroom mirror, its jowls covered in white stubble, its eyes bagged and its pretty-boy hair gone gray, was that the face of the man who'd made it across the finish line at Sebring and the Monaco Grand Prix? The man who had gone four chukkars against Argentina's polo studs? The country club tennis champ? And how about the golden boy of Andover and Yale, where was he? They were gone, those fellows, leaving behind a battered geriatric with enough money left to pay rent and buy food and booze for six months or so. Because he'd never worked, the old yachtsman had not been thrown a Social Security lifeline. His medical insurer was a high co-pay Scrooge outfit with no hospitalization coverage.

Robertson Lowell Weller was running on silver fox good looks, charm and an aging wardrobe of bespoke coats and trousers and shirts, and a rack of deeply creased handmade shoes. It was marry money or take the revolver from the desk in the study. Only the desk was in the study of the house owned by his second wife. Ah well, he still had the revolver.

And then last year he'd come here to Cedar Lodge, lured by the advertisements that promised excellent fishing and four-star food and . . . rest. Oh, how he'd needed rest following the abandoned, humiliating courtship of a tiresome woman of immense wealth who had, at a party at her oceanside manor, introduced him to her friends as the "hottie I'm buying for my golden years." Having arrived at Willow Pond with the feeling that there would be no gigolo-tempting prospects at a bass-fishing camp on a Maine lake, he had nonetheless, to his delighted astonishment, stepped into gold.

God knows Gene had been no beauty, but she had been a barrel of laughs, Bob now lamented. Yes, she'd been outrageous in many respects, but she'd been a superb sportsman, something Bob had always admired in a woman, and she'd been strong, with the hardest body he'd ever seen on an old bird, and she had been remarkably frisky in matters conjugal. She had also been uncommonly honest and forthright. Love was out of the question, both of them had agreed. Gene told him she wanted a hearty, humorous, good-looking companion who would feed her no bull. If he was what she was looking for, she had told him, then she would give him anything he wanted, with the firm understanding that amorous prowling was out of the question. Bob had told *her* that he didn't want anything, he'd had it all anyway, that he was tired—especially tired of the prowling game—and that all he wanted was for someone to take care of him.

And now all that was gone in an instant of murderous violence. A goddamnable fiend had killed her and burned her. Jesus *Christ,* he thought, how, HOW, could someone do a thing like that? The appalling evil of it was more than he could comprehend.

This was the end of the line, Bob told himself. He was hung over and anguished, and he was coming to a moment of brutal self-assessment: *I'm too old for any more of this.* He knew he could not endure any more romancing of faded beauties dripping with diamonds and pearls. I am exhausted, he realized, physically and existentially; I've made it to this age, a good span of years covering a damned adventurous life, and I refuse to suffer the debasement of poverty.

I have the courage to do one last grand thing, he reassured himself now, rising again from the bed to get more water to quench his maddening thirst. I will kill the brute who killed Gene. And then I will die.

Nineteen

Kipper awoke at five-thirty Sunday morning, just as the gentle blue of predawn brightened toward full light. He felt seedy and slightly ill from too much gin and too little sleep. After Jean-Pierre had crept from the room after their argument, Kipper had tossed about as the night's terrible scenes came rushing back into his unsettled mind. Finally, around three, he had fallen into a deep sleep, only to be roused now, as usual, by his cerebral alarm clock, with no hope of further sleep. He knew he was probably facing a grim and painful day.

Through the open window came nature's daybreak symphony heralding a bright, beautiful day. Out on the lake, loons chattered and gulls squawked, while in the trees nearby finches and warblers and chickadees chirped and twittered.

But Kipper was not comforted. The coming week was bound to be tumultuous. And Jean-Pierre had him worried. His little lover was upset and frightened, but surely he would come round. Now, he thought, our dream can come true. We can go to New York. Once the estate has been settled, we can start a new life together, away from Willow Pond, away forever. *I have been chained to this place all my life. Now I am free.*

Now I am hung over and feeling like crap, he thought. Time to struggle up, get down to the kitchen and knock back some atomic-strength coffee.

He showered and shaved and put on fresh khaki shorts and a polo shirt and slipped into his boating moccasins. Cleanliness effected a mild psychological boost but his head was aching. He dreaded slogging through endless hours of a police investigation concomitant with the unavoidable task of getting the lodge up and running and caring for the needs of its guests.

He walked to the window and looked down at the docks to see if anyone else was stirring this early. Ah, good lad, he thought— over by the west dock, Sam, as Kipper had instructed him last night, was trailering one of their largest bass boats into the water; another was already tied up at the dock. Under the gruesome circumstances probably no one would want to go out on the lake, but he wanted two boats in the water because . . . because why? he asked himself. Because it didn't seem right not to have any boats at all by the docks and ready to go, as per Gene's standing instructions. All boats, she had commanded time and again, must be ready to go instantly, with the keys in the ignition. The day was bright, with a gentle breeze rippling the water. All would be well, he reassured himself; just get through this day and all will be well.

The hail had downed younger trees around the lake; Kipper could see a number had fallen into the water. The area around the docks was free of broken trees but it was littered with debris from the storm, mostly branches and little islands of twigs and what looked like the remains of an unfortunate gull. All that would be easy enough to clean up as there didn't seem to be any logs floating in. Wait a minute—something fairly large was on the shoreline on the far side of the east dock. Something dark . . . it was a . . . person. Was some fool nature lover going into the chilly morning water? And wearing black clothes? *Wearing black. Oh, dear God.* Kipper's heart froze and he gasped—it was not a swimmer, he could see that now. It was a body lying face up. *Jean-Pierre!*

Kipper screamed in terror and charged from the room to the stairs, taking them two and three at a time, crying and shouting, "No, no!" He made it to the second floor, scrambled around to the next staircase and hit it full speed; halfway down he tripped, twisted his right ankle and tumbled onto the floor of the front lobby, where he lay writhing and whimpering, "Jean-Pierre! Oh, God, no, oh please no." He crawled to the newel post and pulled himself up. As he stepped forward, burning pain shot through his ankle; he shrieked and crumpled to the floor again. Crawling toward the front door, he screamed as loud as he could: "Help! Somebody help!"

Sam pounded up the porch steps and appeared in the doorway, shocked to see Kipper crawling and screaming.

"Sam!" Kipper gasped, gesturing toward the east. "The dock, the last dock, down there!" Sam looked that way, hesitated, causing Kipper to shout, "Quickly, Sam—please get there!"

Sam ran to the east dock until he saw the body at the end; he stopped abruptly and gaped, his legs weakening at the sight. He turned back toward the front door and saw Kipper on his knees screaming, "Help him, Sam! Help him!" Sam took a deep breath, stepped forward to the body and looked down into the dark, sightless eyes of Bruno Gabreau.

* * *

"Oh, sonofabitch, sweet sonofabitch," Benson groaned. Caleb was driving as he and the sheriff, with Tom Barclay seated in back, sped west across the all-too-familiar stretch of 225 toward 27 north with the siren on and dome lights flashing. Caleb loved tearing through the countryside in a howling squad car. It satisfied his need for occasional pulse-quickening adventure. Of course, he reflected, pulse-quickening most likely was going to be the order of the day judging by the frantic 911 call that had come in at 6:27 a.m.

"This is so bad," Benson continued. "This is so goddamn bad. Are we going to have to call in the state troopers? What the hell is happening at that place?"

"Ayuh," Caleb said, "it's a right horror. Bruno Gabreau dead in the water."

Benson craned his head around toward Tom. "What do you think, Tom? Suicide maybe? He killed Gene and then couldn't take it?"

"Could be," Tom replied. "Thing is, I wouldn't have judged Gabreau to be hampered by an emotion like guilt. I think he is— was—cold and hard. I mean, this is just me reacting to two days' fishing with the guy last year and then seeing him last night. If he was murdered, which is most likely—what kind of accident could he have had?—then we can suppose that the same person who killed Gene Seldon killed him. The thing is . . . why?"

"He saw the killer in action," Caleb said.

"Exactly," Tom confirmed.

"If that's true," Benson said, "why didn't he tell us?"

"Scared maybe. Although he didn't seem like he'd scare easily." Tom was thoughtful. "Blackmail attempt?"

An early-bird fisherman hauling a bass boat behind his pickup truck was ahead of them on the road. Caleb added the deafening honkers to the sirens and the truck swerved to the shoulder, the trailer and boat bouncing and lurching.

"Okay," Benson said, "let's see where we are and then form a plan. We've got forensics and an EMS truck on the way, and we've called the pathologist's office. Our two guys on the road say no one has tried to leave the camp. Now. Gabreau's death changes our situation with the paying guests. I don't know what their mood's going to be . . . nothing hysterical probably, knowing fishermen . . . but we've got to deal with them quickly. And then the family—and I'm including Beauchamp, and the chef. LeMaire and Kipper are a pair, right?"

"Yep," Caleb affirmed. "That's what the professors say. Love is where you find it, I reckon."

From the back, Tom said, "Caleb. You're not prejudiced against gays, are you?"

Caleb's face flushed pink. "I most certainly am not." He cleared his throat significantly and added, "I'm a modern man."

Benson turned quickly to the passenger window and suppressed a laugh, while Tom chuckled.

Caleb gripped the steering wheel tightly, disheartened by the sudden and appalling thought that Tom might be a lesbian. He *was* a modern man, he argued to himself. He didn't have a thing in the world against gay men *or* women. He simply didn't want the woman he longed for to be unavailable in so fundamental a way.

Tom said: "Kipper had a knock-down-drag-out with Gene when he begged for his part of the inheritance so he and LeMaire could move to New York. That strengthens him as a suspect— LeMaire, too, I suppose."

"Yeah," Benson said, "and Merrill wanted her third of the money in order to divorce Beachamp. . ."

"Who wouldn't," Tom muttered.

". . . and Brad wanted to dump his wife."

"Again, who wouldn't."

"Like you said—a pack of rascals."

* * *

The EMS truck was already there when Benson and the others pulled into the campground. They walked up to it and found Merrill, hysterical and rocking frantically back and forth, sitting inside while Warren Cobb attempted to inject a sedative into one of her arms, which were jerking spasmodically. Her dilated eyes stared straight ahead, seemingly at nothing.

"Oh, God, no," Merrill crooned. "Oh, God, no, oh please, oh no, what am I going to do? He didn't kill her, he didn't kill her. I thought he killed her."

Warren, making soothing sounds, finally got the needle into Merrill's arm and depressed the plunger; Merrill continued rocking as he taped gauze to her arm. Then turning to Benson, Tom and Caleb, he said, "Trauma. Bad. Totally non compos. The main action is at the far dock. Johnny's down there."

As the trio walked away Caleb said, "Jesus. She believed Bruno killed her aunt."

"Yep. That's just dandy," Benson said. From the sheriff's acerbic tone and the clenching of his jaw, Caleb knew his chief was angry and worried. Caleb was worried, too, and as he glanced at Tom and met her eyes, she moved her head very slightly back and forth, indicating for him not to say anything more. On the trip over, Caleb had been jarred by Benson's anguished cursing and his suggestion that they might need the state police. He admired Benson for his customary calmness, in emergencies especially, and for his common sense and general sensitivity to others under his command. In other words, Caleb would testify in a second, a damn fine sheriff.

But this situation at Cedar Lodge was like nothing the Somerbec team had ever faced. Rural and small-town central Maine was not New York City. Or Los Angeles. Violence here was never a daily occurrence, and vicious, perplexing murders such as these by the shore of tranquil Willow Pond were blessedly few.

As they passed the long front porch, a number of subdued lodgers watched them go by in fascinated silence. Six and Alicia, Brad, the two deputies and Johnny Bolduc solemnly awaited them, and as they neared, stood aside to let them look. Bruno Gabreau, lying in only inches of water, wore black jeans and a black T-shirt; his feet were bare. His face was bloated and blotched and his eyes were open.

"Drowning?" Benson asked.

"Looks that way," Johnny said, "but I don't want to examine him before the pathologist gets here."

"Of course. She's on the way." Benson looked up. "Six, Brad. You OK?"

"I'm all right," Brad answered. "Merrill's in bad shape. Went crazy, screaming like hell, fell down on his body. I dragged her off, held her while she kept screaming and thrashing. Finally, she went limp and flopped down on the ground, wouldn't move."

"Yeah, we just saw her. Warren's sedating her."

"Did you find the body?" Tom asked. She noticed that Brad seemed unsteady. Was the man actually drinking this early in the morning?

Brad's hooded eyes regarded Tom for a few seconds. "Thomasina," he said, barely audible. Then he paused, shrugged. "Lieutenant. No, it wasn't me. Kipper spotted him from his room. Thought it was Jean-Pierre. Twisted his ankle running down the stairs, yelled for Sam, who was putting the boats in. Sam went over to look, then came to get me. I sent him to get your two guys guarding the road and I came down here."

"Where's Kipper now?"

"He's on the couch in the lobby," Johnny told her. "I've got to wrap his ankle. He can't walk."

Six was staring down intently at the shoreline pebbles as if they were displaying a mathematical formula.

"Six?" Benson said. "You got something for me?"

"Ayuh," Six answered, looking up. "Think I do. Merrill and Bruno shared a room . . . but not last night."

"Oh, yeah?"

"One of the lodgers on their floor told me Bruno was pounding on the door and pleading with her to open up. The guy, the fisherman, said he looked out to see about all the racket and Bruno left, dragging his clothes and a suitcase."

"And now Merrill is in the ambulance going crazy, crying that she thought Bruno murdered Ms. Seldon," Benson told him. He looked at Brad. "When she was here"—he pointed down at Bruno's body—"did she say anything to that effect?"

Brad had his eyes closed. Benson raised his voice. "Mr. Seldon!"

Brad blinked to attention. "Yeah?"

"Did your sister, while she was, as you said, falling on Gabreau's body, say anything?"

"Yeah. She kept screaming, 'He didn't kill her, he didn't kill her.' I couldn't control her . . . she's a strong girl. The ambulance guy helped me."

Benson looked back at the ambulance and said, "I don't know if we can get anything out of her."

"Maybe not. But we better try," Tom said.

"Ayuh. 'Spect you're right. Caleb, can you take one of the boys"—he nodded toward the deputies—"and see if you can find Gabreau's suitcase and clothes? We should find out where he spent the night. When you find them, don't touch a thing. We'll want our forensic hounds to sniff it out."

"Will do." Caleb walked over to the two young men, last year's recruits, who were awed by being in the midst of a case that was as bad as anything they'd seen on TV. Like Benson, they had worked for several years for the state's Department of Inland Fisheries & Wildlife as wardens, and the worst they had confronted was a wrestling match to get the cuffs on two drunken hunters who had bagged an out-of-season buck and chasing bass fishermen with over-the-limit catches. Caleb addressed the smaller of the two:

"Billy, come with me. We gotta search the lodge. Eric, stay with the body until the pathologist arrives."

Six walked to the end of the dock, leaving Eric, the deputy, alone with the frightening corpse with its staring eyes, and looked out onto the immensity of Willow Pond, its waters sparkling with sunlight. The day was cloudless. A "bluebird day," some fishermen called this sort of calm, beautiful weather that often follows the day after a chill or a storm, when the fish, for whatever biological determinants, were reluctant to take a lure.

Over the years, Six and Alicia had fished Willow Pond many times, sometimes trailering their boat to a public landing on the western shore, not far from Cedar Lodge, and other times coming here, to the lodge and renting one of the Seldons' gleaming 18-foot bass boats with 75 hp motors that speared through the water and took you within fifteen minutes to the far northern shoreline. They most often went out on their own, without either Brad or Merrill, preferring their own quirky methods of bringing in the big ones and having the pleasure of discovering good spots themselves.

Six longed to be out on the lake now, just him and his kiddo, the two of them casting into bright water, in a world where the horrors of last night and this morning had never taken place.

The memory of Gene's burned face haunted him, and now, at the other end of the dock, was another tragedy. He had not known his Winsokkett Pond neighbor Bruno Gabreau, except by reputation, and for all he knew, as Gene had claimed, the man *had* been a calculating fortune hunter. But he had also been a vibrant, handsome young man and now he was a cold, forlorn corpse. If Bruno's greatest sin had been fortune hunting then it most certainly did not justify his murder.

The appalling possibility that Gene's murderer, by simulating her death as a lightning strike, was making a grotesque statement about the lightning deaths of Reg and Annice so many years before, led Six toward an inevitable thought: If the murder was a "statement," then by logic the perpetrator was among the family and their spouses and lovers. And if that were true, then what about Bruno? How did his murder fit in? He must have seen something or known something, right? Or . . . Six was amazed at his own devious wondering . . . if Bruno *had* killed Gene, as apparently Merrill had believed, then perhaps he could've been killed in retribution. But who would have wanted to exact revenge? As testimony was revealing, Gene—stating the situation harshly—was in everyone's way financially. So who was there to . . .

Of course, Six recalled suddenly. Robertson Weller. They had forgotten about him, the much-overlooked fiancé of Iphigene Seldon.

* * *

Benson and Tom walked back to the EMS truck. Benson said, "Tom, talk to her, will you? I might scare her."

"Oh, yeah? And I won't?"

"Soft feminine voice, Tom, soft feminine voice."

"Right. I'll try to imitate one."

Merrill had ceased rocking. Warren Cobb said, "The sedative has calmed her down, but I think we better get her over to the Thayer emergency room."

Tom climbed up into the truck and sat beside Warren. She was still for a couple of minutes, thinking it best to let Merrill adjust to her presence. Finally, she said, softly, "Merrill? Merrill?" But Merrill didn't move. "Merrill, I'm so sorry about this." Tom was looking into a pair of glassy eyes that began filling with tears.

"He didn't do it," Merrill whispered. "He didn't do it."

Tom glanced at Benson, and then said, "Merrill, can you . . ."

"He didn't kill her." Merrill began rocking again. "He didn't kill her. Oh, no. Oh, no. I thought he killed her." She doubled over, covered her face with her hands and moaned, "Oh, God, what am I going to do. I want to die. Let me die."

Warren said, "Lieutenant . . ."

"Yeah, I know. I'm leaving"

"I gave her a good wallop and she's still like this. I'll sit with her until we can go. Another truck is coming for the body. What's Johnny doing?"

"He's bandaging Kipper Seldon's ankle. Apparently sprained real bad."

"Please tell him that when he's done we need to boogie."

Benson said to Tom as they walked toward the porch, "Jesus. She believed Bruno killed Gene. Right? What else could she be talking about."

"That must be why they quarreled. But *why* did she believe it? It'd be good to know but I don't want to press her and get her more hysterical."

They stepped up onto the porch, Benson looked both ways along its length and, raising his voice, said, "Folks, I'm very sorry about all this, but could you please come here and talk to me?" Everyone obediently moved toward Benson and Tom and when they'd gathered Benson looked at Colin and said, "Hello again, Mr. Trimble."

"Sheriff," Colin replied. "Bad business this."

"Ayuh. Gruesome. I don't know what the hell is going on but we really have to hunker down on this place."

"Oh, and, uh, sheriff . . . this is my wife, Daphne."

Benson nodded and said, "Ma'am."

"We'll help any way we can, sheriff." Daphne said.

Benson looked around at all the others and said, "As you can see, the situation has changed . . . badly. We won't know until the medical examiner gets here if we're dealing with another murder." A murmur of shock was heard from several people. "I'm going to need everyone's help. I see that there's about . . . oh . . . ." He did a quick count. "There's twenty-one here and I believe there's a total of thirty-six lodgers. After you've had some coffee, some breakfast, then I need to talk to all of you. Please give us your room numbers and then we can get the rest of the guests downstairs."

As the lodgers trooped through the front door, Benson stopped Colin and his wife and said, "Mr. Trimble, you helped a bit last night . . . could I ask you a favor?"

"By all means."

"If you and your wife could just sort of organize folks, make sure they don't wander off and . . . well, I wouldn't mind if you indicated to them that they'll probably be asked for fingerprints and DNA samples. I mean, we're definitely going to do those things, I just want to know if you get any strong reactions."

"Consider it done." Colin threw Benson an abbreviated salute and followed the other lodgers.

"Impressive guy," Benson said to Tom. "Said he was in the British navy. Must've been a captain."

Benson and Tom found Kipper seated on one of the big leather sofas in the lobby getting his ankle wrapped by Johnny Bolduc. "This needs further examination," Johnny told Kipper. "You could have a break. Meantime, use a cane."

"Mr. Seldon," Benson said. "I'm sorry about your injury."

"I don't care about anything right now except that Jean-Pierre is alive."

"We were told that you were the first person to see Bruno Gabreau's body."

"From my window. Oh, my God, I thought it was Jean-Pierre." Kipper choked up. "I'm sorry. I can't help it." Tears ran down his freckled cheeks. "I love Jean-Pierre."

"Well, yeah, I, uh . . . why did you think the body was Mr. LeMaire's?"

"He was in black. I last saw Jean-Pierre at one in the morning, and he was wearing black trousers and a black linen shirt I bought for him in Boston."

"I see. Where is he now?"

"He's cooking breakfast for the guests. His two assistant cooks just arrived. I usually help by serving the tables. Now I can't walk. I'm going to ask the room-service girls to help."

Johnny packed his medical kit, said "Gotta, go, sheriff," and bolted for the door. Kipper flopped back on the sofa and stared at the ceiling. "Merrill's gone crazy and Brad won't be any help. He's probably already on the porch next to his favorite potted plant.

That's where he gets his *spiritual uplift*. That's what he calls it. Oh, how *precious!*"

"He gets spiritual uplift from a potted plant?" Tom asked.

"No, no, *no*. His bottle, he can't do without his bottle. He hides his bourbon in the plant and everybody pretends they don't know it."

"You think he's drinking *now*," Tom checked her watch, "at nine o six in the morning?"

Kipper sat up straight, his eyes sharp with anger. "Oh, well, yes, it *is* just a *little* early isn't it? I mean, really, he doesn't customarily start until ten."

Tom arched an eyebrow and glanced at Benson, who rolled his eyes. Kipper wasn't finished:

"And Merrill. She's *stoned* all the time. How can you be stoned all the time? No *wonder* she's gone crazy."

"Mr. Seldon, your sister has just suffered a terrible shock."

Kipper expelled a heavy sigh and again flopped backward. "I'm sorry. I hardly slept last night and I'm a *wreck*. I'm *sorry* the man is dead. Merrill says she loved him, but the truth is, he gave me the creeps. I'm sorry to say a thing like that, but I can't help it. And I know *damn* well why he wanted to marry her—he wanted her money and he wanted Cedar Lodge."

Benson said, "Did you see or hear anything last night or this morning that could help us discover how Gabreau died . . . or why?"

"*How* he died? I thought he was murdered!"

"We don't know for a fact just yet. He could've drowned. The medical examiner will tell us. Might not know until there's an autopsy."

Kipper just stared at them.

"Mr. Seldon," Tom said, "last night your brother said that all three of you—you, Merrill and Brad himself—had a reason to want Gene Seldon dead."

Kipper sat up so abruptly that he banged his right foot on the floor, causing him to yelp and wince in pain. "I did *not* kill my aunt," he gasped.

"That really wasn't the question, Mr. Seldon. Did you want Gene Seldon out of the way? Did you hope she would die?"

"I *beg* your obnoxious pardon!" Kipper spat the words. "How *dare* you!"

"Gene Seldon told the Godwins that you and she had had a violent quarrel when you asked for your inheritance."

Kipper underwent a remarkable transformation—his face flushed an alarming shade of red, nearly blotting out his freckles, and his green eyes dilated with fury. "Screw the screwing Godwins!" he shouted. "I will *not* tolerate this. I *own* this place. You can't bully me. Get out!"

"We are not bullying you, and we are not getting out, Mr. Seldon," Benson said. "We're investigating a murder. We'll need to talk to you further when you've calmed down."

The heads of several lodgers peeked around the barroom door and quickly drew back after spotting Benson and Tom going toward the front door. In his rage Kipper forgot his condition—he stood up, screamed in pain and fell back onto the sofa. "Get out!" he repeated, pounding a fist on the leather cushions.

Once they got to the porch and out of Kipper's sight, Tom told Benson: "He may not have killed his aunt, but something is sure as hell bugging him. That eruption was way over the top."

"Well. Could be. Maybe he just needs a nap."

"Oh, look. Just as advertised. There's Brad by a potted plant." They walked down to him and sat on a wicker love seat next to Brad's chair. His right hand was curled around a small glass of whiskey and he was staring intently at the deputy and the hapless body by the lake.

"Mr. Seldon?" Tom said.

Brad turned to her. "Lieutenant Thomashina. Would you like a cocktail?" There were the lieutenant's blue peepers boring into him, but Brad decided what the hell, who cares, let her stare.

"Bit too early for me," Tom said.

"Sheriff?" Brad offered, wagging the bottle.

"Some other time."

Brad knocked back the whiskey in his glass. "Sushure self. You don't mind if I have 'nother."

"Be my guest," Tom said.

Brad giggled. "Thass good—be my guest. Just what Renee"—Brad turned to look at Tom—"you know Renee, don't you, the ... whatever she is." Tom nodded and Brad said, "She eats cajones for breakfast."

"High cholesterol."

Brad hooted with laughter. "*Thomashina!* Goddamn. You're all right. Wanna go up to my room?"

"Not right now."

Brad roared with laughter until he choked and coughed and flopped back in his chair in apparent exhaustion. "Ohh, man . . . wow. Where was I? Oh, yes. Ony two days ago"—he wrinkled his brow—"was it two? No, three. Ony three days ago, Renee said be my guest. We were sitting right here and I said . . . Oh, never mind, it's boring."

"Mr. Seldon, you told us last night you hated your aunt."

Brad turned and gave Tom a lop-sided grin. "Juss call me Brad, Thomashina. Are we not on intimate terms now that I asked you for a date?"

"OK ... Brad. So. You hated your aunt."

Brad was silent for so long, staring out at the lake, that Tom finally said, "Mister . . . Brad?"

"Our grandfather founded Cedar Lodge. Fishermen, hunters liked it. But it was our mother and father who made it what it is today. Unnurstand? They made it . . . and they loved us—me, Merrill, Kipper, and they . . ." Brad's voice trailed away. "They loved us," he whispered.

"I'm sorry, Brad."

"Gene hated our mother and father and she hated us. Il duce . . . Il duce hated us."

"Wait a minute, Brad. We were told . . ."

"Oh yeah, oh yeah, I know what you're gonna say. I'm wrong, I'm wrong." Brad smiled and lifted his whiskey glass. "I'm messed up, you see. Forgot. Il Duce hated Merrill and me. She *loooved* Kipper. Just *loooved* Kipperdoo. Him and his little Tinkerbell in the kitchen."

"Yet last night you included him on the list of those you say wanted Gene dead."

"Ohh, yes. Oh, yes yes, lootenerant, my dear. You see, Kipperdoo did *not* love Gene in return. Goddamn phony. It was always, 'Yes, Gene darling' and 'Of course, Gene darling'. She lapped it up. So egotistical. Always thought she had everybody's number. But little Kipperdoo did a number on *her.* He couldn't stand her."

"Do you think he could've killed her?"

"Could've? Very interesting philoshawphical question, Thomashi—Thoma*seen*a. Sorry. Hard to get my tongue around that name. I'm a little under the weather you see. *Could* have is a real possibility with Kipper. He has a very nasty temper when pushed. But kill her and *burn* her body? No. Can't see it. Not him. And whadda 'bout old Bruno lying out there in the sun? Why would Kipper kill him? Same person musta killed Gene and Bruno, right?"

"Gabreau may've been drowned by the killer, or . . . he could've drowned accidentally."

Brad was incredulous. "That guy drown? He lived on the water—in it and on it. And what the hell would he've been doing in the lake in the middle of the night? C'mon, Thomasina. Have a drink. It'll clear your head."

"If Gabreau was murdered then it must be because he saw Gene's murderer at work."

Benson thought he had heard vehicles pulling up and doors slamming, and now that was confirmed as the county medical examiner, Noreen Crepeau, strode past the porch trailed by a forensic technician; she waved vaguely at Benson and Tom and went to kneel next to Bruno's body.

Benson cleared his throat and spoke up. "Brad. You were out in the storm last night."

Brad turned to him and frowned. "I was?"

"Mr. Godwin says you were."

"Oh. Yes. Thass right."

"We were told that you never go out in storms."

Brad turned away and was silent.

"Brad. Mr. Seldon. We have it on good authority that you are terrified of storms . . . of lightning. Is that true?"

"Christ, sheriff. So I don't like lightning. Do *you* like lightning? I don't mean sitting inside with a cozy brandy when there's a storm. I mean do you like go to owsside in middle of lightning to enjoy the thrill? Do *you*, Thomasina?"

"Were you out in the storm, Brad?" Benson persisted. "Mr. Godwin says he found Ms. Seldon's body and started shouting for help and that you ran up to him minutes later."

"Awright, goddammit, I was out in the goddamn storm."

"That means you may have been outside during the time Ms. Seldon was killed."

"I didn't kill her. Wanted to." Brad turned to look at the two officers. "Haven't you ever wanted to kill someone? No? Not gonna say? Well, a lot of times I tried to 'magine what it'd be like to pull out a gun and blow her away . . . juss blow her away . . . right when she was taking my balls off." He gave Tom a crooked smile. "I am a much cashtrated man, rootenant. But they always grow back."

* * *

Six had come down to the foot of the dock and was watching the medical examiner, Noreen Crepeau, at work when Benson and Tom walked up. She rose and faced them.

"Not drowned," she said, stripping off her latex gloves. She was a thin, unsmiling, gray-haired woman who always tried to get conversations completed with as few words as possible. "Stab. Right here." She turned and pointed to the spot at the base of her skull. "Very thin. Awl? Sailcloth needle?" She paused and looked at the ground through her wire-rimmed tri-focals. "Knitting needle?"

"How long dead?" Benson said. Her edited speech always seemed to affect his own when they worked together.

"Not sure. In water. Seven, eight hours? Autopsy needed."

"Anything else?"

"Woman's body. Blow to head, skull fragments in brain. Dead when burned."

"The fire?" Benson was sure she'd know what he meant.

"Ah. Accelerant. Don't know what. Not gasoline." She turned and stooped to retrieve her examination bag. When she turned back to Benson she looked at him silently for several beats and then said, "But . . ." She looked out across Willow Pond. "Something more. Something powerful started the fire."

"Thank you, Dr. Crepeau."

"Ayuh," she grunted and shot off toward her car, passing as she went two men from the mortuary van carrying a black plastic body bag.

"That last bit was actually a complete sentence," Tom said.

"Powerful speaker," Six responded.

Twenty

Huntley awoke with a troubled mind. *I need to get out of here,* he thought. *How* am I going to get out? Goddamn Sheriff Hoo-Hah and detectives and frigging deputies clomping around everywhere. They're going to question me. I need to stay calm, display Beauchamp heartiness and beg to be released for an urgent meeting in Boston to prevent a new client's financial collapse. Huntley smiled at that one, for it was true, in a manner of speaking. The "new client" was himself.

Yes, he had copies of the dummy corporations' spreadsheets created by the "discreet businessman's" operatives (he was still convinced it was that pair of snotty Brits) and last night he had assiduously entered them into Cedar Lodge Enterprises' computerized financial statements. But the grizzly in the living room was going to be Adrian Bucksaddle, Esq. Jesus, what a name. Where did people get names like that? Huntley thought, overlooking the fact that his own name had been assembled from a compilation of fancy monikers. Gene's lawyer would have older statements that showed, in numerous negligible line items, Huntley's embezzling depredations. Huntley had entered them vaguely as such things as "investment in start-up firm" or "green technology bonds." With careful study, a sharp-eyed person would probably notice a certain pattern to such entries. Huntley was aware that the fearsome Bucksaddle had eyes of gimlet. The plan was simple: If Bucksaddle began to note the unelaborated line items, Huntley would swoop in with the new spreadsheets of the phantom companies, explaining to all and sundry that he simply had not devoted time to making the corporate-background entries in the ledgers and that if he, Bucksaddle (or others), cared to examine the freshly ticked out Cedar Lodge third-quarter statements on the computer link, they would see that all was well.

Huntley didn't look forward to dealing with the lawyer but he was confident that all items liable to cause the old man to arch a suspicious eyebrow were sewed up tighter than a gnat's ass. Gene Seldon was dead and Adrian Bucksaddle couldn't prove a damn thing. Anyway, because of the fact that the planned meeting on her rewritten will was now moot, the old man most likely wouldn't show up today.

Nevertheless, he thought, the best prospect for his continued peace of mind was to avoid getting in potential harm's way by leaving Cedar Lodge and Willow Pond far behind him. And soon. Tomorrow? Certainly by the day after.

Well. Time to rise and freshen up and choose one of the handsome leisure ensembles he'd brought with him. What would it be today? He would *prefer* the pale gray gabardine slacks and white bucks, but then white shoes might be looked upon as insensitively jaunty in a setting of murder and police investigations. Very well—the gray gabardines and tan kiltie loafers, topped by a forest green Polo shirt. A Beauchamp personal precept was to never, *ever* go beyond one's front door unless one was immaculately turned out. Appearing in public unshaven, unwashed and rumpled was, he had determined long ago, the mark of a loser.

Deciding to manfully ignore his disquietude regarding lawyers and law-enforcement officers, he strode toward the shower, his gaze casually picking out the large coffee table, made from a slice of oak tree, its intriguing growth rings gleaming under layers of shellac. What he saw on the table—or, more precisely, what he didn't see—puzzled him. He had been working at the coffee table on his laptop last night—diligently spinning more tendrils into his larcenous financial web—but the laptop wasn't there. Odd. He didn't recall taking it elsewhere. Feeling a twinge of anxiety, he returned to the bedroom. Getting absent-minded; probably did some work in bed. But no. The slender black repository of not only Beauchamp Portfolio Investments Inc. but of Huntley's entire vast catalog of business and social contacts plus God-only-knew how many emails, business and social, corrupt and non-, which should never be seen by anyone, was not on the bedside table, the bureau or the dressing table. Fear suddenly choking him, he tore off the bed sheets and looked under the bed; with trembling hands he flung open the doors of the cedar armoire, threw out his shoes, swung his hanging garments back and forth, frantically scrabbled in the upper shelf where there were only brushes and old magazines, pulled out all the drawers of the bureau and the dressing table and dumped the contents of his two suitcases onto the middle of the floor.

Mewling with panic, he flailed through the door into the living room, looked under the sofa, then ripped out the drawers of the desk, side table and sofa end tables. The bathroom. Oh, please God, let it be there let it be somewhere. But the laptop was gone. Huntley stood among the debris in the living room shaking, his eyes wild and staring. The hunted animal caught in the open. How could it be, how could it be. The door was locked, he always locked the door. It was impossible. It was . . .

A terrifying thought weakened his knees; pain speared across his chest. Those hideous Brits. They had struck; they were going to rat him out; rat him out to . . . who? *Why* were they going to rat him out? Those evil bastards—they had stolen his laptop. They were criminals, after all, so what safeguard was a locked door against seasoned crooks? But why had they done it? *Why?* Why would they prepare the elaborate corporate inventions on the spreadsheets passed under his door only to turn around and destroy him? The realization that he had slept through a burglary that could annihilate the creature known as Huntley Wooster Beauchamp made him suddenly ill, and he rushed to the bathroom, vomiting down his legs before he could reach the commode.

A little more than fifteen minutes later, Jennifer Libby and her photographer were bumping along the Cedar Lodge camp road in her clapped-out Honda when a large, black SUV came racing straight at them. Jennifer swerved her car to the right and landed nose-down in the shallow drainage ditch, the impact knocking the camera from the hands of her colleague, Chris Winslow. As the SUV flew past she glimpsed at a big man with wild hair at the wheel.

"That thing OK?" Jennifer asked.

Chris picked up the camera from the floorboard, snapped a shot out the window and checked the tiny screen. "It's fine," he told her.

Jennifer rammed the gear shift into reverse and slowly depressed the gas pedal. The tires spun. She accelerated until the engine was roaring; the tires spun and whined, throwing up rocks and mud. After the third try she put her forehead against the steering wheel, uttered an enraged "Crap!" and opened her door.

"C'mon, Chris. We gotta hike."

The two of them were still trudging down the road when a TV camera truck from an Augusta station came rolling along. The two men inside waved and smiled cheerily as they passed.

"Bastards. Thanks a lot," Jennifer muttered.

"'Action News' it said on the back."

"Thanks for sharing that, Chris."

Less than a half-hour later, out on I-95 North, a certain black car/truck of the kind favored by government officials everywhere, from Western democracies to fascist and communist dictatorships, sped north at 85 and 90 per. The occupant of the driver's seat would've been recognized in certain Boston precincts of the wealthy as "Hunt" Beauchamp, but the man actually doing the driving, psychologically speaking, the one whose eyes, dilated with terror, were trying to concentrate on the pavement streaming beneath his vehicle's whining tires, was a fellow named Jack Spurling, who at the moment believed, with some justification, that the world he had scammed for so many years was closing in on him. And he obviously had *not* adhered to the Beauchamp personal precept—he was unshaven, his hair was a rat's nest and his body rank with heavy sweating. His expensive clothes had been crammed like dirty laundry into his suitcases. Fearing that at any moment he would see the flashing lights and hear the dreadful wail of a highway patrol car, Beauchamp/Spurling scanned the road ahead and glanced continually out the rearview mirror.

Soon, he would have to leave the interstate, turn on the GPS and devise a backcountry route toward Canada. There was no telling how soon they would discover he'd fled and start hunting for him. The attaché case beside him on the passenger seat contained his credentials, including his passport and bank cards, but those particular documents would not have been seen by Canadian customs officers. A zippered and locked panel of the case held a passport, driver's license and bank cards for one Brent Overmeyer, a fallback identity Huntley had created years earlier; the manufacture of the credentials for the fictive Mr. Overmeyer by yet another "discreet businessman" had been enormously expensive, but Huntley felt at the time that the cost was well worth it. How right he had been, he thought now. Two Overmeyer checking accounts had been opened, each currently containing about twenty thousand dollars. Once across the border Huntley Beauchamp could run to ground and emerge shining as Brent Overmeyer, "systems analyst."

As Huntley gripped the steering wheel fiercely, trying to contain the urge to floor the damn pedal and hit 110, he did not register the diamond-shaped yellow road signs with black moose silhouettes. The signs bore indicators—"Next 14 Miles" or "Next 20 Miles"—that first-time tourists thought quaint, believing the state was generously alerting motorists to possible charming sightings of Maine's most famous mammal. Mainers and experienced travelers, on the other hand, knew that the state was warning that on any of the indicated miles, a huge, fearless, stubborn beast that recognized no boundaries to its peregrinations could suddenly gallop onto the highway from the thick forest.

Even had he noticed the familiar signs, Huntley would've dismissed them—the odds against intersection of car and moose were impressively long. Nevertheless, long odds *do* have a bottom figure, confirming that even the most unlikely concurrences will eventually take place.

About twenty miles south of Bangor, Huntley Beauchamp came a cropper on the long odds.

Impending death appeared first as a large, fast-moving blur of brown bursting from the trees to Huntley's right. Seconds later, an 800-pound (according to Maine State Police statistics regarding the wreck) bull moose bearing a heroic rack streaked to the pavement squarely in front of Huntley's SUV. A primal scream of terror ripped through Huntley's throat as he whammed down the brake pedal. It was a quick reaction but it was much too late to matter. The unfortunate moose bellowed pitifully as the car smashed through muscle and bone; his body flipped over the hood and through the windshield, driving dashboard, steering wheel, airbag and shattered glass into Huntley's chest and head. The car spun once, rolled three times, ejecting the moose's body and scattering bits of steel and glass and plastic along the road, and landed wheels up in the wooded median, where it burst into flames. Huntley didn't feel a thing; he was already dead.

* * *

Caleb, followed by the deputy named Billy, clattered down the porch steps and over to Benson and Tom.

"Thought we'd never find his stuff," Caleb said. "Finally discovered this little closet in the room behind the front desk. Gabreau's clothes and suitcase were in there. Where he slept I have no idea. Didn't find a sleeping bag or bedclothes anywhere in the lodge."

Tom was looking thoughtful. "It was a warm night, maybe he just slept on either the second- or third-floor porch. He seemed like a man who could sleep rough."

"We checked the porches, all the way around the building."

"He could even have slept on one of the docks."

Billy said, "Sheriff, we got company."

Bounding eagerly toward them were two men, one carrying what was obviously a small TV camera and the other clutching a microphone and cord.

"Uh oh. Trapped. I look like a sheriff, don't I?"

"Ayuh," Caleb grunted. "Hard to miss."

"Damn. Well, I'll have to say something."

"Pardon me, sir, are you Sheriff Benson Doucette?" said the man holding the mic.

"Yep."

"We're from WCCB in Augusta, and we were informed that there's been two murders here, last night and this morning. Is that true?" The other man had shouldered his camera, so Benson realized his harassed visage was soon to hit the screens probably statewide, so he determined not to look harassed. He would look supremely confident and say little.

"Not quite."

"What do you mean, sheriff?"

"I can confirm that there was a homicide on these premises last night, but . . ."

"I heard that!" Jennifer Libby shouted as she and Chris Winslow came panting up beside the TV reporter, who shot her a glance of acid hostility and said, "If you *don't* mind, I am in the middle..."

Jennifer was impervious to rancor from other journalists. "You're now conceding that Iphigene Seldon was murdered?"

"I am."

The TV reporter stepped forward, thrusting his mic toward Benson while trying to block Jennifer. "Sheriff, have you made an arrest?"

"No."

Jennifer two-stepped around the WCCB man. "Are there suspects?"

"Yep. Can't say who."

When Jennifer and the TV reporter brayed simultaneously, and respectively, "Who was found . . ." and "Is it true that . . ." Benson hollered, "Whoa! I will make a statement, I won't repeat any of it and I won't answer questions. I'm too damn busy. Ready?"

The reporters nodded and tensed for what they hoped was good stuff.

"Ms. Iphigene Seldon, aged seventy-seven, owner of Cedar Lodge, was killed last night sometime between nine and ten o'clock by a blow to the head." When both reporters opened their mouths to speak, Benson held up his hand and glared at them fiercely. "We are awaiting further evidence from the autopsy and from a forensic examination of the premises. A second body was found this morning in the area of the docks. We cannot yet confirm the cause of death—it may've been a drowning—and no we are not identifying the victim until proper notification of next of kin. Thank you." Benson nodded and headed for the porch.

Kipper, hobbling on a hickory cane, appeared in the front entrance, leaned against the doorjamb and pointed at the four journalists, who were reluctantly making moves to leave. "Out!" he screamed. "You get out of here! Sheriff, this is private property. Get them the hell out of here!"

Benson noticed the cameraman starting to shoulder his camera and yelled, "Stop, right there! You film him and you'll never get another thing from me." As the man lowered the camera, Benson said, "OK, all of you out. There's nothing to see here anyway."

As they passed by, Jennifer halted and said, "Chris and I can't leave. My car is stuck in the ditch on the road in."

"Out! Out!" Kipper was reaching a high-pitched shriek.

Benson started walking and signaled for Jennifer and Chris to follow him. "I gotta get you out of sight."

Jennifer said, with awe in her voice, "Who the heck is *that?*"

"One of the family. Tell me what happened. How did you wind up in the ditch?"

"Some crazy SOB in a big black SUV—I think it was an Escalade—came roaring up the road right at us. I had to swerve fast and the car hit the ditch. Tires spun when I tried to get out."

Benson tried not to show a reaction to this alarming news as he silently cursed himself for negligence. Billy and Eric had been pulled away from the road and had not been guarding it for close to three hours. Someone had probably fled. There could be an innocent explanation, of course, but Benson doubted it. A big car speeding up the road and driving others into the ditch sounded very much like a getaway. This could get bad. Not wanting to have this eager-beaver reporter getting any hint of trouble, he kept his voice calm and unhurried.

"All right, young lady, I'll have my two deputies pull you out. They have four-wheel traction. Go back to your car and wait."

"Thanks, sheriff. I really appreciate it."

"Yep." Benson turned and took measured strides toward the lodge. Billy and Eric were by the front steps. "Boys, you need to haul a member of the fourth estate from a ditch." When the deputies looked at him blankly, he said, "The woman reporter, Jennifer, ran her car into the ditch when someone went tearing up the camp road."

"Someone escaped when we weren't there?" Billy looked very worried.

"Not your fault, son. Mine. I should've sent one of you back to the road. When you've got Jennifer out of the ditch just stay there and don't let anyone out . . . or in. Unless it's our pathology team, of course. 'Spect them any minute. If anyone else arrives give me a call and I'll check 'em out."

"Yes, sir." Billy and Eric ran toward their car.

Tom and Caleb were in the lobby. "More trouble, dammit," Benson said. "Somebody left here in a hurry."

"We know who?" Caleb asked.

"That's the other problem—no. Did you get room numbers from all the lodgers who've come downstairs?"

"Ayuh. Bunch more already came down. We only need to roust four rooms."

"Good. Get them down here as soon as possible and let's count heads. Is the Ranger tootsie . . . sorry, Tom . . . is Renee Ranger in the barroom?"

"She is. Looks nervous as hell. If she was a cat she'd be switching her tail."

"And how about Bob Weller? Seen him?"

"Just came down. He's on the porch."

As Caleb walked off Tom said, "You don't need to apologize to me about insulting references to Ms. Ranger. She sort of invites crude remarks by her behavior."

"Thanks, Tom. By the way, you are *no* tootsie."

Tom chuckled. "That'll be the day."

"So let's see who's still in the barn. Brad's on the front porch, his wife's in the dining room, Bob Weller's on the porch, Kipper's here, Jean-Pierre's barefoot and in the kitchen, Merrill's in the hospital."

"Huntley Bee-chump."

"Get his room number."

Benson did a quick survey of the dining room and barroom. No Huntley. The breakfasting lodgers, already subdued, grew silent and watchful as he walked through the rooms and out. When he returned to the front desk, Tom said, "Number fourteen."

When they got to room 14, they knocked, got no reply, tried the knob and the door opened, revealing the chaos Huntley had left behind.

They walked through the two small rooms. "Damn, it's him," Benson said, heading for the door. "We need to get out an all-points. Let's see if he registered his car number at check-in."

"Got it." Tom handed him a slip of paper. "Probably a rental."

"Good man! Uh, I mean . . ."

Tom laughed as Benson flipped open his cellphone, called headquarters and requested a statewide suspect at large bulletin for a large, black SUV, Massachusetts plate number FP1843.

"I don't like the pompous SOB, but I didn't figure him for the murder," Tom admitted.

"Me neither. I mean, he doesn't really have a dog in this fight over the lodge, does he?"

"Well, in a way he does. Six and Alicia said Merrill desperately wanted to divorce him but that he was holding her up for two million. But would that have been enough for him to speed things along by killing Gene?"

Benson drew in a deep breath and released a combination sigh and moan. "Y'know, Tom. You say you don't like Beauchamp. I gotta tell you—I don't like any of 'em."

* * *

The two pathology technicians each commandeered a table in the barroom—one for fingerprints, one for DNA swabs. Benson stood by the door and said:

"Folks, I hope all of you realize the necessity of this intrusion on your privacy. I'm sorry for it, but you know what we're facing here—we've confirmed the murder last night of Iphigene Seldon, whom you all knew, and this morning the body of Bruno Gabreau, a friend of the Seldon family, was found on the shore. Probably most of you did not know Mr. Gabreau. We believe that he, too, was murdered, and we'll confirm that later." That sent a buzz of excitement around the room.

"One other thing, folks, and I hope this isn't a futile request. We're asking you please, in the interest of our investigation and... well, just in the interest of keeping this situation under control, not to initiate any contact with news media."

"Excuse me, sheriff," a voice called out.

Tom saw a tanned, outdoorsy-looking man—well, hell, they all looked that way, Benson realized—standing in the back. "Yes sir?"

"Do you have a suspect?"

"We have several."

A silver-haired woman in a blue-checked fishing shirt and khaki shorts who exuded wealth despite her simple clothing (and they all look rich, too, Benson decided), raised her hand.

"Ma'am?"

The woman smiled and said, in what Benson guessed was a Midwestern accent, "Sheriff, if you are asking all of us to give swabs and fingerprints—and believe me, I have *no* qualms in that regard—does that mean the suspect is among those of us who are guests here?" She looked around the room at her fellow lodgers. "I mean, all of us here in this room?"

That question got everyone's attention.

Got to be careful here, Benson reminded himself. He thought it over briefly and said, "That's a good question, ma'am. Here's how we see it. The killer probably knew the victim, Ms. Seldon, long beforehand. That's what we believe, but . . . but we don't *know* it. Therefore . . . I think you can understand our position . . . we just can't take any chances."

A young man near the front—curly black hair, shaded glasses and the inevitable tan—popped up and asked, "Any chance it's a serial killer?"

Benson was caught by surprise. The notion hadn't occurred to him. "Well, sir . . . that sort of thing is always a possibility, I mean serial killers *are* real, and . . ."

Benson felt a tug on his sleeve; it was Tom.

"Yes, Lieutenant?"

Tom rose and addressed the questioner. "Serial murders were one of my study areas, sir. I'm not an expert, but I have learned that serial killers usually strike in different locations rather than seeking victims all in one location, such as this lodge. We have as yet no indication at all that a serial killer is at work here. Nevertheless, as Sheriff Doucette said, it's an outside possibility. One more reason why putting all of you through these tests and questions is a good idea."

The curly-headed man thanked Tom and sat down; Benson noticed him give her an appraising look, and the sheriff had to admit that if big women were a particular man's object of desire, Det. Lt. Barclay definitely was a dish.

Tory and Nelson Bolston, sitting at the bar, looked upset. "Are the rest of us in danger?" she asked.

"And are you going to protect us?" Nelson chimed in.

"Believe me," Benson replied, "everyone's safety is our prime concern. The five of us here will be at the lodge throughout the day conducting interviews and making a survey of the building and grounds, and two officers are guarding the camp road. Overnight, I'll post two officers in the lodge and one on the road."

A big, bearded man wearing a safari jacket raised his hand and asked, "Some of us have to leave soon, sheriff. I'm not scared, mind you, but I had been planning to leave today and I've got commitments."

"After each of you give DNA swabs and fingerprints, then we'll need to interview you briefly and collect your addresses and contact information. Those of you who wish to leave this afternoon or evening can request to go first."

The silver-haired woman spoke up again. "I'm not familiar with the . . . hmm . . . *dynamics* of Cedar Lodge—it's my first time here—but I have, well, many of us have heard things. How could we not? Isn't it true that the most likely suspects are among the family and, uh, friends and staff?"

Benson smiled at her. "You're right about that, ma'am."

Twenty-One

Six and Alicia dutifully reported to have their DNA swabs and fingerprints. Benson said there was no sense in them doing it, but Six insisted: "The family and staff know by now that we're police stooges"—Six chuckled and shot up two puffs of smoke from his pipe—"but maybe we should keep everyone else thinking we're just part of the gang."

"Well, can't see any harm."

"There's another thing. I've been doing some thinking."

"Uh oh."

"Yeah, I know—makes me nervous, too. This is something that is only a possibility."

"Shoot."

"What if Bruno was killed to avenge Gene's death? Someone knew that he was the murderer and then . . ."

"But everyone supposedly wanted Gene . . ."

"Ah. I know what you're going to say. Not everyone. Bob Weller. He was going to marry her. I have a feeling that she promised she would support him in the style to which he looks like he had been accustomed." Six frowned and said, "If that's a sentence."

Benson chewed his lip and reached in his shirt pocket for a cigar, his somewhat Pavlovian response whenever Six stoked up his wood-burning fireplace, as Benson thought of the large-bowled, curved stem thing now hanging below Six's jaw. "Well," he said, clipping off the cigar end and fishing for his lighter, "that's a damn interesting thing, Six . . . Hey, wait a minute. Weller was passed out drunk during the whole deal."

"Yes, I know. He was passed out right next to Alicia and me. But think about this. By the time everyone was gathered in the kitchen last night, he was up and cognizant but looked so ill that you let him go to his room. Now, we know what state Merrill is in today and we know she locked Bruno out of their room last night.

Weller's room is right next to hers. Brad, Kipper and Merrill all have permanent lakeside suites on the third floor. Gene had put Weller in a small one-roomer next to Merrill. What if Weller was awake and heard Merrill and Bruno fighting? What if he heard Merrill accuse Bruno of killing Gene?"

Benson drew in a satisfying mouthful of smoke, blew it out and pondered. "As a theory I don't like it. Too many ifs and slight chances."

"I don't like it either, to tell you the truth. But it's still possible."

"Ayuh. Can't ignore even slim possibilities, I reckon. But something else just happened that might trash all our theories and bring this case to a quick finish. And I don't want you to mention it to anybody, OK?"

"Should I keep quivering or are you going to tell me?"

"Huntley Beauchamp just roared out of here about forty-five minutes ago. He was going so fast up the camp road that he drove the Waterville reporter into the ditch. I'd left the road unguarded, dammit."

Six looked stunned. "Hoo boy, that's . . . I don't know what to say about that. Do *you* think he did both murders?"

"He would've been my last choice."

"Mine, too. What are you going to do?"

"I've got an all-points out on him. Troopers and local cops will be watchin' for him. Best I can do. Can't go look for him myself."

As they were talking, Six and Benson had strolled out onto the porch to escape the fog they'd created in the lobby. Six pulled a piece of paper from the left breast pocket of his tattered fishing shirt; the pocket itself was disengaging from the shirt as its aged threads gradually decayed, but there was enough still clinging to hold the paper that Six now handed over. "I found this in Gene's office. Tom gave me permission to poke around in there."

"Fine with me," Benson said, unfolding the sheet. "And this would be . . . Oh. This is weird."

"Yeah. It's the death threat. The type is similar to obituary notices in newspapers. Written on a computer. I found that typeface on one of my laptop functions."

"Impossible to trace. In the old days . . . Oh, Jesus, why do I keep saying that? It's so useless."

"Yep. But I understand. Tell me anyway."

"ITOD—that stands for In The Old Days—we could have found the typewriter and matched the key strokes."

Six couldn't help snickering. "Last time I went into the Radio Shack in Waterville, the two young men running the place told me they'd never seen an actual typewriter. Saw 'em in movies."

"Sometimes I think I should just sit down on my front porch for the rest of my life. Ah, well. Thanks for this." As he pocketed the note he spotted Bob Weller down at the far western end of the porch in a wicker rocker. "Looks like Weller down to the end. Would you mind talking to him? I've got too much on my mind, and we need to get the lodgers processed."

"Yep. Be glad to."

"See what you can get out of him. If you do it then it might seem less like interrogation."

"Yep. See ya." Six ambled down the porch leaving a contrail of honey-scented smoke.

* * *

Alicia smiled at Tory and Nelson, who, like her, were waiting to give DNA and fingerprints. As she sat on a barstool next to them she said, "Are you folks leaving soon?"

Tory looked worried and was not displaying her usual bright smile. "We hope to leave in the morning. It's just tragic about all this. Poor Gene Seldon murdered like that and . . . and now this murder this morning. Mister . . . Gabeau?"

"Gabreau," Alicia said. "With an R."

"It's really terrifying. He was Merrill's boyfriend, isn't that true?"

"Yes. Yes, it's true. Merrill's in shock and they've taken her to the hospital."

"Poor woman."

"We heard that her husband is here, too," Nelson said.

"Well, yes, but it's not as . . . hmm . . . *unusual* as it may seem. Huntley doesn't live here, he's in Boston, actually, and he and Merrill are legally separated."

Tory looked up from studying her fingernails. "Huntley? That's her husband? That big guy who looks like the country club president?"

Alicia laughed. "That's a pretty good description. That's him all right. Huntley Beauchamp. Why, have you met him?"

Now Tory smiled. "Oh, yes. He was hitting on me yesterday afternoon. Not my type." Her smile quickly faded. "After all that's happened, yesterday seems so long ago."

"It's hard to believe, isn't it?" Nelson added, standing up. "Would you excuse me? I'm going to, uh . . . well, I see Renee back there and I . . ."

"Of course."

As he walked off, Tory said, "My brother likes Brad Seldon's wife. They're separated, too."

"And I believe you like the other half . . . Brad."

"Oh! Has it been that obvious?"

"Not really. Gene was talking yesterday about all the, uh, friendships that were forming in her lodge, hers included."

"That's so sad. That poor old man." Tory was silent for several minutes as she stared at the floor. "To tell you the truth, Mrs.—it's Godwin, right?"

"Yes."

"Nelson—my brother—and I came here looking for romance as much as for fishing. Does that seem strange? A brother and sister doing that?"

"To my mind, not at all. Six and I have a romantic bent. I mean in regard to others," she added hastily. "He and I have a lifelong romance."

"Nelson and I both had divorces in recent years. Oh, I told you that already. And, yes, I do like Brad very much. But now these murders and . . . well, we don't know who did them . . . and, to be frank, it . . . well, it could be one of the family." Tory touched

Alicia's arm. "And I'm sorry to say that, but . . . you do understand, don't you?"

"Of course I understand."

Tory sighed and looked out the windows at the lake. "It all started so beautifully."

Colin and Daphne walked up to them and Colin said, "All this rather knocks one silly, doesn't it? Bloody damn shame. Hard to believe, especially in an Elysium such as this."

Daphne said, "Most of the others say they're haring off as quickly as possible. I suppose we'll be off as well in the morning. It would seem heartless to fish and have fun, even if they *were* staying open. I do hope the lodge survives all this."

"I believe it will. The Seldons have survived other tragedies."

Colin said, "Where's the professor? Oh, dear. So sorry. I know you're a professor, too."

Alicia laughed. "We *were* professors. Now we're fishermen."

Colin smiled wryly and said, "Um, so I see."

Alicia was again wearing fishing clothes, one of two ensembles that would've gotten her handouts from sympathetic passersby had she been standing on a Boston street corner. "Six and I get used to fishing in the same clothes, and we hate to ever part with them. However, there comes a day . . . This shirt and these jeans, for instance, are replacements for garments that eventually disintegrated."

"Ah! And that was . . .?"

Alicia thought for a minute. "Twenty-eight years ago. My shoes are a good deal older—L.L. Bean, 1974."

Colin was fascinated. Arching a brow, he said, "Is this perhaps a Maine tradition?"

"If it were, Bean couldn't stay in business."

"We've been to Bean. Bloody marvelous."

Alicia reached into a front pocket of her jeans and extracted a wallet so decrepit it looked as though it might've held dispatch papers during the Napoleonic Wars. "Six and I also have a little business." She handed cards to the Trimbles and Tory.

"Ah. Just the ticket," Colin said. "Winsokkett Antiquarian Books. We *do* a bit of collecting. And Winsokkett is a . . ."

"A lake—Winsokkett Pond. Six and I have a camp there. It's the next lake east of Willow. Well, actually, there's a little one, Rocky Pond, in between, that's attached to Winsokkett."

Colin pocketed the business card and said, "Daph and I have already done our criminology bit. Thought I might look up the . . . other professor."

Alicia smiled at him. "Might find him in the lobby with the sheriff, or wherever else the sheriff is."

Daphne looked at Alicia and Tory and said, "See you at lunch?"

"Yep. We'll be here. See ya then."

* * *

Kipper had hobbled and cursed his way back to the kitchen and was now propped on a stool watching adoringly as Jean-Pierre prepared lunch for the lodgers. As his gaze followed the little chef bustling about the counters and stoves and ovens, Kipper's eyes teared when he recalled the horrible moments that morning when he'd thought Jean-Pierre was lying drowned in the lake.

He could not live without Jean-Pierre. If he dies, Kipper thought, I also will die. How could I ever withstand such grief? I wanted to die when mom and dad were killed, but I didn't have the courage to end my life. But now, now, I am so glad now that I lived. Darling Jean-Pierre and I must live a long time. Surely we will. We deserve happiness.

Jean-Pierre, meanwhile, quickened his pace unnecessarily, darting here and there, fussing over the cooks' preparations, keeping busy, busy, busy to avoid glancing at Kipper, to avoid once again seeing those big eyes filled with such prurient devotion. Jean-Pierre wanted to be loved and admired; he did not want to be the object of such ferocious adoration. It made him very uncomfortable. He was not a lapdog, to be squeezed and cuddled and constantly petted and . . . *owned.* That was his fear. Being taken to New York and completely subsidized by Kipper's money combined with being enveloped by Kipper's intense, possessive love was a recipe for tragedy.

There was going to be a wrenching confrontation. Jean-Pierre knew he must make clear his concerns to his emotional lover, no matter how much he dreaded doing so. If he and Kipper were to have a happy life, he must establish in Kipper's mind the incontrovertible fact that he, Jean-Pierre LeMaire, was an intelligent, supremely (in his own mind) talented man with strong, definite ambitions. He could not allow himself to be smothered. Yes, he needed Kip*pair* and his money to obtain his dream of his own restaurant in New York City, where successful chefs became celebrities, and, yes, he actually felt a certain amount of genuine love for his benefactor. But if the relationship became too fraught, too much of a struggle for his own soul, Jean-Pierre was certain that other Kippers were thick on the ground in a place like New York.

Kipper could not catch Jean-Pierre's eyes. He was busy, yes, Kipper thought, but surely not so rushed that he couldn't spare a glance in my direction once in awhile. Then he thought: I am too much of a distraction. If he looks at me his emotions will interfere with his cooking. Also, he probably is still overwhelmed by my storming into his room and crying while I held him. I must have frightened him when I told him I thought the dead body out front was him. I mustn't frighten him. I should leave now.

Dear God, it was a relief not to have Gene stomping around like a chain gang warden. He knew he should feel some sorrow, but he could not; he had never really liked the old tyrant despite her fondness for him. Her affection had actually repulsed him—how could she possibly have thought she could take the place of his beautiful mother? But he'd hidden his feelings for obvious reasons—it made life pleasant and it gave him an upper hand against his brother and sister, both of whom had become so dismissive of him, and so acerbic with their casual insults. He had idolized his much older siblings when he was a child—they were golden youths, and so full of fun.

And then everything had changed. One bolt hurled by a savage God had destroyed paradise in a blazing instant.

"Mr. Seldon."

Kipper started at the sound of Sam's voice. Turning quickly, he said, "Yes?"

"There's three bass boats in the water, Mr. Seldon. Do you want me to put in more? I would've asked your brother but he's, uh, sleeping on the porch."

Kipper snorted in disgust. "Oh, I'm quite certain he needs a nap by now. He had too much ... *breakfast.*"

"Yes, sir."

"I think probably everyone is leaving tomorrow, Sam. No more boats. We'll shut down for awhile." Reacting to the look on Sam's face, Kipper quickly added, "Don't worry, Sam. There'll be plenty of work for you. We have to open again. Probably next week. You're still on for the rest of the summer."

"Thank you, sir. Is there anything else I could be doing right now?"

"Well, yes, Sam, there is. I know it's never been a part of your duties, but could you *please* help Jean-Pierre get food on the tables for the guests? I usually do it. I'll have one of the chamber maids help you."

"Of course. I'll stay here now and be ready when he's ready."

"Good lad." Kipper eased himself off the stool and grabbed his cane. "I've got to get in the office and start sorting things out. There's going to be *such* a load of work getting my aunt buried, changing the corporation papers, dealing ... Oh, I'm sorry, Sam— not your problem. I'm babbling. Not enough sleep."

* * *

Sam told Jean-Pierre he would serve tables, then parked himself on a stool. Just as he was congratulating himself on a successful suck-up to his boss, Sam winced when he realized he would probably be facing the ominous Brits, Colin and Daphne, at lunchtime. He was worried about them studying him with a knowing smirk as he put down their food. An awful scene of knocking over water or spilling food onto them sprang into his mind. What also troubled him, now that he was thinking about them, was that his none-too-sophisticated teenage brain had spawned a sophisticated thought—what if they were *not* British special agents, as they claimed, but were suave criminals, really *dangerous* criminals? What if they were hired killers? Sam had been watching his back all day; he'd locked his door last night, something he had never bothered with before and he'd shoved a desk in front of the door. Today, he had gone to the boathouse where, in addition to all the lodge's boating equipment, there was a room containing hundreds of tools and hardware for general repairs. He'd selected a heavy chain bolt and installed it on his door.

Kipper had said that probably all the lodgers were leaving to-morrow. Sam prayed that among them were Colin and Daphne.

Twenty-Two

Six eased himself into a wicker chair next to Bob Weller, said, "Mornin"—to which greeting Bob turned and nodded—and then knocked his pipe against the porch rail to clear out the ashes, preparatory to another firing. Six customarily smoked two bowls in succession, then waited an hour for the next one. No need to establish unhealthy habits, he assured himself. He refilled the bowl, tamped it down, sucked the lighter flame into it and blew out the first satisfying mouthfuls of smoke. Whoops, he thought—forgot my manners.

"Smoke bother you?" he asked.

"No. Not a bit."

"Feel like talking?"

Bob was sitting scrunched down in the chair with his head resting against the back. He uncrossed and re-crossed his legs and sighed. "I'm incapable of initiating any conversation right now, and I don't mean that rudely. I appreciate your coming over."

"To tell you I'm sorry is a very genuine sentiment, Bob—Gene was my cousin and her death has upset me very much, too."

Bob was silent for so long that Six thought he wasn't going to say anything more. Finally he spoke, his voice heavy with fatigue. "It's not a matter of not wanting to talk—I don't *want* to do anything. I am sitting and seeing and breathing, but those activities are about the extent of my capabilities. If breathing weren't autonomic, I probably wouldn't bother with it."

"Shock is devastating."

"Somehow it feels much worse than mere shock. I am so stunned, Six, that I . . . oh, I don't know . . . I feel unicellular. I will react to stimuli—for instance, if I get hungry enough I will go to the clubroom and, amoeba-like, absorb nutrients. Other than that, I could cheerfully sit right here, doesn't matter how long, and not move until prodded."

"Want me to leave you alone?"

Again, Six wasn't sure he was going to get an answer. Bob continued to stare at the lake but said nothing. After a few minutes ticked by, Six was preparing to make a farewell remark and leave, when Bob spoke up.

"No, I'd like for you to stay, Six. I've changed my mind. Now I want to talk, and I believe it's because it's you. I don't want to talk to anyone else, though I know I can't avoid speaking with the sheriff."

Six thought it best not to respond.

"I don't know you very well, but I like you. And . . . oh, we're . . . well, we're of an age, although I must be fifteen, twenty years older."

"Alicia and I are baby-boomers. Mid-fifties."

"Ah. I was right. That age is nothing these days. Now that I'm seventy-five, I would embrace fifty-five again with joy."

Six stayed still, smoking peacefully. Six possessed the quality of stillness, a seldom practiced art these days, he reflected. Alicia also had stillness. The two of them could sit together for hours in lasting silence, but, then, they were long accustomed to each other. The art of stillness became difficult when practiced socially, in the presence of people with whom one was not intimate, for most people are embarrassed by prolonged periods of saying absolutely nothing to one's immediate companions; the longer the silence, the more acute the embarrassment, until eventually such victims of silence become so ill at ease that they are compelled to blurt out anything. Even mindless chatter breaks the tension. Six was free of such tension and was adept at gauging, in reaction to others' moods, when was a good time not to say anything.

Now was a good time not to say anything, so he began pondering the mystery of bass lures—why bass will strike at purple plastic worms one summer only to spurn them the next, gobbling instead the green ones with black spots. He was just moving on to the contemplation of whether red hooks were actually better than ordinary ones in eliciting a killer response in bass when Bob said, "I never worked."

Six lit his second bowl of No. 79 and worked up a small cumulo.

"Shocks some people. Don't blame them. I'm the kind of SOB most Americans resent. Inherited a fortune, blew it all—racing, women, playing around—now facing poverty." He turned toward Six, his lips curling in a slight, rueful smile. "I am not anyone's idea of a chap who deserves pity . . . and that's the way it should be."

Six simply nodded his understanding.

"I don't deserve *anything*, for that matter. But, spurning suicide, I do have the necessity of finding someone who wants to help me keep my wretched skin and bones out of the ditch. Consequently, here of late, I've been on a self-interested campaign of courting wealthy elderly women." He drew in a deep breath and released it in a long, windy sigh. "And they're a real goddamn pain in the ass."

"Wouldn't doubt it."

"It is more than somewhat asinine to be a septuagenarian boy toy—but . . . as I said, no sympathy. I made my bed."

"Ayuh."

"And then, when I'd grown so sick of it I was contemplating becoming a jewel thief—a la Raffles, of course . . . a *society* jewel thief . . . just after I'd actually purchased several pairs of white cloth gloves, I came here. Not to fish, though I do like fishing, not to do anything except rest. I came here and up jumped this ridiculous seventy-seven-year-old tomboy with a dirty mouth and the voice of a Bourbon street barker. She surprised the hell out of me because I liked her immediately, wasn't sure why at first, but then soon enough I knew why—she was the antithesis of everything I'd begun to despise, the jewels, the designer gowns, the surgical enhancements, the relentless series of elegant interiors, the endless parties—oh, Jesus, the eff-ing parties, the cocktails, the blather, the artery-clogging meals, the incessant braying of the upper classes."

"Think I would've flamed out about two weeks in."

"Took me awhile. I'd had lifelong Olympic-quality saturnalia training."

Bob heaved another momentous sigh and grew silent once more. Six smoked and watched an osprey circling over the water, searching for unwary fish swimming near the surface. The osprey descended and began to hover in one place. Six sat forward abruptly, ready for action, though three feet closer certainly wasn't going to improve his discernment. Suddenly, the bird dived straight down, folding back his primary wing feathers, gaining impressive speed, then swooped up his head, hit the water feet first and plunged in with a big splash. Flapping rapidly, he ascended with a fish in his talons.

"Wow!" Six expostulated. Then, thinking perhaps an explanation to his suffering companion was needed for the outburst, he said, "Osprey dived and got a fish."

Hearing not even an acknowledging grunt, Six turned to look at Bob, who, it seemed, was staring into his own bleak landscape and had neither seen the osprey nor heard Six. *Ah, well. Got a lot on his mind.* Six found himself wondering what it must be like to be a creature like the osprey, burdened by the necessity to constantly hunt for food. But then, that's the human take, isn't it? he decided. What would a bird actually *do* with leisure time?

"It wasn't love, you know."

Six dropped his ruminations and listened.

"That was out of the question. No, we simply enjoyed each other immensely as companions . . . although some of her callous observations made me flinch at times. At least she was honest. Egotistical, yes, but what the hell, we all are to some extent—however, there was nothing phony about her. And God was she funny. Funny, wonderful old broad, and she was . . . ." Bob hesitated, cleared his throat, and said, "She was going to take care of me. I'm too tired to hunt anymore, Six. This is it for me. I'm hanging up the old jock strap."

Six waited, certain that there was more to come.

"Gene lost her life, which she was enjoying so much, and I lost everything that was going to give me a comfortable old age. Quite enough to justify homicide, wouldn't you say?"

* * *

Benson was interviewing a hardy outdoors couple from Wisconsin when Six sidled up to him and said, "Benson, I need to tell you something. Semi-urgent."

"Let me just finish with these fine folks," Benson responded, smiling at the blond forty-somethings who were at the lodge with their blond children, "and I'll meet you by the fireplace."

Six was standing quite still by the fireplace when Benson approached, but mentally the quality of stillness had deserted him from the moment of Roberson Weller's last statement.

"Yessuh?" Benson asked.

"I think Bob Weller may have—and I want to emphasize *may have*—hinted that he killed Gabreau."

"I'm all ears."

After Six had summarized the entire conversation with Bob and concluded with repeating the man's last statement as near to verbatim as he could remember it, Benson said:

"Damn. Whadda you think?"

"I think he could have heard Merrill screaming at Bruno and then decided to kill him. Weller's in a totally messed up mental condition."

"I think what you think."

"What are we going to do?"

"Is he still out on the porch?"

"Ayuh. Indicated he would be coming in for lunch."

"Do you think he's liable to do a Huntley on me?"

"He said he's so depressed he doesn't even want to move."

Benson thought for a minute. "Can't take a chance. I'll have Caleb keep an eye on him. The road is blocked again, but at this point I don't trust anyone about anything. I need to get Weller alone here or I need to take him with me to the station. Meantime, I've got to finish up with the lodgers before lunch." He started to move away then turned and said, "Thanks, by the way. What are you planning to do now?"

"I've got another idea."

Benson smiled. "Take it easy."

"I'm not going to get you worked up until I've done some fishing around out back. Once I've . . ."

"Sheriff!" Benson and Six jumped as Arnaud's voice boomed from the front door. "I've got to tell you something."

"That sounds familiar."

Dressed in his customary plaid shirt, jeans, boots and wide leather belt with a holstered hunting knife, Arnaud strode heavily across the lobby and up to Benson and Six. "At first I didn't think it was all that important, but I worried about it all last night and I believe I better unload it. I just got here from home."

"Tell me," Benson said.

"It's about Brad's wife . . . Renee."

Being constitutionally economical with words, Arnaud proceeded to use as few as possible in relating Renee's peculiar movements at the bar the previous evening when she was talking to Bob Weller. Benson understood what he was being told—it did sound as though Renee was acting a bit strange—but he was not convinced it was significant. Nevertheless, he did not dismiss the information—Arnaud was a calm, intelligent man, not a thrill-seeker who starts seeing killers everywhere. He said, "Thanks, Arnaud. You did the right thing. Are you coming to work now?"

"Ayuh. I usually do lunch and dinner."

"Tell you what. Renee Ranger's still in the clubroom—she's giving DNA and fingerprints. If she stays for lunch or hangs out at the bar, maybe you could keep an eye on her. I definitely needed to talk to her anyway, so what you've told me will help."

"Good. Will do. I'll go on in the bar."

As Arnaud walked away, Benson's cellphone, clipped to his belt, rang sharply. Benson looked at the number flashing and saw that it was headquarters.

"Yep?"

It was the duty sergeant. "Sheriff, Lt. Rene Pelletier of the state police just called. Says they found your escaper. Wants to talk to you ASAP. Here's his number."

Benson drew out his notepad, wrote the number, snapped the phone shut and looked at Six. "This fireplace must be an energy field of some kind. State police. Say they have Beauchamp." He called the number and on the third ring it was picked up.

"Lt. Pelletier."

"Benson Doucette, lieutenant."

"Good to hear from you, sheriff. We have your Massachusetts number FP1843. Cadillac Escalade. That correct?"

"Yes! What about Huntley Beauchamp? You get him?"

"What's left of him, and it's not much, is on the way to the Penobscot County coroner. Worst damn wreck I've seen in years. Hit a moose, flipped, car exploded. Rear license plate was one of the few things not burned."

"Oh . . . damn. Where was this?"

"I-95, eighteen miles south of Bangor. Wanted man?"

"Murder suspect. I've got a bad situation down here, Lieutenant. Two murders." Benson put the phone against his shirt and whispered to Six: "Beauchamp's been killed."

"Yep," Lt. Pelletier said. "Sounds bad. I've got to file a report. Do you have data on this man?"

"Some, but I can get more. Lives in Boston, financial advisor for Cedar Lodge, and I believe . . . You know Cedar Lodge? Willow Pond? That's where we are now."

"Heard of it. Next of kin there?"

"Well, yeah, you might say that. His wife—they're separated— is in the hospital under sedation. Her lover is one of the murder victims."

"The two of them were there at the same time?"

"It's complicated, lieutenant."

"Who else was killed?"

"A woman named Iphigene Seldon, owner of Cedar Lodge."

"How are you doing with all this?"

"To tell you the God's honest truth, Lt. Pelletier, I'm just not sure. We've been working hard on every angle we can think of, we've got forensic work under way, we've had multiple interrogations—all that good stuff. But I've got other things running in the county that I can't neglect."

"Troopers probably could help, sheriff. Want me to put in a request?"

"Well . . ." Benson thought hard for about fifteen seconds and then said, "Let's do this. A number of guests here at the lodge have been cleared and some are leaving tonight, others tomorrow morning. I've got their DNA and fingerprints, contact numbers, everything. I'm leaving two deputies guarding the lodge overnight and another guarding the road. If I don't get *some* kind of break by midday tomorrow—anything at all—then I'll shoot up a flare. Is it possible for you to put in, say, a preliminary request? A just in case sort of thing?"

"Yep. I can do that. You need the fellows in Troop C, over to Skowhegan. I'm upstate aways."

"I've worked with Troop C."

"I'll flag them that you might call. Meantime, get me some more background on this Beauchamp."

"Will do. Gene Seldon's family members are here—I'll ask them."

"Excellent. Over and out."

Benson clipped his phone on his belt and told Six: "Beauchamp hit a moose on I-95 south of Bangor. Car exploded, burned. You can imagine the result."

"Hoo damn." Six winced at the mental image of the carnage.

"When a state trooper says it's the worst thing he's seen in a long time I know it's something I'm glad I missed. I mean, what we've seen here is bad enough."

Six stepped over to the hearth, knocked out his pipe and put it into his jeans pocket. "Benson, this is getting troublesome. Suddenly we've got an overload of maybes. *Maybe* Huntley killed both Gene and Bruno; *maybe* Bob killed Bruno because he believed Bruno was Gene's murderer—and *maybe* he was right, think about that—and just *maybe* Renee slipped something into Gene's drink at the bar that made her weak and vulnerable for Renee's bashing her on the head."

"And then burned her? I know people are saying the woman's a bitch, but do you think she's capable of a thing like that?"

"Nope. Can't say I do."

Sam emerged from the clubroom, walked to the bell hanging to the right of the fireplace and pulled its cord half-a-dozen times, filling the lobby and the stairway with harsh reverberations. Then he went out on the porch and rang the bell there.

"Lunchtime," Six said. "Want to belly up to the trough?"

"Ayuh. I'm running on three coffees and a donut. Tom and I have to grill Weller and Renee. I need to get substantial calories on board."

As they moved toward the clubroom door Benson grabbed his suddenly ringing cellphone. "Yep? Doucette here."

It was the medical examiner. "Noreen, Benson. Man's body. Six-inch blade from base of skull into brain. Very thin. Look for awl. Maybe knitting needle. No other marks."

"Time of death?"

"Midnight to 3 a.m."

"Thanks, Noreen."

"Yep. See ya." The line went dead.

"Like I said, there's an energy field here. Let's go in to eat before the damn thing rings again."

* * *

While waiting for Bob Weller to emerge from the clubroom lunch service, Caleb signaled for Sam to come out in the lobby. Caleb told him: "I know you have to finish waiting tables, youngster, but after that I need your help."

"Sure," Sam said quickly; he was too nervous to say anything more.

"I imagine you know the boathouse and the tool room pretty well, eh?"

"Yes sir!"

"What we're looking for is an awl, or something very much like it, that has a thin, six-inch shaft. We think that maybe one such awl could be missing from the tool room. Now, can you do that for me?'

"Yes sir."

"And don't—as in I mean *don't*—say anything about this or what you find to anyone other than me or the sheriff."

"Yes sir! I mean, no I won't!"

"Relax. You'll be fine."

Something, Caleb decided as he watched Sam head back to the clubroom, has got that boy nervous. Might be good to have another talk with him later. Then he noticed Robertson Weller heading out.

Although he was shaved and suitably spruced up in khakis and a white shirt, and although he held his shoulders straight, Bob glided slowly across the lobby like a man in a trance, his eyes, seemingly, not connecting with anything around him. He drifted by Caleb as if the sergeant wasn't even there, and Caleb Cobb was of a size that was hard to miss in any setting.

Caleb followed him out to the porch, watched Bob reclaim his chair on the western end, and then continued toward the docks, figuring he could diddle around the docks and the water and still keep a wary eye on Bob. Poking around the vicinity, particularly the area where Bruno's body was found, might do some good, he believed. Never know what you might find.

As Caleb neared the water, he watched a squadron of five cormorants swoop by closely overhead, most likely coming from another pond, and land on some large rocks jutting from the lake about a hundred yards out from the shoreline further east. One of the best diving birds in the world, other than the loon, a cormorant usually perched above the water on any object he could find and waited with infinite patience for the opportunity to plunge beneath the water's surface and spear a fish.

Farther out there were six or so fishing boats, one of them speeding east to west, throwing up a big rooster tail of water, just in front of the first island. What a grand-looking day, Caleb reflected, wishing he was in one of those boats with a rod and reel, and what a sad contrast it was to the gruesome murders taking place at this most romantic setting on Willow Pond. It would all pass, he knew, and time would surely heal. Cedar Lodge, whether the Seldons continued to own it or not, would go on, an immutable presence here in this sylvan landscape of dark forests and shining lakes.

Caleb wrote neither poetry nor prose, but he possessed, without realizing that he did, the heart and soul of a romanticist. He had entered college intending to major in botany and study for a career that would have him forever stalking through his beloved woodlands. In those days, biology and natural history had been his passion. In those days, he had . . . Aw, what the heck, he thought. No sense rehashing it all now. In his sophomore year he had read about the opportunity to ensure steady work as a law-enforcement officer in a state where good-paying jobs were hard to find (especially for botanists, he surmised). Police and sheriff's departments everywhere wanted college graduates. So he'd switched his major and here he was fifteen years later—a damn good cop, if he did say so himself, and proud of his work. Only thing was . . . he was getting older and what he needed was a damn good woman.

That thought opened a much-used door in his mind and in walked Det. Lt. Thomasina Barclay. Godawmighty, he was keen on that woman. He imagined what it could be like in a future in which his fantasies had come true: *Unable to quell his aching heart, he finally reveals to Tom his secret passion for her and, astoundingly, she responds in kind, disclosing her own secret desire, and they return here, to Cedar Lodge, long after the murders are only a memory. Together in their room, anticipating their first night of love-making, she takes off her nightdress and moves slowly toward him as he stands naked and aroused, awaiting her enfolding arms.*

Her incredible breasts touch his chest and he caresses her wide hips as she puts her lips to his ears and says,

"I'm going to the boathouse now!"

Visions of conjugal heaven exploded. Caleb wheeled around and saw Sam, waving as he headed off to the boathouse tool shed. Caleb breathed in deeply and released a plaintive sigh. *Whoa!* Bob Weller! Momentarily alarmed, uncertain how long he'd been gathering skeins of wool, he looked up quickly to the porch and was relieved to see Bob still there, unmoving, gathering his own

wretched skeins. Over on the other end of the porch, Brad continued to sleep, his head lolling against the back of the chair and his
arms hanging off the sides.

Stay alert, you big oaf, Caleb told himself. Anything could happen around this place at any time. One more murder would make
it a trifecta of horror.

Six Godwin emerged from the shadows just inside the front
door, ambled across the porch, stopped midway down the stairs
and stood immobile, gazing absently toward the western shore. Oh
boy, Caleb thought—a third daydreamer. Six didn't even notice
Renee Ranger, carrying a canvas fold-up chair, descend the steps
past him. Renee stopped at the foot of the stairs, swung her mane
of dark hair loose from some imaginary constraint, drew sunglasses
from her bag, then strode over to the third dock, unfolded the
chair, sat down and opened a paperback book. Had Caleb been
standing next to Renee he could've seen on the book's cover a lurid
illustration of a body hanging from a grand staircase and the blood-
dripping title "Revenge at Gorham Castle."

Six, meantime, still in a semi-mesmerized state, walked to the
western end of the lodge, continued on around the corner, passed
by the parking lot and went up to the edge of the woods near the
generator shed. So in thrall was he to his own concentrated
thoughts that he didn't remember anything past the moment when
he had left his lunch table, and yet here he was, easing himself onto
a tree stump exactly at his intended destination. Marvelous thing,
the brain, he reflected. Glancing at his watch, he saw that a good
two hours had passed since his last smoke, so, after a good deal of
probing into various pockets, he located pipe and tobacco and began filling the bowl. Then more probing—*where the hell is the damn
lighter?* Ah, back pocket. Puzzling. Why, he wondered, would he
have put it in a back pocket?

A chipmunk skittered by in its species' distinctively nervous
style—*zip, stop, look around; zip, stop, look around.* Squirrels chattered
in the trees, and chickadees, finches, warblers and red-winged
blackbirds sang a contrapuntal symphony. Far away, crows
squawked raucously. Here, the night before, had been a piteous

corpse, harsh lights, fear and trauma. Now, there was only nature's deceptive tranquility.

This was how Alicia found him, sitting on the stump, surrounded by smoke and, like a Merlin in his tower, spellbound by the bubbling retorts and beakers and cauldrons of his mind. She approached with light, careful steps, sat beside him and, in companionable silence, awaited the inevitable eureka.

Six squinted through the smoke at some elusive wraith of a thought that had been drifting in and out of his brain since . . . Since when? He wondered. Last night? This morning? During the past seventeen or so hours since Gene's murder someone—who, when or what now unknown—had said something within his hearing that had, at the time, distinctly intrigued him. But the memory of exactly what was out of reach; each time he tried to conjure it, the thought slipped away into the cerebral mist. He was now certain it had to do with this very site of Gene's ghastly murder and burning. Become still, he instructed himself. Become very still and think about . . .

Burning. That was it . . . was it not? The burning of . . . *Ah hah!* Yes! Noreen Crepeau, the medical examiner—she stood up from examining Bruno Gabreau's body . . . *I was standing right there . . .* and she said . . . something powerful started . . .

Six stood up abruptly and announced to the air around him, "Got it!"

"That's wonderful, my darling," Alicia said.

Six flinched and yelped in fright. "Jesus Christ! I didn't know you'd sneaked up on me!"

"Six. I didn't sneak up on you. I boldly walked up and sat beside you five minutes ago."

"Oh. Sorry. I was casting in unknown waters."

"Catch anything?"

"Ayuh. Come on. I'll tell you about it while we look for Benson."

Twenty-Three

The last commercial—one regarding the joy of having a new muffler installed—was ending. Benson and Tom sat before the big wall-mounted screen in Gene's office awaiting, in grim silence, the expected worse.

Jarring, pulse-beating music descended to a *dit-dit-dah-dit-dit-dit,* an excited male voice brayed, "From the studios of WCCB, Augusta, your two o'clock action news!" and an eager, smiling blonde flashing perfect white teeth appeared on screen and exuberantly announced that she was Joann Jernigan. Joann put on her serious face and said:

"Two people have been found dead during the past twenty-four hours at a nationally known fishing and hunting resort in the Belgrade Lakes district. The Somerbec County sheriff's department has confirmed the death of Iphigene Seldon, owner of Cedar Lodge, located on the south shore of Willow Pond, near Rome, is a homicide. Her body was found in back of the lodge last night shortly after she had been entertaining guests in the popular resort's dining room. According to sources inside Cedar Lodge, her body was burned, although this has not been officially confirmed."

"Goddamn it," Benson rumbled.

"Early this morning a man's body was found in shallow water near the lodge's docks. The sheriff's department would not release the name of the man until notification of next of kin, but, again, our sources inside Cedar Lodge claim that the victim is local fishing guide Bruno Gabreau, a resident of nearby Winsokkett Pond."

"Goddamn it."

"Somerbec County Sheriff Benson Doucette had this to say to our reporter . . ."

Benson winced as the image of his curly hair and worried eyes popped onto the screen. He was relieved to see that he sounded calm and looked intelligent as he confronted the camera and recited his statement.

He punched the remote and the screen faded.

"Coulda been worse."

"Yep," Tom said. "No way to keep people in here from contacting the media."

"Yeah, I know. But I still hate it. In the old days . . ."

Tom stood up patted Benson's shoulder and said, "I know Tom . . . ITOD."

"Then we'll have Jennifer's Sentinel story in the morning."

The office door cracked open and Six's head appeared. "Blowtorch," he told them.

"Is this some kind of password?" Benson asked.

"Gene was burned with a blowtorch." Six came into the room with Alicia immediately behind him. "Had to be. Remember what Dr. Gabreau said? 'Something powerful started the fire.' Some blowtorches use fuel or some kind of accelerant—that would account for the odor we noticed last night—and those damn things will keep going no matter how much rain. Big ones are powerful."

* * *

Sam loped over to Caleb, calling, "Sgt. Cobb! I think I found it!"

"You found *it?*"

"Yes sir!"

"What's *it?*"

Sam was flustered. "The awl, sir. You asked me to look for an awl."

"Oh. Of course. Sorry, Sam. My mind's been sort of wandering."

"Yes sir."

"So the awl isn't missing after all."

"It's uh . . . say what?" Sam looked as though he were struggling to process unfamiliar data.

Patience, Caleb reminded himself. Patience. "The hypothetical awl that the sheriff and I speculated might be missing from the tool room is not missing. You found it."

Sam's flushed pink. "Uh . . . No! No sir, that's, like, not what I meant."

"What *did* you mean?" Caleb asked, wondering briefly how Sam might be doing in college.

"I meant that the awl isn't there but I, like, found where it should be."

"Ah ha."

"There's actually three awls and they've got these, like, little white lines painted around them. All the tools have white lines painted on the walls that, like, show the shape of the tools . . . to show where they should be hung up. There's this awl that's got the longest shaft . . . and it's gone."

The fog lifted and Caleb said, "Good work, Sam. I better go have a look."

* * *

Benson and Tom clattered noisily down the front steps with Six and Alicia hard on their heels. They were looking for Caleb and, as chance would have it, there he was emerging from the boathouse with Sam. He hurried toward them waving his hand above his head. Apparently, he was looking for them while they were vice versa.

Caleb said, "Sheriff there's an awl with a six-inch shaft missing from the tool room. Just the kind of thing Dr. Crepeau thinks may've been used to kill Gabreau."

"Great. We can add it to the blowtorch search."

"I beg your pardon?" Caleb's eyes widened and his brows rose.

"Six thinks maybe a blowtorch was used to set Gene's body on fire."

"Damn. So we start looking for a blowtorch."

"Ayuh."

"And an awl?"

"Well," Benson replied, "if you think about it, searching for something like that around here is probably useless."

"Relieved to hear you say that," Caleb said. "I was just thinking how the murderer, if he used the awl, just flung it out into the lake. Probably never find it."

"For that matter," Benson said, "same thing goes for the blowtorch. Killer could've hurled that into the lake, too." He paused and furrowed his brow. "No. Wait a minute. A blowtorch, even a small one, has some weight to it. Couldn't fling that very far."

Six spoke up. "And the lake grass here is pretty sparse for, oh, maybe fifty or sixty feet out."

"Whattaya think, Tom?" Benson asked, turning to his lieutenant.

"I say let's do it. Let's take a look."

Benson looked at Caleb. "Do you know Steve Libby, over to Oakland? He's helped us in the past."

"Ayuh. Diver."

"Give him a call now and see if we can get him over here right away."

Caleb wandered off and punched in the dispatcher's number so he could get Libby's number.

Benson noticed that Sam was still standing close by, obviously enthralled by the conversation, and called him over. "Sam, have you ever seen a blowtorch around the lodge?"

"No sir. Don't think we'd need a thing like that."

Benson said to Tom: "I bet you know what I'm thinking comes next."

"Calls to local hardware stores, Home Depot, WalMart, et cetera."

"Got it in one."

Benson looked at Six and Alicia and said, "Professors, this is where being secret, temporary cops gets real boring. It would really help us if you could make some calls."

"As many as needed," Six responded.

"Excellent. All right, let's find a PC or a laptop we can use. I'll ask Kipper if we can use a lodge machine. We need to find phone numbers. I know most of the hardware stores in the county but we'll do a Google search anyway for a list. We need to find who bought a blowtorch recently."

* * *

Steve Libby had arrived with his scuba gear and was merrily engaged in one of his favorite activities—looking for something on the bottom of a lake, this time a blowtorch. A blowtorch! The things people dropped in the water never ceased to amaze him. Last year, among other prizes, he had recovered two outboard motors, a sailboat rudder, a shotgun and a $1,500 fly-fishing rod. Why pay so much for a rod? he wondered—it was the fisherman, not the damn rod, that brought in the fish.

This search, he knew—and the thought thrilled him—was part of a murder investigation. Two people had been killed here. He'd seen it on the 2 o'clock news. There he was, sitting at the counter at the Sunset Grill in Belgrade Lakes watching Sheriff Doucette talking to a reporter and then . . . what? Thirty, thirty-five minutes later he gets a call from Sgt. Cobb, and now an hour and a half after he had been sitting at Sunset Grill, here he was right where the TV cameras had been. Looking for a blowtorch. You just never knew, he thought. You just never knew.

While Sam stood at the end of a dock watching Steve's air bubbles trace rectangular and then diagonal paths on the water's surface, several lodgers came to the lakeshore to watch the action. Only there was no action. So they drifted away toward the parking lot in back, where their luggage and fishing gear had already been loaded into their cars. They, like most of the other paying guests, had been interviewed and cleared and given passes signed by the sheriff to get them past Billy and Eric, the deputies guarding the camp road.

Inside the lodge, Caleb searched the premises for a blowtorch as Six and Alicia sat at the reception desk dialing hardware stores and consumer outlets in Waterville, Winston, Oakland, Skerridgewock and Belgrade Lakes.

In Gene's beautiful, pine-paneled office, Roberston Weller sat facing Benson and Tom. All three were sunk deeply and oh-so-comfortably into enormous, dark-brown leather armchairs suitable for an explorer's club where large-bellied, ruddy-cheeked members reclined with brandy and cigars and relived the adventures of their younger, slimmer selves. The seating was an incongruous arrangement for a face-off between suspect and interrogators. Nevertheless, interrogations proceeded.

"Mr. Weller," Benson began, "I know you're probably very upset right now, but we have to ask you some questions. You do understand?"

Bob's eyes seemed to reflect no emotion whatsoever, a result—though Benson could not have known it—of existential numbness. To Benson, the man simply seemed unnaturally calm and self-possessed. Was Weller, despite his avowals of grief to Six Godwin, just a callous fortune hunter after all who was now shrugging off the loss of his murdered trophy? With his finely sculpted features and wavy gray hair and big white mustache, he reminded Benson of a character in some film drama of the 1940s.

"Of course I understand," Bob replied, his baritone voice matching the silver-screen image. "Please carry on."

Benson had decided earlier on a full-frontal assault with no conversational skirmishes. "Mr. Weller, did you believe Bruno Gabreau murdered Gene Seldon?" He was surprised at the reaction to the question—Bob's eyes quickly filled with anger and he abruptly leaned forward in the big chair. He stared with seeming amazement at Benson. "More than that," Benson continued, "did you somehow *know* Gabreau had killed Gene?"

Bob's sudden transformation from dispassionate languidness was startling: His face suffused red and his eyes blazed as he ramped forward to the edge of the chair. "That goddamn bastard killed Gene?" he roared, causing Benson to flinch. "Goddamn! Someone got to him before I did! I wanted to kill—" He choked and coughed.

Benson lifted his chin toward Tom, indicating for her to intervene.

"Mr. Weller," Tom said, leaning close to him, "please listen to me. We do not know that Bruno Gabreau murdered Ms. Seldon. We have no evidence at all that he was the killer." Assuming the possibility that Bob's reaction might be simply convincing theatrics, Tom said, "That's why we're asking you if you knew or suspected that Gabreau was guilty of the murder."

Bob looked long into Tom's large blue eyes, whose basilisk-like gaze purportedly made liars quiver, and was unfazed. *His* eyes, on the other hand, manifested rage. He spoke with slow, emphatic diction. "If I had known who was the stinking animal that murdered and burned Gene I would have killed him. I did not kill Gabreau. I did not suspect him." Pausing, he looked from Tom to Benson and then back to Tom. "Is he the murderer?"

"We honestly don't know." Tom responded.

Ever so slowly, Bob eased his way back into the comfortable depths of the big leather chair. He put his head back, stared at the ceiling and then said, "Then if it is someone else I will find him and kill him."

* * *

Tom Barclay and Renee Ranger could have been female representatives from two different planets at an intergalactic conference: Tom, 6 feet tall and 190 pounds, wore her customary working-cop ensemble of generously proportioned "mom jeans," yellow workman's boots, and a khaki, two-pocket camp shirt with her badge pinned over her impressive left breast; Renee, 5-feet-eight and 140, wore a white silk blouse with a plunging, collared neckline and long, slashed sleeves, an oh-so-short flowered skirt that became rump-high when she sat, and strapless, high-heeled, open-toed pumps that revealed pink toenails; from the sensuous jiggling beneath her blouse it was obvious that she was braless, and the entirety of her tanned thighs was available for viewing.

Sex-cats like Renee Ranger did not elicit strong reactions negatively or positively from Tom Barclay. Her relationships with other females were circumscribed by whether a particular woman was a good person. If a woman for whom she had a high regard as a truly decent human being wanted to dress in screw-me-right-now outfits then Tom figured what the hell—people should be able to dress like they wanted to. As Tom was heterosexual—Caleb Cobb's large heart would've soared with renewed hope had he possessed this knowledge—sexually demonstrative women did not, of course, arouse her; but neither did they offend her, because she never felt the necessity to compete with them. She liked men very much, though currently she was without a lover, but she was determined that her approach to men was going to be totally as her natural self, with no attempt at the kind of artifice in dress or behavior that supposedly attracted hot-blooded males. She was a big ole tomboy—she privately enjoyed the eponymous quality of the description—and that fact was take it or leave it with regard to men. Until a Mr. Superb could love her as she was, then Tom was resigned to enduring a loveless existence.

On the significant other hand, Tom had no use for women like Renee Ranger, whom she perceived as phony and greedy, with irritating coy, affected mannerisms. For reasons she couldn't quite identify—for Tom tried to be as unbiased in police work as was humanly possible—the woman had especially gotten under her skin. She knew she was going to enjoy putting the interrogatory screws to this dolly.

Renee looked everywhere in the room except at Tom and Benson. She examined her fingernails, flicked imaginary flotsam from her blouse, swept her gaze across the photographs on the pine-paneled walls, then, with wrinkled brow, pretended intense interest in the carvings of mallards and pintails arranged on the table next to her leather chair. Because she was unavoidably sunk down into the chair seat, each time she crossed and re-crossed her legs, she offered almost-crotch views to Benson and Tom, as was her intention. Anything to try to fluster "the filth" was her attitude. She just loved the new term she'd picked up from contemporary British police thrillers. Criminals there referred to policemen as "the filth," even if they were Scotland Yard inspectors. What a gas. Thinking of these two sheriff's department lummoxes as the filth helped, somewhat, to allay her barely-repressed anxiety—nobody had said boo about Elavil discovered in Gene's body but then they probably wouldn't, would they? Cops—the filth—were sneaky.

She glanced for an instant at the two cops facing her. God, how she hated the sight of them—so rural and ordinary and boring. So unlike the clever men of London's Met, the Metropolitan Police Service. Even being caught and found guilty would be so much better in such a civilized atmosphere, she believed: The knowing smile of an elegantly tailored chief inspector who lusted after her while stating her rights at the moment of arrest, the ancient paneled courtroom with wigged judges and lawyers, and her standing bravely and ravishingly in the dock while men (and women, of course) in the gallery fell in love with her on sight . . .

"Ms. Ranger."

Renee jerked to attention and glared at Tom. The woman was just the kind of butch she couldn't tolerate. She preferred the women she occasionally bedded to be like herself, slender, long-legged, narrow-hipped and designer-clad. Be that as it may, she knew that, if left alone in a room with Lt. Barclay, she could get this big girl heated up and panting quickly enough. And if it were the sheriff? Hah. Nothing to it. Men were so easy.

For her part, Tom had decided to follow Benson's example with Bob Weller—forgo the usual polite formalities of the "sorry we're just doing our job" variety and throw a punch to the teeth before the opening bell. However, she intended to try a much more dramatic gambit, one that was a bit risky. If it didn't work, then probably no harm done—she could back off and let Benson question Renee.

Drawing on her education and experience in psychology, Tom guessed that Renee was none too bright and was hiding something significant—probably, if her hunch was correct, to do with her odd movements Armand had observed when Renee was talking to Bob Weller at the bar.

"We know what you did," Tom said quietly, daggering her meanest cop stare at Renee's appalled face.

Tom's accusation startled Benson, but he caught himself and did not react.

Renee gasped, "Wha—?" and gaped at Tom. She swallowed and quickly looked over at Benson, who was also glaring at her with cold eyes.

"We know what you did, Ms. Ranger," Tom intoned ominously, then decided to throw a speculative right hook: "You were observed putting something into Iphigene Seldon's cocktail glass shortly before she was murdered."

Fear hit Renee like a defibrillator paddle. *How the hell—who could've seen me?* Lie, she told herself. Lie like hell, get out of this room, and run. Glamorous aristocratic women, she recalled from reading countless thrilling murder mystery scenes, even if guilty and cornered by Scotland Yard, responded with hauteur, disdainful denials and a withering "how dare you."

"How dare you," Renee said, attempting an imperious tone. "I did no such thing." She glowered at Tom from beneath haughtily lowered eyelids.

Tom stared implacably back. I wonder, she thought, if this is going to work.

"The bartender saw you, Ms. Ranger." Oops. Mistake, Tom realized. Crap. Getting careless.

Renee had gained precious moments to get control of her frenzied thoughts. Now a little smile lifted the corners of her mouth. If Armand was the one who had "observed" her then she knew he hadn't seen squat. The moment of spilling the Elavil into Gene's glass was emblazoned in her mind because she'd been so scared. In her mind's eye she could see her every move: Her entire, flowing left sleeve had completely covered the glass and the material was opaque. What Armand, the nosy bastard, had seen she wasn't sure, but she knew damn well he couldn't have seen through the sleeve. Bob Weller had been so drunk he wouldn't have registered a naked sasquatch standing next to him, and she knew for certain that the Godwins had been turned completely away from her. No one else had been nearby.

Tom saw the tiny, gloating smile and knew she was not going to get a knockout.

Continuing with her unconvincing imitation of an outraged woman of breeding, Renee, her voice laden with disdain, said:

"The bartender?" she tucked in her chin and furrowed her brow. "You mean that big Paul Bunyan character? What's his name?"

Tom ground her teeth, thinking, you know his eff-ing name, you absurd little . . .

"Oh. Yes. Armand. That's it."

Oh, spare me, Tom thought, her severely flat affect showing no reaction.

A "gotcha bitch" smile broadened Renee's pinkish, lip-glossed mouth. "Anyone else?"

Tom was furious with herself. What the hell had she been thinking? She quickly decided to try a desperate left hook before accepting defeat by telling an outrageous lie. "The substance was found in Ms. Seldon's body."

Oh, Christ, Renee thought. They found the goddamn Elavil. Swallowing hard and trying to maintain her supercilious smile, Renee figured what the hell, there was nothing to say but,

"What substance?"

For Tom, that was the bell ending the first round in a one-round match. She continued to stare at Renee for about thirty seconds just to make her nervous, then turned to look Benson in the eyes. Recognizing the unspoken request, Benson said,

"Ms. Ranger, you may go now, but we definitely want to talk to you further. Please do not leave Cedar Lodge. Is that understood?"

Renee gave Benson a heavy-lidded look of pretended indifference and said, "Sure." She arose, ran her hands sensuously over her stomach and buttocks, ostensibly to smooth her unwrinkled skirt, walked languorously to the door without looking back and was gone.

Tom allowed herself to wonder what that metaphorical punch in the teeth would've felt like unmetaphorically.

* * *

Steve Libby was determined to give this dive an all-out effort. After all, it *was* his first murder investigation. He'd brought three fully-loaded diving cylinders just in case. Thus far he had seen a number of lures—crank bait, spinners, plastic worms and so forth—two broken rods, a moss-encrusted reel, a small mushroom anchor, sunken logs and branches, and a plastic cooler. Now he saw something a bit unusual, and dived to the bottom to take a gander. When he retrieved it he saw that it was a brand new awl, with painted handle and still-shining shaft. May as well take it back in, he figured. It was obviously usable.

While Steve was exploring the lake bottom, Caleb had methodically searched every closet, cabinet, corner, nook and cranny of the lodge's ground floor; that completed, he searched the rooms of those guests who had checked out and left; then he looked in the boathouse, thrashed through the shrubbery lining the lodge's foundation and ended up at the generator shed. No blowtorch. Leaving the shed he looked around at the encroaching woods and thought with weary resignation that a search in the underbrush was going to be mandatory under the circumstances.

As he turned the northeast corner of the lodge and walked toward the lake, he saw Steve standing on the center dock in his wet suit looking at something small in his hand; he'd removed his tank and fins and pushed the mask to his forehead.

"Hey, Caleb," he called. "Find anything?"

"Ayuh," Caleb grunted, drawing closer. "Two dead gulls out back."

"Lookit this," Steve said. "Somebody dropped a new, perfectly good awl in the water."

* * *

Benson looked at the awl in wonder, as if it was a jewel from a Mayan treasure horde. "Now if that isn't just the damnedest thing," he said.

"Yep," Caleb agreed. "It's a wonder."

Steve was puzzled by their fascination with an ordinary awl. "Don't tell me this is something you were looking for?"

"Ayuh," Benson replied. "I'm telling you just that. We were looking for an awl that's missing from the boathouse. It might've been used as a murder weapon."

"Awesome."

"We figured the killer might have flung it into the lake. But we didn't tell you about it 'cause we thought it was so small and light you'd never find it."

"I don't miss much."

"So we concentrated on the blowtorch, which you haven't found, right?"

"Yep, no blowtorch. I can guarantee you. I covered a big area, went way out. Nobody could've thrown a blowtorch that far."

Steve looked thoughtful. "Course, it could've been dropped from a boat."

Caleb said, "The boats were all out of the water late yesterday afternoon, before the storm hit." He pointed at the two blue-hulled bass boats tied at the next dock over. "Those were put out this morning."

Steve unzipped his wet suit jacket and asked, "Anything more I can do, sheriff?"

"Don't think so. This," he waggled the awl in front of Steve's face, "is a hell of a find. Good work, my friend."

"Anytime, sheriff."

Benson looked down at the diving cylinder. "You need help getting that thing to your truck?"

"Nope. Thanks. I'm used to schlepping it."

Benson handed Caleb the awl and said, "Get this to our lab quick as you can. See if we can get anything off it—prints, blood, anything."

Caleb headed off and Benson walked up the porch, into the lodge and across the lobby, waving at Six and Alicia doing hard time on the phones at the reception desk. The suitcases and bags of departing guests were arranged near the reception desk. Benson continued into the clubroom, where he found Armand serving drinks and beers to Colin and Daphne, two youngish men in shorts and polo shirts, and a hardy old woman with the leathery skin of a dedicated outdoorsman.

"Hello, sheriff," Colin said. "Any joy?"

"We've got some leads." Benson quickly raised his hand, palm outward. "I know, I know. Cops always say that. But we really do, and that's all I can tell you."

"Understood," Colin said.

Armand came over and asked, "What can I get you, Benson?"

"Shot of Johnnie, straight . . . glass of water."

Daphne laughed and said, "In TV films, policemen are always going on about how they can't drink on duty."

"Uh huh," Benson replied. "That's cops on TV. Sheriffs in real life get to calm their nerves."

"We were watching the diver," Colin said. "Couldn't help but be curious." He politely had not asked the question, but Benson answered it anyway:

"We found something, all right. Can't tell you what, of course. But we're getting somewhere."

Benson knew that any of the people facing him could be on their cellphones minutes from now calling the Morning Sentinel in Waterville or the Augusta TV station. That was fine with him. He'd revealed no details, and if intriguing news leaked out to the media then maybe he could be spared dealing with them directly.

"You folks leaving tonight?" he asked the group.

Colin said, "We're leaving early in the morning. Have a flight in the morning from Portland. No sense going down there now just to spend the night in the airport hotel."

One of the younger men gestured to his companion and said, "We're here with our girlfriends. They want to get out now."

The leathery woman spoke up. "I'm staying until you guys catch the bastard who did this. I knew Gene Seldon for years. Been coming here since '82. I still can't believe she's dead. She would've lived to a hundred." She held up her beer glass and indicated to Armand that she wanted another. "I knew Bruno, too. Past several years I hired him to take me out on Winsokkett, Rocky Pond . . . and East Pond. Had him lined up for Great Pond next month." She drank off half of her freshened glass of beer, wiped a hand across her mouth and said, "Who the goddamn hell would be murdering Maine's best fishing guides? Somebody from Massachusetts?"

* * *

At the reception desk, Six was sitting with his back to Alicia as he used the lodge's PC. He had just rung off with Home Depot in Waterville, where a floor manager had confirmed that the store had indeed sold a blowtorch four days earlier but that he wouldn't reveal to whom until he got an official request from the Somerbec sheriff. Without looking behind him he snapped his cellphone shut and said to Alicia, "Got to recharge this thing. Do we have . . . "

"Shhh!"

He turned to see that Alicia, who was using the reception desk phone, was waving him off. "Yes suh, I understand, Mr. Jenkins," she said into the handset, as she scribbled on a notepad. "I know it's private information. I'll have Sheriff Doucette contact you. Thanks very much." As she hung up the phone, Benson came from the clubroom and over to the desk. Alicia tore a page from the notepad and handed it to him. "Over to Blake's Hardware in Oakland. Sold a heavy-duty blowtorch two days ago."

"And I," Six announced, whipping a sheet of paper over the desk toward Benson, "have a Home Depot blowtorch purchase. Don't know what size."

"Excellent!" Benson said, encouraged that there was at least some action, however tenuous. "I'll have a deputy from the station go by those places right away." He had just flipped open his cellphone when Tom came up to him and said,

"I just called over to Thayer. Merrill's awake and looking sane, according to the attending doctor. At least she's quiet. Woke up about an hour ago."

"Can you go over? I've got Caleb taking the awl to the forensic lab and now I've got to get one of our guys to check out two blowtorch purchases."

"Sure." Tom started toward the front door, then turned and said, "We gonna have another go at Kipper and Brad later?"

"When you get back."

"And maybe Jean-Pierre?"

"Him, too. Lots of fun for everybody."

Six was amazed. "You mean you found the awl? In the *lake?*"

"Ayuh," Benson replied. "Look for a blowtorch, find an awl. If Gene's killer got rid of the damn thing in a hurry then he must've tossed it into the woods."

Seizing the opportunity of a lull in phone canvassing, Six began the inevitable many-pocketed search for his smoking ensemble.

"There's no way around it—we have to search the woods," Benson said studying his boots with earnest concentration. When he raised his head to face the Godwins he wore an embarrassed expression. "Professors, I, uh . . . well, things are happening kind of fast and I'm short of manpower . . . and womanpower, for that matter. And I wondered if . . ."

"We would help you search the woods," Alicia finished for him. "Of course we will."

"I'm leaning on you a lot, and I'm sorry."

"Don't be," Six told him, firing up a bowlful of No. 79. "We're in this, all the way. Anything we can do. What's beginning to worry me, though, is that we're searching for a figment of my supposition. I created the elusive blowtorch. We have no proof that one was used."

Benson sighed. "Well, yes, you're right. But it's the best supposition going. Now if a blowtorch or anything like it *was* used, then I believe it's still around here somewhere. After Gene's murder we sealed the place off and nobody got out of here . . ."

"Except Huntley Beauchamp," Six and Benson said simultaneously.

"Mental telepathy, professor. If Beauchamp *was* the killer then he probably had the blowtorch with him."

"The suppositional blowtorch."

"Indeed. I need to contact Lt. Pelletier and ask him to examine the remains of Beauchamp's car."

"How about the people leaving this afternoon?"

"It's hard for me to believe that any of the guests here—and we briefly interviewed them all—could have anything at all to do with Cedar Lodge or the family. About half of them have been here before—this place gets a lot of people returning every year—but the only ones who have any direct connection with the family are you two."

Alicia said: "Do you think it's possible that someone among those lodgers was part of Gene's past? Someone, some events we know nothing about?"

"Well, yeah," Benson answered, "we have thought about that, but . . . really, what the hell do we do? That's a thing that would take months to unravel, supposing if we had even a hint that there was some connection. In comparison, a blowtorch supposition is almost a dead cert."

"A luggage search of the people who haven't left?" Six asked.

Benson chuckled and ran his hand through his hair, which had been getting kinkier during the afternoon heat. "I tell you, Six. You and I have something going here. Some kind of brain lasers. I just had that same thought come trickling in. I wonder how many lodgers are left?"

"According to Kipper's entries in the computer there's about fifteen people in nine different rooms." Six pointed to the luggage stacked several feet away from the desk. "Two men who are here with their girlfriends just put their luggage down right there and went to the bar."

"Yeah, I just saw them."

"Then there's the Trimbles and the Bolstons, who said they're leaving tomorrow morning. So that's eight people in four rooms."

Benson said: "There's the woman in the bar who said she knew Gene Seldon for a long time. She's angry and getting drunk—says she wants to stay here until we catch the killer."

"I know who you mean—she's a single, and there's two other singles, a man from Florida and one from New Hampshire. The woman in the bar is local, has a camp down to Long Pond. And"— Six peered at the computer screen—"there's two more married couples who're staying. Said there's no point in leaving until mid-day tomorrow. Something about connecting flights."

Benson put both fists in the small of his back and leaned as far back as possible, accompanied by a few pops and snaps. "God, that feels good." Then he laced his fingers and stretched his arms back of his head. "Well. I just hate to do it but I may as well. I'll do a quick search right now of the luggage and cars. I'll bring in Billy or Eric from the road to help me. At this point it's just going through the motions. "On the other hand, as the old man said to his wife, you just never know what might pop up."

Twenty-Four

Tom stood beside Merrill's bed in her private room at Thayer Campus, MaineGeneral Medical Center in Waterville. A nurse was seated in a chair on the other side of the bed. Merrill's hair had been combed, and though her tanned, freckled face had a healthy pallor, her eyes seemed lifeless. She was deathly still, her arms beside her, lying inert on the top of the sheet.

"Ms. Beauchamp?" Tom said. "Merrill? Do you remember me?"

Merrill moved her head slowly to the left and looked up at Tom. "Sure. Lt. Barclay." Her voice was flat.

At least no hysterics, Tom thought. Whatever sedatives she'd been given had obviously worked. "I'm sorry to bother you now, but I must."

Merrill turned her head back to stare straight ahead.

"Merrill. You do remember what has happened?" When she got no response, Tom said, more emphatically, "Merrill. Please answer me. Do you remember what happened this morning and earlier today?"

Still nothing.

"Mr. Gabreau, Merrill. You do remember, don't you, what has happened to him?"

Thirty seconds went by and Tom was beginning to fear that between trauma and sedatives, Merrill would be unresponsive to any questions at all.

"Bruno's dead."

Tom's voice softened. "I'm sorry, Merrill, I'm genuinely sorry. We're trying very hard to find out who killed him. We're hoping that you may know something that could help us."

Merrill stared at the wall and did not speak.

"Do you know anyone who may've wanted to kill Mr. Gabreau? Did he have enemies?"

Merrill turned her head again and looked at Tom. "Who would want to kill Bruno?"

Someone, Tom thought, wanted to kill him enough to drive a six-inch steel shaft into his brain.

"That's what we don't know, Merrill. Who *would* want to kill Bruno. Do you know?"

Silence.

"Did he have enemies, Merrill?"

"No."

This was rapidly getting nowhere. "Do you remember what you said this morning in the EMS truck, Merrill? You said, 'He didn't kill her. I thought he killed her.' What did you mean?"

"I didn't say that."

"Merrill, you were screaming it. What did you mean? Did you think Bruno had murdered Gene Seldon?"

"I don't remember saying that."

"What *do* you remember?"

"I remember Bruno lying in the water. I loved him. He was dead. His eyes were open."

"I'm sorry, Merrill. I know this is painful. Do you remember anything after that . . . after you saw Bruno lying in the water?"

Merrill did not speak or move. Seconds ticked by. The nurse was fidgeting and looking at her watch.

"Merrill . . ."

"I don't remember anything."

"You're positive?"

"I don't remember anything until I woke up here."

After Tom gave up and left the room, the nurse took Merrill's blood pressure, drew three vials of blood and then headed for the nurse's station in the hallway to schedule an EKG.

Merrill thought the sedative she'd been given was wonderful, truly magical. Better than coke. Better than grass for sure. She felt as though she was at the center of a universe of grief and despair. And yet . . . and yet, strangely, so very strangely, she suffered no agony, no fretfulness or agitation, nothing remotely like the violent

hysteria that had her shrieking and clawing at the nurses and or-
derlies when they had strapped her down in the emergency room.
Now, she felt nerveless, as if she was sitting beside her own misery
examining it dispassionately.

In this detached state of mind, Merrill remembered everything
with serene, abstract clarity: Bruno's plan to kill Gene, her own
participation in it, Bruno's hideously distorted dead face staring up
at the sky; she also remembered every word of her agonized
screaming. Oh, she remembered it all, but she was not going to tell
those cops anything. Never. Never would she tell anyone what
Bruno had intended to do. She would take her secrets to the grave,
and the grave was where she was going soon, an acknowledgement
that, in her present existential calm, did not trouble her in the least.

She had adored Bruno Gabreau unqualifiedly. He was the only
person she had truly loved since her parents' deaths. She had been
desperately seeking love when she impulsively married the then
dashing and charming Huntley Beauchamp. Now, in her medica-
tion-induced condition of tranquil clarity, she knew that life without Bruno would be unbearable. Once they discharged her from
this hospital she would kill herself. Nothing mattered anymore.
Why not die? The decision held no fear for her—to live would
mean enduring endless grief; to die would be "surcease of sorrow."

* * *

Tom returned from Waterville to find Benson and Eric and the
Godwins thrashing about in the woods in separate locations at the
back of the lodge and near its eastern and western sides. It was
nearly 7 p.m., but the loss of daylight was still about an hour and a
half away. Tom located Benson behind the generator shed and
gave him the bad news about Merrill and said it was a toss-up as to
whether Merrill was lying or that trauma really had wiped out her
memory past the time when she had fallen screaming on Bruno's
body.

"Think we should have another session with her tomorrow?"

Tom thought about that. "Well. Maybe. She was obviously heavily sedated. Even if it is trauma, memory could return. If we knew why she thought Bruno had killed Ms. Seldon we might hold one of the keys to finding out what the hell happened in this place."

Benson's phone rang; he grabbed it and said, "Doucette."

A now familiar Maine accent said, "Crepeau here. Blood analysis on woman's body. Traces of Elavil. Only huge dose could've rendered traces in burned body."

"I've heard of it, Noreen. Remind me."

"Strong anti-depressant. Mixed with alcohol it's like the old Mickey Finn. Enough Elavil with enough alcohol equals fatality. Especially the elderly."

"Jesus. Thanks, Nor—" The line was dead.

"You've got a funny look on your face," Tom said.

"We need to talk to one of your favorite people again."

Renee had returned to the western-most dock and was sitting in a director chair reading; she was absorbed in the thrilling climactic chapter of *Revenge at Gorham Castle* when she heard footsteps behind her. The footsteps thudded onto the dock and a despised female voice said, "Ms. Ranger?"

The filth. Attack first, she thought. "Why the question mark? You know it's me."

Two eastward-pointing shadows rippled across Renee and then Benson and Tom stood before her, staring down through big, aviator-style sunglasses. Tom had thought the sunglasses might have an intimidating effect. Besides, she told Benson, movie sheriffs always wore them.

However, Renee was also wearing sunglasses—big designer horn rims from Saks Fifth Avenue. No eyeballs would be visible during this confrontation.

Tom adjusted her holstered Glock for effect, put her hands on her generous hips and said, "Do you use Elavil, Ms. Ranger?"

If Renee's eyes had *not* been obscured by $800 glare-proof lenses, they would have betrayed her shock and fear. She sat very, very still while her internal voice shrieked.

Deny everything. Call your lawyer. Meantime, you are a ravishing inter-national assassin who has just tried to kill James Bond and you don't give a damn. Sneer at the filth.

"Elavil? Is that some kind of feminine hygiene thing? Never heard of it."

* * *

"Get out of here, I want you out of here!"

Kipper, standing with a crutch under his right arm, faced Benson and Tom across a steel counter and pointed a large carving knife at the astonished officers. They had simply made what Benson thought was a reasonable request—to examine the lodge's investment statements and expense accounts to determine if therein lay any possible clue to Iphigene Seldon's murder.

"Are you threatening us, Mr. Seldon?" Benson said.

A terrified Jean-Pierre had flattened himself against a huge refrigeration unit.

Kipper's red-blotched face was convulsed with rage. He slammed the knife down flat on the counter three times in rapid succession then swept it away; the knife twirled down the counter and dropped off the end.

"There, goddamn it!" he screamed. "I threw it away. Don't you *dare* say I'm threatening you! I am *not* threatening you. I was holding the damn knife because I was *cooking*. In my own damn kitchen. Leave! I want you *out* of here. You're frightening Jean-Pierre."

Benson glanced back at the little chef. He was trembling; tears ran down his face. "I'd say you're the one who's most frightening."

Kipper's face looked as though it was going to explode in a broadside of teeth, hair and eyeballs. He pounded the counter, and his voice ascended to a high, keening screech. "You fascist bullies! Out, out owwwwt! I *own* this place. Get the hell out!" Spittle flew from his mouth.

"We can arrest you, Mr. Seldon," Benson said, trying to keep his voice calm. This was the kind of situation all cops feared. He glanced at Tom; she was wide eyed and shaking her head.

271

"Arrest me? *Arrest me?!*" Kipper was practically squealing. "For what? For *cooking?*"

"Obstructing our legitimate investigation of your aunt's death."

"I didn't kill the old . . . *I* didn't kill her! Are you too damn dumb to find out who did?"

"We need to look . . ."

"No! Nooo! I'm trying to prepare dinner, in case you haven't noticed. I've still got guests in this lodge."

"OK. We'll let you get on with it. But later we want to see those accounts."

Kipper grabbed off his paper chef's hat and slapped it over and over on the edge of the counter, shredding it. "No, no, no, no! *Not* without my lawyer! *Not* without my lawyer! Go away, goddammit!" His crutch slipped from under his arm and fell; Kipper grabbed the edge of the counter and screamed in pain as his injured foot made contact with the floor. This further enraged him. "Get out, get out, get out!"

Benson and Tom got out. They walked down the hall and around the corner to the front lobby, and Benson said, "I tell you, Tom. That hysterical sonofabitch is getting on my nerves."

"Ayuh. Mine too. Way over the top. Kinda scary."

"I wasn't so sure the financial records were all that important in the first place. Now, after that disgusting scene, I'm calling Judge Brenner in the morning to see what our legal options are. I want to see those damn statements."

"There's something else eating him, too. Got to be. That's two championship tantrums in one day."

* * *

Brad was the easiest person to find in Cedar Lodge. Since all fishing and sailing or any activities other than feeding the remaining patrons had been brought to a halt by the murders, Brad had spent all his time drinking or sleeping on the front porch with a grieving Amos curled at his feet, leaving only to get sandwiches and dog food from the kitchen or accommodate bodily demands. Amos accommodated his own demands at the edge of the woods on the lesser-used eastern side of the lodge.

"Well, there they are," Benson said, looking at Brad and Amos. "Sort of a matching pair."

"Ayuh," Tom said. "Kind of sad, isn't it? I mean, the poor old hound takes up with the lodge's other lonesome Joe."

Benson looked at her curiously. "Lonesome? From what everyone's been telling me, women throw themselves across his path."

"Sure. With his looks, sure. But from what I gather, it's only the now and then lodger looking for summer romance. He's peculiar as hell, Benson. Peculiar and a loner. And ten more years drinking at his rate he's gonna be a dead loner."

"Well, I guess you're right. While he's still a live loner we better have another go at him."

"He is interesting, chief—don't you think so?"

Benson gave Tom a long, speculative look. "You getting soft, Tom?"

"You mean am I getting soft as a cop or am I getting soft as a woman?" She chuckled at her own question. "Don't worry, to me he's still a suspect, but the guy is funny as hell, and, of course, I've got to admit, he *does* look like some of those lady-killers I've seen in the old black-and-whites."

Benson smiled at her. "I'm going to try to resist his charms."

"But he *is* sad . . . a real sad kind of guy."

Brad had his feet on a wicker stool and was stretched almost level, with his head on a flowered pillow propped against the back of the chair. He seemed as though he was fathoms deep in slumber, but as Benson and Tom approached his chair he lifted his Panama hat, opened one eye and said, "I didn't kill her."

"Mr. Seldon," Benson said, "if we could just . . ."

"And I didn't kill Bruno Gabreau. So. Now that I've answered all your questions, what's left?"

"Why were you out in the storm at the same time Ms. Seldon was murdered?" Tom said. "Sorry. That's one more question."

Brad looked up at Tom and smiled, holding her gaze. "Are we having another date, Lt. Thomasina?"

"Why were you out in the storm?"

"Jesus. What a hard-ass. How about, where are you from, what're your favorite things, who's your favorite movie star?"

"My dad's mean as hell and I have to be in by ten."

Brad erupted in laughter and nearly fell from his chair, catching himself when his rump was inches from the porch timbers. "Thomasina!" he cried, righting himself to a sitting position. Amos's head came up and his droopy eyes regarded the officers with seeming annoyance. "You are the hottest cop on the planet." He was silent for a few moments as he regarded Tom. "Ah, lieutenant, my lieutenant. Another time, another life. It's been years since I met a woman with a real sense of humor. Not just humor. Wit. You're witty, big lady."

Brad sighed, reached to the floor beside his chair and lifted a half-empty bourbon bottle. "Earlier in the day you declined my offer of a cocktail. Of course, it *was* a bit early for those who must hue to the S and narrow." He waggled the bottle. "How about now? It's damn near sunset."

Tom was amazed when Benson said, "We'll have a snort." He pulled up two nearby wicker chairs and gestured for Tom to sit. Tom was further astonished when Brad reached behind the potted plant whose leaves brushed his chair, "his plant," the one he sat next to every day, and produced two small jelly glasses.

"I always keep stemware on hand in case I have guests." Brad poured bourbon into each glass. Benson and Tom took tentative sips and Benson said, "Damn fine, Mr. Seldon."

"George Dickel. Tennessee's finest. My father always said . . ." Brad stopped, looked out at the lake. "Oh, it doesn't matter what he said."

After a few moments of silence, Tom said, "Brad, now that we've been on a date and you've met my father . . ." She gestured toward Benson, who glared at her as Brad grinned and chuckled. "So, now that we've been on a date, just get it over with and tell me what the hell you were doing out in the storm when it's known that you have a terror of lightning." She tasted some more bourbon and said, "Sorry about that, but we'd like to know."

"Awright, awright. Just give me goddamn minute." After nearly two minutes of silence, during which Benson and Tom figured it was best just to wait him out, Brad said, "This is going to sound like the most utter fragrant bullcrap, but it's the truth and if you don't believe me then . . . then so what. Arrest me. Just let me take Amos with me." More silence, more waiting.

"I was putting myself to the test."

Benson was getting bored with Tom's "date." "Is that right?" he said.

"Ayuh. Damn straight. I screwed my courage to the sticking-place . . ." Brad broke off and looked at Tom. "The sticking-place. Now where the hell did that come from? It just popped out there. Sticking-place."

"Shakespeare," Tom said. "Don't remember which play." Tom glanced at Benson and could see that he was getting irritated. "Brad, just tell us."

"I ran out in the lightning. I ran out drunk and scared and ran around raving at heaven. Amos, here, was with me, but I don't believe he'll be able to testify on my behalf." Brad stopped and frowned, concentrating. "You know, it's the damnedest thing— somebody had shut Amos in a utility closet near the kitchen. He was raising hell to get out."

"So there you were, doing . . ."

"I got out there in the storm, Thomasina, and I danced and I was just mad with joy . . . and then I heard Six Godwin screaming."

* * *

The golden sun sank behind the western mountains and its glorious rays shot upward to greet the first faintly glittering stars. Twilight was brief. Darkness came quickly and profoundly, for there was no ambient glow from towns or cities. Vast continents and rivers of stars shone brightly in heaven's dome. Swallows and bats whipped through the air to catch the fireflies, mosquitoes and drag-onflies that danced just above Willow Pond's surface. Bullfrogs thrummed along the shoreline and far out on the lake loons wailed and chattered.

In these first moments of what in different circumstances would be a beguiling evening, Benson Doucette, Tom Barclay and the Profs. Godwin sat on the Cedar Lodge front porch exhausted and discouraged. All were silent with their own thoughts.

Now that they had come to an inevitable halt for the day, Six could hardly believe the past twenty-four hours had been real: Was it only yesterday evening, he thought, that the storm was raging and Iphigene Seldon was holding her lodgers in thrall with stories of bold adventure? At this time the previous night, Gene, Bruno Gabreau and Huntley Beauchamp had all been alive. To Six there seemed to be a maniacal quality to the murders that had con-founded every investigatory move.

"I can tell you honestly that I'm beat to hell," Benson said, stretching and groaning. "You OK, Tom?"

"Nothing a hot bath and a couple of double scotch-on-the-rocks won't fix."

"Professors? How are you feeling?"

"Oh. We'll get through it," Alicia said. "It's still so hard to take in. 'Thou wretched thing of blood, How came Iphigene by her death?'"

Benson cracked his knuckles and said, "I beg your pardon?"

"Sorry," Alicia said. "I was putting Gene's name into a line from a horribly violent play by John Webster. He was a contem-porary of Shakespeare."

"Ah!" Tom said. "I read that boy in college. 'Duchess of Malfi.' That right?" she asked Alicia, who nodded. "Dead folks littering the stage, as I recall. Coincided nicely with my criminology courses."

"Thou wretched thing of blood," Benson repeated. "Perfect description for Cedar Lodge."

Six cleared his throat and gave voice to the bleak thought that was in all their minds: "If Huntley Beauchamp was not the murderer, then there is still a wretched thing of blood within this lodge."

* * *

Just being back in their own camp on Winsokkett Pond seemed to drain away a great deal of the anguish burdening Six and Alicia. Now, each with a glass of bourbon and water on the table beside them, they sat before their small stone fireplace (the hearth filled with sprays of wildflowers) in their venerable wingchairs. The original chintz on both chairs was so tattered and disreputable that Alicia had thrown quilts over the chairs many summers ago, hers a bear's paw pattern and his a country sampler; the quilts also were getting a bit faded and thin, but were not yet splitting—good for another summer or two, Alicia figured. Rudolph lay flat on his side, legs stretched out straight, peacefully snoring beside Six's feet. Marmalade perched atop Alicia's chair, her front paws tucked under and her contented purring audible.

Six had his laptop open and was cruising Google while Alicia did a pencil sketch for a new watercolor.

"Aha!" Six blurted. "Damned interesting."

Alicia did not look up as she distractedly murmured, "Oh, really?"

"Intriguing is more like it."

"Oh, really?"

"*The Sporting Magazine* my ass!"

Alicia wrinkled her forehead and looked at her husband. "Six! What are you on about?"

"Listen to this. '*The Sporting Magazine*, 1792 to 1870, was the first English sporting periodical to devote itself to every type of sport, thus providing the historian with a reasonably comprehensive source.' How do you like that?"

Alicia put down her pencil, took a sip of bourbon and said, "Six, I don't think I'm on the same channel."

"The English couple at the lodge, Colin and Daphne. They told Gene they'd learned about Cedar Lodge from an ad in *The Sporting Magazine*."

"Ah, yes. We were sitting round the table with them, the Bolstons and Gene. Bob Weller was doing fetch and carry from the bar."

"Well. The damn magazine hasn't been published for a hundred and forty years."

"Perhaps there's a new one with the same name?"

"I've been searching for half an hour. The old magazine is the only one mentioned anywhere."

"Maybe they just said it as a private joke."

"Uh huh." Six reached for whichever of his pipe or pouch or lighter was in his right jeans pocket and was surprised to find all three. In the same damn pocket. Was his mind improving, he wondered? "I think there's a bigger joke going on with those folks," he said, firing up the old 79.

"And what would that be?"

"That they're not what they say they are."

"Really? And why do you think that?"

"Vowels."

"I beg your pardon."

"They slipped up on a few of their vowel sounds. Very tricky, those vowels. American, or possibly Canadian, intonations leaked through their plummy accents now and then, I'm sure of it. I'm going to tell Benson about it first thing tomorrow. No sense worrying him tonight."

* * *

"I know they found something in the lake," Daphne said. "The sheriff and those two deputies were gathered around the diver jabbering."

"Tsk. One of the deputies, as you call them, is a detective. A lieutenant detective no less."

"You mean that great big fellow?"

"My, my, old Daff. Sexist reaction. The detective is the great big woman. That's a lot of girl packed into those jeans. The great big man is a sergeant."

Daphne chuckled. "They look like a matching pair. Except that he doesn't have big tits."

"So. What do you think the frogman dragged from the lake?"

"Something old, something new, something borrowed, something blue . . . which reminds me that we should be getting out of here."

"Right you are," Colin said. "Time to put many a dusty mile between us and this fishing hole."

"Crack of dawn? *Does* dawn crack in this part of the world?"

"Very witty, my dear. Yes. Let's get some sleepy-bye-bye. Early to bed, early to rise, makes a chap healthy, wealthy and unavailable for questions from the police."

* * *

"I'm sorry, Brad, really sorry," Tory said, looking up at Brad with her big blues emanating sorrow. "I just couldn't. I just really couldn't. It's not you. All this has really upset me. *Two* murders. We're leaving early in the morning. Nelson doesn't like this violence *one* bit."

"How about a little cocktail in the bar, then? A farewell drinky-poo."

"The bar? There's someone in there *now?*"

"No. But I own this joint, remember? The bar's always open when ole Bradley's around."

Tory hesitated then said, "OK. One drink, Brad."

Later, as they parted at the foot of the stairs, Tory told Brad how wonderful it had been making love to him and that when some time had passed she would call him and then . . .

"Sure," Brad said, shrugging and giving her a crooked smile. "That'll be swell. You already know how to bait a hook."

* * *

Kipper sat before the computer in the lodge's office, his eyes blood-shot and swollen from crying, his mind hopping about with scenes of violence and rage. Was this madness? Was he really going insane? Is this the way it began for those people he read about on news websites who slaughtered their lovers, their wives, their families and then killed themselves?

Jean-Pierre had become hysterical following the confrontation with the sheriff in the kitchen, especially when Kipper attempted to hug him. Kipper had only wanted to comfort him, only wanted to tell him everything was all right, tell him they would leave, go to New York, that everything would be all right. Please, God, just listen to me, he had begged. But Jean-Pierre had been inconsolable; he had twisted away from Kipper and had screamed and cried when Kipper grabbed for him again, and had said he was terrified of Kipper and that he was leaving and never coming back.

Kipper had gaped at Jean-Pierre, paralyzed for a moment by disbelief, and then a great berserk fury had risen in him and he had lunged, shrieking, "You little bastard! Don't you *dare* say that! Don't you *dare*! I'll kill you, goddammit!"

Jean-Pierre, sobbing and wailing, had fallen backward through the double doors, where he sprawled on the floor in front of the entrance to the clubroom. He'd quickly scrambled to his feet and run to his room, where he had cowered, whimpering with misery, behind a double-bolted door.

Up to this point, the ten lodgers in the clubroom had heard only muffled shouting and had shrugged it off as a possible hissy over something like burned sauce for the grilled salmon they had been promised. But when the howling had reached such an intensity that curses and threats were clearly audible, two men had jumped up and run through the door in time to see Jean-Pierre scuttling around the far corner. Cautiously, they had pushed through the double doors to the kitchen and were confronted by the maniacally staring eyes of Kipper Seldon. As if he were unaware of the presence of the two men, Kipper ripped off his apron, threw it on the floor and walked past them and through the doors.

After about fifteen minutes of excited discussion, the ten diners, sufficiently rattled by two murders to fear yet more violence, agreed to gather in the kitchen, raid the refrigerator and then accompany one another to the safety of their rooms.

Now, still trembling with shock, Kipper sat at Gene's huge oak desk drinking straight gin and trying to get control of his shattered psyche. His breathing was shallow and labored, his chest hurt and when he thought of Jean-Pierre and their last moments together earlier in the night he became dizzy and nauseated.

He had wanted to kill Jean-Pierre.

In one momentary paroxysm of rage, he had wanted to destroy the one and only human he had loved since his mother and father had died.

He drank off his second glass of gin, put his face in his hands and tried hard to calm his thoughts and his breathing.

Listen to your breathing; listen to your breathing. That's better. Now: You did not kill Jean-Pierre, you did not even strike him. You simply screamed out the words of a lover's anguish. You didn't mean it. Everything is reparable. He is frightened, but everything is reparable. Give him some time. You know that he loves you. You know that he loves you.

After spending nearly half an hour with his eyes shut and repeating soothing mantras such as lovers are destined to have their little tiffs and "the course of love did never run smooth," Kipper's seething brain began to quieten and a still extant sense of self-preservation reawakened and compelled him to complete the task before him.

He poured another gin, took a bracing sip, turned on the computer and called up the daily business accounts of Cedar Lodge. As he punched the keyboard he watched the names of his sham distributing companies gradually vanish from the ledgers. The bank accounts for the companies still existed, of course, and to close them out and transfer the money elsewhere would require personal visits to the three banks in Massachusetts and New Hampshire. That needed to be done soon, but at least, he told himself, if the f'ing sheriff stuck his big honker into the lodge's records for the second quarter and July there would be no trace of a certain trio of large but phantasmical warehouse firms.

But there was still a danger. The checks to the phantom corporations were cut on the Cedar Lodge Holdings' Waterville bank account. Could the sheriff's department examine corporate accounts? Weren't such accounts barred to official snooping unless they were ordered opened by a court? And why would Doucette ask for such a ruling? What would he show for probable cause? He would never have heard of the phantom corporations. Only a dedicated bloodhound operation would ever uncover Kipper's three bank accounts that were soon to be closed out, and Kipper thought the likelihood of such an undertaking extremely remote.

After another dreary hour and a half of search and delete, oiled along by a fourth glass of gin, he managed to expunge all entries of payments to his made-up firms for the past two years, ever since the inception of his deception. *The inception of his deception.* He liked that. Very funny. Jesus, he was getting drunk.

During the monotony of the over-and-over process of cleansing the ledgers, which further composed his fevered brain and permitted a modicum of rational thinking, a marvelous idea had occurred to him, a very pleasing idea that brought tears to his eyes when he realized that he could make things right with his beloved little man.

He closed the Cedar Lodge folders and called up a blank Word document and prepared to pour out his heart in a letter to Jean-Pierre. With words of love and adoration he would pledge on his knees, his hapless metaphorical knees, to make Jean-Pierre the happiest, the most successful French chef ever to immigrate from Languedoc, Jean-Pierre's native province. With words of remorse and anguish he would prostrate his wretched metaphorical self at Jean-Pierre's feet and beg his forgiveness.

He would slip the letter beneath Jean-Pierre's door. And then all will be well, he reassured his aching soul, and all will be well.

* * *

At midnight, Cedar Lodge, its long, handsome three-story façade familiar to sportsmen worldwide, was bathed in the pale glow of a bright full moon. All was still—not a zephyr disturbed Willow Pond's flat surface—and all was quiet—no night creatures were heard, though they were most assuredly all about in the woods and water.

Lamplight shone from the lodge's office window. The sheriff's deputy assigned to guard the building throughout the night was aware that one of the owners was working late, and as unobtrusively as possible he checked on him periodically. The deputy was a good deal older than the new recruits Billy and Eric who had been on the scene during the turbulent day and had many years' experience, yet he was nervously wary. This sort of duty was unprecedented. There had been two murders at this place. The deputy standing beside his patrol car on the camp road was also justifiably nervous. He had his car radio on, his radio-phone clipped to his belt and the safety snapped off on his Glock pistol.

Meanwhile, inside the lodge, a tall, bare-footed figure slipped out of one room, padded down the hallway and entered another room.

Twenty-Five

"So, my dearest, how likest thou our new voiture?" Colin said as he and Daphne traveled ever northeastward on Maine's intriguing two-lane county and state roads toward Acadia for a brief hidden layover, their customary routine following especially tedious "free-lance employment." And they agreed that the Cedar Lodge job had been extraordinarily tedious—much too much turmoil for their tastes. Occasional violent escapades had been exciting in their younger years, adding a thrilling dash to life. But now that they had both topped forty, danger held less appeal.

"Le voiture est tres bien for comfort but definitely plebian in styling," Daphne replied.

"Very suitable for our purposes."

"Indeed."

The newish blue Honda sedan, nearly indistinguishable at a distance from hundreds of thousands of other cars on America's highways, had so conveniently offered itself for theft that it seemed to them it would be a shame not to seize the opportunity. It had been parked behind a scruffy pizzaria in a forlorn-looking three-dog village; working in the predawn darkness, Colin and Daphne needed only minutes to open the car, hot-wire its ignition, attach counterfeit Vermont license plates, and toodle along on their way. To such an ingenious couple, rapid thievery was an art form. The old Jeep without license plates they had left in the Honda's place would be quite a surprise, and an enduring mystery, to the Honda's unfortunate owner. Ah well, thus was life, Colin and Daphne felt— self-preservation and all that demanded periodic harm to the well-being of others.

The Honda would provide transportation for only a few hours, and then another car would be purchased by the new people they would've by that time become.

To an interested party, just the exchange of the Jeep for the Honda would provide a nearly complete tutorial on how the very

clever Colin and Daphne—this Nick and Nora of the dark side—
maneuvered their clandestine way through society leaving only a
vaporous trail. People here and there would remember them, of
course, but find them again? Hah-hah, as the late Huntley Beauchamp would say—never.

The Jeep had been purchased with one of a number of credit-
card lines the couple had opened in the names of fully documented
people who did not exist; after each card was used only once, it
was destroyed, along with all of the pertaining bogus personal documents. Both the Jeep and the Honda would be dappled with fingerprints, of course, but none would be Colin and Daphne's, for
they always, *always,* wore white cloth gloves when fiddling about
with autos or driving them. Fresh packages of white cloth gloves
were consistently packed in their luggage and, as the gloves were
so flimsy, Colin and Daphne carried several pairs at all times. The
gloves were understandably necessary for other of their activities
as well. If asked, Colin and Daphne would not have had words
sufficient for the praise of white cloth gloves. For those many
other daily activities that left fingerprints on myriad objects, they
had developed quick, cunning techniques—some of them classic
sleight-of-hand moves—that masked their constant endeavor to
leave no fingerprints and, one hoped, very little DNA. So automatic had their techniques become that very few people ever noticed Colin or Daphne's deft wiping of silverware, glasses, bottles,
metal or polished-wood surfaces, etc. Humans do leave DNA behind in cars and elsewhere, of course, especially in regard to hairs,
but Colin and Daphne's original identities, the ones they had carried from birth, were so buried beneath so many acquired and then
abandoned aliases that fingerprint and DNA searches were 99%
certain never to provide any evidence remotely connected to the
merry couple in the blue Honda heading toward an island hideaway
in Maine's Acadia region.

With them always in their professional life was a compart-
mentalized steel carrying case. One compartment contained phantom individuals' driver's licenses, passports, fake credit reports,

and credit cards that matched those documents. The other compartment held cellphones registered to six of the aforementioned phantoms. Colin and Daphne never owned computers and avoided the Internet as if it were the Black Death.

Sharing the space with the cellphones were license plates from fifteen states manufactured by an artisan who had learned this craft, among others, while lodging at a federal institution.

Fortunately for Colin and Daphne, they were still devoted to each other, for they had to live, of necessity, in their own private bubble and devise entertainments shared by only the two of them. And they never communicated in a social way by mail or telephone with anyone. For "business trips," as they called them, they contacted their "employment agency" through a double layer of secure letter drops.

During the course of such "business" endeavors, Colin and Daphne, perpetually good-natured and humorous, met any number of other people and interacted quite charmingly with them for brief days—even exchanging contact information (though the Trimbles' wasn't worth the paper it was scrawled on) and promising to stay in touch. They were of course never seen again by these momentary acquaintances, any of whom would have been appalled to learn that the delightful and witty Colin and Daphne (or whatever their names were at the one time) actually were polished, elegantly tailored thugs hardened by lives of crime, with a smattering of brutalities to their credit.

One of Colin and Daphne's saving graces, if one could apply that term to any of their attributes, is that they never rationalized their crooked lives or pretended that they themselves were anything other than what would engender the contempt of any law-enforcement officer in most any country in the world.

"We are not nice people, Colin."

"No, dearest, we are not."

"But we've never killed anyone."

"Well . . . there may've been, um, collateral damage."

"Ah, yes. We had to make some rather desperate escapes in the past, didn't we?"

"There *was* a lot of shooting during a few notable occasions. I recall seeing some villains fall down in the midst of our returning gunfire. We may have killed someone, you know."

"Well, regrettably that may be so. But you know what I mean, my love—we've never *murdered* anyone."

"Of course not." Colin gave his wife, who was driving, a brilliant smile. "We are artists of a felonious persuasion. Murderers are evil." He took his cellphone from a jacket pocket. "Which reminds me . . ."

"Oh, oh," Daphne said. "So you *are* going to take care of that little matter."

"That *little matter* is insane in an especially hideous way. I know whereof and all that . . . you weren't with me on that particular job. I was sort of in the background and obviously have escaped the fiend's memory, otherwise the nature of our sojourn at Cedar Lodge would have been considerably altered. Psychopaths do *such* damage to the reputations of decent criminals."

They had a hearty laugh over that one for a couple of miles. Humor was very important to Colin and Daphne, and they never failed to break each other up. Humor kept them psychologically fit for their often nerve-wracking line of work and lifted their spirits when the reality of their being mere villains became oppressive. They were, after all, intelligent and educated and therefore susceptible to periodic bouts of introspection, when they suffered pangs of yearning for the "might have beens" of law-abiding lives.

Daphne pulled the car up to a general store at the junction of two roads covered in aging, cracked tarmac with a few lethal-looking potholes. They had left secondary roads and were now traveling on what could be termed "tertiary" roads. Despite their many protections, the couple felt it was wise to avoid giving the general populace an eyeful of themselves and the car.

Though it was still quite early, two members of that populace—ancient farmers presumably too old to climb aboard the tractor—had already taken up what seemed to be their accustomed stations on a bench in front of the store and were drinking coffee as they swatted at flies.

"So, my dear," Daphne said. "Just how are you going to out this particular psychopath?"

"I'm going to make one strategic phone call."

Daphne arched an eyebrow. "Oh, really? To one of those large sheriff's people?"

Colin chuckled. "No, no. Unh-uh. Bad luck to make unsolicited contact with any member of the carabiniere. You know that. I'm going to call that professor."

"There were two."

"The one who smokes the pipe."

"Ah. And why him?"

Colin stopped in the act of opening the car door and thought. "I think it's because I like him."

"You always wanted to be a professor, didn't you?"

"I would've been especially good at lecturing to students on aspects of the criminal mind." Colin smiled at his beautiful wife. "There is also another reason why I'm calling Professor Godwin and no one else."

"I can't imagine."

"His is the only phone number I managed to collect."

"Very funny."

Colin flicked a business card from his shirt pocket. "You see? Winsokkett Antiquarian Books. Let's get some breakfast."

After purchasing ham sandwiches, hard-boiled eggs and hot coffee, Colin and Daphne pulled onto the road and sped away into the cool, fresh morning.

When they'd been gone for about five minutes, one farmer said, "Don't see many like that anymore."

"Nope. Not since the river camps closed up."

"Nice legs."

"Ayuh."

* * *

The Godwins arose at dawn and walked out on their dock, followed by the ever-vigilant Rudolph, who suspected there might be a boat ride in the offing. Six and Alicia put rods, tackle boxes and thermoses of water and coffee into the bass boat and then settled at the end of the dock for a breakfast of fried egg and mustard sandwiches and grapefruit juice followed by a special treat—coffee from Haiti that supposedly was strong enough to take the hair off a razor-back hog. A camp neighbor had put them onto the thick, delicious brew, and they had ordered the beans from a specialty shop in Bangor. Two bags had arrived while they were at Cedar Lodge.

"Damn fine," Six pronounced after his first sip. "Fire in the belly."

"Is this coffee what they call full-bodied?" Alicia asked.

"I thought full-bodied was big tits and wide hips."

"Six. It's six-thirty in the morning . . ." She stopped and chuckled. "That's kind of funny, isn't it? 'Six. It's six-thirty'."

"I've heard it before."

"Sorry, my love. Anyway, about the reference to a . . . um, fully developed woman. If this indicates a certain incipient ardor on your part, and believe me I am not antipathetic to a bit of ardor, can you please behave yourself until after lunch? I want to go fishing first."

"I'll try to contain myself, kiddo."

Six and Alicia drank their coffee and looked at the clear morning sky and placid lake with deep pleasure. A bald eagle circled above, looking for the silhouettes of fish near the water's surface, and a neighborhood convoy of fourteen ducks paddled by, dipping and bobbing. Cormorants, flying in a V, headed for the rocks surrounding the island near the lake's southern shore, there to perch and watch and dive for fish throughout the day. Large dragonflies landed on the tops of the dock posts.

"Thought I'd try out this new Chatterbait lure," Six announced. "Supposed to be good in the shallows. That is, if we get to the shallows."

"Want to go deep first?" Alicia asked. "Out to McAvoy's Shoal? Put down some Senkos, maybe try the big silver Repalas."

"Ayuh. Let's do it."

"Then why are you sitting there not moving?"

"Worried."

"About . . .?"

"About what I told you last night. The English couple, the Trimbles. Think I ought to call Benson about them."

"Perhaps you should."

"All right, I'm gonna do it." Six retrieved his cellphone from his jeans pocket and before he could open it the phone startled him by peeling a tinny version of Schuman's Piano Concerto in A minor.

He flinched and said, "Jesus!" The phone reprised the opening bars.

"Six, are you going to answer the thing?"

Six flipped open the phone and blurted his name.

"Ah, professor, just the chap I was seeking," purred a dulcet public-school voice.

Six took the phone away from his ear, held it out momentarily while staring at it in amazement, then said, "Speak of the devil."

"Oh, dear, Prof. Godwin, I'm not as bad as all that."

Alicia's eyes widened as Six pressed the phone to his chest and whispered, "It's Colin."

Returning the phone to his ear, he said, "I was talking about you and your wife the minute the phone rang."

"Ah, I see. These things do happen, don't they? Brain impulses whizzing through the air. And what were you saying? How charming it was to be in our company?"

"Not quite."

"Uh-oh. I gather from your terseness, dear Prof. Godwin, that you are displeased about something."

"*The Sporting Magazine* was last published in 1870."

Warm laughter came through to Six's ear. "I see. Well, yes, I suppose Daff and I *were* being a bit too precious with that one."

"And you dropped some of your vowel formations."

"Damn." More chuckling. "Well, we're out of practice."

"Just who are you?" Six was nervous and his palm was sweating. He very well could be talking to Gene and Bruno's killer.

"Who we are isn't important. What I have to tell you is."

Minutes later, Six snapped his phone shut, jumped from his chair and seized Alicia's arm. He looked panicky.

"Sweet suffering Jesus!"

"Six! What is it?" Alicia was alarmed.

"Whose cell numbers do we have at Cedar Lodge? Do we have *any*? Do you? I don't even have Gene's number."

Alicia stammered, "I . . . I, uh . . . Let me think. No! I don't have anyone's number. Six, what's happening?"

"Oh, Christ!" Six howled, striking his forehead. "I don't even have *Benson's* number! Do *you* have it?"

"Uh . . . no, Six. No, it never . . ."

"Do you know Cedar Lodge's main number?"

"I believe I have it written in my date diary."

Six began trotting down the dock toward the camp, dragging Alicia by the arm. "Quick, please! Look it up. I'll get the sheriff's department number on Google. We've gotta move fast."

* * *

As fate would have it, and fate was to be most unkind this day, Brad was the only person around and about at Cedar Lodge by 6:30. He was also sober—customarily, his first visit to the potted plant on the front porch did not take place until nine, or possibly ten, depending on his mood. Kipper had burned himself out at the computer until about three and was asleep on the big leather sofa in the office. Jean-Pierre had decided that as far as he was concerned the remaining lodgers could loot the kitchen or hunt for squirrels to eat—he was packing his bags for an early getaway. The eleven lodgers still resident, exhausted and wary, had not emerged from their rooms. The deputy who had made rounds of the lodge and its grounds throughout the night had greeted the dawn with relief, made two cups of coffee in the kitchen and was now walking out to the camp road to share a cup of morning Joe with his buddy in the patrol car.

Brad, stretching and yawning, stood at the front door admiring the day's rosy-tinted advent. Amos sloped past him, found an acceptable spot by a nearby chair, turned in tight circles three times and slumped to a comfortable heap.

Willow Pond was serene, disturbed only by the peeps and warbles of birds busy with le petit-déjeuner. Two bass boats were tied to the docks, but Brad was certain there would be no fishing; the guests who remained would surely be leaving, he thought. So there would be no work for "one of Maine's premier fishing guides." Fine. That was just fine with him. It suited his current existential fatigue. Yesterday seemed unreal. Today seemed unreal. Perhaps all the days from now on would seem unreal. The possibility of a future of blissfully meaningless days, one melding pleasantly into another and spent on the front porch of a blissfully empty fishing lodge, seemed like just the ticket. Nothing to do, nothing to do. The lodge and the docks would age and disintegrate through the seasons, through the years, and there ole Bradley would be smiling and dreaming and then one day they would gather up his bones and only the jelly glasses behind the potted plant would remain.

Sam emerged from behind the lodge's western corner and moved slowly across the front lawn, the rocky beach and onto the center dock and up to the first blue-and-white boat. He went aboard the boat, started the motor, revved it a few times. Everything seemed fine. Then he went to the other boat and did the same. Sam was following Cedar Lodge routine, even if there were to be no fishermen: Each morning, according to Gene's rules, all the boats were fully gassed, the oil checked and keys put into the ignitions, the idea being to avoid any troublesome delays when paying lodgers were eager to get out on the water.

Brad slouched out to the porch rail, put down his empty coffee mug and watched Sam. Interesting watching Sam. Well, not really, but it was something to watch. One thing was as good as another to watch. Just sit and look at stuff. He couldn't have known it, but directly above him Robertson Weller was sitting on the second-floor porch looking at stuff that only he could see. Bob saw the faceless form of Gene's killer staggering backward, blood spurting from the chest as Bob squeezed off round after round from his .38 revolver. It was a big, loud gun that he'd used many times in shooting competitions in the past thirty-five years, and now he could almost feel the heavy recoil jarring his empty hand. A distant jangling broke his trance. Somewhere below. A telephone.

Brad was certainly aware of the persistent ringing of the telephone on the reception desk, but did he care? Could be reporters. Screw 'em. Let it ring. It would stop eventually. If anybody was calling for reservations then the dumb bastards hadn't been watching TV or looking at news web sites, because the "fishing camp murders" near "the fictional setting of Maine's Golden Pond" had hit the big time. Any minute now, he figured, media hounds would come bumping down the camp road. If the deputies stopped them then they'd probably come through the woods. That's what he would do. Crash through the trees with the cameras. Like those nature shows on cable TV, with a Crocodile Dundee type pursuing terrified beasts.

Here we are in the treacherous wilderness behind the ill-fated Cedar Lodge, where two brutal murders have traumatized this popular lakeside resort. Watch out! (The voice begins whispering.) *Did you see that? Those are chipmunks! Running away!*

The ringing stopped. Then it started again immediately. Ten rings. Stop. Three rings. Stop. Three rings. Stop. Brad turned and glared at the doorway, whence came the offending clamor discomposing his zen. The day may seem unreal, but it was impossible to relegate the piercing jangle of a telephone to nonexistence. There. It stopped.

Brad retrieved his mug, walked through the door and headed through the lobby toward the kitchen. Even an existentialist needed coffee. He eyed the phone suspiciously as he passed the reception and sure enough it rang, startling him. And continued to ring as he tried to retreat down the hall.

"Goddamn it!" he yelled. "Why isn't the goddamn answering machine on?"

When the ringing stopped Brad sprang to the desk and turned on the machine. Now he was curious about all the fuss, so he waited, and was rewarded a minute later with another call. The answering machine stopped the call on the fifth ring and then there was silence while the "Thank you for calling" etc. message played. An urgent voice burst onto the line:

"Kipper! Brad! Are you there? Is anyone there? For God's sake please pick up!"

Brad stared at the phone. It was Six Godwin's voice.

And now he was shouting. "Brad! Kipper! Somebody. Pick up the damn phone!"

Brad snatched up the handset. "It's Brad, Six. What's happening?"

As Brad listened to Six he thought he might be dreaming, which would explain why the day seemed so unreal. What Six was telling him was ludicrous.

"I don't believe a damn word of it."

"I'm not sure I do either, but do you want to take that chance?"

"Who are these bastards, anyway?"

"I don't know who they *really* are, but I can damn well tell you they're not Colin and Daphne Trimble of Anywhere, England."

"Then why should we believe them?"

"Again, Brad—we can't take a chance. The guy sounded damn convincing."

"Why didn't he say anything while he was here?"

"Fear. He and his wife wanted to get out first. He said we've got a psychopath on our hands. A very dangerous one. His words. And Brad . . . he gave me a name. Vadik."

"Vadik? What kind of name is that?"

"Don't know."

Brad was silent, trying to take it in. It just didn't make sense.

"Brad, listen to me. Are the deputies still there?"

"Yeah, they're out on the camp road."

"You've got to tell them, Brad. You've got to tell them not to let anyone leave."

"Ayuh. You're right. I'll tell 'em."

"Take down my cellphone number. Got some paper?"

Brad pulled the desk register toward him and found a pencil. "Shoot."

Six gave Brad his cell number, repeated it, then said: "Keep my number with you . . . and give it to the deputies. Have them call me. I've got to talk to them. Oh—and give me your cell number."

Brad replaced the handset and stood motionless, mesmerized by images of the past three days rampaging through his mind; familiar faces assumed grotesque masks, their lying mouths twisting and smirking. He shook his head. No. No, it just couldn't be true. This had to be a bad. . . . He wheeled around in fright at the sound of footsteps on the stairs behind him, fearing the face that might be there.

Relief washed over him as he saw the unsmiling visage of Janice Bloget, the tough old trout from Long Pond who came to the lodge every summer.

"Morning, Janice."

"Mornin'. Any coffee?"

"Couple of pots in the kitchen."

"Breakfast?"

"Gotta find your own, Janice."

"Figures."

Janice, who rocked back and forth like a sailor as she walked, shambled past him and down the hall.

Brad tore off the top corner of the ledger page where he'd written down Six's number, stuffed it in his shirt pocket and headed for the camp road.

Twenty-Six

Tory and Nelson came downstairs looking outfitted for a day on the Savannah Plains—both wore jeans, hiking boots and khaki safari jackets. They put their bags by the reception desk and walked into the clubroom to find Janice Bloget, whose face bore the aspect of an ill-tempered bulldog, sitting at the bar drinking a mug of coffee. She stared at them balefully.

"Mornin'. Gotta get your own coffee. Kitchen." She gestured with a nod of her head toward the service at the end of the bar. "No staff. No nothin'. Least there's no dead bodies."

Tory gave Janice a cheery smile as she and Nelson passed by and said, "How nice."

Janice curled her lip at Tory's back. Bouncy little hussy, she thought—coming here with her big stud brother. Brother, my aching ass. They looked nothing alike: She was short and plump, all tits and wiggly ass, and he was tall and trim. That long face with the high cheekbones reminded her of some movie star, couldn't think of the name, could see his face . . . Anyway. He wasn't her brother. She was bonking that guy.

Brad walked through the door from the lobby, stopped just inside and nodded to Janice.

Now there was a real man, Janice thought. A man of the lakes, the best fishermen she'd ever known, and she'd known a lot of them, having grown up and lived in fishing camps all of her seventy-three years. Look at him. Wide shoulders, narrow waist, curly auburn hair. She liked the way he was dressed, too—khaki shorts, white fishing shirt, boat moccasins. Back in her day she would've . . . ah, well, no use going down that road.

Janice Bloget had not always looked like a bulldog, for her face when young had been cutely round and pug-nosed, and though she'd had a short, stocky body, the stockiness had been voluptuously contoured, and she had never lacked for the attention of men.

Men. Well, I had a few. If some of those studs back then could see me now, sun-roasted old bag with hooters down to my waist.

It occurred to Janice that Brad had been standing in one place for a spell with his eyes cast down at the floor. Probably worried as hell, she figured. These murders could ruin the lodge. He looks like he needs a drink, she thought, and sure enough Brad came out of his funk, walked behind the bar and began searching through the two shelves of bottles. He located the George Dickel, got a shot glass, turned and put them both on the bar near Janice.

"Care for a little spiritual uplift, Janice?"

"Christ, Bradley, it's what . . ." She looked at her big waterproof watch ". . . eight in the mornin'."

"Ayuh. No fishing. Everybody gone. May's well drink."

Janice thought Brad was acting peculiar. He wasn't jolly. That's what she loved about him, that's what everybody loved about him—he was always jolly. And now she noticed that his hand trembled at he poured a full shot and lifted the glass to his lips.

Oh, what the hell, she decided. The man obviously needed company; probably needed to get something off his chest. And why wouldn't he? Gene murdered, Bruno Gabreau murdered.

"OK, I'll have a snort," Janice said. "Just the one."

Brad didn't evince any surprise at her decision, just got another glass and put it on the bar. "Straight? Water?"

"Water, no ice. Thanks."

Again with the shaking hand, Janice noticed. Maybe the DT's were finally getting him.

"You all right, Bradley?"

"Yep, I'm . . ." He paused, his eyes flicking around the room, then he knocked back the jigger of bourbon. "Look, Janice. There's something, uh . . . there's something cooking around here. Could be trouble. You might want to . . . well, I don't know. You might want to just stay in here for awhile."

Janice's brows lowered over her worried eyes. "Yeah? What's wrong, Brad?"

Brad flinched as the service door swung open. Tory sailed through with Nelson in her wake. They were carrying mugs of coffee. Janice was disappointed to see Brad break into his familiar crooked grin, the one that dazzled women who were ready to be dazzled.

"Oh, hi, Brad." Tory came up to the bar and leaned over, revealing a generous amount of breast from the deep V of her mostly unbuttoned white shirt. She smiled brilliantly at Brad, as she had the first day. "We're leaving."

"Archie Rivera," he said.

She cocked her head in puzzlement, still smiling. "I beg your pardon?"

"It's a pun . . . a pun on arrivederci. Not so funny, huh?"

Tory giggled. "Cute."

Janice wanted to barf. Goddamn little prick tease. She turned away from the sight of Tory's boobs and found herself looking right at another piece of work, only this one was tall and slender— Renee Ranger, wearing a blue shirt (open and tied over her stomach) and not much else except her legs and barely existent white shorts. Her long black hair flowed and curled to her shoulders from beneath a man's straw fedora, cocked at a saucy angle. Christ, Janice grumbled to herself—now I *am* going to get drunk.

Renee did a Lauren Bacall across the room and up to the bar. She glanced at Janice with the same interest she would've shown a tree stump, then saw the bottle and shot glass in Brad's hands.

"What's this?" she smirked. "Bourbon sunny side up?"

Brad didn't say anything, which surprised Janice. Brad always had a smart comeback. Now his hands slid away from glass and bottle and gripped the edge of the bar, his rigid fingers spread like claws. What the hell was going on, Janice wondered. She didn't like the bad vibes.

Renee shrugged at Brad's lack of response and stepped around Janice and up to Tory and Nelson. After exchanging a look of cyanide with Tory she swept past Nelson and said, "See ya, stud. Keep in touch."

"At your service," Nelson replied, watching her vamp through the service door. Then he turned to Brad. "We need to check out."

Brad downed another double-shot of bourbon and said, "Yep. Follow me."

Nelson paid their tab with cash, then he and Tory got their luggage and started down the hall toward the back lot. Tory threw Brad a smile and a wink over her shoulder.

When he returned to the bar Brad found Janice watching him like a hawk. "They gone?" she asked.

"Ayuh."

"You OK?"

Brad grabbed the George Dickel, poured another double shot and drank it off.

"Jesus Christ, Bradley. You trying to kill yourself?"

"Not yet."

"Something's wrong. What's happenin'?"

"I can't tell you right now, Janice," Brad said. "But I am telling you this." He looked into her eyes and pointed a finger. "You stay in here. I mean it." He turned and strode out of the clubroom, leaving an astonished and apprehensive Janice behind him.

Janice was trying to decide if curiosity should trump caution when the service door swung out and Renee barreled through with a cup of coffee; she passed by the bar without a glance and disappeared into the lobby.

Brad, meanwhile, had gone out to the end of the center dock. His view took in all of the lodge, the grassy open areas on both sides and the camp road. The deputies must have contacted Six and the sheriff, because they had stopped two SUVs and were talking to the drivers, who seemed to be conducting a futile argument. He recognized the people in the first vehicle—the two younger men with their girlfriends. The SUV behind them had to be one of the single men.

Nothing to do now except watch and wait. He was ready. Calm. The six shots of bourbon were doing their stuff, and he was calm. He held out his hands. No shaking. He'd gotten his fishing knife and scabbard from the tackle room in the boat shed and was wearing them on his belt.

Watch and wait. The morning was warming up fast. No wind as yet. Clouds were building up in the west. He saw Robertson Weller standing by the second-floor porch and gave him a quick salute. Bob waved back and then walked away. Oh, Christ, there she was.

Renee walked through the front door and across the porch and leaned against one of the big posts at the top of the stairs, hand on her thrust-out hip like Daisy Mae waiting for Li'l Abner. She and Brad stared at each other through their sunglasses. Each of them regarded the other with loathing, though Brad doubted their looks of mutual hatred would penetrate the dark lenses.

Movement out at the camp road caught his eye—a black Range Rover eased up behind the other vehicles. Nelson got out of the driver's side, had a brief exchange with the man in the car preceding him, then walked up to the deputies. The distance was too far for Brad to hear what was said. If a shouting match started it would be audible, but apparently no one was getting exercised. Finally, Nelson stalked off, got in the Rover, backed away and drove to the front of the lodge onto the beach and up to the center dock and came to a brake-slamming halt, scattering beach stones.

He climbed out and walked down the dock, stopping a space-invading two feet away from Brad, his face showing no particular emotion, happiness included.

"The cops aren't letting anyone leave," he said. "Why?"

"I don't know. What did they tell you?"

"Said the sheriff's coming. Thought you might know something."

"I don't."

"Why not? Aren't you the boss around here now?"

"That's an optimistic description."

Nelson smirked and said, "Funny. Look, Seldon. We have a pass signed by the sheriff to let us leave. So . . . what the hell?"

"I can't tell the deputies what to do. Personally, I'd be happy to see you go."

Nelson seemed to consider that statement but made no reply.

Tory got out of the Rover and came down the dock to join them and stopped beside Nelson, standing to his left. She smiled and said, "Hi, Brad. Why can't we leave?"

"He says he doesn't know why," Nelson told her.

Tory stepped up to Brad and pressed her body lightly against his while slowly stroking his right arm with her left hand. "Brad, honey," she said, "you look so fierce. What's wrong?"

"Beats me."

"We have to leave, Brad. We have a flight to catch in Augusta."

"Nelson!" Renee called out. "What's the prob? Thought you were going to boogie home."

This seemed to irritate Nelson, who muttered, "Crap," and turned to walk away.

Despite the warnings, Janice had wandered out onto the porch and Sam emerged from the boathouse and was looking their way. Christ, Brad thought—let's get everybody out here having fun. This was it, he decided. The courage of bourbon was ready to speak. "Hey, Nelson," he called out. "You ever hear of a guy named Vadik?"

Nelson froze for an instant and then turned slowly around and Brad saw the frightening change in his face. He didn't look like the man named Nelson Bolston. Tory's nails dug into the flesh on Brad's arm. "You complete bastard," she whispered.

Brad broke free of Tory's grasp, stepped backward, unsnapped the scabbard and whipped out the thick-bladed knife.

"Anka!" Nelson barked. "Watch the knife!"

Anka? The strange name hung in the air. A nasty little sneer transformed Tory's baby-doll face into something not so nice. She reached under the left side of her safari jacket to a belt holster and drew out a small, black pistol—a Beretta 8045. Brad was so transfixed by horrified fascination that he did not drop the knife, as was obviously indicated by Tory's gestures with the gun. When he had first looked out at this day he'd thought it seemed unreal, and this was about as unreal as it could possibly get.

Nelson pushed past Tory and smacked a blackjack across Brad's wrist. Brad yelped at the sharp pain and dropped the knife as Nelson whipped out a gun from a holster strapped in the small of his back. Grabbing a wad of Brad's shirt in his left hand, Nelson jerked him forward, jammed the barrel of the gun against Brad's neck, and said:

"All right sucker, now you *are* going to get us out of here. Anka, get Renee. Quick!" As Tory—Anka—ran off, Nelson noticed Sam by the boathouse and pointed the gun at him, gesturing for him to get inside. Sam stepped back, tripped and fell and then scrambled on all fours through the door, slamming it shut and throwing an inside bolt.

The strange confrontation on the dock and Brad's howl of pain alarmed Janice, who moved with impressive alacrity down the porch and into the front door. Renee, unfortunately, was not so quick off the mark. She thought the angry sounds meant a fistfight. When she saw Anka come tearing down the dock with a gun in her hand she screamed and dashed for the doorway, but it was too late to get away. Tory sprinted across the lawn and up the stairs, catching up to Renee in the lobby. She snatched the taller woman by her hair, knocked off the straw hat and yanked her around and slammed her against the staircase. Renee felt her breath explode from her chest.

Anka put the gun under Renee's chin and said, "If I pull the trigger the top of your head will hit the ceiling. Move!" With a painful jerk of Renee's hair, Tory wrenched her back and hustled her forward out the door and down the stairs.

Renee begged, "Please don't hurt me!"

"Oh, shut it, bitch," Anka spat out. "Move ass." She yanked Renee's hair and shoved the gun against her spine.

Amos began pacing the porch baying in fear. Bob heard the hound just as he was fixing himself a whiskey in his room upstairs; the incessant ululating began to worry him, so he moved to a window and was astounded to see Anka holding a gun to Renee's head and shoving her along on the dock. And her brother was holding a gun to Brad! *Jesus Christ!* Bob ran to his dresser, grabbed his gunbelt from the top drawer and strapped it on.

Out on the dock, Nelson jammed the gun barrel hard against Brad's neck and said, "Vadik at your service, sucker." His black eyes widened and glared as a menacing leer spread across his face. "You know what this is? It's a Magnum .357. One shot now would separate your head from your body. We wouldn't want that, would we?"

"Probably not."

Nelson—Vadik—snarled, "Always the joker. Always got a wisecrack. Funny, aren't you, *stud?*" Vadik prodded his neck with the gun. "Huh . . . *stud?*"

How strange it was, Brad thought. He wasn't shaking, he wasn't pleading for his life. He felt detached, as if he were watching a movie. He did wonder how it was going to feel if the trigger was pulled. Would there be a searing flash of pain, or would he be conscious long enough to feel anything?

Renee, sobbing and pleading, stumbled down the dock with Anka jerking her hair and jamming the gun in her back.

And then suddenly Bob Weller was at the end of the second-story porch shouting at the deputies, who had moved away from the squad car and were reaching for their sidearms. "Guns!" Bob yelled. "They've got guns! Hostages!"

"You old bastard!" Vadik swung around and fired at Bob. The shot exploded like thunder and struck the banister and sent chunks of the top railing flying as Bob hit the porch deck. Vadik giggled and squeezed off another round, blasting off an upright from the banister.

"Vadik!" Anka yelled. "Leave him. The cops, goddamn it, the cops!"

One deputy ran toward the docks as the other ran behind the lodge in order to approach from the eastern side. As the first deputy pounded across the front lawn, Vadik, grinning and sniggering, raised the Magnum at arm's length and fired. The man screamed and hit the ground writhing.

Amos ran frantically back and forth on the porch howling and barking.

Vadik laughed. "Hah! Got him! Good shot, Vadik. Why thank you very much, I thought so too."

He pulled Brad forward, got behind him and prodded him forward until they were beside Anka and Renee, and now Brad could see Renee's face. Her horrified eyes were darting around wildly. "Oh God please oh God please," she whimpered. Brad was appalled to see that her shorts were wet—she'd lost control of her bladder.

Vadik released Brad's shirt and swung the back of his left hand across Renee's mouth, hard; she bawled and grabbed her mouth and slumped forward. Anka yanked her back up by her hair, put her gun to Renee's ear and said through her teeth: "You want to die right now, bitch? Shut up!" Renee got quiet; blood ran from under the hand she had clamped over her mouth. She stared at Brad with pleading, terrified eyes.

"You stinking animals," Brad said.

Vadik spun Brad around and kneed him in the groin. The pain shot up Brad's body like fire and seemed to explode in his brain; he crumpled to the dock groaning and clutching himself.

"Uh-oh. Did Vadik hurt the stud? Naughty, naughty Vadik."

"Goddamn it, Vadik," Anka yelled. "We've got to get out of here!"

"Oh, we're getting out right now. Stud and his wifey are going to march before us like . . . what is that army thing? Oh, yes yes yes. The *vanguard*. They will be the vanguard. The sacrificial troops, the cannon fodder. Get up, stud!" Brad stumbled to his feet gasping from the pain in his balls.

"Watch it!" Anka said. "That other cop is over there to the left. He's got a rifle."

"Easy. He won't take a chance of hitting precious or stud." Vadik wrapped his left hand around Brad's belt and then shoved him forward. "Keep hold of the bitch's hair. Let's go."

A macabre tableau moved slowly down the dock. Renee gasped and grunted as Anka's grip tightened in her hair. Vadik pressed against Brad closely; Brad felt the man's breath on his neck.

"Keep her close," Vadik told Anka. "Now everyone, we're changing the dance steps. Turn toward the funny cop with the rifle and walk sideways." Renee and Brad complied and the four of them crab-walked toward the lodge.

The deputy got on one knee, leaned against the corner of the lodge and got the quartet in his rifle's sight. No way. There was no way he could get a clean shot.

Bob Weller, on the other hand, had an angled view of Vadik and Anka's backs—he lay face down on the porch boards with his big .38 revolver propped on the bannister's bottom railing. His heart pounded as he tensed. Sweat trickled from his forehead into his eyes; he wiped it away and gripped the gun barrel. No. No, it was much too dangerous. Were this twenty years ago when he still had a keen eye, he wouldn't have hesitated. He eased his finger off the trigger and watched as the four figures struggled toward the foot of the dock. The wounded deputy was still now, blood spreading across the front of his shirt, and Bob wondered if he was dead.

A distant wail caught Bob's ear. The sound faded away for a few moments then returned, faded, then came again stronger and stronger until there was no doubt—sirens.

Amos bayed hysterically and whined as the sirens' wail grew louder. The group on the dock lurched to a halt. Movie images flashed through Brad's traumatized mind—the cavalry, the boys in blue, pennants fluttering, guns blazing.

Anka was afraid. Vadik, the psychopathic bastard, would get them killed if she didn't do something fast. Getting shot to death had not been in her plans for the day.

"Vadik!" she said. "A boat. Get in one of the boats."

"We're on a lake. There's nowhere to go, you dumb broad."

"There's a way out. Brad showed it to me. A creek goes over to the next lake."

"You'll never find it," Brad said. "You're dead meat."

"Oh yes we will. You're gonna take us there, stud." Vadik and Anka dragged their hostages toward the first boat and Vadik untied the stern line. "God dammit!" he yelled. "The keys, the keys—we don't have the boat keys."

"They're always in the boats. Christ! Hurry!"

"Watch the rifleman," Vadik said. "Keep them in front."

Anka squatted by the first bass boat, pulling Renee down in front of her. She released her grip on Renee's hair, clutched her shirt collar and pressed the Beretta alongside her cheek. "OK, bitch. We're going to jump in the boat together. Try anything and you die. Got that?"

Renee, trembling with terror, murmured, "Yes."

"Now!"

They tumbled backward, hitting the gunwale painfully—Renee cried out, Anka cursed vilely—and slamming onto the deck just behind the driver's seat, which caused the boat to rock madly and bang against a dock post.

"Stay down!" Anka commanded. She dragged Renee forward as Vadik and Brad crashed down beside them. As the boat lurched and bucked, Vadik got to his knees and stuck his gun in Brad's face. "Get the bow line, stud. Fast!" Brad crawled along the deck up to the forward fishing seat and reached for the bow-line cleat. He froze when he heard Kipper roaring "Stop, stop!" and Amos barking and yipping insanely. Peeking up, he was horrified to see Kipper hobbling as fast as he could on his sprained ankle down the dock holding a shotgun. Amos was out in front of him, long ears flapping.

"Kipper, no! God, no!" he cried. Too late. Vadik stood and fired. Amos emitted a last, heart-breaking howl of agony as the first shot propelled him backward into the water and Kipper was lifted off his feet and slammed backward on the dock boards as Vadik's second shot blew open his chest.

Brad sobbed with rage and screamed, "You evil bastard!" He leaped over the driver's wheel and tackled Vadik, striking at knee level. But Vadik was too big and too strong. He kicked out of Brad's grasp and stunned him with a glancing blow across the top of his head with the gun. Brad saw stars and whirligigs and fell on his side under the dashboard. Renee shrieked and babbled.

Vadik saw the deputy crouch and move away from the corner of the lodge, and he squeezed off a round that kicked up dirt by the man's feet and sent him scrambling back behind the building.

Up on the porch, Bob was sickened. Blood flowed from the wound in Kipper's chest and spread over his body, and Amos's sad, inert body floated beside the dock. But Bob held his position because now—now!—he had a clear shot. Vadik had climbed into the driver's seat and started the motor. *Steady, steady, just like the old days. Take a bead just below the target. Hold the barrel steady, steady . . . and squeeze!*

Vadik bellowed in fear and lurched away as the fiberglass molding on the steel gunwale a foot from his right arm exploded into shards.

"Weller! On the porch!" Anka shouted. She fired two shots at Bob that hit the bottom lower railing and drove splinters into his check and forearm. He grunted in pain and rolled away.

Anka was getting frantic. "Go, go, go!"

Vadik turned the wheel to the left, pushed the accelerator handle forward slowly and eased away from the dock and gained speed gradually through the shallows. Then he rammed the handle to full speed and the motor roared and the bow sprang up; the hull shuddered as it slammed back down in the water and the boat leaped, settled and shot forward at 50 mph.

The deputy ran across the lawn toward his wounded colleague as he put in red alert calls to the EMS and the sheriff. When he got to the other man he found that he had a horrific shoulder wound but was still breathing.

Ignoring the sting of his cuts and the blood trickling down his right cheek and forearm and cursing himself for a miserable, weak old fool, Bob Weller holstered his .38 and plunged down two flights of stairs. Vadik's boat was already abreast of the first island as Bob ran across the lawn and the stony beach. On the dock he hovered over Kipper's body and, just to be certain, felt for a pulse in his neck; gore had seeped from the hideous hole in his chest and soaked his clothing; death must've been instantaneous—Kipper's open-eyed face still wore a ghastly, twisted expression of shock.

"Poor fellow," Bob whispered, "poor fellow." He choked up at the dreadful sight and tears trickled through the blood on his cheek.

Then he brought himself to attention and ran toward the remaining boat. His mind was in a turmoil of rage and grief as he ripped loose the bow and stern lines and leaped aboard.

Twenty-Seven

All along Route 225, astounded drivers of cars and trucks swung onto the dirt shoulders as three Somerbec County Sheriff's Department vehicles sped past with sirens howling, horns blasting and tires squealing around the treacherous curves. Neighbors in Rome remarked to one another about the extraordinary sight of three patrol cars at once tearing through the countryside. That was big-city stuff, that was. What the hell, they asked themselves, was going on?

Sgt. Caleb Cobb drove the lead car. His big hands wrapped around the wheel in a death grip and his lips curled back over gritted teeth. In truth, he enjoyed this sort of manic cops-chasing-the-villains action, but on a road like 225 it was also extremely dangerous. The curves, of course, were bad enough, but he could handle those; it was merciless fate in the form a child or a pet darting onto the road or a vehicle pulling from a hidden intersection that he feared.

Two deputies were with him. Another sergeant was at the wheel of the car behind with Benson Doucette beside him; Tom Barclay and another two men were in the third car. All the vehicles were equipped with rifles, shotguns and Kevlar vests.

Benson snapped his phone shut, dialed, heard the pickup, then said, "Tom, we've got two people down from gunfire, and one of them is Jack. He's alive, the other is dead."

"Has he been I.D.'d?"

"Middle-aged man. Cyrus doesn't know his name."

Tom closed her phone, shut her eyes and leaned back against the headrest. She was an ace shot on the indoor shooting range, but she'd only had to draw her Glock 17C three times in the line of duty; she had never fired it during police action. She wondered now if she was headed into her first gun battle. Tom had no misgivings about her courage—she wouldn't panic under fire. But the thought of opposing gunfire was daunting, and she realized that her heartbeat and her breathing had quickened.

Surprisingly—well, perhaps not so surprisingly if she were truthful to herself—she found herself praying that the dead man was not Brad Seldon.

With just a glance to check for oncoming traffic, Caleb took the sharp turn from 225 onto 27 North on two wheels. Not for nothing had he raced stock cars at the Skowhegan State Fair in his youth. He heard Benson radioing to all three vehicles:

"Everybody wears vests on this one. Caleb, stop on the camp road and we'll suit up."

* * *

Benson felt the weight of failure oppressing him. What, he asked himself, could he have done to prevent this tragedy? What had he not seen, or understood? The Bolstons, the damn *Bolstons.* Mild-mannered computer-guy brother and sweet-faced, sexy little sister. They were killers marking a trail with blood. Why had nothing pointed to them? And why, *why* were they killing? Especially here, at this beautiful lodge on this gorgeous lake? What evil was loose in this small paradise?

Benson and Caleb hurried over to where two emergency medics were strapping the wounded trooper into a gurney. The trooper's eyes were fluttering and Benson said, "I'm sorry, Jack. Goddamn, I'm sorry," though he didn't know if Jack could hear him. The medics got him into the EMS truck and one of them joined him and slammed the doors shut. The other hurried to the cab, turned on the flashers and siren and then the truck went bumping and wailing over the grounds and up the camp road. Another big EMS vehicle was parked by the center dock, and two medics were examining Kipper's body.

Tom removed her hot, heavy Kevlar vest and went down the dock and stood over Kipper's body and looked into his ghastly-white, blood-drained face; like Bruno's, his sightless eyes stared upward at a benign Maine sky. Tom was secretly relieved that Brad

Seldon was not lying on the dock with his chest pulped and his heart shredded, and felt immediately guilty for the emotion—dear God, how could she not feel it?—when it was his brother instead who lay slaughtered at her feet.

As the newly arrived troopers rounded up the traumatized lodge guests and took them to the big lounge just to the right of the lobby, the rifleman deputy described for Benson the confrontation on the dock and the hostage-taking—he'd had them in his gunsights nearly the whole time. There was no doubt: The Bolstons had beaten and captured Brad Seldon and Renee Ranger. He also said that as he was going to the aid of his wounded comrade an old man wearing a gunbelt had run from the lodge and jumped in the second boat.

"Weller," Benson said. "Christ! He's gonna get killed." He turned quickly and clutched Caleb's arm. "Jesus, oh, Jesus, Caleb. This is bad. They're all going to get killed. We've gotta get some boats and get out there."

Caleb called a trooper over and told him, "Get the rifles and shotguns out of the cars. We're gonna create ships of war."

The man hurried off and then Benson saw Sam in the water pulling Amos's body toward shore using a fishing net. "Sam!" he shouted.

"Yes sir!" Benson had never seen anyone come to rigid attention while standing in waist-deep water, but this boy, he was amazed to see, managed it. "We need two boats, now! We'll help you get 'em in the water."

"Yes sir!" Sam dropped the net, thrashed out of the lake and raced across the beach toward the boathouse. Amos's pitiful body floated away.

An anguished shriek split the air. Benson and Caleb turned toward the lodge in time to see a deputy grab Jean-Pierre as he bolted down the front steps and toward the dock where Kipper's body lay. He thrashed and kicked so violently, screaming all the while, that another deputy ran up to help the first, and together they dragged him back up to porch.

"Kee-pair, Kee-pair!" he sobbed. "No, God, please noooo!" The troopers got him back inside, where he continued to keen and beg God's mercy.

Caleb squinched his eyes shut and said, "Jesus."

"It's gut-wrenching, Caleb, but we gotta get moving." As they followed Sam, Benson said: "This is a big, damn lake, Caleb, but we've got them trapped. If they put ashore they'll be on foot and we'll get them. Why the hell did they take hostages? I don't get it."

"They're not really trapped, chief. There's the serpentine up in the northeast. Goes to Rocky Pond."

Benson slapped his forehead. "Oh, damn, *damn*. Of course there's the serpentine. It's been a lot of years since I was a warden but I can't believe I forgot about it. I went through the thing once."

"It's real hard to find, though, tucked back in the trees and you gotta go through a marsh to find the entrance. Even when you get there you hardly know it cause it's so overgrown."

These details surprised Benson. "Criminy, Caleb. You been there recently?"

"Oh, yeah. I go around all over the place on my days off."

"But the Bolstons don't know where it is."

They got to the boathouse as Sam threw the doors open. Three bass boats were on blocks but one was already trailered-up. Sam said, "I'll get the truck and have this one in the water in ten minutes."

"Good man," Benson told him.

"But Brad does," Caleb said.

"Brad does what?"

"Knows the serpentine. Has to."

Benson thought about that. "And that's why . . ."

". . . they took him hostage," Caleb finished.

A deputy trotted up to them. "Sheriff, Billy and Eric have got reporters blocked up at the road."

"Newspaper or TV?"

"Two newspapers, two TV stations."

"Damn."

"One woman's raising hell, shouting about public safety."

"That'll be Jennifer Libby." Benson gave it some thought. "She's right, you know." He called Tom over from the dock and explained what was happening. "We've got to give them something."

"Of course we do," Tom said. "The question is, how much? Should I tell them about Kipper's murder and our trooper getting shot?"

"Let's do it, Tom. There's nothing for us to be coy about at this point. We're in the middle of a goddamn disaster and we better get the word out."

"Will do," Tom said, taking off her Kevlar vest.

"Tell them armed suspects, with hostages, are heading into Rocky Pond and Winsokkett and they'll be doing a public service getting the word out, especially on TV."

* * *

Brad crawled from under the dashboard by Vadik's feet and dragged himself painfully to center deck and propped against a tackle box. The blow on his head from the gun had rendered him momentarily semi-conscious and now his scalp was raw and he had a vicious headache.

He studied the two figures at the stern: Renee sat on the transom, rigid with fear, hands between her trembling legs and her eyes staring ahead at death; Anka held her Beretta pointed at Brad, there obviously being no fight left in Renee.

Brad stared at Anka with revulsion. Most of his life seemed to have been one nightmare after another, but this nightmare was grotesque in a special way. He felt like some pagan whose soul had been raped by a demon, one that now boldly regarded him with cold eyes. How, he wondered, had those eyes danced so merrily, how had that face lit up so prettily? The memory of how he'd preened before her and turned on the force majeure charm filled him with disgust. He hadn't charmed her—she was a killer, and while she was killing she wanted a good screw. Better to die, Brad

315

decided, than live on burdened by a humiliation that would be with him every day.

Vadik brought the boat to a halt and left the engine running in neutral. "Get up, stud," he ordered Brad. "Get in the driver's seat."

Brad stared up into Vadik's black eyes. So this, he thought, is what a psychopath looks like. Charming. "Screw you," he said.

Vadik moved close to him and put his foot in Brad's crotch. "You want another kick in the balls? I wouldn't mind kicking them right up your ass."

The thought of enduring that hideous pain again made Brad struggle to his feet. He was probably going to die anyway, but he didn't need to suffer such agony before the end. He slumped into the seat and Vadik said:

"Where is the goddamn creek?"

"I don't know. I'm lost."

"You're lost? This is *your* goddamn lake. You know where it is—move!" He prodded the gun against Brad's temple. Slowly, Brad pushed the accelerator handle forward and took the boat in a large figure eight.

"It's around here somewhere, I just can't see it," Brad said.

With a scream of rage, Vadik charged the stern, grabbed Renee by her shirt and yanked her up next to Brad. He spun her around and squeezed her cheeks until she cried out and then he forced the gun barrel into her mouth. Renee's eyes widened and she whimpered in terror.

"What does this look like, stud? It looks like my gun in your wife's mouth. It looks like if I pull the trigger, her brains will land in your face. Do you think I won't do it? Ask your faggot brother." Vadik giggled. "Oh! That's *riiight*. You can't ask him. He's dead."

All around this floating tableau of horror was the serene beauty of a Maine wilderness—water birds fishing, turtles slipping from a log, a gentle breeze riffling the bright water. And yet it all faded away and the center of the universe for Brad was the dreadful, pleading look in Renee's eyes. "I'll do it," he said. "Please take the gun from her mouth. I'll take you. Now."

Brad got the boat underway and in ten minutes he was at the northeastern-most reach of Willow Pond and heading for the small marsh that he knew led to the serpentine. Some two hundred yards into the marsh's thick spread of tall reeds there was an obvious gap in the midst of the forest. All here was peace. Communities of small birds chattered in the trees. Strangely—perhaps it was because he was about to die—Brad recalled that when he was a boy and a young man, when he gloried in each day because life seemed so perfect, he could identify every kind of finch and warbler and sparrow and oriole simply by its song.

And now, suddenly, so very suddenly he wanted desperately to live.

"There," he said, pointing at the wrong place. "See it?" Vadik took a step forward and stared.

"No. Where is it?"

Brad stood, leaned over the steering wheel and lifted his arm straight out. This time he pointed directly at the gap. "There, right there!" He hoped he had the bastard diverted.

"Yeah. I see it." So concentrated was Vadik's gaze that he wasn't aware that his gun hand had drifted down until the barrel was pointed at the deck.

Brad moved like a cougar, seizing Vadik's arm with both hands and sinking his teeth into the man's forearm. He ripped at the flesh and Vadik shrieked in pain, dropped the gun but then dived on top of it. Brad barreled into Anka as she fired her gun and he felt the shot burn across his cheek. He kicked Anka's arm as she raised the pistol again, grabbed Renee by her hair and shirt and catapulted the two of them off the stern and into the water.

"Dive!" he screamed. "Dive, dive!"

The motor lurched to starboard and the boat swung in a circle, throwing Vadik and Anka hard against the portside hull. Vadik came up raging and grabbed the wheel just as the boat crashed into brambles at the water's edge. He lunged into the driver's seat, reversed the boat and turned it back toward Brad and Renee, whose heads popped into view as they came up for quick gasps of air. He pulled off two rounds that threw up small geysers just as their heads went under.

"Leave them!" Anka screamed. Vadik cursed and shot twice more into the water. "Vadik, you crazy bastard—leave them! Get us into the creek!" Anka prevailed and Vadik swung the boat around and headed for the serpentine.

They were not prepared for what greeted them as they entered the narrow waterway, for it appeared to be the Maine equivalent of an Indiana Jones jungle, with thick vegetation choking the shores, moss-covered tree trunks and rocks protruding from the water, and a canopy of branches blocking out the sun. Birds flitted back and forth over the creek; lily pads carpeted its surface. Mosquitos swarmed and Anka and Vadik cursed and slapped futilely at their necks and ears.

Bob Weller saw the boat slip through the marsh and into the serpentine. He'd been tearing across the lake like hell wouldn't have it until he saw the other boat churning the water far ahead. Then it had stopped, dead in the water, so Bob had slowed and cut south of the island with the abandoned camp, thinking to ease around the north of it and come at them from a hidden position. And then, when he'd arrived at the north end, he'd heard raging voices and gunfire. He'd continued at 5 mph past a towering rock formation and then sighted the boat heading into the marsh.

What he had not seen was Brad and Renee going into the water.

Brad struggled on foot, knee-deep in the murky water, through reeds and thick growths of lily pads; a mass of sunken moss and branches caught at his feet and he pitched into the water, instinctively landing with both arms out and screaming as the pain in his ripped and bleeding left arm, which had been hit by Vadik's second shot, came in contact with the marsh floor. He rose, gasping, to a kneeling position, with his head and shoulders above the water. Dizziness and nausea overcame him as he tried to crawl forward and loss of consciousness swirled in on a black cloud.

And then consciousness returned and he was vomiting water and gulping for breath. Hands were in his armpits and someone was dragging him onto the rocky, bramble-covered bank of the marsh. The hands gently rolled him onto his back and he looked up into Renee's water-scoured face—no eye shadow, no lip blush, no delicate coloring of cheeks, just plain skin. Her sodden, weed-strewn hair hung in black tendrils that touched Brad's face.

She took off her shirt and began ripping it into strips. "I won't let you die, Brad," she said. "I won't let you die." She tied a tourniquet of sky-blue, Ralph Lauren linen around his arm above the bicep and then wrapped strip after strip around the deep, ugly gash in Brad's arm until the bleeding was stanched. Her large, tanned breasts swayed above Brad's face, but he wasn't interested in breasts at that moment. He was trying to remember the name of the warbler piping a sweet melody in the nearby brambles. And then, once more, he blacked out.

Fifteen minutes later, two more of Cedar Lodge's blue-and-white bass boats roared toward the marsh, with the sheriff and his big sergeant in the lead boat. Caleb scanned the tree line with his binoculars until he located the serpentine's entrance and pointed it out to Benson, who was at the wheel. Benson slowed to a 5 mph crawl as they motored through natural channels in the reed-choked marsh. As they neared the serpentine, Benson said:

"They'll be in Rocky Pond and damn near across it by the time we get there. Put in a call to headquarters and tell them to get one of our boats over to Winsokkett. I'm going to call Six Godwin."

He had already calculated that the other boats had at least a 30-minute lead, but there was no way they could speed through the many hazards in the twisting creek without risking the motor. Hitting any sunken rock or log at speed could damage the prop or the Evinrude's entire lower unit, possibly even breaking it off.

Caleb looked around the marsh as he opened his phone and was about to dial when he saw two figures lying in a tangle of brush on the bank to their south.

"Yo, chief!" he blurted, raising the glasses, which were powerful enough to bring the figures into sharp focus. "Godawmighty. Brad and Renee lying in the weeds. Look beat to hell."

"They alive?"

"Renee's moving."

"Tell the boys to pick them up."

"There's one other thing."

"Yeah?"

"Renee's upper-body womanhood is entirely exposed to view."

"Caleb. Your way with words amazes me sometimes."

The other boat was nearly alongside. Caleb pointed toward Brad and Renee and yelled, "There, there!" at the two deputies. "See them?"

One deputy raised his binoculars. "Got 'em in sight," he shouted.

"Pick them up, get them back to the lodge."

"Will do."

* * *

Six felt that if he got any more anxious he would break out in hives. He paced up and down his dock with his cellphone in a shirt pocket—the pocket that was still mostly sewn onto the shirt—and willed it to ring.

"Puh-*leeeze*, somebody call me, dammit, dammit, dammit," he muttered.

He had been smoking pipe after pipe of No. 79 and not enjoying it after the first two bowls, but he continued to fill up and light up because it was something to do. His throat was getting raw.

Shortly after his call to Brad he'd heard from the deputies guarding the camp road; he alerted them to the probability of two murderers on the grounds and ready to run. They obviously had quickly contacted Benson Doucette, because the sheriff had phoned Six shortly after that he was headed to Cedar Lodge with three cars of armed troopers.

But that had been nearly an hour back, and since then not a word. Six had rung Brad's number repeatedly, kept leaving messages when there was no answer, and now, calling again, there was nothing—no ring, no voicemail, just ominous, dead silence.

Alicia sat on the top left end of their T-shaped dock and watched her husband and the dog, who was doing what one would call dogging his master's steps and pacing along behind him. Ordinarily, Rudolph would've observed such a useless activity from a comfortable position, but Six's loud phone calls and cursing and general carrying on had made the Labrador worried and fretful. Alicia was reminded of caged tigers.

Six stopped, peered down at his moccasins, looked at the sky, turned, stopped again, went down the dock to their boat, kneeled and retrieved a rod rigged with spinner bait. Anything to calm his nerves, he thought—Zen fishing, his term for casting without expectation of disturbing any fish. He walked to the right side of the T and cast the spinner into the weedy shallows. By the fourth cast Rudolph assumed the crisis had passed, executed a few turns and flattened himself against the boards and sighed in satisfaction, the expelled air flapping his dewlaps.

Six's mind was a Boschian landscape of scenarios at Cedar Lodge, but the repeated casting began to work somewhat like a chant. Lift rod, snap, whizzz, ploop, reel in rapidly. Lift rod, snap, whizzz . . . There were no fish in the shallows; everybody knew that. Nothing but minnows sucking up nutrients from the bottom muck. But that wasn't the point; the point was the soothing mantra of Zen fishing. Lift rod, snap, whizzz, ploop . . . Six nearly dropped the rod in shock as the water erupted with churning and thrashing. A bass had torpedoed through the grass, hit the lure, and now the line whined as the fish darted for deeper water.

Recovering, and with instinctive skill from a lifetime of hauling 'em in, Six grabbed the reel handle, jerked the rod back over his left shoulder, which set the hook, and began pulling and reeling. It was a fish with a lot of fight. Alicia got up and walked to Six's side just as he snarled, "Goddamn it! I wasn't supposed to get a damn fish."

Alicia was stunned. She turned and frowned at Six. "I beg your most humble pardon." Angrily cursing because one has caught a fish was akin to angler blasphemy.

"I was doing Zen fishing. This has destroyed my *om*."

Alicia looked at Six as if he had absolutely lost his mind. "Six, have you absolutely lost your mind?"

Six was having a struggle with the fish, which was coming in, but not without one hell of a show first. It leaped and dived, leaped and dived, and pulled hard on the line as it swam in circles.

"Smallmouth. Two pounds at least, maybe more."

Six's phone played Schuman in his pocket. "Oh, dammit, I *knew* it!" he yelled. "Here, take it!" He thrust the rod into Alicia's hands and clawed his phone from the pocket. She was delighted to take over the action and began battling the fish toward the dock as Six opened his phone:

"Six here!"

It was Benson Doucette's voice. "Six, are you at your camp?"

"Yep. What's happening?"

"They're coming your way—the bad guys. You were right, or I reckon Colin was right. It's the Bolstons sure enough. They're heading for Rocky Pond. Through the serpentine. Might be there already."

"Jesus."

"And there's worse. They killed Kipper, wounded one of my men and grabbed Brad and Renee for hostages."

Six groaned. "Oh, dear God." Alicia turned and saw the shock and sorrow in his eyes. "Kipper's dead," he whispered to her.

Alicia was so stunned that she let her line slacken and wasn't aware when the bass rose high and threw the hook.

"Brad and Renee," Benson continued, "got out of the boat, God knows how, and were lying in the weeds near the serpentine."

"They're alive?"

"Believe so. Other boat's taking them back to the lodge."

"Where are you now?"

"We're entering the serpentine. Six, listen to me. We're way behind—we can't catch up to them. I'm sending a boat to Winsokkett. Can Alicia meet them at the state road and get them down to the lake at your place?"

"Why not me?"

"I've got a job for you, and I want you to listen carefully. You don't have to do it—could be dangerous."

"C'mon, Benson. Tell me."

"If you could put out in your boat and try to keep them in view when they come out of Rocky Pond, then you could call the troopers in our boat and tell 'em where the bastards are."

"I'm leavin' right now."

"Six! Listen to me! *Don't* go near them. Just keep them in view. They've both got guns—not rifles, but I believe Nelson's got a .357 Magnum. That's a bad gun, Six."

"I've got a rifle in the camp—Ruger 30.06."

Benson's voice came through Six's cellphone loud and angry. "Goddamn it, Six! I'm telling you now to leave that rifle in the camp. I'm ordering you to."

"Actually, you can't do that."

Benson got steamed: "Don't you dare go all professor on me. I've already got a dangerous situation with Weller."

"*Weller?* What about him?"

"He's following them in another boat. According to my deputy at the lodge, he had on a gunbelt."

"Oh, crap."

"Yeah. Right. Now please take down the cellphone number of Trooper Delaney . . ."

"Wait a minute wait a minute!" Six leaped into the bass boat and scrabbled for the paper and pencils he kept in a bag for fishing notes. "OK, shoot."

Six took down the number and Benson told him: "Delaney will be one of two guys in the boat. They will have rifles. They'll try to put holes in the hulls before they shoot anyone. Now. Alicia up to the road, you scouting the lake."

"We're on it." As he started to close the phone, Benson's voice shouted, "Six!"

"Ayuh?"

"Don't go near that goddamn boat."

* * *

Vadik and Anka had soon realized their mistake when they'd entered the serpentine at 20 mph with the motor down. Within minutes they had struck a submerged log that jarred the boat violently and cut the motor. Now, with the motor tilted so high that it was spluttering water and Anka hanging over the bow spotting logs and big branches and rocks, they negotiated the last stretch of the serpentine and emerged into Rocky Pond from a tree line just south of Bert & Betty's Summer Camps, a collection of decrepit, sun-bleached fishing shacks with rusty screen porches arranged around a semi-circular sandy beach. Children on plastic floats splashed and whooped next to their parents in the shallows. They all waved merrily at Vadik and Anka. Mad killers in a 16-foot motorboat look like anyone else in a motorboat.

Vadik got the boat to half-speed for several hundred feet and then full speed, and they were cutting across the lake at 40 mph, sending up a big V of water from the bow and a rooster tail from the stern.

"Vadik!" Anka screamed, flapping her right arm up and down. "Slow, slow!"

As Vadik cut the speed, a daunting sight greeted him and Anka. Not for nothing had Rocky Pond gotten its name. Small archipelagos of boulders broke the lake's surface in all directions, and, as all locals knew, beneath the occasional areas of open water treacherous rock formations, deposited by glaciers millions of years previously, had brought many a boater to grief and paid for college educations for progeny of the owners of several nearby maintenance-and-repair marinas.

Consequently, the lake was dotted everywhere with buoys warning, "Hazard!"

Vadik glared in rage at yet another obstruction that he couldn't eliminate with a gun. "Goddammit!" he snarled.

"We've got to go easy, Vadik. We can*not* wreck the boat."

Vadik gave Anka a sneer. "You don't say? Well, my goodness." He paused to look her up and down. "You stupid broad."

Anka's face flushed angrily and she shouted, "Don't call me that again, you bastard!"

"Or you'll do what? Kill me? Yeah?" He snickered. "Stupid broad." Before Anka could move or utter a sound, he raised the Magnum quickly and aimed at her head. "Now that we're on the subject, what do I need with you? I'll move faster alone." Anka's eyes widened in terror. Vadik lowered the gun and said, "Changed my mind. Get up to the bow and look for rocks." Anka complied with alacrity.

Some five minutes later they approached another dismaying sight: The entire narrow passage to Winsokkett Pond was strewn with boulders stretching several hundred feet east and west, and scattered among them were seven fishing boats, for The Narrows was a prime spot for bass feeding on crayfish. On board one of those boats was a lanky gentleman of considerable height wearing a tattered shirt and grungy brimmed hat.

Vadik again tilted the motor until it was spluttering and Anka anxiously scanned the clear water for rocks. Once they had cleared the last boulder, Anka used the binoculars to gaze back across the lake to the serpentine. She adjusted the focus, easily located Bert & Betty's camps, twitched the glass left and, yes, there was the creek's outlet, and emerging from it was another blue-and-white boat just like theirs.

"There's another boat coming into the lake from the creek," Anka said. "Blue and white, just like this one."

"Who is it?"

"Can't tell. Too far away."

Vadik grabbed the glasses from Anka, homed in on the boat, but couldn't distinguish the driver. But it seemed to be only one person. "Probably that damn Smokey the Bear sheriff," he growled. Vadik loathed all police of any kind, as might be expected from someone pursuing his specialty of murder for hire, but he especially loathed policemen in hats.

Bob Weller also had binoculars, for he and the killers were both beneficiaries of another Cedar Lodge rule of the late Iphigene Seldon: In addition to always being gassed up and with keys in the ignition, each boat was to be equipped with binoculars and foul-weather jackets. Being unfamiliar with Rocky Pond, he had to stop and scan the tree line on the opposite shore until he found The Narrows, and . . . aha! There they were, creeping through the rocks. They had been out of sight by the time he'd gotten underway at Willow Pond, so he knew they had no idea he was following.

Bob had a plan. It was natural, when fleeing in any vehicle, for escapers to look behind them. Just so with boats. However, a pursuer on water had no roads or hills and dales or anything else to obstruct an encircling move on the pursued, thereby effecting a surprise assault from the front. Whichever direction they headed, he would go the opposite way and make a big arc across the lake at full speed, stop, get them in sight again, and then plow straight at them.

I'll kill them, and then I will die.

Twenty-Eight

Six cast with a metal sinker tied to the end of his line to prevent the risk of a strike smack in the middle of his surveillance routine. As Vadik and Anka (he still knew them as Nelson and Tory) slipped by only two big boulders away from his boat, he tried to look as nonchalant as possible—just a nowhere Monday, nothing going on, only a shabby-looking duffer whiling away the time. He pulled down his hat brim and cast in a different direction so that he could turn his back on the other boat. He usually fished in his long-billed cap but had chosen this khaki porkpie so that he could partially hide his face. He noticed that his heartbeat had quickened and his hands were sweaty. He wondered if James Bond ever had sweaty hands, nervously wiping them on his trousers before lunging into action.

When he heard the sound of their motor increasing in volume, he glanced over his shoulder and saw them picking up speed. He cranked up his tilted motor and put-putted through the rocks and into open water. Then he dialed Trooper Delaney's number.

"Delaney."

"Six Godwin. The villains have just gone through The Narrows into Winsokkett. Where are you?"

"Just turning onto 8 north."

"My wife will be at the top of the camp road to guide you in."

"Beautiful. I'll call you when we're on the water."

Six lowered his motor and proceeded at 20 mph, staying far back of the other boat but keeping it in view. There were few other boats on the lake, so he headed first in one direction and then another as if seeking a particular place to cast. So far so good, but two things worried him: One, where was Bob Weller about now, and two, how the heck were the Bolstons going to get away? The entrance to the wide serpentine that drained into North Pond was on the southern shore, but did they know that? Unless . . . oh, damn. Gene always had Cedar Lodge boats fully outfitted with gear other than the state-required floatation vests, oars and running lights—foul-weather jackets, binoculars and, as fate would probably have it, U.S. Geological Survey maps of all bodies of water in the Belgrade Lakes area.

How smart were these particular killers?

***

"Here, here, look!" Anka jabbed the Winsokkett chart she was holding before Vadik.

"What is it?"

"It's another serpentine. Leads into North Pond. See that island? Head for that—the serpentine is right in back of it."

Bob didn't know Winsokkett either, but he by God knew boats, from sculls to canoes, cabin cruisers, sailing yachts—and especially speedboats. He had raced in Miami, the Bahamas and Australia, tearing through courses at 110 mph, going airborne over wakes at 90. That had been so many years ago, and, yes, he knew—he was now old and weakened. But there was a significant extra factor on this brilliant July day as he circled northeast after observing Vadik heading southeast: He had no fear. He had already determined he would end his life on this day by his own hand were he not to be killed in the coming waterborne battle.

He mentally rehearsed his tactics. In an attempt for complete surprise, he would bear down at full speed straight at Vadik and Anka from a port-side angle; Vadik, if his guess was correct, would panic and jerk the boat starboard, lifting the port side hull from the water just as Bob swept in, swerved hard to *his* starboard, and gave the other boat a hard, glancing blow. As the driver's seat was starboard, the anticipated effect was to throw Vadik overboard.

And if that didn't work, well, he'd just swing around and ram them broadside with his .38 blazing away.

Six, meantime, was getting increasingly anxious. The Bolstons were on a course aimed directly at the serpentine into North Pond. Was this simply an accident? Delaney hadn't called him and the other boat was nearing Eagle Island. He eased the accelerator forward and picked up speed, and as he closed the gap he tried to see if the others were looking at a chart. Before he realized what he was doing, he'd gotten much too close. He pulled back the lever but it was too late—Tory had turned and spotted him.

The opening bars of the Schumann concerto that he loved so dearly scared the bejesus out of him; he seized the phone and flipped it open.

"Godwin."

"Delaney. Where are they? "

"To the west of Eagle Island. You know it?'

"Yep."

"Serpentine to North Pond is just south of it."

"Our boat's going in the water now. Be underway in two minutes."

As he returned the phone to his pocket, Six was astonished to see a boat speeding toward the Bolstons. Couldn't be Delaney, so he thought it must be some wild-hair fisherman racing to his favorite spot. Good God, it was bearing straight at the other boat. He cut the engine and picked up the binoculars.

"Oh, damn," Six whispered to himself. "Oh, goddamn." It was Bob Weller.

The boats collided with a sickening crash. Vadik's boat nearly tipped over to the starboard, and Vadik was propelled from the driver's seat into the water.

Anka grabbed the shaft of the forward fishing chair as the boat shuddered with the impact and reared to starboard. She heard Vadik scream. The boat righted itself and spun crazily at full speed, slamming Anka against the hull as she crawled toward the driver's seat cursing and railing in fear and pain. She finally managed to grab the lurching steering wheel and swat the lever into neutral.

Just before he had slammed into the other boat, Bob had stood with knees bent in the middle of the deck with his right hand gripping the steering wheel and his left hand holding a line looped around a portside cleat. With this cushioning stance he had survived the crash still on his feet. Now, he flung himself into the driver's seat, cut his speed and swung the boat around, and was astounded to see that his attack had worked: Vadik was in the water thrashing and yelling.

Bob drew his .38 from its holster and bore down on Vadik, who realized a couple of seconds too late that a boat was approaching from behind. His head snapped around. Bob aimed, fired and, with a last expression shock and fury, Vadik's face exploded.

Six shouted and waved his arms frantically—Anka was coming full speed at Bob, who didn't see her. She fired at him, the shot thumping into the aft fishing chair. He came about hard, sending up a curtain of spray, and fired back at her, but she was squatting behind the wheel housing and looking out through the steering wheel. She popped up, fired twice, her shots going wild, then ducked back down.

Six looked toward the northeastern shore, desperately seeking a sign of Trooper Delaney's police boat. He held up the binoculars and . . . yes, right there—a larger boat was plowing break-neck toward them, but it was at least a half-mile away. How could he sit here dead in the water while Bob dodged bullets from a murderer's gun? Nothing for it, he quickly decided, pushing the lever full forward and heading for the action. As he closed in, he saw Anka rise and fire the shot that ended Robertson Weller III's long life of adventure, a shot that put a bullet through his heart. He fell to the deck on his back and bled to death in 30 seconds. As his boat sped away to the west under its own power his last sight was that of a lone osprey circling high above, silhouetted against a clear blue sky.

Forgetting, in a moment of unthinking anger that he was *not* James Bond, Six aimed his boat straight at Anka, coming at her broadside. As he neared, she saw him, fired and missed—*thank you for that one, Jesus*—and he swung hard to port, drenching her with his wake.

When he came around he was appalled to see Anka close on his stern. His bunged-up old boat with a 60-horse motor was no match for the new 75-horse Cedar Lodge boats. He quickly swung to starboard but she stayed right on his tail then closed in, fanning out and coming alongside starboard. The roar of both engines was deafening and added to the terror of seeing Anka, her face distorted with rage and screaming curses he couldn't hear, aim her Beretta at him. He ducked, yanked the wheel to port and her shot struck his hull just behind the driver's seat.

Six found himself raving in fear, "You goddamn bitch! You goddamn bitch!" He was going to die, he *knew* he was going to die and he was going to die howling and wailing.

Their circling, swirling combat had taken them close to Eagle Island. Panicked, Six ran straight for it, thinking irrationally that there would be some measure of safety dodging among the rock formations on its western side. Anka roared up abreast of him on his portside and squeezed off a shot that hit his dashboard as he hunched to a fetal position.

Anka swung hard to port as Six's boat spun crazily without his hands on the wheel. His motor coughed, sputtered and died.

"I've got you now, shithead!" she screamed, coming alongside as Six desperately cranked his motor. Too late. She pulled up and stopped. Six was only 10 feet away. She aimed, squeezed and . . . *click, click, click, click.*

She had loaded the gun with an eight-round magazine, and she'd just fired the eighth cartridge.

"Goddamn you!" she raved.

(Six later told everyone who wanted to hear, which was everyone he knew, that as he looked into that little woman's furious, deadly blue eyes, a black madness overcame him, like that which possessed the "berserker" Viking warriors who suddenly charged into the enemy throng slaying those around them with wild strokes of their battle axes. She had humiliated him, he elaborated—had him cowering and whimpering in fear—and the need for revenge had inflamed him. Having been a history professor, Six now and again liked to reach for dramatic metaphors from the pages of long-ago conflicts; embarrassed by his florid simile, he quickly explained that his actions were, of course, a good deal less savage than those of a demented, ax-wielding Norseman. It was the, er, "black madness" to which he, ahem, referred.)

Knowing Anka would speed away, Six grabbed the only weapon he had at hand, a rod and reel, a weapon of awe only to various species of fish. He'd rigged the rod with his largest Repala pike lure, a vicious thing constructed vaguely in the form of a small fish and fitted with three hooks, each having three razor-sharp barbed points. Anka thrust the gear lever full forward, the motor roared and the boat's bow reared up. Six whipped the rod to twelve o'clock position, aimed for Anka's head and the lure hissed out as he snapped the rod with his wrist. The lure caught Anka's neck as her boat pulled away; Six jerked the rod back over his left shoulder and heard her shriek in agony as she fell backward clawing at the hooks ripping her flesh. The lure tore loose and blood streaked from her neck as her boat shot forward and crashed into a huge rock, shattering the fiberglass bow. Terrified cormorants and gulls flew in all directions from adjacent rocks. The boat began sinking. Anka jumped and flailed toward the shore of Eagle Island.

Six cut his motor and drifted to a halt, so shocked by what he had just done that he could only stare in disbelief as Anka thrashed ashore and stumbled into the thick stand of pines and oaks.

A siren startled Six and he turned to see the police boat coursing toward him, full speed ahead.

Twenty-Nine

"Vadik Bazhukov and Anka Beckenbauer—hired killers," Benson Doucette announced to Six and Alicia. All three were sitting in the canvas chairs on the Godwins' dock. "FBI had Bazhukov on its bad guy list, but it seems they didn't know how bad he really was. Beckenbauer, would you believe, they never heard of. Somerbec County therefore has the pleasure of prosecuting her."

Six completed packing his pipe bowl with No. 79, lit it and stoked up a miniature cumulo formation. "And I came here for the quiet life," he said.

"Please!" Alicia exclaimed. "We're practically drooling to hear the details."

Benson took a sip of the cold beer Alicia had brought him and said, "Ayuh, it's just the damnedest thing. Bazhukov was from British Columbia, parents immigrated there from Russia. Served in an elite Canadian special forces unit . . ." he pulled a note from his pocket ". . . Joint Task Force 2 under the Canadian Special Operations Forces Command. Quite a mouthful. It's a counter-terrorism outfit. Canada's real secretive about information on the group. Anyway, after he left the army he disappeared from all public record. That was twenty-one years ago. How the hell people can do that just amazes me."

Six smiled. "Don't forget Colin and Daphne Trimble."

"Yep. Them too. Yet two *more* people who can't be traced who just *happened* to be at Cedar Lodge at the same time. The mind reels. Believe me, we've tried to track the Trimbles. More about them later."

"Why were hired killers at Cedar Lodge, of all places, and *why* would they kill Gene?" Six asked. "This is not some Mexican drug cartel."

Benson took another pull on his beer and said, "We've got the answer to that, and it's pretty wild. Little miss gun-slinging Tootsie-cake . . ."

"Ugh," Six growled. "Stinking little animal."

"Ayuh, I know how you feel. Anyway, tootsie, Beckenbauer, is singing an opera. She and her lawyer are trying to cut some deals for her because she's ratting on the whole Murder Inc. type of operation in Boston. You see, Maine doesn't have the death penalty, but Illinois does, and Illinois wants to extradite her. She's a Chicago lassie who was involved—under another name, mind you—in the murder of a prominent businessman."

As Benson described it to Six and Alicia, Vadik Bazhukov and Anka Beckenbauer specialized in business-related hits, but not always involving murder. The outfit that hired them evidently had other highly skilled criminals on its payroll. A businessman who was desperate to get himself out of trouble and who had no conscience about how he extricated himself, contacted this anonymous group, which then contacted the criminal operatives, who themselves were kept completely in the dark about who their paymasters were.

"In this case," Benson continued, "the killers knew who had requested the, er, service . . ."

"Awful way to think of murder, isn't it?" Alicia said. "Simply horrible."

"Ayuh. That's how our little killer refers to it—a service. Anyway, she and Bazhukov knew who had requested Gene's murder because he was there at the lodge at the same time and because it necessitated them passing him bogus financial papers for Cedar Lodge to cover theft. And that person was . . . want to guess?"

"It has to be Huntley Beauchamp, right?" Six answered.

"Right you are. From what we can piece out from Beckenbauer, this crime syndicate includes rogue financial experts."

"So . . . Beauchamp must've been stealing from Cedar Lodge."

"Bigtime. Millions, according to Gene's lawyer. Fella named Adrian Bucksaddle."

"That's quite a handle," Six said, chuckling.

Alicia fixed him with speculative look and an arched eyebrow. "Hmmm. People with odd names. It just makes you wonder how they got them, doesn't it . . . *Six.*"

Six harrumphed and muttered, "Well, yeah, I see what . . . well . . . hmph."

Alicia and Benson laughed heartily and Six had to smile as he puffed vigorously and studied a dock post.

"Well, it's Mr. Bucksaddle's belief that when Gene called that family conference then Beauchamp panicked. Thought he'd be outed when the lawyer *and* the accountant got hold of the investment statements he'd been giving Gene."

Six looked thoughtful as he turned to face Benson and Alicia. "So it all comes down to him and his greed—Gene, Bruno, Kipper—Christ, even the dog. Essentially, he killed them all."

"And then died a horrible death running away," Alicia said.

"Kinda scary, isn't it?' Benson said.

They were all silent for a time and then Benson spoke up: "About the murders. Pretty gruesome. Want to hear it?"

Six said: "We want to know."

Beckenbauer says Bazhukov bludgeoned Gene with a rock and then used a blowtorch on her. You were right, Six."

"Yeah, well . . ."

"She says the blowtorch was his idea, that he likes to get quote *artistic* unquote with his murders."

"Oh, Jesus," Six said.

"He got the idea after hearing all the talk about how the Seldons' parents had been killed. Beckenbauer insists that she thought the idea was crazy but that Bazhukov was a psycho. Said he was sadistic. I just love it—one murderer calling the other a sadistic psycho. Claims that whenever they worked together, he did the murders—she was the strategist, he the tactician. Didn't soil her dainties with murder."

"Tell that to Bob Weller."

"Oh, yeah. She doesn't consider that murder. Her lawyer's going with self-defense."

"Lying little bitch!" Six burst out, then quickly said to Alicia, "Sorry, kiddo. Beckenbauer chased him down."

"Don't worry. You'll be a prime A-1 witness when this thing gets to trial. By the way—odd thing. A former wife came to claim

Weller's body after she saw the news on TV. Claims she still loved the old guy. We made national network. Your name got mentioned."

Six grabbed the pipe from his mouth and wheeled around toward Benson. "Oh, no! Dammit! If they had quotes from me then they're lies—I didn't say anything to anybody. I didn't answer the door or return calls."

Benson held up his hand. "Don't worry, don't worry, just your name was mentioned as having witnessed the gun battle. Just like you asked, we didn't mention your, uh, hmm, *expert casting* there at the finish."

Six sighed and looked relieved. "Thank you."

"However, Beckenbauer is raising hell about it through her lawyer. She's got three ugly gashes from the base of the neck, across the right shoulder and down her back."

Six slumped over with a hand to his head. "Oh. God. Damn. It. Am I going to be charged with assault?"

"The DA is sure we can avoid that, but Anka and her lawyer are trying to use it as a bargaining chip. If that lure had caught her a few inches further along the neck, you might've slashed her carotid artery."

Six moaned. His former buoyant mood was getting hammered.

"What about Bruno?" Alicia asked.

"Bazhukov was sure Bruno had seen him during the storm when he went out to the generator shed to cut the line to the lodge. And get this—she says he used those extender tree-pruners to cut the main line from the road. When he ran across Bruno sleeping in the rough after the fight with Merrill, he lifted that awl from the boathouse, killed Bruno and carried him out to the lake. This Bazhukov was a strong sonofabitch."

"One more evil bastard off the face of the earth," Six growled.

"We grilled the hell out of Tootsie about the falsified financial statements, but she started raving at us that she doesn't know how they were done. Her job was to deliver the things. I've got to believe she's telling the truth, because she's desperate to escape the long arm of the state of Illinois. If she knew any more she'd be reaching for a high C."

Another short silence ensued during which they all contemplated the strange vagaries of fate, then Alicia asked:

"How are Brad and Merrill?

"Thayer hospital kept Brad two nights. Going to have a nasty sort of scar on his right arm. I just saw him. He's busy as hell right now sorting out funerals for Gene and Kipper. He was sober, shaking a bit. Solemn, too, which is not like him."

"It was a horrendous experience," Alicia said. "We don't watch TV, but we read the accounts in the *Morning Sentinel*. Got other papers' versions on line. Renee Ranger was the source for most of it. She talked about Brad's incredible bravery saving their lives."

"She'll probably sell her story to a magazine," Six suggested, "complete with gorgeous babe photos."

"I wouldn't doubt it," Benson grumbled. He sighed heavily, took a long pull from the beer bottle, then said, "I can't prove it but I know damn well she gave Gene Seldon that Elavil. Noreen Crepeau—you remember her, the medical examiner?"

"Yep."

"She said the dose must've been huge. I believe Renee was trying to kill Gene, but what the hell should I do about it now, after all that's happened?" Benson grew thoughtful, his eyes focused on two dragonflies on a dock post attempting to make more dragonflies. "It's like getting away with . . . well, damn. It *is* getting away with attempted murder. But what the hell's the use in pursuing it?"

"I agree," Six told him. "More trouble than it's worth at this point. The Elavil isn't what killed Gene, after all."

Alicia offered her thoughts on Renee. "You might say that her terrifying experience of almost being killed was something of a payment for her sins."

"Reckon so," Benson said. He very much doubted that a person like Renee Ranger would be morally altered by what had happened at Cedar Lodge. On the other hand, you just never knew, did you, he concluded.

"And what about Merrill?" Alicia reminded Benson.

"Not much change. Won't talk, acts like she's somewhere else. Brad says as soon as the doctors OK it, he's going to get her back to the lodge and take care of her. Says he'll hire a full-time nurse to look after her. God knows he's got the money. Despite the lodge being closed and despite the millions Beauchamp stole, there's still a big fortune there."

"He *is* going to reopen the lodge, eh?" Six wanted to know.

"Well. I just don't know *what* he's going to do. I didn't really want to press him on anything."

"Of course not."

"The chef, Jean-Pierre is gone too—to New York City. Brad's a kind-hearted guy, when you get down to it. He gave Jean-Pierre enough money to get to the city and live for awhile. Told him he'd invest in a restaurant if Jean-Pierre finds one he likes. Jean-Pierre told me this, not Brad. Poor little guy is heartbroken over Kipper. Can't even say his name without crying."

"That's just amazing about Brad," Six said. "Maybe we're getting to see the man who was underneath all the booze and carrying on."

"Maybe," Alicia said, "it's also a way to honor Kipper."

"Yep, probably so," Benson agreed. "All these deaths are going to haunt me, but that young man's death is going to especially grieve me."

Alicia looked around at the beautiful day before them. "It's still hard to believe the whole thing happened."

For his part, Benson was still shocked that such murderous professional thugs had been running loose on his own turf. And thinking of suspicious characters, he said, "You asked about the English couple, the Trimbles."

"They weren't English," Six snapped. "I by God found them out of that one. Their accents slipped just enough for me to give them the jaundiced eye."

"Well, yes, that sort of fits with what I was going to say—I think everything about 'em is made up. They've vanished like morning dew on a turtle's ass."

Six and Alicia both gave Benson the arched eyebrow treatment. "I beg your pardon?" Alicia asked.

Benson's face flushed. "I made that up. Just now."

Six chuckled. "Next thing you know, Benson, you're going to be sitting on a front porch whittling decoys and telling tourists they can't get there from here."

"What are you talking about? You're the character, not me."

Six regarded him with a look of mock outrage. "*I'm* a character? News to me."

"Well, anyway," Benson said, "I don't think we'll ever know what the hell those two were doing at Cedar Lodge. But I suspect they were up to something."

"It's very strange, isn't it?" Alicia said. "They recognized that horrible murderer. Makes you wonder."

"I've been thinking about that," Six told them. "It's a wild thought that two sets of criminals—and I'm convinced Colin and Daphne are criminals of some kind—were at a bucolic place like Willow Pond at the same time. One hell of a coincidence, if that's what it was."

Benson looked intrigued. "Oh? Meaning?"

"What if they were also part of the gang making a hit on Gene and the lodge? What if they were the financial experts, the ones drawing up the false documents?"

"Do you also think they might be killers?' Benson asked.

"Hard to believe, isn't it—I mean they were so British and so charming. But then who the hell would've ever suspected old 'regular guy' Nelson Bolston and his sexy, giggling sister?"

Alicia suddenly looked very cross and pounded a fist on her knee. "I will never, never forget the way that evil little hussy just took me right in." Alicia put on a cutsie voice: *It's just so tragic about Gene. It's so terrifying. Nelson is sooo upset. We came here looking for romance and now it's sooo awful.*

Alicia snorted with disgust. "Ghastly woman."

All three were quiet for several minutes, absorbed in contemplation of the macabre charade that had ensnared them.

Benson gazed longingly at Winsokkett Pond, basking in 75-degree sunshine graced by a mild breeze that riffled the water and the leaves of nearby maples and oaks and pines. Everests of white cumulo clouds unladen by storm-heralding dark areas surmounted the western mountains. Oh, how I'd love to go fishing right now, Benson thought. He was dressed in mufti for his day off—jeans and new L.L. Bean fishing shirt, hoping that the shirt might hint to the Godwins of his desire to get out onto Winsokkett for an activity other than pursuing killers. He hadn't had the opportunity to fish the lake in years.

Perhaps cerebral telepathy was in the air at that moment, for Alicia said, "Benson, would you like to go fishing?"

Benson brightened and turned to her. "Ma'am, that would be just about the best thing I could think of. Do you mean today?"

"Why, yes. Six and I went out this morning and we'll soon be heading out for the afternoon. No sense wasting perfect weather. Plus, as we discovered earlier, the fish are ravenous."

"Excellent. I want to go back home and get my two favorite rods and a tackle box." He rose to go, stopped and looked down at Six sternly.

"One more thing about your, shall we say, *alleged,* assault on Beckenbauer—damn it to hell. Why didn't you listen to me, professor? We would've caught her. I mean, Delaney was on the way in our boat. Why did you go wading into it?"

Six knocked the ashes out of his pipe into the water and busied himself cleaning the bowl, trying to avoid an answer.

"Professor? You damn near got yourself killed, didn't you?"

Six cleared his throat and sighed and squirmed in his chair. "I don't know, Benson," he said in a small voice. "I don't know what came over me."

Silence.

Finally, Six sat up and looked straight up at Benson. Grinning widely, he said:

"But you got to admit—it was a damn good cast."

October

Brad Seldon sat by his favorite potted plant on the long porch of the big lodge and contemplated the incomparable beauty of the forests surrounding Willow Pond, with their reds, oranges, yellows, browns and greens glowing in the melancholy October light. The air was enjoyably chilled, with the smell of wood smoke from nearby camps drifting in. Readings were somewhere in the 40s, Brad guessed; he had stopped looking at temperatures. Those instruments still active in his little meteorology lab upstairs continued to quietly register their data, but no eyes studied their prognostications. He would get back to them someday, he thought complacently.

Merrill was up in her room with a nurse, and Brad talked with her each morning and evening, though she seldom responded—otherwise he was alone. Except for the first-floor windows looking toward the lake, the kitchen windows and those in his and Merrill's rooms, the lodge was shuttered and dark. Fallen leaves lay everywhere—they covered the lawn and were scattered heavily over the beach and the docks. On the porch, curled brown leaves were strewn from one end to the other—and all around the sides, for that matter. The grounds in back, the parking lot and the camp road to Red Fox Lane were all carpeted with leaves. Why bother to clean them up, Brad had decided. No one was coming to Cedar Lodge. Besides, he enjoyed rustling through leaves wherever he walked, including from the front door and down the porch to his chair.

The huge weeping willows that draped so charmingly over the boathouse during summer had turned brown, and before long their hundreds of spidery branches would be bare and rattling in the winter winds. All the boats had been winterized and locked in the boathouse, and the dock had been claimed by grateful ducks and gulls and Canada geese. Their droppings made the docks a hazardous proposition, but then what the hell, Brad thought—no one's going to be putting out in a boat. For every October of his life that he could remember, Brad had been fishing—here, Winsokkett, North Pond and East Pond, Great Pond, the Kennebec River. Barring a spell of nasty weather, fall fishing was a delight in the crisp air of an uncrowded lake surrounded by the colors of autumn's palette. Fall angling, of course, wasn't anything like summer's bounty—the bass and other fish were going deeper as the top layers of water got colder, and they were harder to locate. However, Brad, with his instinctual skill, could bring some up on any autumn day, but now, during *this* autumn, he had no desire other than to sit and watch nature's progress into winter.

He was at peace. No urgencies intruded into his life. There was plenty of money, and there was plenty of time. Let the rest of the world go by. Old song, right? he asked himself . . . *and let the rest of the world go by.* Yes, that was it. Couldn't remember any more lyrics and the tune was on the edge of his memory. A song from his parents' time. He could think of them now, his wonderful mother and father, without agony. Somewhere along the way during the nearly three months since the summer's hideous traumas, the coil of anxiety and bitterness that had lain beneath his boozy charm for eighteen years had dissipated. Strange that, he thought.

He wondered if he might have become a Buddhist. No—a Taoist. He remembered how in college he'd become beguiled reading about Taoism: Strength through "non-action," placing one's will in harmony with the natural universe. *Don't struggle. Like a reed, bend with the wind and the water.* So, here he would sit and dwell in Taoist serenity, happy merely to be alive.

Well, yes—there was the familiar bottle of George Dickel beside the plant; it was no longer necessary to hide it *behind* the pot. Actually, he could've put the bottle on the porch rail—who was here to see? He simply liked the tradition of bottle by the potted plant. One must maintain some verities, he reasoned.

There was a difference in this ritual now, however: The bottles of bourbon lasted a good deal longer. As an example, here it was deep into the afternoon and Brad was not drunk; he was not even really tight. He was simply mellow. He lingered over every glass of "spiritual uplift," sipping it ever so slowly, savoring the delicious tang. Just enough to enhance bodily warmth, was his dictum. Clothes weren't enough when you got down to it. Today, he was bundled in thick cord trousers, boots, a high-necked fleece sweater, a black-and-red-checked hunting jacket and a wide-brimmed Moose River hat.

Good lord, he thought. Are those footsteps? Yes, here they come, rustling and crinkling through the leaves. And then . . .

At first he didn't believe his eyes, so he continued to sit and stare for several moments, and then he saw that yes this was not an illusion, so he sprang to his feet and called out, "Thomasina!"

Tom Barclay came across the lawn to the stairs, where she stopped and said, "Hello, Brad. Anybody home?"

Never before at a loss for a comeback, now Brad was at a loss, so he just smiled. Maybe I'm getting *too* calm, he thought.

"Just me and the birds." Brad gestured toward the avian community squatting on the docks. "Come on up on the porch, Thomasina." He was surprised to see that Tom was wearing a tweed skirt, V-neck pullover and a brown tweed jacket.

Tom smiled and said, "Thanks. And just call me Tom. Only my mother calls me Thomasina."

Brad looked sheepish. "Well. Yeah. I guess I made a big thing of your name when we were, uh, well. . ."

"When I was the enemy."

"Oh, I don't know. I was being a real hard case." He chuckled, took off his hat and ran a hand through the long, unruly mass of russet curls. Taoist non-action had also resulted in not getting haircuts. "The truth is, Thoma—Tom, you made me . . . well, that cold, hard stare . . ."

Tom laughed loudly and gave Brad a warm smile. "See, Brad, this is what I look like. That stare is a put-on. It isn't me. I developed that bit of theatrics at the academy when I was learning how to interrogate people. I was trying to be super-cop."

"Oh, I know what you look like, Tom. You're a very fine-looking woman."

Tom blushed and Brad, having gotten himself flustered, fidgeted and looked this way and that as if seeking something in a strange place.

"Tom, sorry, please have a seat. I, uh, haven't been a host to anyone recently except squirrels and chipmunks." As they both sat down, Brad grinned at Tom. "Could I offer you some nuts and berries?"

Tom looked thoughtful. "Hmmm. Not right now. I just raided a bird feeder."

They laughed together, and Brad held up the bourbon bottle. "Here's the old familiar," he said. "I've, uh . . . I've cut way back, and that's the truth, but I still have solitary afternoon and evening cocktail parties." Adopting a formal, house-servant voice, he said, "May I interest you in some refreshment, madam?"

"Why, thank you." Tom looked pensively at the porch roof. "Perhaps a . . . let's see . . . bourbon and water. Do you have that?"

"As a matter of fact, I do. Pardonne-moi for a few seconds." Brad disappeared into the darkened lodge and returned within minutes with another glass, a carafe of water and a bucket of ice. He fixed Tom's drink, handed it to her and said, "Cheers." They drank a toast and then Brad continued with, "Tom, do I gather by your ensemble that you are not here on a constabulary undertaking?"

"Day off," Tom said. "Damn, this is good bourbon."

"Only the best served at the Café de Front Porch." Brad paused and looked out at the lake. "Why did you come, Tom?" he asked without looking her way.

"I came just to see how you're doing."

"Really?"

"Yep."

Brad's voice was barely audible. "I'm honored, Tom. Thank you."

"And, so, how are you . . . really?"

"Actually, I'm fine. I really am. I'm . . . what's the word? Composed. Yes, I'm composed. I have acquired, remarkably, an attribute that Six Godwin told me was important to him—the quality of stillness. The ability to sit for long periods of time and simply think, even in the presence of others." Brad looked at Tom and smiled warmly. "And so, for the time being, I'm just right here, being still. And how about you?"

"Everything's fine. Hoping to get in some serious hunting this winter. Speaking of which, are you going to reopen the lodge?"

"Not this winter. After that, I don't know. I think I'll sell the place."

Tom sipped her whiskey and thought about that. "Kinda sad."

"Yep. It is sad. Been here all my life."

"Brad, I'm very sorry about Kipper. I wish we could have prevented that happening." When he didn't respond, Tom said, "How is Merrill?"

"Ohh, not so good. She reads, watches movies—DVDs—occasionally. Starts getting upset and then hysterical if she watches television. Can't say I blame her. Mostly she reads, takes her meals, falls asleep in her chair. Sometimes, she sits out here in the sun. I . . . I can't get her to say much of anything. I talk to her every day, and she'll maybe smile or give monosyllabic answers to my questions. Doctor has her on strong meds. Getting her off coke was an awful battle. I don't know . . . maybe eventually there'll be a breakthrough."

"Give her some time. I bet she'll come out of it."

"Hope you're right. I'm always worried about suicide, so I've got a nurse with her all the time. God knows I can afford it. Half owner of forty-eight big ones. Oh. Yeah. Forgot to mention it. I had Amos cremated and I put his ashes out there by Duck Island. I miss him."

"You could get another dog."

"I could. Yep. Been thinking about just that."

They both grew silent and tested each other's quality of stillness. After awhile, Brad said:

"Tom, why did you come see me?"

"Like I said, to see how you were doing."

Brad turned and looked into Tom's magnificent large blue eyes, so different in texture and so different in the humanity that shone through them from the blue eyes that had so grotesquely enraptured him in July. "But why, Tom? Why do you . . ."

"Why do I care?"

"Yes."

"I think you can guess." Tom blushed and looked away.

Brad stared at her in wonder; a quickened heartbeat ruffled his quality of stillness.

"I was very relieved you weren't killed, Brad. I came to tell you that. I'm glad that you're alive."

"Thank you. Thank you, Tom. And I'm glad you're here. Would you like another, er, cocktail . . . madam?"

Tom grinned at him. "I've got to go, Brad. Anyway, a DWI cop is a terrible thing."

"I wish you could stay longer. Maybe some other time?"

"Of course, another time." Tom looked out at Willow Pond and thought how exquisite it was, the quintessential Maine lake, unspoiled, unpolluted, lonely and serene. How sad, how very sad, she thought, that it had been desecrated by such murderous evil. "Brad?" she said.

"Yes, Tom?"

"You're a very brave man."

Brad started to speak but felt a catch in his throat, and re-mained silent, fearing he would show his emotion. He turned and studied Tom's profile and realized that her words were probably the single best thing anyone had ever said to him in his entire life.

She turned her face to him and smiled and they held each other's gaze for long moments, until Brad looked away, sighed, drank some whiskey and studied the weeping willows on Duck Is-land. Softly, he said, "Uh, Tom . . . I, uh, I'm not sure just how to say this, which is, hm, different for me"—he forced a chuckle—"silver-tongued devil and all that. But, well, Tom, you're different from any woman I've ever known. And that's not a cheap line. I've gone through too much for any more cheap lines. You're funny as hell, and smart and . . . I was wondering . . ."

Tom drank the rest of her whiskey, put her hand on Brad's arm and said, "Brad, I know what you're going to say. And the truth is, I was thinking along those lines myself."

Brad turned and beamed at her. "You were?"

"Yep. However . . ."

Oh, damn, Brad thought. Here it comes.

"However, there's real problems. First, there's me, a cop—and I love being a cop, and . . ."

"And then there's me, a lush. Although, like I said, I *am* getting better."

"I'm sure you are. But, like you also said, you're a hard case. That's beyond me to deal with now."

"I understand."

Neither spoke for a while. Brad broke the silence.

"And then there's age. How old are you, Tom? Twenty-eight, twenty-nine?"

"Thirty-one."

"I'll be forty-nine in January. Kind of a gap there."

Tom sighed. "Let's say . . . let's just say that for now . . ."

Brad raised his glass to her and smiled. "That for now, it's not to be."

"Thank you, Brad. You're actually one hell of a guy."

"And you, my big darling," Brad said, putting his hand on hers, "are one hell of a girl."

* * *

"I know they're down there," Six proclaimed, placing a well-aimed cast about three feet from the nearest rock looming from the water. "We got two here last fall—remember?"

"Yep. But they were sort of junior-sized," Alicia reminded him.

"Nevertheless. They were still pike. This year, one of us is going to get a champion. Hope it's me," Six stated from the stern fishing chair; Alicia was in the bow chair. He turned to her and twinkled merrily. "Just joking."

"No, you're not."

"Of course I am. I would never be so selfishly inclined."

Alicia shot an arched-eyebrow look in his direction and said, "Six, I know you. If you were fishing with Jesus Christ and he got a six-pound largemouth and you caught a two-pound smallie, you would glare at his back with scorching envy."

"You amaze me, kiddo. I am the most generous of sportsmen. Did I not insist that you take the forward fishing chair. Everyone knows the person in front gets the most fish."

"What a comedian you are, my darling. That applies only when the trolling motor is being used. Bow fisherman is the first to get a line into the new water. We're stationary, as agreed. No wind, fish in each new spot a half-hour."

Six chuckled smugly. "In that case . . . I hope it's me."

"And I hope it's me."

"Are you using a Rapala?"

"I am indeed. New one, just out this year. It's called the Thug."

Six laughed loudly. "Oh, that's rich. I'm fishing with the very same Rapala I used to hook a real thug."

Alicia reeled in and glared at her sometimes insufferable—though, generally lovable, she had to admit—husband. "That little escapade was the stupidest damn thing you've ever done, Six! I could have been a widow."

"Sorry, kiddo. You're right, of course. But if you do become a widow I'm sure you'll have plenty of gentlemen callers. All fisher-men, of course."

"I don't want any goddamn gentlemen callers, whether they've got a rod in their hand or not!"

Six let that statement float on the cold October air for a few moments. He could tell by the way Alicia had quickly twirled her chair around so that her back was to him that she'd realized her mistake.

He waited a few beats, cleared his throat, and said, "Would you like to re-state that sentence?"

"DAMMIT!"

They fished in profound silence until the thirty minutes for that particular spot were almost expired. Alicia burst out, "OK. C'mon, c'mon. Take it again, take it again." She abruptly jerked her rod over her left shoulder and shouted, "Whahaa!"

Oh, dear, Six thought—it's going to be her.

"It's for sure a pike!" Alicia exclaimed. Six went forward to watch her reel in and, yes, he agreed—no circling, no jumping, no thrashing, just a tremendous pull at the end of the line. Definitely a pike.

Alicia reeled and pulled, reeled and pulled. "Can't let any slack get in there." At last, a pike appeared, all teeth and black eyes and long, torpedo-like body. In customary pike behavior, he rolled over on his side next to the boat and stared at them, seemingly giving up, but the Godwins knew he was just foolin', working the line to the back of his mouth and waiting for slack so that he could crunch down with his teeth and shoot forward to freedom.

"Kind of on the small size," Six proclaimed.

"Ayuh. Still a pike. Be careful with that net—he'll tear loose."

Six eased the net slowly into the water behind the fish and toward his tail and then—whoosh. He netted him just as the pike snapped the line; he scooped him up and emptied him onto the deck, where he thrashed until he threw the lure. Alicia put on steel-tipped gloves, seized the pike by his lower jaw and held him for Six to snap a photo. Then she lowered him back into the lake.

"Nicely done, kiddo," Six told her.

"The next one's yours, dearest, and I hope it's a whopper. Sorry about my, er, rather emphatic outbursts earlier."

"And I apologize for my intemperate statements."

"Excellent. Now that we have that settled, let's get another pike."

And an hour later they did do just that, another team effort. Six's large, old, paint-chipped Rapala must have looked like a hotdog to the biggest pike either of them had been close to in a long time. It was a real champion among northern pike, and the fish and Prof. Godwin went *mano-a-mano* for more than fifteen minutes before the pike, reminiscent of a miniature submarine, surfaced and rolled over with an evil glare in his black eye.

Photographs were taken and the pike was hefted back into the water to hunt again in Winsokkett's depths. He would've looked impressive mounted above their fireplace, but they both agreed that he was too magnificent to kill.

The autumn-colored forests surrounding Winsokkett Pond gleamed in the late-afternoon sun as Six and Alicia motored home in leisurely triumph. A V of Canada geese flew over them toward the eastern shoreline, where tendrils of smoke rose from fireplaces in the camps; wood smoke scented the air. As they came within sight of their dock, Six announced in a stentorian voice, "Oh gods of the lake, I dedicate my brother fish-of the-many-teeth to the memory of Iphigene Seldon, sportsman extraordinaire."

Epilogue

Adrian Bucksaddle, Esq., was an honorable man. Not completely and always, of course—a human being who was always and ever honorable in every aspect of life would be one who was either touched by the divine or mad (or possibly both). Likewise, a human being engaged in a prosperous, effective pursuit of law for most of a long lifetime could not possibly have avoided instances wherein cunning and subterfuge were necessary.

Nevertheless, Adrian Bucksaddle was as close to consistently honorable as one in his position could be. This aspect of his personality was still giving him trouble now, all these months later, in respect to his involvement in the Cedar Lodge murders. Oh, he was by no means in moral turmoil, he was simply concerned that his, shall we say, *clandestine* actions the previous summer had placed him indirectly in contact with possibly evil people.

At this moment, as he pondered these unanswerables, he was sitting at a window table in the dining room of the Copley Plaza Hotel and gazing down at a snow-and-ice covered, wind-swept Copley Square. So Arctic were the conditions that the few people visible were wrapped like Admiral Perry's crewmen and were hunched and darting frantically toward whatever doorway awaited them.

Other than in the dining rooms of his two clubs, this table at this window in the Copley was Adrian's favorite place in Boston to take a meal. He'd just finished an outstanding tender sirloin followed by a soft crème brule, and was lingering over coffee and brandy. In keeping with his maintenance of the old virtues was his maintenance of old standards in clothing. On this frigid Friday evening only days before Christmas, Adrian wore a Harris tweed jacket whose weave was a brown, heather and blue mélange, a buff wool vest with horn buttons, gray cavalry twill trousers enhanced by argyle socks and dark brown, perforated captoe Peel & Co. oxfords.

On Christmas, he would be at his sister's home, reveling in the company of her children and grandchildren, his only family, for though he was decidedly heterosexual, he had never married. ("Oh, but I had my day with the ladies," he would sometimes affirm with an enigmatic smile.) He led a solitary life, but he was not lonely—he had his books (favoring novels of the 1930s through the '50s) and his music (favoring Wagner and Liszt) and his movies (DVDs of all the film noir classics). He had a small and agreeable stable of friends and occasionally he was an appreciated dinner party guest. For the most part, though, he was blissfully comfortable with his own company.

When Adrian was at one of his clubs, he dined companionably with fellow members, but when he took his meals at this table at this window, he always dined alone, quite by choice. A copy of John O'Hara's *Appointment in Samarra*, one of his favorites, lay open by his brandy glass, yet he'd given it scant attention, distracted as he was by thoughts that returned relentlessly to Cedar Lodge, to Iphigene Seldon, her niece and her two nephews, one now tragically dead.

Despite his requests, Gene had seldom given Adrian a look at the investment statements for Cedar Lodge Holdings, as managed by Huntley Beauchamp, declaring that it was a waste of Adrian's time, as he was not a finance expert and, what the hell, she insisted, old Huntley, despite being, in her estimation, "a pompous gasbag," was doing a bang-up job of bringing in the capital-gains bacon. Yes, it *was* true that finance was not his forte—nevertheless, Adrian had become convinced during his meticulous examinations of the few statements he'd received that Beauchamp had an embezzling snout sunk into the Cedar Lodge trough. Though he saw what he believed to be suspicious entries and fiddling about with numbers, he just couldn't prove it.

And so he took action that was anything but honorable.

A certain colleague of the bar, who was a fellow member of the club in which attorneys-at-law were heavily represented on the roster, a man whose reputation for discretion in matters large and small was impeccable, had once mentioned to him during whiskeys

by the fireplace late one night in the club's library, that for gentlemen faced with, shall it be said, an intractable situation, there was
a certain drawer in a certain private postal store wherein inquirers
could leave a description of the aforesaid intractable situation and
request availability of service. Answers to such requests were left
in the box within forty-eight hours. A breath-taking fee was "suggested," which the inquirer was to leave in a provided zippered
envelope bag of the kind used by banks. Once received, the fee set
in motion the desired resolution. One simply had to trust that one's
money had not been shoved into an oubliette. Time went by—no
telling how long any particular service would take—and the inquirer's growing anxiety was relieved only when, voila, the source
of his initial trouble had been neutralized, so to speak.

Adrian had chuckled jovially and dismissively that night before
the fireplace when told of the very special service. His colleague
was a friend of long standing, and a man whom he admired.

"Don't tell me, old fellow," he had said, "that you of all people
have made use of this cloak-and-dagger outfit."

"Ah, yes, Adrian," his friend had replied. "I have indeed put
my cash into that mysterious drawer, once, and to great effect. I
was told about this by another lawyer who had a similarly successful outcome."

"Good Lord," Adrian had exclaimed. "Shades of the Green
Hornet in mask and cape."

"I believe that was The Shadow. You may laugh now, Adrian,
but there may come a day. And if it does, I will be only too happy
to guide you to that fascinating drawer."

And that day did come, of course.

At Adrian's home, locked away in the desk in his study, the
laptop computer of the late Huntley Beauchamp awaited its coming destruction, once all relevant details had been withdrawn.
Adrian was currently mulling various methods of secretly oblite-
rating the thing; the risk of his possession of it becoming known
was too dreadful to even think about. It had been delivered to his
office—*his* office, not his secretary's nor at the receptionist's
desk—in a steel briefcase. His office door had been locked and so

had the firm's outer door, and yet there it had been, underneath his keyhole desk when he'd come to work early on a morning in the first week of August. Adrian had believed that an examination of Huntley's laptop would reveal his nefarious financial deeds, and he had been absolutely correct. The dreadful fellow's entire life of crime was rendered in hundreds of electronic redirections of Cedar Lodge funds into his own bank accounts and by thousands of emails chronicling an entire life, both in business dealings and in personal relationships, of double-dealing, blackmail and bribery.

Adrian had learned from Sheriff Benson Doucette that the surviving killer, Anka Beckenbauer, alias God knows what else, had identified Huntley Beauchamp as the person who had, through an intermediary, hired her and Vadik Bazhukov, though he had never known who they were.

That scenario sounded uncomfortably familiar to Adrian. Without revealing the source of his knowledge, he provided details to Sheriff Doucette that bolstered Anka Beckenbauer's contention that Huntley had been stealing from Cedar Lodge Holdings, Inc. He also learned from the sheriff and the Profs. Godwin about the mysterious English couple Colin and Daphne Trimble. It seems the Trimbles had broken the baffling case by revealing the identities of the murderers to the Godwins; they had done this with a phone call, during which they admitted that they, the Trimbles, were not who they said they were and that it would be utterly futile to attempt to uncover their identities or trace them, an assertion that had proved to be all too true.

That last bit of information had considerably dismayed Adrian—he was certain that this Colin and Daphne had been the thieves conjured into action by his deposit of the hard green in the "fascinating" drawer. If they had recognized Vadik Bazhukov as a murderer, then how came they by that knowledge? Had Bazhukov also been hired by means of the fascinating drawer, and did that mean that the Trimbles had been on "jobs" with Bazhukov and that they were also murderers as well as burglars?

And that was the imagined contingency now troubling Adrian's otherwise composed and orderly mind: By paying for a burglary job had he given money to an organization that also murdered people for money, the most soulless of mercenary enterprises?

Never, ever again, he vowed, would he be tempted to act in such a manner.

He sighed, closed his book, arose and walked through the dining room, giving his usual generous tips to the waiters and maître d'. A Christmas concert awaited him at Trinity Church on the square below. For several minutes he would be one of those frozen figures dashing for warmth.

After the holidays he would communicate with Bradley Seldon concerning his wishes for the continued legal advice of Bucksaddle, Putnam & Wrisley. And then he would authorize a banker's check in the amount of $2.3 million to Mrs. Bradley Seldon. Those involved in the Cedar Lodge tragedy had expressed great sympathy for Mrs. Seldon, known as Renee Ranger, in regard to the terrifying ordeal she had undergone, but several of them also had hinted that she was a tiresome, narcissistic person.

Well, Adrian allowed as he collected his outer garments from the restaurant's coat-check desk, at least she wasn't a murderer.

About the Author

For 32 years Ned Crabb was an editor, writer and illustrator for The Wall Street Journal; he still free-lances for the Journal. This is his second novel. He and his wife Kay live in New York City and spend most of each summer at their camp on North Pond, in the Belgrade Lakes chain. They have two daughters.